HOUSE OF TRANSFORMATION

A NOVEL BY ASTREA TAYLOR

This book is dedicated to Kristl,
the copper triangle,
and all my muses

.

Hieronymus Bosch, *The Garden of Earthly Delights*. 1515. Oil on oak panel. Museo del Prado, Madrid, Spain.

Ananda
/ah-NON-dah/
noun: perfect happiness, bliss, one of the highest states of being
origin: Sanskrit

Prologue

Ananda dreamed she was lying on a warm beach, a cocktail sweating in her hand — that is, until she lifted her head from an overblown airbag. Black smoke erupted from her crunched mini-coupe rental. The smell of burnt rubber scorched her nose. Broken glass from the windshield lay all over the dashboard and in her lap. Over her steering wheel, she saw the chipped gray building she must've hit.

What had she done?

A tap on the window startled her. She looked up and saw several people gathered around the car, shouting her name. A camera flashed, and then another, momentarily blinding her.

"Ananda, are you hurt?"

"Ananda Dawn!"

Fear electrified her nerves. She couldn't let them know she was as high as the next solar system. They'd smear her all over the tabloids again if they caught the slightest hint of anything scandalous. Getting into a car accident was bad enough.

She unbuckled her seatbelt and rummaged around on the floor until she found her signature giant sunglasses. With trembling hands, she slid them on. The voices continued, some of them speaking French.

"Did she lose control of the car?"

"Do you think she relapsed again?"

Ananda knew she had to get out of the car, but she didn't want to. Why couldn't she go back to the beach?

She wiggled her fingers and toes. Except for a few gashes on her arms and a headache, nothing hurt too much. Nothing was broken. She grasped the door handle, but stopped — the paparazzi were already there. They'd capture every angle, every moment.

She found her studded Karl Lagerfeld purse on the floor and pulled out her favorite lipstick. With a deep breath, she willed strength with every stroke of Rapturous Red, and then finger-combed her white-blonde hair.

She opened the door onto a gray morning and a crowd of concerned faces. A policeman helped her step out onto the pavement in her Louboutin heels. Cameras flashed. She popped glass shards from her blouse and tugged down her miniskirt.

"Are you injured?" an officer asked, his thick French accent crisping the words.

"I think I'm okay," she whimpered.

A microphone plopped in front of her face. She turned to it, channeling as much angelic energy as she could muster.

A paparazzo with greasy brown hair and a nice suit barged in front of everyone, shoving the microphone aside.

"Ananda, are you sober or did you relapse again?" he asked, a shit-eating grin spread across his face.

She ground her teeth. So 'the Greaseball' wanted a fight. Didn't she have a restraining order against him?

"Are you afraid of going to jail for what you've done?" he asked.

Her eyes darted to the car smashed at the bottom of a building. But there was no blood, no body. She slowly let out her breath. She hadn't hit anyone, although she could have. She should've been more careful. She barely remembered anything after her liquid lunch.

"Miss?" the officer asked. "What happened?"

"Someone blinded me with a camera flash when I was driving. I couldn't see where I was going," she said, hoping it sounded true.

The policeman nodded. It was easy enough to believe. For years, she'd been running from the paparazzi, ditching them down side streets, and entering restaurants and clubs from the rear. It was exhausting. She rarely went out anymore for fear she'd end up on the National Enquirer again with a bad picture and a worse caption.

"Do you know where you are?" he asked.

"Of course I do. I'm in Paris."

"But do you realize you crashed into a national monument?"

"What?" She looked back at the wreck. She'd hit a building,

hadn't she? Then she noticed the building had a gray crisscross design in steel that swept upward for several stories into the sky. She gasped.

"No." She ambled toward the Eiffel Tower, running her hands along the rough stone base. It was like a xyritav dream, except it was real. She tried to focus. Had she really jumped the curb and drove into the park?

The traffic on the *Quai Branley* had come to a halt. Horns blared, and still more people arrived and whipped their phones out. Multiple cameras flashed.

The policeman shook his head and said something into a walkie-talkie. Ananda could imagine the cover of the Enquirer now. *Ananda collides into Eiffel Tower, police blame drugs.*

She swallowed. How was she going to get out of this? She had to spin it to her advantage.

In the distance, sirens wailed. The blue twinkling lights of an ambulance approached. The reporters fired questions again, but one voice trumpeted out above the others.

"Would you like to say anything about the hazards of driving while intoxicated?" the Greaseball asked.

A plan came to her. It was so crazy it wouldn't work for anyone except the most beloved of celebrities. That was her once, before the media twisted everything she did. She hoped she could pull it off.

"This may sound crazy," she said, trying her best publicity smile.

A shush ran through the crowd. All eyes were on her.

Ananda walked out of the shadows of the Eiffel Tower and into a beam of sunlight. She gazed directly into an HD news camera.

"This may sound crazy, but part of me always wanted to crash into the Eiffel Tower!"

The crowd laughed. A few people shook their heads or exchanged knowing looks. The paparazzi shouted questions again.

Ananda waited, timing her answer. She leaned toward the microphones, a smile parting her lips. "Ever since I was a little girl, I had a fantasy of meeting my true love here." She paused for effect, her hands trailing to her heart.

"In the fantasy, I had a fender bender near the Eiffel Tower with a cute French guy. We fell in love and lived happily ever after. It's so funny — I just thought of it this morning. But that's not what happened. I was driving to the *Rue Saint-Honoré* when a camera flash blinded me, and I lost control of the car."

The crowd smiled sympathetically, heads tilting. It was working. Only the Greaseball frowned, pushing through the throng.

She turned away from him. The reporters shuffled and moved with her.

"I always imagined us dancing under the Eiffel Tower, just like Audrey Hepburn and Fred Astaire."

"Are you saying you crashed your car on purpose?" the Greaseball asked.

She flashed doe eyes to the cameras. "No, of course not. But after it happened, I thought maybe my fantasy had come true. This is a lot more serious, though, and no handsome man helped me from the car... unless you count the policeman, I suppose."

Several cameras swung at once to the blushing policeman.

"You don't have to say it." She laughed. "I know. I'm a hopeless romantic."

The crowd laughed with her.

She couldn't believe it worked. She had charmed them all. Was there anything she couldn't do?

Questions started up again, but police officers parted the crowd to make way for a large ambulance. The show was almost over. The ambulance parked nearby and medics jumped out. The crowd stepped back, cameras still rolling, capturing everything.

Paramedics set up a cot and made her sit down on it. One of them shone a flashlight into her eyes, listened to her heart, and took her blood pressure. He nodded.

Ananda turned to the crowd and gave them two thumbs up. They cheered. A few people even whistled.

The paramedic bandaged the cuts on her arms, then a ruggedly handsome officer with a swoop of black hair approached. He said something in French and beckoned toward the open door of the police car.

Ananda froze. Was he really going to arrest her? After all this? She couldn't let him. She had to make a graceful exit, or else a photo of her being shoved into the back of a police car would be all over every news outlet. The tabloids would win again.

She leapt up, her heart beating fast.

"It's you!" she shouted. "I can't believe it. You're the man from my dreams!"

"*Qu'est que c'est?*" he asked.

Whispers flew from one officer to another.

"What?" he asked, leaning toward her.

She kissed him square on the mouth, inhaling his expensive cologne.

After a stunned moment, he kissed her back. Catcalls erupted from the crowd. The other officers laughed and shook their heads.

"Dance with me," she whispered. "Please?"

"Dance? Here?" he asked, his dark eyebrows arching.

"*Oui.* Dance with me, then take me to the ambulance. Please. Do you understand?"

The police officer threw a desperate glance at his senior officer. The older officer shrugged and threw his hands in the air. The black-haired officer faced her again, beaming, and clasped her hand.

From the crowd, a man with an accordion rushed forward and began to play a waltz from *Amélie*.

Ananda couldn't believe her luck. The officer stepped on her foot once, but after a beat, they glided together as perfectly as if they'd practiced. Police and paramedics laughed in disbelief, while hundreds of phone cameras followed the couple as they swept beneath the gigantic arching structure.

Ananda glowed with relief at the serendipity of the moment. She threw back her head and laughed, giving the photographers ample time to capture the moment. Then she looked into the officer's smoldering brown eyes.

"What's your name?" she asked.

"Bertrand."

"You really are a dream come true. I'll never forget this."

When the song's last notes died out, he dipped her low. The crowd applauded. He helped her up and they walked toward the ambulance, his hand lightly touching the small of her back.

Ananda climbed in and waved at the crowd. They waved back, even after the ambulance doors shut and they were out of sight.

She closed her eyes and leaned against the wall. She'd saved her reputation once again.

Chapter 1. Abandonment

I picked up a file and read the name of the fourteen-year old runaway scowling at me on my sofa. My office was cramped, but I insisted on having a sofa. People felt comfortable on them.

"Tanya, my name is Margaret Woods," I said, "but you can call me Mag. I've been a therapist at the New Beginnings Center for five years. Why don't you tell me about yourself?"

She crossed her arms. "What do you want to know? Everything sucks."

I pursed my lips. I could imagine what she was thinking. I had an air of privilege, from my Ann Taylor blouse to my conservative, short haircut. But despite my degrees and Board Certification, we weren't so different. I shifted in my chair, adjusting my skirt so it sat on my waist instead of squeezing the fat rolls around my hips.

"Look, I know how hard it is to be out there — barely eating, just surviving. I've been there myself."

She cocked her head and lifted a single eyebrow. "You ran away from home?"

I nodded, and looked at a picture of San Francisco on my desk. "When I was sixteen, my parents and I had a huge fight about what I should study in college. They wanted me to have a 'real job,' but I wanted to be an artist. So I ran away to California and lived out of my car for a few months, until it got towed. Then I lived on the street. It was harder than I imagined. I would've starved if it hadn't been for a shelter. They helped me get back on my feet and inspired me to make a difference. That's why I work here."

Tanya sucked on her lower lip.

"It's rough out there," I continued, "but we can help you. You don't have to worry about where you're going to sleep, or if you're safe or not. You don't have to worry about your next meal. And we can help you figure out what you want to do with your life. How does that sound?"

She looked around the room. Her shoulders unhunched a little. Something in her eyes shifted, as if she was tired of being tired.

"I'll try it. It's getting really cold out there. But no promises."

My heart melted and I felt myself break into a smile. I'd saved one more person from the harsh Minnesota winter, drugs, and who knew what else. She was getting a fresh slate, just as I had.

"You're going to like it here, I promise. Let's show you around."

After giving Tanya a room, I went back to my office and took a big slurp of creamy hazelnut coffee. My cellphone blinked with three voicemails. I pressed play on the first one.

"Hey Mag. It's Darren, from SoulM8s? I was wondering if you want to do anything this weekend. There's a holiday concert downtown-"

I grimaced and pressed delete. Darren was good on paper. He had a steady job, a 401k, and a nice car. The only problem was he had no personality whatsoever — he was the human equivalent of a gerbil. Why I'd slept with him last week, I'll never know. Something to talk with my therapist about.

I played the second message.

"Congratulations Miss Woods, you're now a published author," my agent Cleve Burns purred. "You couldn't have picked a better time to write *Analyzing Ananda*. The publisher wants an extra chapter about the Eiffel Tower event in the next week or so."

My eyebrows furrowed. Eiffel Tower? What was he talking about?

"Send it to me by next Monday. We'll tack it to the end of the e-books as soon as you're finished."

I deleted the message and felt a twinge of hope. Ever since Ananda's biography was published a few years ago, I was a running joke about 'the need to preserve one's character in this modern age.' Finally, with my book, I was able to set the record straight about my friendship with Ananda, specifically that I was never her girlfriend or the high priestess of a pill-popping nude colony known as 'The House of Transformation.'

The last message was from my best friend Kitty. She and I talked every month or so, always about Ananda, never really about ourselves. Our lives hadn't changed much in the seven years since Ananda left. I'd received an MA in Psychology, and Kitty had narrated a few bestselling books, but that was nothing compared to Ananda getting Musician of the Year and gracing the covers of Vogue and People.

"Mag, it's Kitty. Did you see what she did today? She crashed into the Eiffel Tower! She looks really messed up."

Hmm. So that's what Cleve was talking about.

"I still don't know why you published that book," Kitty said, "and why did you say she has sociopathic tendencies? Call me back."

I flinched. Had I said that?

I went to my laptop and downloaded my book. While it loaded, I googled 'Ananda Eiffel Tower.' A picture from earlier today showed Ananda's bandaged arms wrapped around a police officer as they danced under the Eiffel Tower. In the background, the front end of a tiny car was smashed into the base.

Someone knocked on my office door. Mary, the other therapist at New Beginnings, walked in. We were both in our early thirties, but she had a deep-fried southern demeanor, from her frosted hair to her acid-wash jeans, that made her seem older.

"A new girl just arrived," she said, zipping up her puffy down coat. "I have a dentist appointment in half an hour. Can you take her?"

"Sure."

"Thanks. She's in my office. Her name's Ella."

Mary waved on her way out the door. I'd started to close my laptop when another photo caught my eye. Ananda smiled, a streak of blood in her hair, her eyes lit with xyritav. My heart ached for her. She'd been in pain for years and now she was running on fumes. Maybe no one else could tell, but I could. I said a prayer for her and closed my laptop.

I walked to Mary's office and knocked. "Ella?"

The old brass knob twisted in my hands. The office was empty, but the blinds were ratcheted up and the window was open a crack. I looked out the window. Under the streetlights, a solitary trail of footprints cut through the fresh snow.

I frowned. I could run outside to find her, but it would take too long to get my snow boots and coat on. She'd be three blocks away, and I'd never find her. I stared outside at the twirling flakes for a moment. As much as I wanted to, I couldn't save all of the girls who came here. Just the ones willing to stay.

Later that night, I ate dinner with the girls and the house moms. Tanya walked in with another girl, chatting about boys at their high school. I smiled. She might be alright after all.

After three slices of pizza, I left to investigate what Kitty said about my book. I was pretty sure she was mistaken — I've called Ananda a lot of things, but a sociopath wasn't one of them.

I drove my beat-up Honda Civic to my apartment, threw my stuff by the door, and turned on TMZ. Just like every other night, I made a cup of tea in my favorite mug, a chipped, blue-glazed cup from the only man I'd ever loved. It made me feel better, as if my life wasn't a disappointment, only a rather long hiccup.

As I waited for the peppermint tea to steep, I flipped open my laptop. I saw an email from the Journal of Psychology and felt a rush of hope — maybe my PTSD research would get published. Then I read the words 'does not offer any novel insights,' and my heart sank. They'd declined it, just as several other journals had.

Tears dashed into my eyes. I'd hoped by my tenth rejection letter, it wouldn't sting so much, but it did. My research was good. They were idiots for rejecting me. I didn't even want recognition — I just wanted the information out there, even if it helped only one therapist counsel someone with PTSD.

I opened *Analyzing Ananda* and scrolled through the opening pages, but something was wrong. It didn't look like the document I'd sent them. The intro about Ananda's good points was missing. A passage that was supposed to be in chapter eight was at the beginning. And then there it was, on page five.

Ananda can make anyone in her presence do anything she wishes. It's one of her most dangerous abilities, since she believes herself to be above the law and common decency. Her beauty, narcissism, and sociopathic tendencies enable her to use people for personal gain and make her utterly unstoppable.

My stomach bowed into my spine. I opened the drafts I'd sent Cleve and combed through them. I didn't see the word sociopath anywhere. Had he made it up? Then, I found it, in an instant message I'd sent to him.

Ananda definitely has more sociopathic tendencies than the average person!

My hand flew to my mouth. I'd been tipsy when I wrote that! I hadn't thought he'd publish it.

I tried to calm my raging heartbeat by listing my top three fears.

1. *Fear of career loss*
2. *Fear of being misunderstood*
3. *Fear of facing Ananda after calling her a sociopath*

Naming my fears was an old trick I'd picked up in college, and sometimes, it worked. I took a deep breath and felt a little better. My therapist always said 'it's never as bad as it seems.' I hoped he was right.

"And now for the latest on party girl Ananda Dawn," the TMZ reporter said.

I turned the volume up. Graphics bustled on the screen.

"Ananda cancelled the remainder of her European tour after she crashed into the Eiffel Tower with a rental car earlier today. She was released from the hospital soon after with no major injuries. Authorities didn't press charges against her, even though she put a two-inch chip in the concrete. Here's footage taken from the scene earlier today."

Ananda, in her big sunglasses, smiled dopily. "I had a fantasy of meeting my true love here... I always imagined us dancing under the Eiffel Tower, just like Audrey Hepburn and Fred

Astaire."

I recoiled. Had she even seen *Funny Face?* They danced *on top* of the Eiffel Tower, not below it.

TMZ continued. "The pop star danced with police officer Bertrand Le Fevre before going to the hospital. The rumor around Paris is Le Fevre might propose to her to make her Eiffel Tower dreams come true. Sources say he broke up with his girlfriend of two years after that steamy kiss. Next on TMZ-"

I turned the television off and sat back on the couch. I'd been so worried Ananda might've been hurt or gone to jail. But she'd gotten off so easily, like she always had. She probably dazzled everyone with her smile and snuck out the back door.

My doorbell rang. I looked up with a start. No one came to my apartment at seven at night, or ever, for that matter. Could it be Darren from SoulM8s, wanting another late night hook up? I hoped not.

I walked to the door and stood on tiptoe to look through the peephole. A girl slouched in the apartment lobby, her head turned away. Her black leather jacket was out of place in the Minnesota winter. Was she one of my former patients?

I opened the door. When she turned to face me, my heart stopped and my blood froze in my veins.

"Surprise," Ananda said.

Chapter 2. Hostage

My heart clenched as Ananda and I looked at each other for what felt like eons. Her makeup was smudged, like she'd been crying. Did she know about *Analyzing Ananda*? Did she come to make me take it off the shelves? Sweat erupted from my pores, despite the chill in the foyer.

"Magdalene, I've missed you."

"I thought you were in France," I said, my voice higher than normal.

"They made me come back to the States." She shivered. "Apparently I wore out my welcome."

I blinked at her. I could barely speak. Why was she here?

She cowered, looking over her shoulder as if my neighbors would emerge from their apartments at any moment. "Can I come in?"

My hand flew up to the doorframe. Years of therapy taught me I needed boundaries, especially when it came to her, but I never thought I'd have to use them without notice.

"I- I don't know," I stammered. "I mean, you could have called first."

"I ditched my phone in France. I didn't want the paparazzi to track me. Please. I need to talk to someone who knew me before-" her voice caught in her throat, her eyes pleading toward me. "Before all this."

"But you ignored me for seven years. You never called me back, or wrote, or anything, and now you want to be friends again?"

She raised her glassy green eyes to mine. Her chin began to twitch. "I can explain. Can I please just come in?"

I swallowed, considering. Her tears made my heart break, even though I was still mad at her. I sighed. I supposed I could let her in for a moment. I moved away from the door.

I snapped my laptop shut, but not before seeing the last sentence from *Analyzing Ananda*.

Her beauty, narcissism, and sociopathic tendencies enable her to use people for personal gain, and make her utterly unstoppable.

I crossed my arms. I'd have to keep my boundaries up.

"How'd you know where I live?" I asked.

"Kitty gave me your address ages ago." Ananda dumped a duffle bag by the door.

"Really? When was the last time you spoke with her?"

"It's been a couple of years. I think she's mad at me about something." She laughed nervously.

"What's so funny about that? Maybe she has a good reason."

"Magdalene, Kitty's crazy, we both know that. Remember when she lost it?"

"Yeah, but..." I couldn't finish my sentence. My thoughts were blown to pieces by the fact that Ananda, my ex-best friend and international pop star / scandal was in my living room, looking over my secondhand furniture and my barely decorated apartment.

I took a deep breath and cleared my head. There was no way I was going to let her get to me.

"You still have this painting, after all this time."

She gazed at the only thing I had on my walls, a Bosch painting that used to hang at the House of Transformation. I used to love it, but I seldom looked at it anymore. It was a ghostly reminder of everything I left behind from those days.

The silence grew uncomfortably long. Guilt about my book curdled my stomach.

"So why are you here?" I asked.

"The paparazzi don't know about this place. They follow me everywhere. I can't powder my nose without them knowing about it. They'd go nuts if they knew I came to you, of all people."

I scowled. "Is that because of the story you made up about us? Ananda, we never had drug-induced orgies! Why did you lie?"

"My ex-manager wrote that book, but it's okay. I fired him. He was all about my sex appeal and didn't understand who I really am."

"Why didn't you stop him from publishing it? You could have done something about it. Retracted the quote or something?"

"I wanted to. I didn't know about it at first. Once I found out about it, I wanted to take back the whole book, but my contract said he could say anything about me. I probably should have read it before I signed it," she said absently.

I seethed. "You know, the reputation your manager gave me hasn't done a lot for my career. I'm a joke to most psychologists."

"You're not a joke to me."

"Well, you're not a professional psychologist."

She shrugged. "I could be."

I turned away. I hated her for saying that. As if my six years of college and Board Certification meant nothing. I massaged my left temple. She'd been in my apartment for five minutes, and already my head ached.

"Look Ananda, I have boundaries now. I'm different than I was seven years ago."

A phone bleated from one of her bags. Her eyes went wide.

I glared at her. "I thought you said you ditched your phone."

"Well... I ditched one of them."

I nodded. Great. She was going to lie about everything again. "Do you want to answer it?"

"No, I'm listening to you."

"You screened my calls for years. Why bother listening to me now?" I walked away from her, fuming. Why did I expect an apology? She never admitted guilt. Why did I think she'd be any different?

"Magdalene..." She smiled her million-dollar bullshit smile.

"What?" I snapped.

"I'm sorry. Time is different on the west coast. I was always so busy. By the time I had a free moment, it was four in the morning and I couldn't call you back."

"Well, email works 24/7."

"Mag, come here." She walked toward me, arms open.

I slapped her hands away. "Don't touch me. You can't hug

someone if you've hurt them. You need to ask."

She gaped, her waterworks starting up again.

I looked away. It took all the energy I had to stay grounded in my own emotion and not be manipulated by her tears.

"Mag, I wouldn't have come back unless I needed your help. You're the only person I can trust. And I'm sorry about the past. I can't say it enough."

I looked at her body language, ready to throw her out of my apartment if she showed the slightest sign of acting. But she looked more honest in that moment than she had in all her years of being a celebrity. And she'd apologized — that was a huge step for her. The old Ananda never would've apologized. I relaxed the tension in my shoulders and exhaled.

"Okay," I muttered. "Apology accepted. It's just... when you didn't respond to any of my emails, I felt rejected."

"I wouldn't reject you. I was just so busy."

I nodded and met her eyes. I believed her. She lived in the moment — out of sight, out of mind. And of course she was busy.

She bounced on her heels, beaming. "I knew you'd come around. So, can we get something to eat? I'm starving."

"Yeah, sure." I reached for my coat.

She grasped my arm. "But I don't want to go out there, you know? People might recognize me. Does Indian sound alright? And could you pick up some organic strawberries and hemp milk too? I'll pay."

I took a step back. "Are you kidding me? I'm not doing that for you. Don't you have personal assistants to run your errands?"

Her lips pressed together and her gaze turned to the carpet. "I fired them. My assistants, my bodyguards, my manager, everyone. I'm all alone now."

"Why'd you fire them?"

"They treated me like I was a child. They talked down to me."

"Really? Even your bodyguards?"

"No. But they were with the manager, so when I fired him,

they went too."

"When did this happen?"

"A week ago. My label dropped me too. It's been pretty hard since then. The paparazzi know I don't have bodyguards anymore, but I don't think they followed me here. I really am starving."

"Okay. Let's get some food."

We stepped out of my apartment and into the hushed night. The falling snow made white lines on the tree branches. I shoved my mittens into my coat pockets and dug out my car keys. Ananda shivered in her jacket. She reached into her studded purse and retrieved huge sunglasses.

"It's night time," I said. "You don't need those."

"I do need them," she pouted as she slid them on. "I might get recognized."

"No one's going to recognize you on my street." I looked down the road at the placid pastel houses and apartment buildings.

"You'd be surprised. Will you drive?"

I noticed the Lexus parked across the street with one tire on the curb and almost laughed.

"Sure."

My car was a mess with folders and paperwork, but Ananda didn't seem to notice. I started the engine, then brushed the snow off the car while it warmed up.

Something nagged me in the back of my mind. She probably didn't come to St. Paul just to eat curry with me.

I climbed in and turned to her. "Before we go anywhere, you have to talk. Why did you come to see me?"

I flinched when her cold hand touched my cheek. I wasn't used to being touched.

"Mag, I need to remember who I am. I've had a few nervous breakdowns, but this was the worst yet. That Eiffel Tower crash — it wasn't exactly an accident."

I took an involuntary breath. "Are you saying you tried to commit suicide?"

"Maybe. I've been driving under the influence a lot lately. I know I'm not supposed to, but I need to take xyritav or I get anxious."

I touched her hand. If she'd been behaving recklessly, that meant she was depressed. It could be a precursor to suicide, too. Her life really was as terrible as I suspected.

"I just want my old life back," she said.

I nodded. After a moment, I shifted the car into drive, maneuvering carefully on the snowy streets.

Lately, the paparazzi photos showed her dining and walking alone, head bent, sunglasses on. Maybe she didn't have any other friends. I glanced at her sidelong. For a moment, she looked like her old self, from our times of all-night parties, art, and lust. I stopped at a red light. Thick snow swirled around the car.

"This is so weird," I said. "I feel like no time has passed, like we're still close friends."

"We *are* still close friends. You know me better than anyone else."

"Ananda..." I wanted to tell her about my book, except the words didn't come. I shook my head. "I'm going to wake up and this will all be a dream."

She touched my face again, and this time, I didn't flinch. I relaxed into her caress.

"Life is but a dream," she said spacily. Her sunglasses caught the streetlights. For a moment, she looked drug-addled, propped, obscene.

I drew away from her. Was she high again?

The light turned green. We rode in silence, passing our old haunts, until I turned into the nearly empty parking lot of the Indian restaurant. We got out of the car and crunched through the snow.

"Did you know I'm performing at the Grammys this year?"

I nodded. Of course I'd heard about it. Her act was the finale. The commercial slots were auctioned at some of the highest prices to date. I couldn't imagine the pressure she was under.

I opened the door to the Indian restaurant and swooned at the aroma of cumin and garlic simmering in the air. My stomach clenched when I realized this was where the Swami had taken me on our 'date.' I started to think it wasn't a good idea, but Ananda walked in and sat down at a booth. I shrugged out of my coat and sat down across from her.

"What are you going to order?" she asked.

"I'm not that hungry. I had pizza at the center." I glanced at the list of entrees. But chicken curry did sound pretty good.

"So, Mag, we've just been talking about me. What do you do these days?"

I shrugged. "Mostly I work, come home, and unwind."

"Do you still make collages?"

I gave her a tight smile. "Do you know how hard it is to be a successful artist?"

"Who said anything about success? That was your dream, what you always wanted to do."

"Well, it was a stupid dream." I unfolded a napkin and dropped it in my lap.

"Anyone who ever created anything felt that. But have you really given up without even trying?"

"I tried–"

"Stevey's 'Art Parties' aren't trying. Those are the precursor to trying."

"But I need to work. It's unsustainable to do both."

"You can still do things and work. What do you do at the end of the day? Watch tv? Online dating? More work?"

I swallowed. "Yeah, so?" I could've added 'write books about my former best friend too, but my heart hammered just thinking about telling her. Hopefully, she'd be gone by the end of the night and I'd never have to deal with it.

"Mag, where'd your dreams go?"

I cringed. She might not know much about the real world, but she had a point. I'd given up on those childish dreams. She didn't have to be so condescending. She was testing my boundaries, and I needed to keep her on the right side of them.

"So, where are you staying tonight?" I asked as the server

walked past us with steaming entrees.

She toyed with the menu. "I don't know."

"Well, my apartment is too small for two people..."

She stared at me and then yawned. "I think I'll get the *saag paneer*. I'm so tired. I must be jet lagged."

"Wait. So you're okay with going to a hotel?"

"Yeah, I was planning on that anyway. Goddess, Magdalene, you look the same as the last time I saw you."

"Well, thanks. So do you." It wasn't true. She looked more fabulous, while I was forty pounds heavier. I hated it, but it was part of getting older and working a desk job. Not everyone had a metabolism like hers.

"I can't believe it's been seven years since we saw each other," she said. "It feels like we were just hanging out last week at the House of Transformation."

I nodded. Those days were always on my mind. It was almost as if everything she'd done over the years was just a ridiculous xyritav dream. But it wasn't a dream. I had a whole crate of magazines and biographies under my bed to prove it.

After we ordered, Ananda excused herself to the bathroom. I stared up at a painting of a multi-armed Goddess. I still had no idea what Ananda wanted from me. Did she need a friend? A therapist? Did she want to rekindle our romance? She might be disappointed. I wasn't ready to be besties again. And there was the issue of my book. I never thought I'd have to tell her about it face to face — I never thought I'd see her again. I bit my lip. If only I'd waited one more day to release it.

I shook my head. She'd probably leave in a couple of hours and I wouldn't see her for another seven years. What was I worried about?

Ananda came out of the bathroom with fresh makeup and plopped into the booth just as the appetizers and drinks arrived. The server did a double take at her transformation, but she didn't notice.

"Anyway," she said, "like I was saying, my life is so confusing. People follow me everywhere, trying to get a picture of me so they can say I did something stupid."

"People always liked to take pictures of you. Remember Jared?"

Jared's photos of Ananda had become famous. He was a talented photographer, but that didn't excuse him for what he did that night at the House of Transformation.

She sneered. "I've never been sicker of people in my life. Sometimes I just want to be left alone. Everyone in the world knows everything I do, but not who I really am. They only know a fraction of a fraction."

Her eyes glassed over for a second. My mind flashed back to the night she took too much xyritav. '*I am the cerulean doll,*' she'd said, slumped against the wall.

I took a deep breath and munched on a piece of fried *paneer* to clear my mind. "How was France?"

"Not bad. I went shopping with the French First Lady, what's-her-name."

"That's cool."

"Yeah, but I miss our old times more than anything, when it was just you, me, the collages, and Kitty. We had the best parties. Do you still talk to Kitty?"

"Yeah."

"I think Kitty's forgotten about me."

I laughed. "Of course she hasn't. Who could forget about you? You're Ananda."

She grinned at me like a fox. I smiled back, but clenched my hand under the table until my fingernails dug into my palm. I needed to be more careful. I was playing into her sense of entitlement.

"Could we drive by the House of Transformation?" she asked.

My breath caught. Didn't she know what'd happened to it? "I don't think that's a good idea."

"Why not?"

"It's getting late and I need to wake up early tomorrow morning."

"Why?" she asked, dumbfounded.

I raised my eyebrows. "I have to work."

"Take a day off."

"I can't just take a day off work." I looked at her balefully.

"Come on. When was the last time you took a day off?"

I tried to remember. Had it been June? "Six months ago?"

"See?" she asked. "You deserve a day off."

"Ananda..." I sighed.

She was getting her way all over again. Worst of all, it was so tempting. To be off work with my superstar ex-best friend — wasn't that what days off were for?

"I'll think about it."

Our server returned and set down the entrées, his gaze lingering on Ananda again. We ate in silence. The only other customers paid and left. A bus boy appeared and poured water into our glasses. He stared at Ananda, spilling water on the table. I was used to people staring at her — she was gorgeous — but I was surprised when he whipped out his phone.

"Ananda, I love you." His Indian accent made the words rounder.

"Thank you." She smiled at his phone as if they were old friends.

The camera swung to me. I froze.

"This is my friend Magdalene," she said. "*Namaste.*"

He aimed the camera back to her. "*Namaste.*" He closed his phone and walked back to the kitchen.

She turned to me with a smirk. "They love me in India. My name means bliss in their language."

I nodded. I remembered that from our old days. I poked at my food, but I was full. After Ananda finished, we waited five minutes for the check, and then ten. When there was no sign of the server or the bus boy, Ananda walked behind the counter to get a box.

"Did you make a hotel reservation yet?" I asked.

"Not yet," she said, returning to the table to spoon the rich gravies into the box. "But don't worry. The hotels around here never fill up."

The restaurant was eerily quiet.

"Where is everyone?" I asked.

The kitchen doors banged open. Five or six Indian men ran toward us with cameras and camcorders.

Ananda flashed frightened eyes at me. I grabbed my coat and purse and we rushed toward the exit.

When I opened the door, I startled. Bright lights beamed at us, as if we'd just walked into four lanes of oncoming traffic. I shielded my eyes. A small crowd amassed in the parking lot. Video cameras swiveled, cameras flashed, and voyeurs raised their cellphones, all to capture Ananda.

I froze. Ananda walked in front of me and waved, sunglasses on again.

"Ananda Dawn, over here!"

"Ananda! Are the rumors of your pregnancy true?"

"Hey, isn't that her psychologist friend?"

I hurried after her, my hands shaking so much I could barely unlock my car. We piled in. The crowd surrounded us, pressing against the car, clamoring and shouting questions. Cameras flashed in our faces.

"What the hell?" I said. I dropped my keys twice on the floorboard before starting the car.

Ananda smiled as serenely as if we'd just come back from the spa. "Just back up slowly."

I backed up, then gunned it through a gap in their ranks. "Holy shit. That was insane!" I said, breathless.

"This is my life, every day."

I glanced in my rearview mirror at the paparazzi rushing into vans. My stomach soured. I ticked my fears off as I peeled out onto the main road.

1. *Fear of public ostracization*
2. *Fear of career loss*
3. *Fear of the unknown*

"Drive around until we lose them," Ananda said, looking over her shoulder.

I turned onto side streets and back alleys, sped through yellow lights, and without thinking, drove back to my apartment. They were there waiting for us. A gaggle of cameras and lights on tripods crouched in the snow like sci-fi creatures.

We ran inside and drew the blinds and curtains in a mad rush. When we were done, I collapsed into a chair, my heart still racing. Ananda put the food in the refrigerator and leaned against the wall, the trace of a smile on her lips. My breath caught. Was this exactly what she'd wanted to happen?

"Now you see what's it's like for me," she said.

"Yeah. It was a nightmare."

Someone pounded hard on the window. I jumped.

"Ananda!" someone said from outside. "I just have a few questions for you. Open the window!"

"You might want to call the police." She slipped into the bathroom, closing the door firmly behind her. Seconds later, the shower ran.

After calling the police and talking to an incredulous officer, I turned on the television and set the kettle on for tea. Soon enough, flashing blue and red lights shone through the blinds. Officers drew the crowd back to the edge of the property.

Entertainment Tonight played a video clip of us exiting the restaurant. Ananda moved like a diva through the crowd. I scurried behind her like an obese mouse. I shook my head. Great.

"Ananda Dawn is the subject of controversy, back in her home town of St. Paul, Minnesota. Rumor has it she's pregnant, though we could neither confirm nor deny this. She was recently released on bail for public misconduct at SeaWorld in Florida, and earlier today, damaged the Eiffel Tower due to a car accident. Ananda Dawn is presently at the apartment of long-time friend, psychologist, and ex-girlfriend Margaret Woods. Some think it's a cry for help."

They cut to live footage of my apartment lawn. A woman in a red coat held a microphone, her scarf flapping in the wind.

"Margaret Woods, known as Magdalene in Ananda's biography, is a psychologist at the New Beginnings Center for Teen Runaways in St. Paul, Minnesota. She just published a book about Ananda earlier today that's rising to the bestseller list–"

I flipped the channel and saw a reporter in a black pea-coat in front of my apartment.

"–ex-girlfriend Margaret Woods, who works as a therapist, writer of the book *Analyzing Ananda...*"

I couldn't believe how many reporters swarmed in front of my apartment! And could Ananda be pregnant? I felt sick to my stomach. I got up and swatted the lights off.

"I guess they're going to bed," the reporter chortled.

"I guess so," the anchorman laughed.

I grimaced and fell on the couch. When they showed a photograph from my college graduation, I couldn't take it any more. I turned the television off, but the image lingered. That picture was taken a few days before I rented the House of Transformation. In the photo, I leaned against a tree trunk, graduation cap in my hands, wearing an exasperated smile, as if to say 'Mom, Dad, enough pictures already.' The show must've gotten it from my alma matter. I wondered what else they had.

Ananda emerged from the bathroom, one of my towels wrapped around her. "I feel so much better." She dug through her bag and pulled out fresh clothes.

"Hey, uh... are you pregnant?" I asked.

"What? No, I'm just not dieting anymore. And I haven't worked out for a while."

"On the news, they said–"

"It's a food baby." She flipped up her blouse and touched her tiny belly.

The teakettle whistled. I got up, but she stepped in front of me.

"I'll get it. What do you want? Peppermint? Chamomile?"

I nodded, surprised she remembered. I drank one of those two teas every night for years.

After she walked into the kitchen, I played some relaxation music I'd bought years ago for yoga, but had never used until now. My brain hurt, like I had psychic whiplash. I tried to breathe, but it was hard.

Moments later, Ananda, clothed in yoga gear, brought my teapot into the living room and sat on the carpet. I heaved myself onto the floor to join her.

"I made a little of everything. I threw in some red clover from my bag. Remember how we used to pick the blossoms when we walked home from the coffeehouse?"

I nodded, sipping the tea. I tasted chamomile, clover, and an unfamiliar herb... Valerian root?

We drank in awkward silence, Ananda the superstar, and me, the homely house-mouse. I wanted to tell her about my book, but I didn't want to spoil the near-perfect moment.

The curtain lit up from a light outside again. Someone else must've been reporting live.

"So, I guess you're staying here tonight after all," I said.

"Well, I don't want to impose, but I didn't think they'd find me so quickly."

"It's okay. I understand. It must be weird to be hounded by them all the time."

"It is. It's like I'm living for everyone but myself."

Something strange happened. The room shifted. The walls seemed to be breathing, and geometric markings arose from the carpet. The music became mysterious and multi-layered. I looked up and saw Ananda had vanished. Then the room went dark.

Something crackled behind me. When I turned, I saw Ananda, lighting a candle, her face illuminated from below. She looked like a monster. I dropped my teacup and watched it fall in slow motion to the floor.

Xyritav.

"You drugged me," I said, shifting in and out of pools of awareness.

"Mm hm." She placed the candle on my coffeetable and fixed me with a glare. "I drugged both of us. You can't lie on xyritav, remember?"

I swallowed a lump in my throat. As much as I wanted to escape, I couldn't go outside. I couldn't let the whole world know I was on drugs — it'd ruin my psychology career. I was a hostage in my own apartment.

Ananda must've found out about my book. I shivered, a wave of nausea rippling over me. The last time I'd taken xyritav, death was so close I could touch it.

"Ananda, I'm sorry I said those things. I never meant to hurt your feelings."

She looked at me serenely. "You don't have anything to apologize about. We need to talk about what happened at the House of Transformation."

I paused, biting the inside of my lip. Did she not know about my book?

"I want to know if everything was as real to you as it was to me," she said.

"What- what do you mean?" I squeaked.

"The spirits, the ghosts... what happened to me in there."

I took a deep breath and looked at the swirling carpet. "What happened to you is subjective-"

"Don't give me your demeaning psycho-babble, Mag. It doesn't work on me. Look, you were there too. I want to know what happened to me, from a psychic and professional point of view."

I glared at her. "My 'professional point of view' doesn't mean anything right now."

She caressed my back. "I'm sorry. It's been a while since you partook, hasn't it? Since Yes died?"

I nodded. An image of Yes lying on a slab in the morgue flashed in my mind. Yes was so young. Our whole community had fallen apart that night.

I tried to slow my breathing, knowing it would be better if I didn't resist the drug, but I couldn't. A dam broke behind my eyes and I started to cry.

"I've thought about that night so many times. I wish it could've been different. I'm so sorry." She took my hand.

I couldn't think of anything to say. It was all I could do to keep a tiny sliver of sanity. I held onto that, as slippery as it was.

"Let me try another way of asking." She brushed her hair with her fingers. "Tell me about the ghosts at the House of Transformation."

I huffed. "I don't know what you want me to say. At the time, they seemed real. Now, I think it was just the drugs."

"But you had proof, remember? You knew one of the ghost's names. She helped me when I was sick. They were real, so tell me what you know about them!"

A chill lifted the hairs on my arm, as if she'd just conjured the spirits that lived and died at the House of Transformation.

I took a deep breath. "I didn't really know their names. Plus, rational psychology doesn't lend a lot of credibility-"

"Fuck rational psychology! Is this what you've become? What happened to you? It's like you turned off your ESP and you're living among the once-born as if you're one of them."

I glared at her. "Maybe I am one of them. There are worse things to be."

"But your potential, Magdalene — you're barely scraping the surface. You're living like someone who gave up."

I turned my hands over. "I don't know what you want me to say."

"I want you to tell me I'm not crazy," she said, baring her teeth, her eyes gleaming in a crazy kind of way.

"I can't say that," I grumbled. Stupid xyritav and not being able to lie on it.

"So I *am* crazy," she said.

"No, it's not that easy."

"Fine, tell me. What does rational psychology have to say about me?"

"Well, first of all," I paused, my training coming back to me. "It seems you're very upset, and I feel very uncomfortable. I wish you'd calm down."

How many times had I said that in therapy, pretending she sat across from me?

She pointed a finger in my face. "You're condescending."

"No I'm not!"

"Yes you are. It's your biggest obstacle. All book sense and no common sense."

"At least my biggest obstacle isn't paying the rent!"

"Fine. You know what?" She snatched her purse up from the floor.

My heart clenched. I reached for her. I didn't want her to

leave. Not now, not seven years ago either.

"Don't leave," I said. "I'm sorry. I'm disoriented. I'm saying things I'd never say sober. Why did you dose me?"

"I wanted to know how you really felt, without all your college brainwashing. How much do I owe you, anyway, for rent?"

"Seriously? About two thousand." I watched in disbelief as she scribbled on a checkbook.

"Here. I made it for ten, though I should make it for less. You never paid for any of the clemeral or xyritav back in those days."

She ripped the check out and it floated to the carpet like a leaf, landing face up. All the zeros looked like holes.

My stomach clenched. I stood up and blood rushed from my head. I ran for the bathroom, stumbling into a wall. I lurched toward the toilet just in time to hurl up all the Indian food and pizza into the porcelain bowl.

Ananda brushed my hair out of my face with soft fingertips. She put toilet paper in my hand.

I wiped my mouth and spit.

"Now will you call in sick?" she asked.

My stomach twisted again. I heaved, but nothing came up.

"This is why you never got into xyritav, isn't it?" she asked.

I couldn't answer. Bliss was taking over my brain, making the situation laughable. I should've been angry at the fact that she manipulated, drugged, and kidnapped me in my own apartment. I should've stood up to her and gone somewhere else — anywhere else. But being trapped with her seemed more and more like the best thing that had ever happened to me.

"Look, I got you some water," she said, offering a glass.

"Ananda," I croaked. "Why did you do this to me?"

Her irises shifted like emerald puzzle pieces. "I need you. I've always needed you, Mag. I don't have any real friends, not like you. Everyone expects something from me, except for you. You never did. You just let me be myself." She stroked my arm.

I slumped onto the bathroom mat. She massaged me all over — hard and deep, and then soft. I must have fallen asleep for a moment, because I awoke to her voice.

"Do you remember this scent?"

I inhaled vetivert, jasmine, and cinquefoil, like black flowers. Of course I remembered it. It was the oil she wore when we'd first met.

She rubbed it into my temples and down my spine. "You are now cleansed of negativity," she whispered.

A weight lifted from my shoulders. I wiped my mouth and sat up.

Ananda smiled at me — not the practiced starlet smile, not the smile she wore when she wanted something. It was an innocent smile, one I hadn't seen in years. Despite everything she'd put me through, I smiled back.

"So will you help me?" she asked.

I looked at her pleading eyes. The nausea had passed. A burst of happiness surged within me. My Ananda was home again. She had come back for me.

"Of course."

Chapter 3. Acceptance

I awoke to the lilt of a woman's voice coming from outside my bedroom door. I sat up, confused. My alarm clock was blank. I tapped it but nothing happened. My head throbbed as if I'd pounded shots all night.

Then it hit me — I should be at work.

I ran into the living room. Ananda sat on the sofa, talking on her phone. As soon as she saw me, she shot up.

"Yes, that's right. She's working for me now," she said into the receiver.

"Who are you talking to?"

She hung up the phone and gave me a shaky smile. "I just called your work and told them you work for me now."

"What?!" I reached for the phone. "Why would you do that?!"

She staggered back. "You said you'd work for me, remember? You said you'd be my new manager."

"I said what?" I looked around my living room. My coffee table was pushed against the wall. Candles and tarot cards cluttered every surface, and one of Ananda's tapestries hung over the television. Pillows that normally lined the couch littered the floor. In the three years I'd lived there, I hadn't changed a thing. Now I had a lounge in my living room.

"Magdalene, don't you remember? You said you didn't trust Hollywood managers. I offered to pay you what I paid my last manager and you accepted the position."

Revulsion gurgled up within me. Flashes from the night before played in my mind — being drugged, throwing up, the massage, Ananda burning sage, doing yoga, reading tarot cards, talking for hours in the candlelight... And then it came back to me. I'd accepted the job and a salary of $500,000 a year without a single thought about my career, the New Beginnings Center, or what my parents would think.

I groaned and ran my hands over my face. Of course I'd do

something like that when I was on drugs. But had I told her about my book? I held my breath, thinking back to the conversations from last night. Somehow, the topic never came up. I felt a twinge of relief, though I knew it wouldn't last. I'd have to tell her about it sooner or later.

"Do you want me to call them back?" she asked.

I rubbed my eyes. I wanted to call them back myself, but I was still so foggy from last night. "What time is it?"

"It's a little after one. The paps are still outside."

"The what?"

"The paparazzi. The news people."

"Still?" I peeked behind a curtain.

The paparazzi crowded on the sidewalk about fifty feet away, cameras ready for us to make an exit. Fans had joined the milieu too, gawking and waving signs.

"How do you live around them?" I asked.

"I don't live. Look, if you don't want to be my manager, you don't have to. I just thought last night was so fun, like old times. Remember how much fun we used to have?" Her eyes pinched with sorrow, then she turned away from me, withdrawing into the couch.

I bit my lip. She'd become a shell of her former self, even if her personality still was larger-than-life. In a lot of ways, she was like the runaways I counseled. She looked like them in the eyes — the eyes that said how lost they were, how they felt they had no one in the world. If what she said was true, she didn't have anyone either.

I sighed. I couldn't let her do this alone, though I wondered what she'd think after she found out about my book.

"Look." I crossed the room to face her. "Give me some time to think about it. Anything I said last night doesn't count because I was messed up."

"But it was real. We had intimate discussions."

"Those emotions weren't genuine. They were a product of xyritav. Will you promise not to drug me again?"

"Fine, but it was for a good purpose. Just look at us. We're like best friends again." She smiled.

I narrowed my eyes. I couldn't tell if I was getting through to her or not.

"I made coffee," she said. "Want some?"

"Is it just coffee? Nothing else in it?"

She nodded.

I walked through the swinging kitchen door. Maybe it was the residual xyritav in my system, but everything seemed a fraction out of place. I straightened my tea tins and tried to take a calming breath, just like John had taught me. My brain ached. I could only hope the coffee would make me snap out of it.

I took a cup into the living room and sat on the floor cross-legged. If I was going to even consider being her manager, I wanted to know what I was getting into.

"So you're addicted to xyritav, right?" I asked.

She flopped back on the couch and rolled her eyes. "Define addiction."

"Are you doing it every day? Do you worry about running out?"

"Magdalene, people take xyritav every day. That's how doctors prescribe it."

"Are you really one of those people?"

She shrugged. "Yeah, I guess so."

"Well, if you were one of my patients, I'd suggest you go to a rehab–"

"Are you crazy? I can't go to rehab!"

"Why not?"

"The media would eat me alive. I'd never live it down. For the rest of my life, I'd be known as 'that pop star who went to rehab and never had a career again.'"

I shook my head. "You don't know that."

She pointed to the window. "Look outside. I have no privacy. No wonder I need an anti-anxiety drug. And yeah, I do know I'd never work again if I went to rehab. Think about it. How much work does Lola Whalen get these days? Huh?"

The image of Lola going to rehab popped into my mind. Every newspaper carried the photos and her story. It was all TMZ talked about for a while. She hadn't been in any movies since then, and that was five years ago. It was like she was toxic.

"Okay," I said. "I get it. Just give me some time to think about it." I picked up my phone and peered at it, blinking. Could I really have thirty-two messages? I sighed and started going through them.

"Hi Mag, it's Kitty. Call me."

"Hey Mag, Darren here. I haven't heard from you since our last date. Just wondering how you were doing. Call me if you get a chance. Uh... bye."

"Me again," Kitty said. "Call me when you get this. I'm dying to talk."

"Margaret Woods, this is Tracy Carter from Fox 9 News, wanting to know if I could set up an interview. You can reach my personal cell at 651-"

I rolled my eyes and pressed delete.

"Margaret, this is Cleve from Kukaroo Books. We have a best seller," he sing-songed as I punched the volume down. "Just wanted to let you know. Have a great day!"

"Kurt Hayrick here, from CBS. We're all ears if you want to comment on the-"

"Margaret, this is Richard Trucco. I need to speak with you about Ananda. The people of the world need to know she's okay. I'd like to come by for photographs."

I deleted at least twenty more messages from news people, then Kitty's voice came on again.

"Are you there? Pick up! Come on, it's not fair you're having a reunion without me. I'm coming out as soon as I can. Call me already."

I shook my head and pressed delete. Kitty's intensity was more than I could handle at the moment. The messages continued.

"Hello, Mag? It's Mary from New Beginnings. Are you there? It's ten o'clock and I usually see you by now. Hold on, what?"

A muffled voice murmured in the background, no doubt telling her the news from the night before.

I exited voicemail and called her office, adrenaline pumping through my blood. It rang three times before she answered.

"New Beginnings Center, Mary speaking."

"Hey, it's Mag."

"Oh... I saw on the news you're with Ananda Dawn." She sounded cold, as if I were a stranger.

"Yeah. She's a little-" I faltered. I didn't know how to finish the sentence.

"When one of the girls told me about it, it just floored me, and then Ananda Dawn called here and told Caroline you quit. Is that true?"

I cradled the phone in my hand. "I don't know. I haven't decided yet. It's all so weird."

"The girls are going crazy here. They can't stop talking about her. They've been playing her music all day. We cancelled the activities because, well, you were going to lead the workshops, but they just can't focus. And get this. Caroline's already talking about posting your position."

My heart burned. Of course, cautious Caroline would replace me at the first sign of preoccupation. I couldn't even take a day off without things going crazy.

"Tell Caroline I haven't decided yet."

"You really can't decide? You know, I defended you to the board members after Ananda's book came out, and now you're thinking of working for her?"

"I told you, Mary. Most of the stuff in her book isn't true."

"That's what I told them, but how does it look, now that you're buddies again? It looks like I lied to them."

My face flushed and my heartbeat gunned it. "Look. My friendship with Ananda is complicated. It'd take me hours to explain everything we went thr-"

"You can tell Caroline yourself when you decide. I'm backed up with all the extra work you're leaving me."

"I'm sorry, Mary. I wish I could be there."

"You better think really hard about it. If you take that job, Caroline will make sure you never work in this profession again."

The phone went dead.

I looked at it in disbelief before dropping it onto the coffee table. How could Mary mistrust me after we'd worked together for so many years? How could Caroline think about replacing me so soon? I'd done so much for that place. The thought of someone else in my office made my stomach curdle. Years ago, when I'd painted the walls raspberry red and it took two weekends and five coats, I'd justified it as an investment. I thought I'd be there for the rest of my career. Now, someone else might hang their diplomas on my walls, or paint over them altogether.

My hand hovered over the phone, ready to call Caroline, but I hesitated. Mary was right. I needed to think about it before rushing into a decision either way.

I went to my room, closed the door, and opened the dream journal I never used. I created two columns. Pros and cons.

On one hand, Ananda needed me. I might be able to help her, unlike her former manager, who treated her like she was sex on a stick and threw pills at her. Plus there was the money. With half a million dollars every year, I could pay off my student loans and fund the sorely needed expansion of the New Beginnings Center.

On the other hand, I still didn't trust Ananda completely. Would I be able to put up with her habitual lying? My privacy would be invaded, and the media might make up stories about me. The safe world I'd built for myself would disappear and my career could be jeopardized.

And then there was my book. Would Ananda still want to be friends after she discovered I'd written a book about her? I doubted it. But she, of all people, would know what it's like to have words put in your mouth. Maybe she'd understand and forgive me, and we could pretend like it was a publicity stunt.

I wondered if my therapist might be able to help. John had a way with words. He could make her see it was a mistake, but completely forgivable, just as I'd forgiven her for the same thing.

I thought about my PTSD article rejections. They still burned in my heart. I'd just wanted to help people. And there Ananda was, right in front of me, begging for help. If I worked for her, I could help her, and my salary could fund more PTSD research and a nice website to publish it. The information would be out there, just clicks away from those who needed it.

Lastly, I was certain if I declined the position, Ananda would ask Kitty to be her manager. Kitty wasn't a bad person, but I couldn't remember a time when she was sober. Ananda would spiral further downward. None of her problems would be solved.

I shook my head. I couldn't let that happen.

I went into the living room and sat down on the armrest of the couch. Ananda played with her phone on the floor.

"So about being your manager..." I said.

She turned to me and brightened. "You'll do it?"

I held my breath, praying I'd chosen the right decision. "Yes, but–"

She whooped and got up to embrace me. "Thank you, thank you, thank you!"

"I'll be your manager on one condition. You have to start meeting with my therapist.

She tensed. "What? Why?"

"You're finally going to therapy."

Ananda withdrew and slumped against the couch. "But I don't need therapy."

I shook my head. "It's not negotiable. You're doing it or I won't be your manager."

She looked at the carpet. "I don't know. I don't trust anyone these days. Why can't you be my therapist?"

I pursed my lips and steeled my breath. "It's better if you don't know your psychologist."

"He won't sell my stories, will he? The media can't know about xyritav or my past."

"He won't tell anyone. He would've sold my stories about you a long time ago if that was the case."

"Fine." She frowned. "If that means you'll be my manager."

"Okay. I'm going to see if he can come over tonight." I reached for my phone.

"Can you schedule a massage too?"

"Sure. Hey, how much longer will the paparazzi be here?"

"Beats me," she said, getting up. "I'm going to take a shower."

After I heard the shower running, I dialed John's number. His secretary answered.

"Hello, Dr. Brengleman's office," she said crisply.

"Is John available?"

"He's with a patient right now. Can I take a message?"

"This is Margaret Woods. I need to schedule an emergency home visit as soon as possible."

"Oh, wait, you said Margaret Woods? Hold please."

After a moment, I heard a click.

"Mag, how are you?"

John's warm voice put me at ease despite my predicament.

"Hi John. Did you hear Ananda's at my apartment?" I watched the bathroom door in case she happened to come out.

"Yes, it's all over the news. Are you okay?"

"Yeah, but it's weird. I'm calling because- I'm wondering- would you be interested in a new client?" I held my breath.

"Are you saying what I think you're saying?"

"Yep. I need to see you too. She's running over my boundaries again. And then there's the issue of my book."

"Oh, that book you wrote." He sighed.

"Could you mediate a conversation about it tonight?"

"I suppose so. That's probably the only way you can preserve your friendship. I can't guarantee anything. It's a really harsh critique, one I didn't expect from you. I thought you were getting over your issues with her."

"The publishers added something I never thought would be published. And they edited out most of the positive things I said about her."

"That's no excuse. You let them publish some very cruel things."

"That's why I need your help. Can you come over tonight? We're stuck at my apartment. The paparazzi are watching us like vultures."

"Sure. I'll come over after my other appointments."

I breathed a sigh of relief. "Thank you so much."

When I hung up the phone, I felt a little lighter. I'd tell Ananda about my book tonight. It'd finally be out in the open. If she got mad and stormed out, I could still go back to New Beginnings. Caroline wouldn't have hired anyone that soon.

I googled a massage therapist and made an appointment for her to come to the apartment tomorrow. Then I squinted at an online menu for a Thai restaurant. Xyritav still coursed through my system, making the text a little fuzzy. By the time I ordered, the windows were dark.

I peeked through a crack in the blinds and glared at the news crews, still milling about like a circus. Fifty or so people lined the sidewalk, even in the freezing weather. White vans with gigantic antennas cluttered my usually serene street. A newscaster light flicked on. A reporter babbled into a microphone in front of a camera, then they tore it down and went back to waiting. They stared at my apartment like it was a television show. No doubt, they'd be ready to strike if we made the slightest movement.

When I googled Ananda to find out what the media was saying, I found several links with speculations, which ranged from the blithe *Ananda Dawn visiting hometown for the first time in seven years*, to the shocking *Ananda shacks up with former lover after Parisian fiasco*, and even the scandalous *Ananda's addictions came to a peak when she demanded entry to Woods' apartment, where the two went out to dinner, then stayed in isolation since last night. They could not be reached for comment.* A sidebar advertised *Analyzing Ananda*, with a link to buy it. I sank my head into my hands. What had I gotten myself into?

Chapter 4. Isolation

I was drunk, or at least tipsy when I first met Ananda. I'd been invited to a party by Dahlia, a Polish exchange student, who was in town a few more weeks until her visa expired. She was my only friend from St. Anne's who hadn't gone back to Long Island, Santa Clara, or some other fascinating city. We were both outsiders to St. Paul, only I was from Eau Claire. She had said the party wasn't to be missed. The only problem was she wasn't there.

After hours of tepid conversations with strangers about sports, mainstream music, and pothead movies, I swallowed the last of my beer and set the bottle on the counter. Nothing waited for me at the big empty house I'd rented, but no company was better than bad company. An Irish Goodbye was in order. I tiptoed down the hall and out the front door.

On the porch, I yawned in the sweet June air. I searched my pockets for my keys and cursed. No keys. I'd walked to the party because Dahlia said she'd give me a ride home.

I ambled toward the sidewalk but stopped short. A woman with long orange hair sat on a wicker sofa on the porch. I almost didn't see her. She placed an empty wine glass on a table and gave me a lopsided grin as if we were already friends.

"Pretty lame party, huh?" she asked in a low voice.

I couldn't tell if she had a slight English accent or if her voice was affected by the wine.

"You can say that again," I said.

"So you're from St. Anne's College?"

"Yeah, I just graduated. How'd you know?"

"I heard you talking to those pigs in there."

I laughed. "You mean the frat boys?"

She wrapped a black velvet jacket around her lean frame and stood up. She towered over me — she must've been almost six feet tall. Her eyes glinted like green sea glass.

"What do you think is their purpose in this world?" she

asked. "Why are they even here?"

I shook my head, befuddled, as if my earlier conversations about football and beer had made me stupider.

"I don't know. Business? Money? Organized sports? Why, are you studying philosophy?"

She smirked. "Why be a philosopher when you can save souls?"

"Save souls from what?"

"From being frat boys."

I started to laugh, but footsteps thundered toward us. As if they'd heard us talking about them, the dudes waded through the crowded foyer.

"Come on." She grabbed my hand.

We ran onto the sidewalk and into the shadows. I looked back. The boys blustered onto the porch and looked around drunkenly.

"There's another party a few blocks down," she whispered. "Want to go?"

I nodded. She smiled then paced down the sidewalk. I followed, running after her through the historic neighborhood. We ran past tulips and lilac clusters, still fragrant in the night air. She looked back and laughed. I laughed too. It wasn't just the beer — I'd been drunk before. I'd seen those flowers before when I walked the same sidewalk earlier that night. But somehow, in that moment, they were ten times more beautiful because I was chasing a fantasy.

We rounded a corner. I stopped, breathless, and watched as she loped into a park, then stepped into a dark gazebo. I hesitated, hands on my knees. I wasn't sure if I should follow her. It was late. I didn't know her. She seemed wild, feverish.

I've often wondered what would've happened had I not followed her. I would've returned home to my paintings of blue women, would've tried to paint with depth, and would have missed the mark again. After a month or two, I would've quit painting. I would've gotten a job or another degree, would've started paying off my student loans, and might've even fallen in love and gotten married.

But following her felt so right, as if it was the only thing I could do. She burned with a kind of artistry, and I wanted to burn too. It was my whole reason for living in St. Paul on my own.

I traced her steps and found her sitting among a throng of bodies against the inner gazebo walls. The guys had stubble and funny hats, and the girls had long hair or partially shaved heads. A dready guy played long chords on a guitar that rang out like fragments of a song I almost recognized.

I sat down in the circle and someone handed me a bottle. I drank instinctively, wincing at the sharp punch of liquor. I started to pass the bottle when the girl from the porch intercepted it. She took a long drink before plopping down beside me.

"Jesus, Ananda," some guy heckled from the darkness. "You drink like a lumberjack."

"I'm catching up. Besides, I brought more."

She produced two bottles of wine from her coat pockets and clunked them in the center of the circle.

"Did you get those from the party on Westerby?" he asked.

I looked at the bottles and recognized the Shiraz to be the one I'd bought. It still had the Emporium price tag of $10.39. I laughed. No one at that lame party was drinking wine, anyway.

A cool gust blew into the gazebo, raising bumps on my arms. I ran my hands over them. My jacket hung on a chair at the party. I thought about going back for it, but I didn't want to leave. I was in much better company. Even if I shivered, at least I wasn't bored.

"Are you cold?" the girl asked.

"Just a little."

She started to take her jacket off.

"No, don't–"

"I'm not giving it to you, if that's what you think." She draped it over our backs.

I curled into it, which smelled like a fog of black flowers. "Thanks."

"No problem. I'm Ananda, by the way."

"I'm Mag."

She gasped. "Please tell me that's short for Magdalene."

"Ha. No, I wish. It's short for Margaret, but I hate that name."

I was one of many Margarets, Maggies, and Margies in every school I attended. Mag was the most original name I could think of, even though it rhymed with unflattering words such as hag, nag, and sag.

"Pleasure to meet you." She grasped my hand with hers awkwardly on top, as if I were about to lead her to a dance in Edwardian England.

I shook her hand before laughing self-consciously.

"I can tell you're a sweet girl," she said. "In Europe, the women are so mean. They laugh with you at the bar, then stab you in the back as soon as you walk to the bathroom."

"I always wanted to go to Europe. Where'd you go?"

"I just got back from England. I'm a model. I've been to Europe five times, and I'm sick of it. Sick of the architecture, sick of the attitudes, the high prices, the small portions... Another thing I can't stand — French men. Never date one. Seriously, they're all players."

"Are English guys any better?" I took a bottle from the guy beside me and drinking a swig.

"Oh God, no." She rolled her eyes, grabbed the bottle from me, and drank. "They have this fascination with Americans because we're supposed to be fun, but in the end, every one of them tried to make me more British."

I laughed. "What do you mean?"

"They were like, *do you think you could wear a collared shirt more often?* or *I know this lovely place for a haircut, and I've made you an appointment — don't say no! Or somebody needs a new pair of shoes. Who might that be?*"

I laughed. "But modeling must be exciting."

"Yeah. It's nothing like the sweatpants capitol we live in."

"I know what you mean." I slumped, feeling underdressed in my corduroys and thrift store shirt. Her blouse looked as fragile as a crocus. "At least Europe has good art museums."

"Yes. They're amazing! The funny thing is- well, you've seen Monet's paintings online and in books, right?"

"Yeah."

"On the wall, they look different somehow — like they're alive, or like they were conjured instead of painted."

"I know what you mean. I'm a painter. It's so hard to really make a painting come alive."

She peered into my eyes. "Do I know you from somewhere else? Maybe London?"

"No. I never left the country. I did live in San Francisco when I was sixteen."

"Are you an army brat?"

"No. I ran away when my parents told me I couldn't be an artist. Apparently it's not an economical decision."

I breathed in the cool air and let it out slowly, my heart settling. It was still a point of contention between me and my parents. They'd cut me off completely when I told them I wanted to spend my graduation money trying to be an artist for the summer.

"I lived in San Fran too." She grasped my arm. "When did you live there?"

"Six or seven years ago."

"I lived there about four years ago."

"What part?"

"The northern part."

I tried to remember the neighborhoods. "North Beach?"

"Yeah." She smiled. "I surfed North Beach every day I could. It was amazing."

My breath caught. North Beach was the concrete-lined bay where people boarded ferries. Had she confused North Beach with Ocean Beach?

"Hey Mag," a familiar voice called from outside the gazebo.

I turned. Dahlia was silhouetted against the trees. Her short blonde bob was illuminated as she lit a cigarette.

"I didn't see you at the party," she said.

"I just left. Did you know anyone there?"

"They're a bunch of douchebags. The cool people showed up

here instead. It's almost two in the morning. You want a ride home?"

"Yeah, just a sec." I lifted the velvet jacket off my shoulders and stood up, stretching.

Ananda stood too, a ballpoint pen poised over her arm. "What's your number, Magdalene?"

My heart sank. My phone had gotten turned off when my parents refused to pay the bill. "I don't have a phone right now."

"Your address, then."

"47 Hazelwood."

I watched as she wrote it down on her arm. I never expected her to come. But she did.

Chapter 5. Airs

For the next two weeks, whenever I heard a noise on the porch, I ran to the door, expecting to find Ananda. It was only ever the mail carrier, or a stray cat, or sometimes, nothing at all.

Whenever I left, I taped a note to the door with my destination. I braved the heat and the humidity to go to museums, the library, or hipster coffeehouses, always looking for her. I couldn't forget the way her eyes twinkled when she spoke about art.

I knew I should be painting, but I'd come to an impasse. My blue women looked alien and lifeless. I kept trying to capture cheekbones, but their faces looked as flat as pancakes. I wondered if I'd ever get the hang of it.

On one of my visits to the Arts District coffeehouse, I was leafing through a book about pre-Raphaelite painters when I heard a haughty feminine voice.

"Excuse me?" the voice said.

I dropped the book to the table and saw a woman wearing a black minidress and a red feather boa. She swung her long black hair over her shoulder and peered at me over designer sunglasses.

"Have we met?" she asked.

"I don't think so. I'm Mag."

"I'm Li Xia, but my friends call me Kitty. You look so familiar." She evaluated me for a moment. "Do you know the warehouse people?"

I shook my head. "I don't know anyone here. I just moved from Bedlam Hills."

She frowned. "Then you must know the nudists."

"I don't think I know any nudists," I said, my forehead crinkling.

"Why not? Are you modest or something? I'm not modest but I've always had something against nudists. It's so egotistical, like 'Look at me, I'm naked,' you know?"

She sat down at my table. Her eyes blazed so intensely I could barely look at her. There was something about her that put me on edge, like smelling smoke and knowing there's a fire nearby. She drew a fan from seemingly nowhere, cracked it open, and fanned herself.

"God, it's hot. Anyway, do you go to college there, at St. Anne's?"

"I just graduated from there."

She sat back in the chair, her eyes passing over my thrift store clothes. Her boa slid to the floor and pooled beside her fancy shoes, but she ignored it.

I'd just started to look at my book again when she tapped her fan hard on the book, just inches from my face. I looked up at her, startled.

"I know you from somewhere. When did you move here?"

"Um," I swallowed. "Four weeks ago."

"And what do you do?"

"I'm a painter." That sounded strange. I didn't want her to think I painted houses. "I- I'm an artist."

"Are you a trust fund baby?" Her eyes lit up.

I laughed. It would've made being an artist a lot easier. "Uh, no."

"Me neither." She shrugged. "What was your degree?"

"Psychology."

"I got my BA in communications a few years ago. I do voices for the radio." She leaned conspiratorially across the table and whispered. "You know that commercial, 'the quickest upper hand in intimacy'? The one about erectile stimulants? That was me. Did you hear it?"

"I only listen to public radio."

She swatted my arm. "Now I remember. God, why didn't I see it before? You're Ananda's friend, the one she brought to the gazebo for my birthday party."

I tried to remember if I'd seen her that night. We certainly hadn't been introduced.

"Fun times," she said. "We finished that whole bottle of cognac I brought. Courvoisier VSOP too, not that it matters. So what neighborhood did you move to? The Arts District?"

"No–"

"Where do you live?"

"Hazelwood Rd."

"Ugh. That neighborhood is going to the cockroaches if you ask me. I mean, what kind of mental malfunction happens where people think it's okay to litter?" She whipped her boa up from the floor. "I gotta run. Here's my number, in case you need a cup of flour in the middle of the night or anything."

She scribbled onto a napkin, kissed me on the cheek, and whirled out the door.

I stared at the magenta ink on the napkin.

Kitty

651-538-7760

XOXOX

The next morning, I thought about using a payphone to call her to track Ananda down. It was tempting. I was tired of being a recluse. I decided if Ananda didn't stop by in a few more days, I'd call Kitty and ask to meet up for wine. She seemed like a wine person.

As it turned out, I would've been better off calling Kitty as soon as I got her number. It would have gotten us off on a much better start.

A week after meeting Kitty, I still hadn't seen Ananda. The faces of my blue women still refused to pop from the canvas despite all my attempts at shading. As if to add insult, my cheap paintbrush was falling apart. One of my ladies looked like she was growing a patchy beard. I considered throwing my paintings in the alley behind the house, but I stacked them against the wall, facing away from me.

I picked up all my 'inspirational' images – pictures from Vogue, National Geographic, and other magazines, and opened up the blue vintage suitcase. All the images I'd saved from over the years looked up at me. I'd stuffed them in there in the hopes I'd be able to paint every single one as soon as I left college. But if I couldn't make a face come off the canvas, I wasn't a painter at all. I was wasting my time.

I glared at the images, wishing they could tell me how I could be a real painter. I *felt* art. Why couldn't I make it?

I picked up the image of a ballerina, then water lilies with the same blue color, then ocean waves under a luminous moon. Something came to me, like a forgotten dream, or a ghost of my subconscious. I put them on the carpet and moved them around until the images flowed. They worked together somehow, like alchemy.

A mysterious feeling rose within my chest. Painting was hard, but what if I didn't have to paint? What if I could create art by combining images with different contexts and colors? In this modern age, maybe collaging was an evolution, the next step, of modern art.

I dumped the images from the suitcase and spread them out all over the floor. I matched movements with explosions, flowers with statues, and mountains with crystals.

I made three collages that night. When I couldn't make any more, I went to the thrift store, bought magazines, and made two more collages.

I felt like I was part of a giant, unfathomable puzzle I'd only seen from the ground. Only now, I was above it, and it was all coming together.

I was an artist, at last.

Chapter 6. Talking Back

I'd been in a collaging trance for hours when bells pealed out. I stood up — so that's what the doorbell sounded like. I crept toward the front door, unsure if I wanted to deal with a Jehovah's Witness or a vacuum salesman. I'd barely showered in the past couple of days, and I couldn't remember the last time I'd brushed my hair.

I peeked through the beveled glass window and saw fragments of red hair. I gasped, surprised Ananda had come after all this time. I opened the door.

"Hi Mag." Ananda wore a floor-length bohemian-print dress that seemed to mold to her form.

"How are you? Come in." I felt a little self-conscious in my clothes, but I didn't care. I was just happy to see her.

She kissed my cheek and walked into the foyer, a giant rectangular package under her arm.

"What's that?" I asked.

"The painting we talked about."

I racked my mind, trying to remember what paintings we'd talked about. "Monet's *Waterlilies?*"

"No, I told you I had a framed print I needed to store somewhere for a few months, remember? Wow, you need artwork in here. It's like a nunnery. You don't even have any furniture."

"Did we talk about that?" I leaned against the foyer wall, my head swimming.

"Are you alright?"

"I'm fine. I just forgot to eat."

"Where should I put this?" She turned the package around.

It was a framed painting reproduction. The left panel was heavenly, the right hellish, and the middle looked like the wildest party ever. A flower grew from a man's rear end, birds were the size of people, and a parade encircled a lake, which looked like a giant eye. I took a step back. It mesmerized me to the point of being lost in that other world.

"Pretty cool, right?" she asked. "I used to stare at it when I was a kid. It's *The Garden of Earthly Delights*, by Bosch." She put the painting on the mantle and looked at my collages spread out over the floor.

I blushed. "These aren't done yet." They were missing something, like a portrait missing a mouth.

"They're good," she said, turning to face me with excitement in her eyes. "You should be in the next art show."

"Okay." I tried to sound nonchalant, but I was thrilled. A show! I was still so surprised she'd even remembered me. "Do you want some coffee?"

"Always!"

She followed me into the kitchen, where I started up the ancient Mr. Coffee with oily Ethiopian grounds.

"Do you have any modeling gigs coming up?" I asked.

"Not right now. I have enough money to keep me afloat for a while, though."

"Are you from around here?"

"Yeah, but I went to boarding schools in Vermont until I dropped out. There was too much pressure to conform, you know? Like, wake up early, wear a uniform, and for what? It doesn't matter. Nobody cares if you have a GED or a diploma."

"Are your parents still around?"

She rolled her eyes. "Unfortunately, yes. My mother is a tiresome bore who competes with the neighbors for the best azaleas. My father is devoted to work and his mistress, in that order. Magazines and tv raised me. I got into modeling at fifteen. I haven't seen them much since then. What about yours?"

"They're psychologists in Eau Claire."

"No fucking way." Her mouth gaped. "So did you have a perfect childhood, or what?"

"No, they don't really understand me. They don't want me to be an artist. They want me to go back to school, but I can't stand the idea of two more years in hell, you know?"

"Yeah. Fuck that."

"Yeah. And collaging is going really well."

The coffeemaker gurgled and steam clouds formed. I poured two cups and took a sip. "Do you live around here?"

A furrow appeared in her forehead. "I don't want to think about that right now."

"What's wrong?"

She sighed heavily. After a moment, she lifted her face to meet mine. "It's just — the guy I'm living with is all over me, and we're just friends. It's like he's stalking me, except we live in the same apartment. He lectures me on what I should and shouldn't do, and how I shouldn't bring guys there, not even friends. He's been creeping me out lately. He walked in on me when I was changing clothes."

"That's terrible. Can you move out?"

"I have to. I never want to go there, but I supposedly live there."

I took a deep breath and looked around my empty house. I hadn't considered a roommate, but if she helped with the rent, I could spend a few more months doing collages. I'd just found my art, after all.

"You should move in here. I have two extra rooms."

Her brows shot up. "Seriously?"

"Yeah. Unless you have somewhere else to go."

"I don't have anywhere else. You'd let me move in here? You don't mind?"

"No, I don't mind. I'd love the company. Just me and my collages get a little spacey from time to time."

A sliver of tears shone in her eyelids. "He's going to want his deposit back, and he'll probably ask for next month's rent too."

"If he's as weird as you say he is, you don't owe him anything."

"I only moved in with him because he had a broken soul. I wanted to help him, only he's taking it the wrong way. Once, he didn't know I was there. He got out of the shower and he stood naked in the hallway. He was yelling 'stupid, stupid, stupid!' He was crying and laughing at the same time, and then he punched a hole in the wall! I hid in my room until he left, then I packed a bag. I haven't been back since. Kitty says she doesn't mind, but she only has one bedroom, and she really needs her space."

"Well, if you want to live here, I could help you move your stuff in. What's his work schedule?"

"He's a nine to fiver. He works at the BMV."

"The Bureau of Motor Vehicles?" I laughed. "Figures. Let's go over first thing tomorrow and move your stuff out."

Her eyes filled with hope. "Are you serious?"

"As your psychologist," I smiled, half-joking, "I think we need to remove the source of pain and start the healing process."

"Okay, psychologist." She laughed.

"You'll feel so much better."

"Yeah. God, I just hate conflict like this. It's so draining."

"That's what hitting bottom feels like. But now you have a way up."

Slowly, she smiled. "Okay. Let's do it."

We worked for hours on collages, over several pots of tea and several sticks of incense. We talked about everything. Her stories of traveling abroad were so glamorous. I'd never met anyone like her.

Just before sunrise, when the birds chirped in the dark, we crept upstairs and crashed on my bed. She fell asleep instantly, her breathing heavy and rhythmic.

I watched her slack angelic face for a while, wondering what mysteries hid behind those eyelids, before I slid into sleep.

I awoke with Ananda's hair in my face. Thick afternoon light shone through the window. I unwrapped her arm from around me and tiptoed downstairs to make coffee.

The living room stopped me in my tracks. I'd forgotten we'd taped the collages to the walls last night. The house had the distinguished air of a gallery. Each collage looked like its own world, with art that flowed strangely and beautifully. I gazed at one, rapt with appreciation at its nuances — the tilt of the queen's head to the gravestones, the field of poppies and fireworks exploding above them. Ananda had added something to each of my collages — the missing element. They sang with completion, each with a story and energy all their own.

"It's late. Let's get my stuff from Brad's tomorrow," Ananda said, walking down the stairs.

I pursed my lips. "But tomorrow is a Saturday."

She shrugged. "Then we can wait 'til Monday."

"Won't you feel better if we at least got one bag?"

She eyed me warily, but took a deep breath and nodded.

Brad's apartment building was five-stories of maroon brick surrounded by pine trees and an asphalt lot. We walked up two flights of stairs enclosed in glass and trod down a beige-carpeted hallway, stopping halfway at 221. When Ananda opened the door, the smell of rotten food made me wince. I could see the source of the stench from the hallway — stacks and stacks of dirty dishes by the sink.

Ananda gagged. "Brad never liked to do his own dishes. Let's run."

We ran into her room. She shut the door behind us and lit a stick of incense. A stack of trunks teetered against one wall, bits of cloth hanging out like tongues. Three scantily clad mannequins intertwined in the corner. Silk hung from the ceiling to the bed, and tapestries covered most of the walls. A futon hid beneath a pile of pillows.

"Everything will fit into my car," I said. "We'll have to make a few trips, but it's only one o'clock. We have plenty of time."

"Okay. Let's throw everything into those trunks."

My fingers tingled as I stuffed the intricate fabrics from her closet into the trunks. After twenty minutes, the closet was bare and the trunks were full. We hauled everything downstairs, drove back to the house, and dumped it in the living room.

On the second run, we shoved the futon, bedding, and pillows into my car.

On the third run, we leapt up the stairs and gagged again at the smell of rotting food. It was four o'clock. We had an hour to pack the mannequins and take down the fabric from the walls. Ananda started to remove the silk while I carried the mannequin parts to my car.

As I shoved the last mannequin's body parts amongst the pile of tangled limbs in my backseat, a black Lexus coasted into the parking lot. A man with sunglasses and blond highlighted hair exited the car and walked up the glass-enclosed stairwell. I glanced at my watch. It was 4:30. It couldn't be him.

A heavy feeling hit me in the stomach as I saw him walk to the second floor and go halfway down the hall. I jimmied the last mannequin leg in, slammed the door, and climbed the stairs two at a time. I raced down the hall and saw Brad's apartment door wide open. I bit my lip. I'd closed it on my way out, I was certain. I crouched by the door, listening, my heart thundering.

"Just like that, you're leaving?" a man's voice boomed. "What about everything you promised? Didn't that mean anything?"

"I can't be here any more," Ananda said. "I found someone who supports my visions more than you ever did."

He laughed cruelly. "I'll bet he does."

"It's not a man. God, why are you so obtuse?"

"Are you at least going to wash the dishes before you go?"

I peeked around the corner and saw the back of Brad's head. His arms were crossed as he confronted Ananda.

She saw me in the doorway, and something about her solidified. He glanced over his shoulder in my direction. I ducked behind the doorframe before he could see me.

"I have to go," she said. "My real friend is here." She walked out of the apartment and into the hallway, the last bag of her belongings in her hand. We ran down the hall.

"You owe me an explanation," he shouted. "And three months rent!"

We beat down the stairs to the car. As we piled in, Brad watched us from the glass stairwell, his face impassive under his sunglasses. I started the car as fast as I could, then yanked it into reverse and floored it.

"Asshole!" I shouted.

Ananda cowered by the car door, sunk low in her seat.

"I can't believe he yelled at you like that. He had the nerve to ask you to do the dishes! But at least it's over now. You got out."

"Mag, will you do something for me?" She clutched my arm, her eyes desperate. "I need healing from his energy. Would you do a cleansing ritual on me?"

I had no clue what a cleansing ritual was, but I supposed she'd tell me. "Sure. Anything you want."

We hauled her futon into the bedroom right beside mine. She stood on a chair and nailed swaths of silk to the ceiling, so it hung around her bed. Then she lit a candle and left to bathe.

I waited in her room with an art book, leaning against the wall. Candlelight bounced around the room, making something near the door light up in flashes, like morse code. I crawled toward it. Someone had scratched the doorframe. Raw wood glinted beneath the mahogany stain like a golden fire. I ran my fingers over the words.

Help me.

I leapt back, my heart thumping furiously. The words were written in a childish scrawl. My mind whirled. It came to me, in a haze of dreamish wakefulness — a young girl with curly hair, like a ghostly Shirley Temple.

I shook my head. What was I thinking? I must be tired.

Help me.

The candle guttered and sank lower. I had the distinct feeling I wasn't alone. I told myself it was paranoia, but I couldn't shake the feeling someone was watching me. A movement caught my eye. I whirled. Nothing.

From the corner of my eye, another shadow moved. I pressed my back against the wall, my eyes darting around the room. The hanging silk swayed. My mind raced with paranormal visions of the little girl's curly hair and baby-doll dress.

I tried to breathe, telling myself ghosts don't exist. My psych teachers had drilled the paranormal out of my head. It was insane to believe something without any proof.

And yet, part of me wanted to reach out to the girl, because if there were monsters in the world, she wasn't one. I wondered what her name was, and a single thought entered my head.

Rosie.

A whooshing noise erupted from the bathroom. I half-expected Ananda to scream and run into the room. Instead, the bathroom door creaked on its hinges and she walked in, rivulets of water running from her hair and naked body. She crashed onto her futon and lay on her back.

"Remove the negative," she said. "Hurry, the new moon is almost peaking."

The candle sputtered again. Shadows jumped around the room.

"Wait. I need to trim the candle wick."

"No." She clutched my shoulders. "The full moon is about to peak. Remove the negative energy." She closed her eyes. Her nipples swam in mounds atop her ribs.

I didn't know what to do. I didn't believe in energetic healing any more than I believed in the Easter Bunny, or ghosts before that night.

I put my hands on her body, one on her belly and one over her heart. I took a deep breath, called upon all the holy names I could muster, and asked them to cleanse her. I fell into an unbound space, as if she and I were the only beings in the universe.

I felt the little ghost girl nearby. Why was she still on our plane? Was she trapped?

Ananda yawned and rose from the bed. Her arms wove around me and she pulled me close. I lay down beside her. The candle lapped a few more times, then extinguished itself.

Chapter 7. Nesting

Our first three weeks of living together, Ananda and I didn't leave the house except to buy magazines, coffee, and food. When we went out, she dressed me in her clothes. We stood out among the other grocery shoppers like exotic flowers.

People at the coffeehouse gave us free coffee, and people at the market gave us free bread. Everywhere we went, people waved to her or shouted her name as they drove past. Everyone knew her, and everyone loved her. I felt beautiful for the first time in my life, as if I were from the same painting she seemed to have walked out of. Sometimes, on our journeys into 'the mundane world,' as Ananda called it, our hands clasped and she leaned into me. For hours afterward, her black perfume oil lingered on my skin and clothes.

We slept together every night, sometimes in my bed, sometimes on her futon. Nothing happened, not really. We talked like teenagers, about dreams, ambitions, and stories. She'd drape an arm or a leg over me, and even though it crushed me, I never moved it away. It felt so natural to embrace her or brush her hair away from her face. Sometimes it felt like we were the same person in two different bodies.

Our lives were in sync. We woke late in the afternoon and worked for hours on collages. Days seemed to last forever, and nights were quiet except for the pulse of crickets and music. Timelessness fell upon us. A world existed outside the house, but it didn't compare to our rich world inside the house. A deep peace settled in my mind for the first time in my life. I didn't know if I could ever go back to small talk.

One night, deep in a collaging trance, gunshots rang out. We locked eyes. Ananda gasped and reached for me. A second round of gunfire went off, then a third. We ran to the windows, expecting to see gunslingers or gang members prowling the street, but instead, we saw fireworks bursting in the sky in magenta, blue, and sparkling white. It was the Fourth of July, and we hadn't even noticed.

"I know who you remind me of now," Ananda said, cutting from a new magazine from the thrift store. "You remind me of a French model named Annabelle. She and I worked on a photo shoot in Italy. She used to sing to the birds wherever we went. It's weird. You have the same facial structure and hair."

"I bet Italy was amazing."

She finished cutting the image out and laid it on the carpet. "I'll tell you what. The next time I have an international modeling gig, you should come too. I don't have very many now that I'm in my mid-twenties, but they still pop up every now and then. If our art takes off, we could tour Europe together! I'll show you all the best places."

My heart fired at the thought of traveling Europe. "That sounds like a dream come true."

"It'll happen. I can see it."

I reached for a new magazine. I hoped it would have the images that would open the doors of the art world to us.

One night, Ananda found opium in one of her trunks ('from Amsterdam!' she squealed). We smoked it and did yoga while trance music poured from the stereo. When we finished, my head felt like it floated a few feet above my shoulders.

Hours later, as I toweled off from a bath, a faint tangle of lights hovered, slowly making their way toward me. My neck prickled with an otherworldly sense. The lights swayed, playful. I thought about shouting for Ananda, but I hesitated. I didn't want to scare them away.

"Rosie?" I asked tentatively.

The lights moved where a head would be.

My insides clenched with fear and wonder. Could it really be a ghost? My heart beat a little faster as I tried to think of what to say.

"How are you?" I asked.

The lights floated for a moment, then descended the stairs until they faded from sight.

I toweled off, threw on clothes, and ran downstairs. "Ananda, you'll never guess–"

I stopped, shocked to see fabric and silk covering the walls, like a giant Kasbah tent had sprung up in our living room. Christmas lights hung from wall to wall. Ananda teetered on her tiptoes, hanging ornaments from several long tree branches sticking out of the old bronze chandelier.

"Do you like it?" she asked.

"I love it." Our lives were a symbiosis of movement, color, and cultures. It made sense that we lived in a place that echoed that.

"What were you going to say?" she asked.

"Oh. Nothing. I just thought I saw a ghost upstairs." I laughed.

"Really? What happened?" She dropped an ornament on the floor and gazed at me, eyes wide.

"I'm joking. Ghosts don't really exist."

"Mag, just because there's no evidence doesn't mean they don't exist. People thought wireless technology was crazy, and now look at us. Cellphones are everywhere. Tell me what happened."

I sighed, unsure how to even explain it. "I saw something in the bathroom. I said hi, but she didn't respond, she just sort of floated away."

Ananda shivered, running her hands over her arms. "I think I feel her. Is she in the room?"

I looked around but I didn't see Rosie's lights. "No."

Her eyes burned with zeal. "Show me."

We went upstairs and I showed her the place I saw Rosie. Ananda screwed up her eyes at the area.

I touched her arm. "You don't have to try that hard. It's more like seeing something in the corner of your vision. But it's just a trick of the light, or maybe my eyes are bad."

"No, I feel her too," she said, arms stretched out.

The writing on the doorframe flashed through my mind.

Help me.

We were living with some kind of ghost, even if she was just in our imaginations.

Chapter 8. Truth and Lies: excerpt from Analyzing Ananda

Ananda Dawn, *neé* Jennifer Clark, is adept at reinvention and disguise. She surrounds herself with people who support her illusions so as to not reveal or encounter her true nature. She flatters people and takes them into her confidence without revealing the totality or truth of herself. Her outright lies, including her name, origin, hobbies, job history, financial status, and relationships (footnotes 36-41) combined with her lies of omission are staggering. This, with her known history of petty theft (footnotes 42-45), reveal her to be a person utterly incapable of facing reality and her past. Her familial background is particularly interesting, as her mother was declared unfit to raise her and her father is unknown. This psychology, combined with permissive drug use and abuse, fostered escapism.

Lies are the building blocks to recreating her world. In her biography, *Ananda Dawn, Face of a New World,* she claims she and I were girlfriends, however, we never slept together. Likewise, there were no orgies, nor was there a cult known as the House of Transformation with a sexual initiation. Another notable difference between Ananda's imagined life and real life is that she and I were friends for a few months only, not life-long friends.

Her falsified portrayal of our relationship demonstrates her disregard about slighting those she purports to care about, and also demonstrates to herself and to others her desirabilty, in which she ultimately does not believe.

Ananda makes friendships seem larger than life because the illusion of being loved covers up her inability to maintain friendships and simple relationships. She especially befriends people who could be called 'givers.' She takes as much as she can and gives back shallow compliments and empty promises of love, which always fall flat.

Chapter 9. The Doctor

I sat at my dining room table, unable to touch the gingery Thai delivery growing cold. My gut felt slimy with worry about what Ananda was saying to John in the spare room. On one hand, she needed therapy so much. I wanted her to learn more about herself. On the other hand, John was my friend, and Ananda's habitual lying might change that.

I looked at the closed door, my leg bobbing under the table. After his talk with her, John would help me tell Ananda about my book. It was nerve wracking, waiting to tell her. I should've told her last night, only I hadn't realized she'd still be in my apartment. At least I had John to help me. I exhaled and felt a little of the cortisol trickle away.

I opened my laptop. Gossip blogs and fake news sites elevated our situation to a near overdose, a pregnancy concealment, and a forced abortion in my apartment. A picture of Ananda blinking was plastered all over the internet. They speculated she was wasted and closer than ever to overdosing. It amazed me they could get away with saying that. When did speculation become an acceptable substitute for the news?

I knew what I had to do. I opened my email, took a deep breath, and typed a letter to my agent.

Dear Cleve,

I wrote Analyzing Ananda from a place of anger, and since seeing her, I no longer believe the psychological verdicts I assessed. Besides, a couple of sentences from my instant messages were used out of context, and I never intended those to be part of the book. I'm sorry to do this, but you must pull all the books from the shelves. Please follow up ASAP.

Thank you, Margaret Woods

I pursed my lips. Pulling my book from the shelves was the least I could do, but it didn't take back what I'd said. Cleve would hate me, of course. Only a lunatic would pull a Top 10 book from the shelves, but I couldn't let it go on any longer, not with Ananda under my roof.

My computer pinged with a reply.

Is this your idea of a joke? If so, it's not funny.

I sighed, my fingertips hovering over the keys as I tried to command the strength to respond.

It's not a joke. As you're probably aware, Ananda is living at my apartment right now. This is the best way to keep our relationship moving forward. Please proceed with my instructions. Thank you.

I pressed send. The knot in my stomach loosened a little.

I typed xyritav into the search bar and clicked on the National Physician's page.

Classification: Upper, mild hallucinogen

History: Used in diet pills and energy drinks until it was banned in 2010. From 2005–2010, it was distributed in dance clubs in New York City. It is still manufactured, prescribed, and sold in Europe, South America, and other parts of the world.

Side Effects: Anxiety, delusions of grandeur, paranoia, nausea

I searched through addiction websites. My heart burned as I read xyritav detox stories about all-consuming yearnings, black depressions, and self-recriminations. One doctor compared the first week of xyritav detox to alcoholism withdraw, with vomiting, headaches, and body aches. It sounded terrible, though several people said it got better after a few days.

Another email from Cleve popped up. I opened it and saw a wall of expletives. I closed it, but not before seeing his words.

I'll make sure you never publish again!

The bedroom door opened. John walked out and locked eyes with me. For all his excitement about meeting Ananda, he looked like he'd rather be anywhere else. His short brown hair looked grayer, as if she'd sucked some of the life out of him.

"How'd it go?" I asked, snapping the laptop shut.

"How do you think it went?" he mumbled. He slid into a chair and picked at the takeout with a plastic fork. Brown sauce dribbled onto his sweater vest.

"How is she?"

"She's crying. Did she tell you her dreams? About being naked in public again?"

"No."

"It's a classic vulnerability dream. It sounds like her childhood wasn't very good. She's addicted, depressed, she has PTSD, and she may have general episodic histrionics and narcissism." He looked at his watch and patted my shoulder as he stood. "I should go."

I bolted onto my feet. "What about telling Ananda about my book tonight?"

He winced. "How about tomorrow?"

I swallowed, blinking to hide my disappointment. I desperately wanted John to help me tonight, but he was wiped out. I supposed I could wait another day, even though I wanted to rip the bandaid off.

"Have you set boundaries with her?" he asked.

"Yeah, but she's a bulldozer. She doesn't know any limits."

"You need to be firm. Just try not to be too condescending."

"Condescending?" What had she told him about me?

He gave me a look.

"Okay, fine," I said. "What about the xyritav addiction?"

"She's going cold turkey, starting tonight."

"Here? In my apartment? But I never studied detox or withdraws. I don't even understand addiction!"

"Just be her friend. All you need to know about addiction is that her brain is like Swiss cheese. She has unhealthy pathways, and she needs to fill in the holes. And you're just the one to help her with it." He put on his coat.

I stared at him, my palms sweating. "Maybe we should take her to rehab or a clinic — somewhere that knows how to deal with detoxes."

He stopped. "Not if you want her to come out of this with a shred of dignity or sanity. The tabloids would make a mess of this. They'd never let her live it down. No one knows she has an addiction, and they shouldn't. It's none of their business. She'll detox here, and you and I will work on her. No one will be the wiser. Problem solved."

I shook my head. "I don't think I can handle this."

"There's no other way, unless you want to throw her to the wolves. But you won't have to do this alone. You'll have my help."

My throat constricted. I fought to take a breath. I couldn't believe my own therapist was making me do this. Especially after how I told him about her manipulating me. I thought about running. I could go to my parents' house. It was tempting. But I'd promised Ananda I'd help her.

I ticked off my fears.

1. *Fear of losing control*
2. *Fear of being obsessive-compulsive*
3. *Fear of losing my father figure to Ananda's lies and my terrible book*

As if he sensed my thoughts, John patted my arm. "It'll be fine. Xyritav detox isn't that bad. Just be her friend and I'll take care of the rest." He zipped his coat, donned his scarf, and splayed the blinds with his fingers to peek at the paparazzi.

I stood beside him and looked out. They were having a snowball fight, laughing, while we were trapped inside. Three of them ganged up on one of them, pelting him with snowballs and then shoving them down his back.

"You're right." I shivered. "I don't want to let them win."

"So you'll try?"

"Yes." I blinked back tears.

He adjusted his scarf. "Thanks for calling me. You know I'm a big fan."

"Yeah, who isn't?"

"I'll see you tomorrow around three."

After he left, I locked the door and pressed myself against the wood just to feel anything beyond the sinking feeling in my soul. I closed my eyes, but the dread didn't leave. He said we'd tell her tomorrow. I could hang on for one more day. Maybe she'd be more receptive then. It was probably poor form to bring it up right after her first therapy session, anyway.

Ananda emerged from the bedroom with red, puffy eyes. My heart ached to see her so raw. I'd cried my eyes out during my first therapy session too. She embraced me and I held her, inhaling her black perfume.

It took me back to those days at the House of Transformation, when we spent all our time together and finished each other's sentences and collages. Of course, we'd moved far beyond that, into venomous territory and back again. But once, she was my best friend, and of all the people I knew, only she had believed in my dreams of being an artist.

I didn't know what to say to her, but John's advice came back to me. *Just be her friend.* "Ananda, I'm so glad you're in my life again."

She sobbed against me, her body convulsing. My shirt grew wet beneath her. "He took away all my xyritav."

I drew back. Was that why she was crying? "Yeah. I guess you're quitting tonight."

Her face twisted with rage, just like when she was mad at me all those years ago. The blood chilled in my veins.

"I didn't want to quit like this. I wanted to cut down *and then quit.*"

"But you don't need it. It gets in the way of awareness. Remember when we used to collage all day for hours on end? You didn't need it then, right?"

"No," she sniffed. "But I was on clemeral the whole time."

My face clouded over with confusion. Was she high the entire time I knew her? Did I even know the real Ananda?

"I thought you knew about that," she said.

I shook my head and sat at the kitchen table.

"So, I guess that means I am crazy." Her hands flopped in the air.

"Ananda, you're not crazy. Drugs manipulate your senses, and long-term use can change your brain. That's why it's good you're quitting."

"But John said I'd need therapy every day. Doesn't that mean I'm crazy?"

"No, the same thing happened with me," I lied, hoping to make her feel better. "Calm down. I'll make us some tea." I walked into the kitchen.

"Can I talk to you about something?"

I put the kettle on and held my breath. "Sure."

"How are you going to make this look like a rose garden when it's bullshit?"

I shrugged, trying to think of an answer. My mind had gone blank. I didn't know what to say.

She sniffled. "Maybe I should fake my death and go into hiding."

"No. Don't think like that. That's a terrible idea. But you can take a break from the limelight if you're not feeling it, or you can drop out altogether."

"I can't afford to miss the Grammys, though. The worst part is I don't even know what I want. All I know is I hate my life. I can't stop thinking about Yes." She pressed her face into her palms and cried.

I swallowed hard, admonishing myself. Of course Ananda wasn't a sociopath. The fact that I'd joked about it with someone who had the power to print my words made my book even more terrible.

I reached out to touch her arm. "Let's just take it one day at a time. But if we're going to rewire your brain, you'll need to think positively."

She nodded, biting her lip. "I should've come back here years ago."

"At least you're here now. Kitty will visit soon." I hoped it would cheer her up, though the thought of Kitty's lackadaisical habits were unsettling. I made a mental note to ask her to get rid of any drugs she had with her.

Ananda wiped tears away and looked around my apartment. "Maybe we could start collaging again."

"Sure, but I don't have a lot of magazines. The paparazzi are still outside."

"You could hire someone."

"Yeah, maybe I should." One of my former patients popped into my mind. I wondered what she was doing. It'd been years since I last saw her.

"Just make sure they can keep their mouths shut. They have

to be loyal." She opened the cupboard and looked at my teas.

My heart rose. How many times had I wished we could hang out, make tea, and talk about our lives? And here she was. I laughed.

She raised her brows at me.

"Sorry, it's just so funny you're a pop star. It feels like just yesterday, we had our art show with all those weirdos."

She laughed a little. "I know what you mean. It's weird being a singer. Sometimes I wonder — do I really get in front of thousands of people and do that? It's ridiculous. You must feel the same way about being a therapist."

My smile stiffened. "Well, that's a little different." Being a therapist was nothing like her 'career.' She caught someone's eye in a dance club and the rest settled into place. She probably didn't think anything about my six-year sacrifice in library basements.

The kettle started to whistle. I tossed a couple packets into the teapot and poured the boiling water. Ananda reached for a cup from the shelf and her arm brushed against mine. We stared at each other, waiting for the tea to steep. My breath slowed.

"I don't mind if you sleep in my room," I said.

She took a step back, averting her gaze to the tile. "Would you mind if I slept on the floor of the guest room? Beds hurt my back."

I blushed. "Of course." The rejection stung, but a sense of lightness came over me. Being that close to her again would only complicate things.

"Mag, thank you so much. What would I do without you?" She clasped me into a hug.

I held her back, but I couldn't answer. I could only smile and hope she didn't see the shadow behind my eyes, the lie I couldn't reveal just yet.

Early the next morning, the doorbell to my apartment rang over and over. I pulled the covers over my head and groaned.

Ananda crept into my room and crawled in bed with me,

shaking me awake. "Mag, wake up."

I yawned. "What? Who is it?"

"It can't be the paps," she whispered. "They're not allowed to come this close to the house. But it might be Kitty. Will you get the door?"

I grumbled but dragged myself out of bed. When I looked through the peephole, bouquets covered the foyer like a carpet. A guy with a clipboard waved in the middle of them.

"Please just leave them in the hallway," I said.

"I need a signature," he shouted.

I grunted. "Can you slide it under the door?"

He pushed the papers under. I scribbled on them and pushed them back. I watched him pick up the papers and walk out the door, then I opened the apartment door.

Rose bouquets, all colors and sizes, cluttered the foyer. I bent to pick one up when the apartment door across the foyer flew open.

Mrs. Gutesberg, dressed in a tracksuit, eyed the flowers, her arms crossed. "What's all the fuss about? And what are those reporters doing out there?"

I tried to smile, but it probably looked more like a grimace. There was no way I could tell Mrs. Gutesberg about Ananda. The last time I'd talked to her, when my cat Serena died last year, the other tenants and the mail carrier knew within days. People I didn't even know apologized about Serena for weeks.

"I can't talk about it," I said. She knew I was a psychologist. I could always fall back on the client-patient confidentiality clause. I set the first bouquet on the floor of my living room and started bringing the others in, one enormous vase at a time.

She put her hands on her hips. "Do you have a celebrity in there?"

I shrugged. "I really can't talk about it."

"Can you at least tell me if anyone passed?" she asked, her face lined with concern.

"No one passed." I hauled the last vase in and kicked the door shut.

"What's going on?" Ananda called from the bedroom.

"You got some flowers." The understatement of the year.

"Check them for cameras."

I paused, looking at all of them. "Are you serious?"

"Yeah. That's how the Greaseball got those naked photos of me. He still sends me flowers."

I rifled through the bouquets, unsure what to look for. "I don't see any cameras. I think you're safe. It looks like you have one from John, one from Bertrand... Who's that?"

"The Eiffel Tower cop." She walked into the room.

"Oh. Actually, a few are from him. Here's a card. But it's in French. I can't read it."

"Let me see."

I gave her the card.

She smiled. "It says he doesn't know my favorite color, so he got roses every color. He wants to take me out on a date." She smirked and flipped the card away.

I squinted at her. "Did something happen between you? Besides that kiss?"

"No way. Don't you remember what I said about French men being players?"

"Yeah, but..." My voice trailed off. She'd lied about that, like she had with so many other things. But I didn't want to remind her of the past. She was detoxing, and I was trying to be her friend.

"Who else sent me flowers?" she asked.

I looked through the cards. "The rest are from fans. Why are they all roses?"

"I said they were my favorite flower in some old magazine interview. I meant they were my favorite flower that day. Now all I ever get is roses."

Another knock sounded at the door. I looked through the peephole and saw a teenage boy loaded with several bags of groceries. I almost forgot I'd ordered them the night before.

"Set them in the hallway please," I shouted through the door.

He obliged and left. When he was gone, I opened the door and hauled the bags inside.

"Please tell me he got hemp milk," she said.

I rifled through the bags and found a carton.

"Thank Goddess." She ripped off the tab and took a long drink.

"Hey, how are you feeling?" I thought she might be sick — that's what the website said would happen during the first day of detox, but Ananda looked fresh.

She set the milk down on the counter. "I'm a little queasy."

"Hang in there. It might get worse, but we'll get through it together."

After we unpacked the bags, she threw her hands in the air. "Where's the chocolate?"

"Um... I don't see any. I asked for four bars." I looked in the foyer for a forgotten bag, but didn't see one. "The teenager must've forgotten to pack it, or maybe it's rattling around the back of his delivery truck."

I looked at my car keys, hanging by a hook on the wall. I wanted to go to the grocery myself.

I peeked through the blinds. Paparazzi and fans still mashed up the snow on my sidewalk. There was no sign of them letting up anytime soon. I didn't want to go out there, not until I was sure Ananda still wanted me to be her manager after I told her about my book. It'd be too much for me. My heart sped up just thinking about their video cameras and pointed questions.

It was time to hire a personal assistant.

Everyone at the New Beginnings Center called Hayden an old soul. Now, she was twenty-one, and one of the smartest young women I knew. I doubted Ananda would intimidate her, and I trusted her more than I trusted most people.

I listened to the phone ring until it went to her voicemail, then left a message with the offer.

"So, when's my massage?" she asked when I set down the phone.

"About an hour. I'm going to make coffee." I walked into the kitchen. At least the grocery service hadn't forgotten that.

She walked in and leaned against the counter. "You'll need

to print out a privacy form for the massage."

"A what?"

"It's called a confidentiality form. Look it up online. And can you tell her not to talk during the massage?"

"Sure."

The coffeepot bustled with steam, and soon the aroma floated in the air. I felt more awake just inhaling it.

Ananda's face crumpled. She turned, trying to hide it, but I could tell she was bothered.

"What's wrong?" I asked.

She sniffed. "This is when I usually have my first xyritav, with my morning coffee."

I gave her a tight smile. "Do you want to try meditating?"

She pouted, but nodded.

We sat on the floor, hands in our laps. I closed my eyes and tried to let my mind go, but my thoughts wouldn't stray from my book. Would Ananda hate me when I brought it up later that night? Would she storm out? It didn't seem fair that she came back to me hours after it was published. After a few minutes, I got up.

"What's wrong?" she asked.

I shook my head. "Nothing. Just worried about the time. The massage therapist will be here soon and I need to find those papers."

Her shoulders drooped. "I might as well get ready too." She got up and walked into the bathroom.

I closed my eyes and released the air from my lungs. Was this how Judas felt? I went online and found a confidentiality agreement. I printed the papers just as the doorbell rang.

A dowdy woman with a graying bun stood in the foyer, a folded up massage table beside her.

"Thanks for coming," I said. "Please come in."

She walked in with her table. I shut the door behind her and handed her the paper.

"I have a confidentiality agreement."

She signed it with barely a glance and handed it back to me.

I held my breath. "You didn't read it."

"Don't worry. I won't talk to the press."

"It's not just the press," I said. "You can't talk to anyone. If you do, there could be a law suit."

"Yeah, I know. I took a confidentiality course to get my license. I won't tell anyone anything."

I set my mouth, determined to keep from flying off the handle. It wouldn't do any good. Besides, Ananda needed a massage. Detoxing was no joke. She was probably in a lot of pain.

"Okay. You can set up in this room. By the way, she doesn't like to talk."

"Fine with me." She lugged her table in.

After the massage was underway, I went back into the kitchen and opened a cake mix. Baking always relaxed me, and I hoped it'd help Ananda's cravings as well.

Once the chocolate cake was in the oven, I checked my phone and saw a voicemail from Kitty. When I played it, her anger was audible. At first, I was afraid it was directed at me, but then I realized she was upset because she couldn't make it out to St. Paul due to recording deadlines before Christmas.

I also had a text from Hayden.

R U 4 REAL?!?!?!?

I laughed and called her. She answered immediately.

"Hey. Yes, I'm for real."

"Are you serious?!"

"Yeah. You'd run errands and make appointments, that kind of stuff. We'll pay you."

"Hold on..."

I heard some rustling, and faintly, I heard her shout. "I quit! No more smelling like french fries!"

Then I heard her laugh and a jingling that sounded like keys. My heart clamored. Had she just quit her job? I should've told her it might be temporary.

"Are you there?" I asked.

"Oh my God, thank you so much. When can I start?"

"Today if you want."

"Sweet! Text me your address."

"Okay. There are some reporters here. Just ignore them."

"No prob. See you in a few."

Knowing Hayden, she probably screamed with excitement after we hung up. I texted her my address and checked the time. John would be back in a few hours. I'd finally get to talk about the book. I took a deep breath and hoped for the best. Things were going so well with me and Ananda, but everything could crumble if she got mad about my book. She might leave and start taking xyritav again. I could be without a job, with a worse reputation than before. I could only hope she'd let me explain, that she'd like my plan and Hayden enough to stay.

I told myself John would help me. I closed my eyes and repeated it like a mantra.

Chapter 10. The Assistant

Chocolate cake began to aromatize the air when Hayden arrived. I opened the door and saw my old patient and friend, her cheeks flushed, her curly hair peeking out from a winter hat. I hadn't seen her for a few years. Her face had gotten more slender, some of the baby fat gone. My heart warmed, seeing her so grown up.

"Hi." I embraced her.

"Hi. I'm so excited!" She squealed.

"Shhh. Ananda is in the other room getting a massage."

"Sorry. How've you been?"

"Good. Not much is different, except for Ananda, of course." I smiled and pushed my hands into my pockets. Truthfully, since I'd last seen her, I went through three failed relationships, gained twenty pounds and three pants sizes, and only paid off about $3,000 of my student loans, but she didn't need to know that. "What's new with you?"

"I'm going to Richmond Community College. We're on winter break right now. Mostly I've been working at McDonald's and going to indie rock shows."

I peered at her. "Are bands from Indiana that popular these days?"

"No, *independent bands*. It means they're not on a label. Oh mom." She laughed, shaking her head.

I smiled back weakly, my heart a little bruised. I thought of her more like a little sister.

I handed her a confidentiality form. "Can you read this and sign before we start? The paparazzi will try to trick you into saying things. They'll offer you money. You just need to ignore them."

She took the form and read it, front and back, and signed it.

I glanced at the massage therapist's form with contempt. Hayden was half her age and had twice as much sense. She'd do just fine around Ananda.

"What do you want me to do first?" Hayden asked, glancing around the messy apartment.

"Before we start, there's something you should know. Ananda's detoxing from xyritav. She's having therapy sessions in the apartment. In fact, her psychiatrist will be here soon. We don't want to bring her down, so don't tell her any of the gossip going around. Also, she's not allowed to have any drugs besides ibuprofen. If she asks for anything else, let me know."

"Didn't you write a book about Ananda that said she was a sociopath? They're always talking about it on the news."

The timer went off with a loud *brrrrrrrnnng*. I nearly jumped out of my clothes. I shot her a tight smile and slipped into the kitchen.

She trailed behind as I pulled out the cake and tested it with a toothpick.

"Uh, yeah. I did write that book, but don't mention it, okay? It's not the right time yet."

Her eyes bulged. "She doesn't know?"

"No." I took a deep breath. "But I'm going to take care of it tonight."

The massage therapist emerged from the spare bedroom and walked to the bathroom. Ananda came out a moment later, dressed in my terrycloth robe, her hair rumpled with oil.

I turned off the oven and walked into the dining room. Hayden followed reluctantly, eyes wide.

"Ananda, this is our new assistant Hayden. She's an old client of mine from the New Beginnings Center."

"Lovely to meet you." Ananda flashed her million dollar smile.

Hayden held out her hand. Ananda grasped it so hers rested on top, just as she always did.

"It's such a pleasure to meet you," Hayden said. "I'm a huge fan."

"Thank you."

The massage therapist opened the bathroom door and retrieved the massage table. "Drink lots of water," she said to Ananda.

"I'll go get you some." Hayden leapt into the kitchen.

The massage therapist put on her snow boots and left. I locked up just as Hayden reappeared with a glass.

"Thank you," Ananda said. "Mag, did you make a cake?"

"Yep," I beamed. "You're one day sober. I thought we should celebrate."

"Thanks. You're the best." She smiled and took a drink of water.

"So," Hayden said, teetering on her toes. "Are you pregnant?"

Ananda almost spit the water out. I shot Hayden a warning look. The last thing Ananda needed in her sensitive state was to be riled up by the gossip mill.

"No. I'm not pregnant," Ananda said with cold eyes. "The last time I checked, you have to have sex for that to happen."

"Well, sorry." Hayden fidgeted. "I was just asking because TMZ is saying that you are, and you're in denial because of that French guy."

"That's insane." Ananda slammed the glass onto the counter and glared at me. "I told them I wasn't pregnant."

"Maybe we shouldn't talk about this," I said.

"They're also saying the two of you are shacked up with enough drugs to last until the apocalypse. You should think about releasing a statement."

Ananda shook her head. "I can't do that right now. I'm detoxing and I need my space."

"Wait a minute," I said. "Hayden has a point. We don't know how we look to the outside world, but she does." I turned to her. "What do other people do in this situation?"

"You can pretend like nothing's wrong, like Amy Winehouse or Marilyn Monroe, but we know how those stories ended. Or you can tell the truth and move on. Like Lola Whalen."

"I can't tell the truth," Ananda said. "It would kill my career, just like it killed hers. And I still have to do the Grammys."

"If you can't tell the truth, you need to at least add to the dialogue. You can say you're visiting an old friend."

Ananda rolled her eyes. "Duh."

"Maybe you're writing an autobiography?" Hayden asked.

Ananda straightened. "That could work."

"Or you're working on a new album?" I asked.

"Yeah, I like that. But I can't go out there and release a statement. Those news people would eat me alive."

"You don't have to go anywhere," Hayden said. "We can do it online. By the way, I noticed you don't have a blog, just social media, which you rarely update."

"So what? I'm busy."

"You need to reach out to your fans. I can help you with that."

"You can?"

"Yeah. I'm studying public relations in college."

I gazed at Hayden appreciatively. Of course — social media was the perfect way to reach out without being on the news. Hayden would know exactly what to say. She was practically raised on it. I breathed a sigh of relief.

"Take some selfies." Hayden handed her phone to Ananda. "I'll upload them and start a blog about your new album and autobiography. We have to get your message out there so people understand you. You've done some crazy stuff lately. It looks pretty weird."

Ananda crossed her arms. "You mean it looks pretty awesome."

Hayden shook her head. "No more weird stuff. Otherwise, that's all you'll be remembered for. Remember when Michael Jackson dangled his baby over a balcony? One minute he was the King of Pop, the next, he was a baby-dangler. Same with that guy who started dancing on a talk show. My generation only knows them for their weird stuff. You have to be careful."

"I'm not dangling any babies," Ananda huffed, her face turning scarlet.

I bit my lip, wondering if bringing Hayden in was a good idea. What she said made sense, though.

"Hey, I'm on your side," Hayden said. "I'll tell you what. I'll work on something and let you approve it before it goes out, okay?"

"I guess," Ananda said. "No promises."

My phone rang from the living room.

"I'll get it," Hayden said.

"These are good ideas," I said to Ananda. "If the public wants a piece of you, let's decide which piece it'll be."

She sighed. "It's just so scary to do anything."

"Um, Mag?" Hayden asked, the phone dangling from her hand.

"What is it?"

"That was Waverly Hospital. Someone named John Brengleman was in a car accident."

"Oh my God." A sudden chill hit me at my core. "Is he okay?"

"He's stable, but he has some broken bones, including his collarbone. It sounds pretty bad. He's going to have surgery."

I squeezed my eyes shut and collapsed on the sofa. John was my dear friend, but he was also going to mediate when I told Ananda about my book tonight. Without him, I didn't know if I could bring up the book. Ananda was too unpredictable, too volatile, and besides, who knew what she'd do in the midst of her detoxes?

Ananda crumpled into the sofa beside me. "I knew he was too good to be true."

I held her as her tears flowed, but my thoughts were on my own problems. If I told her about my book, she'd crack like an egg. I needed to keep her whole a little bit longer, at least through the detox phase.

Chapter 11. Ego

"Maybe Stevey isn't here."

I looked down the warehouse hallway. Dust bunnies collected on the well-worn wooden floor, and the pastel green walls were covered with a layer of grime. Fluorescent lights overhead spasmed and blinked. It looked like the setting for a chase scene in a horror movie, where the heroine trips and falls.

Ananda adjusted the digital camera strap over her shoulder and banged on the old wooden door again. "He's here. I can feel it."

"Let's just get some magazines at the thrift store and make more collages."

Footsteps sounded from the other side of the door. A lock clinked and the door creaked open. A haggard man in a rumpled t-shirt stood before us. "What do you want?"

I swallowed. If this was Stevey, I wasn't sure I wanted to be in his art show.

"Is Stevey there?" Ananda asked, gazing over his shoulder.

The man looked us up and down. After a moment, he stepped back from the doorway. Ananda strode over the threshold and into the room. I scrambled in after her, trying to keep up with her long paces.

The foyer contained several lamps and mirrors, clustered together like a room out of Alice in Wonderland. In the next room, enormous oil paintings hung from the ceiling, fabric emerged from the walls, and ceramic figures clustered on the ground like fungi.

Ananda walked into an open-air two-story living room and threw her arms around a plump, middle-aged man wearing a black t-shirt.

"Stevey baby!"

Dimples rose from Stevey's ruddy cheeks as he smiled. "How's my sweet Ananda?" He kissed her cheek.

Ananda sat down on a black leather couch. Three others

formed a living area. She patted the seat beside her. I scurried over and sat on the edge. Above us, skylights blazed with the afternoon sun. Giant paper cranes and mobiles rotated on invisible wires.

"Stevey," Ananda said, "this is my best friend Magdalene. We've been working on collages for your next Art Party." She handed him the camera.

He thumbed through the pictures she'd taken of our collages the night before. "I like them. They're kitschy. What kind of scale?"

"Whatever you want."

"The bigger, the better. I have space." He gazed at his mostly empty loft. "To be honest, no one at the next show has any talent. I'd like to display something besides photography and pop art. I don't know why pop art is so hot right now, do you? But I get it, Lichtenstein and the 60's are in." He passed the camera back. "You know my deal, right? Fifty-fifty."

Ananda nudged me in the ribs. "Is that okay?"

"What? Sure." I said.

"Can we have a room for the show?" she asked him.

He shook his head. "Those 'performance art' nut jobs pay a lot for those, and I can't turn away the money, you know? But I'll tell you what. Blow up your stuff and I'll think about it."

Ananda's eyes danced. "You'll love it so much. I just know you're going to buy one."

"We'll see. But I have a meeting in a moment, so..."

He stood up. Ananda and I followed suit.

"By the way, Ananda, do you still model?"

"Of course."

"Have you done anything lately? We could make it a double feature. That stuff sold so well last time."

Ananda blushed. "I haven't done anything like that in ages."

"That's too bad. You're so photogenic. Everyone loved those prints, except Kitty, I guess."

"When did you say we could drop off the prints?" she asked.

"Whenever."

"Stevey's kind of weird, isn't he?" I asked.

We sat in the Arts District coffeehouse patio. Cars and pedestrians bustled beside us. The July humidity had increased to near unbreathable conditions. Our iced coffees sweated on the black metal table between us. Ananda slid on sunglasses and slumped in her chair.

"What did he mean about you modeling?" I asked, playing with my straw.

"I did some nude modeling a few years ago, but I don't anymore. But Stevey's not bad — he just thinks art peaked in the 80's. Plus, he toots his own horn about having his art in the Art Institute, but it's just a bunch of clay slabs with holes in them. It's lifeless compared to our work."

"Do you think we'll sell some prints?"

"Of course. Our collages are ingenious."

A photographer in black crouched a few feet away, his camera poised at Ananda. Dark curls stuck out behind a Nikon.

I made a face at the photographer and grabbed the bag of thrift store magazines. "Let's get out of here."

Ananda smirked. "Wait."

She stood and walked toward the photographer. He lowered his camera and eyed her warily. His face was pinched, as if his tongue tasted sour. His nose protruded far over his teeth.

She held out her hand to him. "Fifty bucks."

He reeled back. "What?"

"Come on. I know you're going to sell those photos. I get paid to model. I'm not doing it for free."

He gulped. "Fifty bucks is a lot of money."

"Then how about deleting them? I know the guys who work here, and they have no qualms about taking a camera away from an asshole with no common sense."

The photographer sputtered and blinked, avoiding Ananda's gaze. Finally, he pulled out his wallet and handed her a few bills.

"Thanks for not being an asshole," she said sweetly, pocketing the cash. "Here's my card with my hourly rates if you want to do anything worth your time. I'm between projects, so you're lucky. I'm usually international. I'm Ananda."

She extended a hand, and he took it. Mid-shake, her hand slipped on top of his. His face scrunched in confusion. I laughed under my breath.

"I'm Jared. Sorry."

"Sit with us for a minute," she said.

I side-eyed her. Why was she asking him to sit with us?

"Tell me more about yourself," he said to Ananda, pulling up a chair and leaning forward, his nose leading the way.

She smiled as she repeated things I'd already heard. I listened politely, but after ten minutes neither of them acknowledging me, I couldn't take it. I sat back in my chair, trying to relax, but my legs wouldn't sit still.

I stalked off to the bathroom, locked the door, and looked in the mirror. My moony face gazed back at me. I grimaced. No photographer, no matter how greasy, had ever tried to steal a picture of me.

I shouldered my purse and walked out, but stopped at the dark alcove of the bathroom to spy on the patio. Ananda threw her head back, laughing at something he said, and slapped his arm. He looked surprised and quite pleased with himself. He leaned in, his spindly fingers animated as he talked.

Something heavy fell on my heart. I'd never seen her flirt with anyone but me before. She should have been talking with me. We needed to do our art, not indulge some weirdo. Our work was sitting at home and she was wasting our time.

I avoided the patio and walked through the coffeehouse, my heart in my throat. Someone called my name. I turned on my heel, nervous someone had caught me, afraid Jared would reach out to me. But it was one of the coffeehouse guys, the one with the spiky brown hair who'd given us free iced coffees.

"Hey." He held out a white paper bag. "I thought you might want these day-olds, since you and Ananda aren't working and all."

I took the bag. Bagels, muffins, and pastries jostled together, each wrapped in cellophane. "Thanks. How'd you know my name?"

"Word gets around about who Ananda's hanging out with.

I'm Ricky, by the way." He wiped his hand on his apron and offered it.

I smiled at him and took it in mine like Ananda did, with my hand on top. "I'm Mag." I tried to twinkle my eyes.

His blue eyes matched the ceramic mugs on the shelf behind him. Despite trying to keep my cool, my smile grew to match his.

The patio door swung open. Ananda walked toward us, Jared in tow. She took the pastry bag from me. "Thank you Ricky. You're so sweet." She leaned close and kissed him on the cheek.

"Anything for you," he said.

I shrank toward the door. She outshone me, effortlessly. I took a deep breath and walked toward the door, my mouth set into a hard line.

"Nice meeting you," I said to Ricky. I pushed the door open, pounding out into the hot afternoon. The bright sun whitewashed the sidewalk, and I had to put a hand up to avoid the glare. Someone's footsteps followed behind but I didn't turn around.

"Mag!" Ananda shouted.

I turned, hoping Jared wasn't with her. I was relieved to see her rushing after me, Jared nowhere in sight.

"Good news," she said, breathless. "Jared wants to-"

"That guy is a creeper." I continued walking as soon as she caught up to me.

"He's is harmless. Besides, he knows Stevey. His pictures are going to be in the show too. He reminded me that there's a party the night before the show, for the artists to hang their stuff. It's called the Hanging Party. He said he could photograph us for our bios. He can come over anytime."

"What are bios?"

"Headshots and biographies. It's stupid, but we have to do it."

"I don't want that guy knowing where we live. He seems like he wouldn't go away. I'd have to kick him out every time I wanted to work."

"Oh Magdalene." She sighed. "You don't even see it, do you?"

"See what?"

We reached the gazebo and wandered inside. I sat down on the cool stone ledge, my legs dangling over the wall. Ananda straddled it and gazed into my eyes.

"Jared is a lost soul, can't you tell? He doesn't know who he is. Don't you feel compassion for him?"

"No. He seems like a stalker."

"He just needs acceptance. Don't you want to do good in the world?"

"Of course I do." Heat rose behind my face. "But we need to keep people like him at arm's length. We can't let strangers into our house just to prove we're good people."

"You and I were once strangers, and look how that turned out."

"That's different. We clicked over a conversation about art. He's a weirdo who takes pictures of girls having coffee."

"Magdalene, we're all lost souls — every single one of us on the face of this earth. And contrary to popular desire, we don't leave our mark on this world. Maybe some DNA or a piece of art for a while, but in the end, there's only evolution, culture, and the advancement of technology. Since we don't have anything to do with the tech stuff, we should help people. Do you know how many broken people there are in the world?"

I pressed my lips shut. Her lecture was humiliating, especially since that was one of the reasons I chose to study psychology — to help the downtrodden.

Looking back, that moment was the beginning of the end, the crack in the plaster that brought the house down. Had we just stayed in our own world, we might still be living together to this day. We might've become artists and left our marks in museums and history books like I dreamed.

"Wait," I said. "Didn't you say the same thing about Brad — he had a broken soul or something? You tried to save him, and he took it the wrong way?"

"Jared's different. He's an artist like we are."

I closed my eyes and named my fears.

1. *Fear of rejection*
2. *Fear of the unknown*
3. *Loss of Ananda*

"I don't want to weaken what we have," I said.

"You're so sensitive." She pulled me close.

I worked through my internal resistance, but softened. I let her embrace me. She caressed my face and stroked the nape of my neck, her fingertips as light as feathers. I felt my anger drain from me. She held me until my breaths subsided.

"Are you better?" she asked.

I nodded, wiping my eyes.

"Good. I need to talk to you about something. I think we should model. Jared can pay us by the hour."

I frowned again. "I have a camera too. I can take pictures of us."

"How are you going to capture both of us in the moment if you're not even in the frame?"

I slumped back and shook my head. "I won't feel comfortable modeling in front of him."

"Don't worry about Jared. Trust me. He doesn't know who he is, so he takes on the personality of whoever is around him. In our case, it'll be like we have another girlfriend."

"So you don't... like him like that?"

She cracked up laughing, and after a stunned moment, I did too. I didn't know what I was thinking. It was ridiculous to think she'd go for him.

"No, I'm not into him. But he is an artist in need of genuine people."

The maelstrom of my anger blew over. "Okay."

"Magdalene, I love you." Her arms wound around me and she sank into the embrace.

"I love you too."

"Homeward? We can make some more collages."

I smiled and nodded. That was all I ever wanted.

Chapter 12. Taboo

Ananda conned her way into free prints at an all-night copy place by flirting with the guy behind the counter. She twirled her hair as he printed our collages.

"We're artists. We don't even have day jobs."

I stacked the prints together on the counter.

"Can I get your number?" he asked her, handing me the last one.

"I don't have a phone, but I'll come back sometime."

"Promise?"

"Come on, it's getting late." I grabbed her hand.

She blew a kiss as I dragged her away.

"I hope Stevey's still awake." I glanced at a dust-covered clock in the warehouse hallway. It was after midnight.

"Don't worry. He's a night owl." Ananda banged on his door.

A moment later, it opened a crack. A fat man stood in the doorway. He was wearing a white oxford shirt, a black apron, and red lipstick. He grinned at us. "Password?"

"The black rose weeps tears of blood," Ananda said, running a hand over her face dramatically.

"Enter, my darlings." He swung the door open.

I reached for Ananda's hand as we walked in. The foyer looked different. I could barely see the floor in the half-darkness and the heavy *nag champa* smoke. The lamps and mirrors threw shards of light across the room.

We found Stevey and a few other men lounging on the leather couches. Overhead, the skylights were open to the night air, revealing stars between the mobiles.

The man in the apron passed us and walked into the living room. I shuddered when I saw he wore no pants behind his apron. Ananda snickered.

"May I present to you," he said, "Ananda and her friend."

"Girls," Stevey said in a playfully stern voice. "What on earth could you want at this hour? It's way past your bedtime. Our butler let you in, and for that I'll have to punish him. What do you have? Are those presents for me?"

Ananda nudged me. I looked at her, confused. We hadn't talked about how to present the prints. I shuffled them, trying to figure out which one to show first.

"Oh, that one will have to be spanked too," one of the men said.

"Show them our work, Magdalene," Ananda commanded.

I looked at her balefully. My limbs ached with exhaustion. I didn't want to play this game, but I held up our best one anyway.

"I call this one Awakening Spirit," Ananda said.

The men gazed at it appreciatively.

I looked down and saw it was one of my collages, one I didn't even have a name for.

"And this next one is Cerulean Bliss," Ananda said.

"Well. The names suck," Stevey said. "No offense, sweetie, but I don't want any titles that sound like they might be a relaxation album."

Ananda licked her lips. "Those are just rudimentary titles."

"Let me see." Stevey rose from the couch and took one from me. He set it against a pillar and stepped back to look at it. "Sell it to me."

"You want to buy it?" Ananda asked.

"No, I want you to sell it to me, like I'm someone at the show."

"Okay. First of all, I won't be dressed like this. I'll be wearing something much more glamorous."

"Good, good." He nodded.

"I'll say 'we wanted to see what happens when worlds collide.'"

"I'm impressed. I'll give you a good space at the Art Party. But I want you to upload them into a computer program. Make the black blacker and get rid of those tacky crinkle marks."

"Alright." A smile lit up her face.

I breathed a sigh of relief. The pitch went better than I'd expected.

"Yay! I'm so excited." He hugged Ananda with one arm. "Do you want to hang out? There's wine in the kitchen, and there might be some food left."

"Absolutely." She took my hand and led me to an open kitchen, separated by the rest of the warehouse by cupboards that didn't reach the ceiling. They were painted robin's egg blue, with silver handles shaped like branches. Black and white tiles lined the floors, and the countertops appeared to be made of black granite.

"Magdalene, we did it. We're going to sell a ton of prints!" She hugged me and lifted me into the air.

Being picked up always reminded me that everyone towered above me. But this time, it shot me with a rush of exhilaration. We'd just procured a good space at the art show. It was the next step in becoming artists — first the art, then the show.

I slid down her body until my feet touched ground. She released me and turned to pour two very full glasses of white wine. I picked up one.

"To us." She clinked her glass against mine.

"To us," I repeated, and drank.

"Let's catch up with them."

"Okay," I laughed, and took another gulp.

She drained her glass and poured again. "We've never been to a party together."

"Except the one we met at."

"That wasn't a party." She snorted. "That was a gathering of idiots."

I laughed, the alcohol starting to sing in my blood.

Ananda pulled me close again. "We did it. After all that work, we're going to show our collages. We're going to be artists!"

She pressed me against the counter, her warmth enveloping me. She leaned close, her lips brushing mine in long, intoxicating sweeps.

I became all sensation, lost in the mesmerizing sway. It'd

been so long since I'd last been kissed. The guys at college pawed and slurped more than they kissed. This, on the other hand, was delicate, soft, and sophisticated.

"It's a good day to be gay," sang a jolly voice.

My eyes flew open.

The butler opened a bottle of wine on the kitchen counter. Ananda drew away and laughed drunkenly. The butler laughed too, his belly rumbling. It made me laugh, more out of nervousness than anything else.

Ananda picked up her glass and swatted my ass on her way to the living room. I tried to look nonchalant, but my lips still tingled.

"She's the definition of beauty isn't she?" the butler asked. "Just open the dictionary, look it up, and her picture would be right there. Here, have some more wine. I'm Barry, by the way."

"Thanks, I'm Mag. I love this warehouse space."

"Oh yeah. Stevey has an eye, doesn't he? I'm going to have him re-do my flat. He costs an arm and a leg, but he's worth it. He understands the need to look at pleasant things. Speaking of which, I love your collages."

"Thanks. You're coming to the show, right?"

"Where else would I be?"

"Oh, butler!" came a voice from the other room.

"Coming!" he sang, setting the wine on a silver tray and whisking away with it.

I trailed behind him. Someone had dimmed the lights. Ananda sat on a couch, looking like a cat among dogs. I sat beside her and she gave me an exhilarated smile.

A crack rang out. I looked up and saw Stevey brandishing a ping-pong paddle, his eyes on Barry's ass as Barry poured wine. Stevey swung again, then another guy spanked him. I laughed nervously and glanced at Ananda, who also held a paddle, a mischievous grin on her face.

There was wine — they opened bottle after bottle that night. The guys threw back pills, and Ananda bargained the collage prints for some. I asked what they were and she said they were like drinking a beer.

We had deep conversations, draped on the sofa. Stevey disappeared and reappeared in drag. I danced until I couldn't move, then danced more.

At one point, I looked around and saw all the men were gone. Soon after, we heard moans and grunts coming from a room with a closed door. We laughed behind our hands, trying to be quiet while dawn peeked through the skylights.

When I awoke, my body ached as if I'd been beaten. I sat up on the crinkly leather couch. Ananda lay on another couch, still asleep. On the coffee table sat a silver tray with two glasses of water and a bottle of ibuprofen.

I took a few pills and downed the water. I hunched over, trying to unmuddy what happened the night before. I had no memories after the pills, like my mind was wiped clean.

I wandered through the warehouse but didn't see anyone. In the kitchen, empty wine bottles lined the counter like soldiers. The cold light of day made the place feel toxic.

I woke Ananda up and hustled her outside. The sun slashed like bright sharp knives into my eyes, making the drive home painful. Once home, I crawled into bed and slept like the dead.

My eyes blinked open slowly. The sky outside was dark but my hangover still hammered within my head. I padded down the stairs and found Ananda doing downward dog on a yoga mat in the living room.

"Good morning," she said from upside down. She looked radiant, as if we'd had two completely different nights.

"What happened last night? I barely remember anything."

She slid into a svelte cobra. "You drank so much I had to take away your glass. But you didn't get sick on Stevey's furniture or anything. He's going to give us a room for the show. Did you have a good time?"

"Yeah, from what I can remember of it. I just never blacked out before." I rubbed my head. Blacking out wasn't something I'd factored into my life plan.

"You'll be fine. You just need some food."

"Maybe." I couldn't shake the feeling I'd done something bad to my brain.

"I'll tell you what. Let's go out to one of those all-day breakfast places, and then spend the rest of the day collaging. We have a show to get ready for."

She was right. We had a show. We might even sell prints.

I checked the foyer mirror and combed my hair with my fingers. I smiled at my reflection for the first time in recent memory.

I was living the artful life, finally.

Chapter 13. Reversal

Three days before our art show, five collages sat by the door, ready to be copied. Another ten were in various stages of completion. We worked for hours at a time, breaking only to buy more magazines or to eat.

I saw the world as an artist for the first time. Everything was alive and connected, pigmented and pure. A poppy wasn't just a flower — it was fire, silk, lust, and anatomy. My creative brain burst to life while my rational brain loosened its vice-like grip. I'd spent years sharpening it, and then it became the least important thing in the world. I didn't miss it at all. Art was all I was, all I wanted. I'd never been more proud of anything my entire life, and I knew our show would be wonderful.

Ananda and I had just started cutting images from fresh magazines when someone pounded on the front door. We stared at each other with wide eyes, unable to move. No one knew where we lived except Dahlia, and she'd moved back to Poland.

The banging came again, louder and more insistent.

"What if it's Brad?" Ananda asked, cowering against the wall.

I bit my lip. "I'll see who it is."

I crouched by the door stealthily and saw a figure refracted through the beveled glass window. It was too dark and petite to be Brad. A closer look revealed Kitty, in black leather and leggings. I swung open the door. "Kitty! How are you?"

She looked different from the last time I saw her. Her eyes were tinged with red and her forehead was creased.

"Hi. Is Ananda here?"

"Yeah. Is everything okay?"

"Kitty!" Ananda ran to the door and embraced her.

"There you are!" Kitty said. "God! I was so worried about you."

"I'm fine. Come in. We're getting ready for the art show."

She didn't move, just clutched her purse tightly. "Why

didn't you call me?"

"I don't know. We've been busy."

"Too busy to call me?"

"Whatever." Ananda swatted her playfully. "I'm so happy to see you. Wait 'til you see our collages. You're going to love them!"

Kitty shuffled into the house. She gazed at the chandelier clustered with tree branches and her lips curled into a sneer. Her eyes passed dully over the grasses growing in makeshift pots and the altars overflowing with pinecones and rocks. She barely glanced at the collages.

"Are you going to get any furniture, or do you like living in a cave?" she asked.

My skin tingled with embarrassment. Why was she so mean? I tried to catch Ananda's eye, but she wasn't paying attention.

"I'm going to make coffee," I said. "Anyone else want some?"

"Sure," Kitty said, her face screwed up as if she was about to cry.

As I walked into the kitchen, all I could think about was how scathing and weird she was compared to when we met at the coffeehouse. I made the coffee and washed some dishes until it was done.

When I brought the coffee out, Kitty reclined against several pillows, Ananda tending to her. Kitty's eyes were still puffy and red, but she gave me a weak smile. I set the coffee on the carpet.

"Thank you," she said, then inhaled sharply. "What, no cream?"

I shook my head.

"You don't have cream packets or anything?" she asked. "You just drink it black?"

"*Dahling*," Ananda said, "would you take cream in your wine?"

"*Dahling*," Kitty said, "this isn't a Malbec. But I was in the neighborhood, and I was thinking-"

"You were thinking again?" Ananda interrupted. "I thought I smelled something burning."

Kitty's hand fell down hard on Ananda's rump. She laughed.

"I was thinking, tomorrow, a monk is teaching a workshop on creativity and enlightenment. Do you want to go?"

I perked up. My heart burned at the thought of meeting someone enlightened. I imagined my life would be different after I met him or her — easier, more creative.

"How much is it?" I asked.

"It's free."

"It's not really free," Ananda said to me.

Kitty rolled her eyes. "Free to you."

"Like a scholarship?" I asked. "Are we at the bottom of a sliding scale?"

"I'll pay for you both if you go with me. I don't want to go alone."

"I'll go," Ananda said.

They looked at me expectantly, but I held my tongue. I was hesitant about being in Kitty's debt. I could imagine her holding it over my head.

"What about a trade?" I asked. "I'll wash your dishes a few times or something."

"Done, and the best deal I ever made in my life! I'll pick you up here at one tomorrow."

Ananda clapped her hands in joy. "We're going to meet a monk!"

I glanced at our unfinished collages on the floor. We might have enough time to finish them if we worked through the night and after the workshop.

"Do you have a blender?" Kitty asked. "I brought stuff to make smoothies."

She opened her purse and revealed a carton of strawberries, orange juice, and a bottle of Gray Goose.

We walked into the kitchen and I got out the blender from a shelf. Kitty dumped the ingredients in and revved it. It jolted, juice flying onto the counter. She jammed the off button and poured the frothy liquid into glasses.

"A toast!" Kitty said in her radio voice. "May sweet music echo throughout our lives as we dance and play this human game."

We drank. The liquor was strong, but we drained the glasses.

"Oh, Kitty!" Ananda said. "I had a marvelous dream last night. I was a bird, but with a human face."

"A harpy?" she cooed, a flushed smile on her lips.

"Yeah, I was a harpy, and I flew over a pasture, and a boy harpy noticed me. He was beautiful, with black wings, and his eyes were black too. He was testing me."

"Mm hm."

"I fluffed up my feathers, and he said, 'you passed the test. Now you can be one of us.'"

"Hmph." Kitty frowned. "That reminds me. I have to pick up my black feather boa from the cleaners. It's been there for two months, ever since we dropped it in the mud that one night."

"In the GOD DAMN mud?" Ananda laughed.

"The GOD DAMN mud." Kitty cackled. "What a freak. I swear, I'm a magnet for crazy people."

"What happened?" I asked.

"Ananda and I were careening around the Arts District, and we're dressed up like-"

"Like usual," Ananda said.

"And we're crossing the street to go to another bar, and this poor hobo sees us, and says 'GOD DAMN!,' like he's on crack or something."

"And we're so tipsy on Shiraz and zalfadins that I'm like, 'GOD DAMN TO YOU TOO!'"

"And he says 'GOD DAMN!' again, and starts following us," Kitty said. "Can you believe it? Like, seriously, he's following us around, saying 'GOD DAMN! GOD DAMN!' Finally, I got tired of it. I turned around and said, 'GOD DAMN SOMEONE ELSE, GOD DAMN IT!'"

Ananda laughed. "You should've seen his face!"

"And then I dropped my boa in the mud." Kitty smiled softly at me. "By the way, I like your place. I get it now."

A surge of affection raced through me. "I should give you a tour." I wanted to grab Kitty's hand and run through the house, but I resisted. Instead, I led her around, Ananda following behind.

Kitty gazed at everything with interest, though she frowned when Ananda opened her bedroom door.

"That's my tiger-print nightie." Kitty gaped at the mannequins. All three were dressed in animal-print lingerie and cat headbands, entangled together on their hands and knees, as if in a sensual game of Twister.

"I hope you're not mad," Ananda said.

"Nah. That nightie is too long for me anyway. Could you fix it? I could bring your sewing machine by. Is it my imagination, or does that mannequin even look like me?"

"You're only my biggest inspiration," Ananda said. "You always have been."

Kitty's eyes met hers, growing large. "Really?"

"Of course."

I walked to the window and pretended to look outside. A stab of jealousy pierced my heart, same as when she talked with Jared. I supposed some part of me hoped she only spoke like that to me.

"You're the apple of my eye," Kitty said.

"I'd rather be the pineapple," Ananda said, slinking off toward the bathroom.

"What?" Kitty called out.

"I'd rather be the pineapple of your eye. It's more exotic."

Kitty started to follow, but stopped by the door. She bent low to peer at the scratches in the wood. In the sunlight, they were more blatant than ever, almost as if they'd been carved deeper into the wood.

Help me.

"What the fuck is this?" Kitty asked.

My stomach sank. She seemed like the kind of person who could nurse a worry into a full-blown panic attack. She might try to take Ananda away from our house, away from me.

"What is this, some kind of joke?"

"No," I sighed.

"Did she do this?" Kitty pointed toward the bathroom, where Ananda was singing.

"I'm pretty sure it was here before she moved in."

"Did you sage the house?"

I shook my head.

Something in Kitty's eyes scared me. "You don't know what you're dealing with here. This could be a disaster!"

"A disaster?" Ananda asked, walking into the room. "I know it's messy, but–"

"Did you see this?" Kitty asked, pointing to the words.

Ananda craned her neck to look at them and stiffened in surprise. "No, I never saw that before."

Help me.

The ghost girl could be standing next to me, tugging at my clothes.

Help me.

Kitty pulled away and gasped. "There's a ghost in this house. You can't stay here another night, Ananda. You should come back to my condo."

"It's not so bad," I said. "It's just a little girl."

Kitty threw a wild glance at me.

I dug my fingernails into my palms, regretting speaking. Why had I just said that out loud?

"You can feel her too?" Kitty asked.

"She can see her," Ananda said. "It's a little girl named Rosie, right Mag?"

I bit my lip. I didn't like the direction this was going. "It's just my imagination. Ghosts don't really exist."

And yet, as soon as I said it, a chill rushed up my spine and all the hairs on my arm stood on end. I smoothed them with my hands. How had it gotten so chilly in the house?

Kitty and Ananda exchanged a glance.

"What does she look like?" Kitty asked.

"I'm serious. I can't see ghosts. I just have an active imagination."

Kitty pursed her lips as if she didn't believe me. Ananda produced a bundle of white sage and lit one end until smoke billowed out of it like a stink bomb. My mind searched for the ghost girl, but she wasn't around anymore. I wondered where she went, and instantly, the attic popped into my head.

"Better?" Ananda asked Kitty.

She nodded and dug in her purse until she drew out a decorative golden box. On top of it, the words *Eat Me* were embossed in black. She opened it and offered it to me. Several indigo pills rolled around on a bed of navy velvet. They looked just like the pills at Stevey's. My mouth watered. I could almost taste their sweet cotton candy flavor, almost feel the floating sensation.

Ananda snatched two up and popped them into her mouth.

"What are they?" I asked.

"Clemeral, same thing as before," Kitty said.

I searched her eyes. "Same as before?"

"Same as what I put in the smoothie," she said, eyebrows raised defiantly.

"You put this in the smoothie? Without asking me?"

"Yeah, so what? Don't take one if you don't want any."

"Maybe I won't." I stormed downstairs and paced the living room, arms crossed over my chest. Now it made sense. I'd opened up to her and spoke my mind because she'd snuck pills into the smoothie. Everything Kitty had done since she'd walked in the house was a ploy. She wanted Ananda to move back in with her. She didn't care if she hurt my feelings.

I glanced at our unfinished collages on the floor and my heart crushed with anxiety. Our show was three days away, but we had to have everything ready in two days for the Hanging Party. I wanted to be done with them by now. I supposed we could work on them before the workshop, but I had a bad feeling.

"Hey," Ananda said from the foyer, biting her lip. "You okay?"

I clenched my jaw and looked away. I couldn't meet her eyes. I wanted to ask how long Kitty was planning on being around, but I was so mad I couldn't speak.

She caressed my arm. "Talk to me."

I sighed and looked into her clear green eyes. My defenses crumbled. "Did you know she put them in the smoothie?"

Ananda swallowed and her mouth turned down. "Yeah, but I thought you'd be okay with it because of last night. You're supposed to take clemeral with food, and it's better when it's in the food. There's some kind of organic chemistry that happens — it makes you feel it more. But I don't know what you're upset about. It's all good. Kitty's hilarious when she takes it."

"Good, because she's being a bitch right now. She doesn't like me."

"Of course she likes you. She's like a cat. Just give her time to warm up to you."

I threw my hands in the air. "We're running out of time to finish our collages too. We still have to print them."

"We have plenty of time. We'll finish them in the morning and print them tomorrow night, I promise."

She rolled a pill into my hand. It looked like a bead made of lapis luzuli. I knew the risks — the potential for brain damage, toxicity, and even death. But thousands of people took them every day for anxiety, so could it be so bad? And maybe I could use a little medical therapy. Wasn't my obstinacy proof of that?

I put it in my mouth, and the cotton candy flavor exploded on my tongue. As it dissolved, my anger dissipated until I smiled, then began to laugh.

Ananda laughed too. Her green eyes had taken on another quality. Gold flecks flared within them, like a dancing fire. She stared at me as if she were seeing my eyes for the first time too. My heart pounded. Desire burned inside me again, but it was nothing compared to the deeper soul connection we had.

"I told you so," she said, the warmth in her voice echoing in my ears.

She went to the stereo. A moment later, a bevvy of notes pealed out. Bass and percussion built up a trance, and then I heard the mysterious feminine voice of Cypress, the pop-star-gone-independent singer who recently released a mesmerizing album. The music unlocked patterns in my mind, like the rhythm was a key.

"I am in heaven!" Kitty moaned from the foyer.

I jumped. I'd completely forgotten about her. Strangely, she was completely drenched. Drops of water jettisoned off her hair, and her blouse had dark blotches.

Ananda and I burst out laughing. Kitty laughed too. We laughed so hard tears sprung in my eyes and my face hurt, and even then, we couldn't stop.

Our house looked like another realm. The Christmas lights gave each room an ethereal glow, and the fabric on the walls looked lustrous. I stared into a collage Ananda made, feeling it stir my soul. I don't know how long I stood there, but I noticed Kitty nearby, staring at one of my collages, tears in her eyes.

"I understand your art now."

A weight lifted from my heart. I'd been so afraid Kitty disliked me, but now that seemed ridiculous. She had a hard exterior, but she could also be nice.

"*Who will dance the dance of life?*" the singer asked on the stereo. It sounded like Cypress' sultry voice, except it was more playful.

"It's your song!" Kitty cried, clasping Ananda's hands.

"Is this you singing?" I asked Ananda.

"Yes." She swayed back and forth. "Do you like it?"

"But- how did you make it?" I asked.

"Before Brad was creepy, we made music. Come on, dance with me."

"*Who will dance the dance of life?*"

We danced, listening to the song on repeat until we collapsed onto the carpet. I stared at the branch-chandelier. The Christmas ornaments shone in the low lighting.

The pills were wearing off. Kitty must have felt it too, because she rummaged in her purse and pulled out the pillbox again.

"How late is it?" I asked.

She made a face. "Darling, it's ten thirty. Live a little."

"It's only ten thirty?" I asked, my mouth falling open. It felt like we'd been up for hours, as if the sun would rise any moment.

She passed the box around. I looked at the pills again, like drops of the Mediterranean Sea. I picked one up and ate it.

Sweetness flooded my entire being again. A cool night breeze blew through the windows, so fresh it felt healing just to breathe it. The song started again.

"Who will dance the dance of life?"

Kitty stayed in Ananda's room that night. My stomach knotted as I watched them climb the stairs, and again when I saw the closed bedroom door. Until that night, Ananda and I had slept together every night. We hadn't spoken about our relationship, but I thought it was special. We weren't lovers, but that kiss felt like something real.

She confused me, bewildered me. Was I special to her, or was everyone special to her? Maybe she did whatever she wanted, and everyone just wanted to be near her light, like moths to a flame. Perhaps that was why I also felt burned.

I slogged into my room and slumped into bed. I stared at the ceiling, trying to think of anything except what was happening in Ananda's room.

A minute later, when thick snoring resounded through the walls, I almost laughed with relief. Blue lights danced behind my closed eyes until I fell asleep.

Chapter 14. The Swami

We all slept in, but once Kitty was awake, everyone was awake. "We're going to be late for the workshop. Are you guys awake or what?!"

"Awake," Ananda sang from her room.

"Where are all the clocks in this house?" Kitty yelled.

I threw on clothes and brushed my teeth. On my way out the door, I paused by the unfinished collages and my heart sank. We hadn't worked on them this morning like Ananda had promised.

I stopped Ananda by the door. Through the beveled glass window, I saw Kitty getting into her Firebird.

"Ananda, we only have a day and a half to finish and copy our collages, and we both wanted to make more. Maybe we shouldn't go to this workshop."

She turned her palms up. "We'll be fine. We can always finish them when we get home." She tied a scarf around her neck and walked out the door.

I pressed my lips into a line. My artistic aspirations rode on that show. If we didn't sell any, I might have to get a job. I looked around at the spacious house and shuddered at the thought of the heating bill.

Kitty drove fast, speeding when she could, and cursing at every red light when she couldn't.

"Can we stop for breakfast?" Ananda asked. A mascara wand hovered in front of her eyes as she peered at her reflection in the passenger mirror.

Kitty gave a beleaguered sigh but swung into a Dunkin' Donuts. "Make it fast," she said, her teeth on edge. "We can't miss the opening meditation." She climbed out and stormed inside.

"I forgot my purse," Ananda said to me. "Would you get me something?"

"Sure." I contorted out of the back seat, trudged through the line, and brought back coffee and blueberry muffins.

We arrived at the convention center early, much to Kitty's surprise. We checked in and were given name tags, with spaces for name, occupation, and 'mystical name.' I wrote *Mag, Artist* on my sticker and walked into the fray. The room was clogged with tables displaying prayer flags, incense, and crystals of every size and color. I didn't think they had anything in common with enlightenment, but I held my tongue.

Ananda and Kitty made a bee-line for the display tables while I looked for a trashcan. I wandered among monks dressed in saffron robes, wealthy new-agers, disheveled college students, and yoga teachers. A petite blonde in light pink yoga gear waved at me from a table covered with schedules and pictures of people doing yoga.

"Would you like some tea?" she asked. "It's Enlighten Mint."

She offered me a steaming cup of brown liquid, her smile managing to show all her teeth. Her nametag read *Bethany, Yoga Teacher, Tiny Bosom.*

I laughed under my breath until I read it again and saw it said *Tiny Blossom.* I blinked. How could I have misread it?

"No thanks. I have coffee." I lifted my Styrofoam cup.

"I'm Tiny Blossom, but my friends just call me Blossom. *Namaste.*" She folded her hands and bowed her head, her cerulean eyes blinking closed for a second.

"I'm Mag. Have you been to one of these workshops before?"

"Oh yeah. Swami is so wise. I wanted to join his monastery, but they don't allow women because they're supposed to be celibate."

I picked up a schedule. "What kind of yoga do you teach?"

"I teach hatha yoga, but I'm really into karma yoga, you know? Helping people? I teach disadvantaged people."

"That's nice."

"Yeah, and I get to write it off my taxes too." She laughed in a cascade of notes that sounded like tinkling glass. "So, you're an artist?"

"Yeah. I have a show at the warehouses this Saturday. You

should come."

"Hey Blossom," Ananda said, sidling up to us. "You found my new bestie Magdalene. How've you been?"

Before Blossom could respond, Ananda produced a softball-sized cluster of crystals from a purple gift bag and hugged them to her chest.

"Are those Maliesberg points?" Blossom asked, studying them up close. "Those are so rare! I bet they cost you a bundle."

I bit the inside of my lip. If they cost so much, how had Ananda paid for them? She'd forgotten her purse at home.

Blossom turned them over in her hands. "It's said to invoke feelings of love and to activate the fourth chakra."

"Well, I love them." Ananda smiled at Kitty.

Tibetan bowls rang out, drowning all the chatter in the room. The monks opened a door at the end of the hall, and people started lining up. A little door opened, and a monk let one person enter at a time.

"Let's get good seats." Kitty took Ananda's hand and walked to the line.

"See you," Blossom said, running to get in line.

I sank against the wall and drank the dredges of my coffee, replaying the conversation in my mind. The more I thought about it, the more I was certain Kitty was in love with Ananda. I was also pretty sure she thought I was the other woman. I sucked air between my teeth and stared off into space. I hadn't even realized I was in a strange love triangle.

After twenty minutes, when no one was left in line, I got up and went to the door. A young monk ushered me into a coat check room. A wrinkled monk in white stood in the center. I felt breathless all of the sudden — I hadn't realized I'd actually meet the enlightened monk in person. We gazed into each other's eyes for a moment. His brown eyes were clear and prismatic, like a kaleidoscope. The room faded away, until it was just the two of us. My drama with Kitty was petty compared to the ocean of peace he had. He was soul and spirit — no conflicts. He was the real thing.

He broke the connection to dip his finger into a tiny clay pot before touching my forehead. "*Namaste*," he said in a weathered voice, bowing.

"*Namaste*," I repeated.

Someone pulled at my sleeve. I blinked as a young monk in orange robes pointed me toward the way out.

I entered an amphitheater. The ceiling must've been at least two stories high. A white silk parachute hung behind the stage, illuminated with a pink light. People lazed on gray berber carpet, propped up with giant pillows. Everyone's foreheads blazed with a red mark. I didn't see Kitty or Ananda anywhere, so I sat near the door beside a yuppie couple and some college students. They smiled at me as if we'd known each other for ages.

"Is this your first time seeing the Swami?" the yuppie woman asked. Her short brunette haircut was so sharp I wondered if she'd just come from the hairdresser's.

I nodded.

"You're in for a treat. We come every year. This is my husband Alfred, and I'm Sherry. I see you're an artist. What kind of art do you do? Photography?"

"Sherry has a sixth sense," Alfred said. He was balding from the top down, his creased khakis at odds with the floor-lounge atmosphere.

"Sort of," I said. "I'm working on collages for an art show."

"What kind of an art show?" she asked.

"All sorts. Photography, collages, paintings, sculptures."

"Tell me more." She scooted closer.

Before I thought better of it, I told them all about the show. I knew I should shut up, but they kept asking questions and they were so nice. They reminded me of a cooler version of my parents.

"Magdalene?" said a mousey voice behind me.

I turned and saw Ananda shivering, crouching by the door.

"Can I borrow some money? I need to buy something else to wear. It's so cold in here."

"Sure." I dug my money out of my purse and handed it to her.

She gave me an icy kiss on the cheek before running to the lobby.

Kitty plopped down beside me. "Where'd she go?"

"To buy more clothes." I laughed.

"I told her not to wear that outfit. She looks like a groupie."

"Well, at least the monks are celibate."

"I don't know why she dresses like that. I mean, everyone wants attention now and then, but she does it for all the wrong reasons."

"Like the nudists?" I joked, recalling our first conversation.

Kitty didn't laugh. Instead, her face fell. "Did she tell you about them?"

"No, you did, at the coffeehouse."

"No, I mean what they did to her?"

"No, what?"

Kitty leaned in close. "Ananda signed a consent form. They gave her a ton of drugs and got her naked and took pictures."

"Ugh." The undercurrents of what she said chilled me. "Isn't there something about consenting under the influence?"

"I don't know. She just loves to be in front of a camera. The monks say the world of the senses is secondary to the world of the spirit, but that's something she's never grasped."

I straightened — it was the first time Kitty had ever said anything wise. "Well, I guess that's what happens when someone is 'raised by television and magazines.'"

Kitty started to say something, her brow creased, but several Tibetan bowls rang out. The old monk in white robes walked among the audience, touching people on the head as he passed.

Ananda entered through the side door, dressed in saffron robes just like the monks. She sat down beside us, just as the Swami approached. He chuckled and stopped to freshen her smudged forehead mark. The yuppies grinned at us. As I looked around, I saw everyone in the room smiling.

The monk nodded to the yuppies and several other people, then walked up the stage steps. He ceremoniously lit candles and incense on the stage as the parachute color changed from pink to purple. He fumbled with the cordless microphone, then breathed heavily into it.

"Anjay, please turn off the overhead lights." The Swami's Indian accent curled the words like silk over gravel. He sat cross-legged at the edge of the stage, his spine straight and his palms open. "Welcome." His voice boomed over the speakers. "You may lay down if you wish. Close your eyes and let your spirit soar in meditation."

I lay down beside Ananda and Kitty. I must've fallen asleep, because the next time I opened my eyes, the clock had spun ahead an hour. Everyone around me slept on the floor like preschool naptime. The Swami was the only other person awake.

"Welcome back." He winked at me.

I smiled weakly. More people awoke and stretched.

"It's time to return our consciousness back to Earth, and live fully from this moment onward. *Namaste.*"

The Swami bowed and walked offstage to a smattering of *namastes* and applause. Kitty and Ananda still slept beside me.

"Wakey wakey," I said, running my fingertips down Ananda's arm.

Kitty bolted upright and looked around in confusion, while Ananda awoke slowly, stretching like a time-lapsed flower in bloom.

"I have a meeting with him," Kitty said. "I'll be back."

"Hello spiritual beings," a feminine voice sounded through the speakers. Blossom sat on the stage, a yoga mat rolled out before her. "I'm going to lead a free yoga class now. You're welcome to stay."

Ananda poured her heart into her eyes. "Let's stay. It'll be a while 'til Kitty gets back."

"What about finishing the collages for the show?"

"She's our ride home. And we'll be back soon, don't worry." She leaned close and kissed my cheek.

Without Kitty around, Ananda was much more affectionate. She touched me more often, looked into my eyes more. The chemistry from Stevey's kitchen was still alive. I thought about asking her what she wanted from me right then and there, but I couldn't. Strangers surrounded us. The silence in the room was so thick I could slice it.

Ananda slid into a yoga pose. I reluctantly followed suit. After a while, Kitty returned.

"How'd it go?" I asked.

"Fine. Let's get out of here."

Blossom announced another pose to the class and waved goodbye to us.

Outside, the heat had picked up. Ananda shrugged off the orange robes, revealing her tiny clothing.

"Don't be mad about this Mag, but," Ananda winced, "Kitty and I invited Blossom and the Swami over tonight."

I gasped. "But what about–"

"I know you want to finish the collages. We can finish them tonight before they arrive. Besides, we've worked so hard. We deserve a little party. So what do you say? Do you trust me?"

I bit my lip, but nodded. I trusted her, even though my intuition told me not to.

Chapter 15. House of Transformation

Kitty jerked the car into a grocery parking space. I braced, almost hitting the dashboard. She fumbled with the keys before dropping them.

"Damn it. I'm losing my fucking peace of mind!" she growled. She wrenched the door open, got out, and slammed it shut.

Ananda and I followed after her into the grocery. My mouth twisted. Kitty's mood had taken another wild turn. I couldn't figure out why Ananda and I did everything she wanted. Was it because she paid for it, or was she just that controlling? Or was I just a third wheel Ananda dragged along, foiling Kitty's attempts at winning her heart?

"Get some fruit," Kitty snarled at us as she browsed the chocolate section.

Ananda and I walked to the produce section. She picked out a few cherries while I tried to locate the kiwis. I found some, a few bins over, and tossed a couple into the basket. Then I spotted Ananda talking to someone with a camera and a mop of dark hair.

I bit my lip. Jared had found us. I'd hidden the scrap of paper with his contact information in the fireplace, but he'd found a way.

I ducked into a canned goods aisle and peeked around the endcap. Jared snapped pictures of Ananda posing in front of bell peppers.

My stomach soured. I wished we'd never met him, or that he was more of an asshole — anything but another person to contend with for Ananda's time and affections.

Kitty walked toward them. A secret thrill lit me up. She'd rip him apart. She made a snide remark, then she laid into him, her arms crossed over her chest. But after a moment, her frown turned into a smile. She threw an arm around Ananda and stood in front of a pyramid of pineapples as he aimed his camera at them.

"Where's Magdalene?" Ananda asked in a loud, airy voice.

I slid back into the aisle. I didn't want Jared to think of me as a friend. He'd feel entitled to show up at my house unannounced. I couldn't imagine the long, boring conversations he'd try to have with me. I wandered down the aisle, so furious I couldn't even read the labels on the cans.

After a few minutes of sulking, Kitty and Ananda found me.

"There you are," Ananda said. "Are you alright? You look peaked. What's wrong?"

"I'm okay." I slumped against a shelf. "I'm just stressed about the art show."

"Don't stress." she cradled my hand. "Kitty said she'd help us."

"Guess who we just saw!" Kitty said.

"Who?" I asked. My voice sounded flat.

"Jared! He took pictures of us with fruit and vegetables. Isn't that silly? We invited him to the party tonight. Ooh, we should make an exotic fruit platter." She shot Ananda a loaded look and skipped back to the fruit bins.

My muscles tensed. It was as if another Kitty had taken her place. I was getting psychological whiplash from her mood swings.

"Magdalene, take these." Ananda dropped something into my hand.

I looked down at two blue pills.

"We took ours a few minutes ago. I thought you might want to catch up."

I sighed. So clemeral was behind Kitty's improved mood. Of course.

"Does Kitty do these every day?" I asked.

"Yeah. It was prescribed for her anxiety."

Tears formed in my eyes. I just wanted to go home. I wanted to tell her how stupid it all was, but my words wouldn't come out. "I have a headache."

"Clemeral helps that."

I glared at her.

"It takes away my headaches," she purred. "Plus, I want us all to be on the same page."

I blinked hard at the pills. I knew I'd rather have bliss over a meltdown. Maybe I could just take one so my headache would go away.

I put one in my mouth and rolled my tongue over it, tasting the cotton candy sweetness. I put the other one in my pocket in case my headache came back. After a moment, the vice on my head loosened a notch, and then another.

Ananda took my hand in hers, knitting our fingers together. We walked to the produce section. Kitty swung a basket of fruit, eyes bulging and chest heaving, as if she'd just run a marathon.

"Are you okay?" Ananda asked.

She gasped. "I feel like I can't get enough air."

"How many did you take?" I whispered.

"Same as always, three. I'll just meet you at the car." She set the basket down and ambled toward the exit.

"But- I don't have enough money," I shouted.

She turned and slung her purse in the air. I reached for it, but fell short. Her Prada purse hit the floor and slid toward me. Kitty walked out of the store without a backward glance.

Ananda picked up the purse. "Come on, let's get out of here," she said. "I don't know why she takes so many. I think she likes to test her boundaries."

We paid with Kitty's credit card, then walked through the hot asphalt lot. When we got to the car, we found Kitty curled up in the backseat. The keys were on the console.

"You'll have to drive," she said.

I don't remember driving, but somehow, we made it home. I shifted the car into park, thanking my guardian angels. I wondered if they were horrified with my reckless behavior. I should've been furious that Kitty made me drive in this condition, but my raw emotions were buried under blankets of bliss.

A sweet breeze flowed through the house. I looked at all the beautiful objects we'd created and took a deep breath. I felt more at home at this house than any other place I'd ever lived.

"Why are there no goddamned clocks here?" Kitty's hands trembled as she looked at her phone.

I side-eyed Ananda. I didn't know much about clemeral, but it looked like Kitty had taken too much.

"Give this to me." Ananda took her purse and phone. "Go lie down in my room. We'll take care of everything. You've done so much for us, it's the least we can do."

Kitty's eyes darted around the room. I turned away. Even though clemeral made me feel wonderful, Kitty's drama sucked it out of me.

"I'm so tired." She rubbed her eyes. "Lie down with me, Ananda."

From the corner of my eyes, I saw Kitty kiss her on the lips greedily.

"Okay," Ananda said. "Mag, I'll be back in a minute to help with everything."

They trod upstairs noisily.

I picked up Kitty's phone from the floor and breathed a sigh of relief when I saw it was still unlocked. I opened a web browser, googled 'clemeral overdose symptoms,' and waited for the page to load. I wasn't above calling an ambulance if it got Kitty out of our house. But the page said it was nearly impossible to overdose. People who took more than their recommended dose got jittery, and then sleepy.

I dumped the phone back onto the floor. She wasn't going anywhere. I didn't even want to have a party, and there I was, the only one preparing for it. What were Ananda and Kitty doing? Was Kitty demonizing me, trying to win her over with more workshops and crystals?

I opened a drawer and pulled out a knife. I sliced the head off the pineapple and had just started jimmying the ribs when someone walked down the stairs.

Ananda walked into the kitchen. "Hey." She leaned against the counter. "Thanks for being so nice about Kitty. She's one of my best friends."

I didn't say anything, just sawed hard. She sidled next to me and picked up a paring knife and a kiwi.

"Whenever I smell pineapples, I think of the time in the Mediterranean when my friends and I rented a yacht. Did I ever tell you about that?"

I shook my head but didn't look at her. I wasn't in the mood for her stories. I just wanted to collage.

"It was me, a few other models, and a couple of our guy friends. We only packed fruit, water, wine, and cocaine. We didn't know there was no real food until we left the shore. There was a full moon one night. It was one of the best weeks of my life – until now, that is."

I stopped sawing the pineapple. I knew our time together was special to me, but I had no idea about her feelings. "What are you saying?"

"I've had a growth spurt here. My life is finally falling into place." She slid the kiwi slices onto a plate and wiped her hands on a towel. "Let's pick out something to wear tonight."

"What about the rest of the fruit? We haven't even touched the mangoes yet."

"Leave them. We bought too much anyway."

She folded her hand in mine and led me upstairs. On the landing, we heard a monstrous snore from her bedroom. We burst into hushed giggles and tiptoed into my room. Once inside, I shut the door. Crisp, sunlit air blew through the open windows, billowing the multicolored scarves I'd hung earlier that week.

Ananda wriggled out of her halter-top and whisked her shorts off, revealing a purple bra and panty set. Her fingers trailed on the hangers in my closet. She withdrew a sundress and pressed it against her body.

I licked my lips and tried to find words. "There's something I want to ask you."

"What is it, love?"

"Were you– were you and Kitty ever together? I mean, as a couple?"

She laughed, her eyes flashing incredulously. "Of course not. Why would you think that?"

"Because... she's in love with you. She doesn't like me because she thinks we're together, and we're not." I watched her, daring her to contradict me.

She could've turned to me, could have made it real at that moment, but she didn't. She returned the sundress to the closet and continued browsing.

"Don't worry about Kitty. She's stronger than she looks. She's one of those people who could survive a nuclear attack."

"But-" My breath went out of me. I eyed the door, afraid Kitty would storm into my room at any moment and start a fight.

"Kitty's just a big baby who needs pampering. I mean, think about it — she has to work for a living. I just try to make her happy."

She stepped into a black vintage dress and turned her back to me, red hair lifted, so I could zip the dress. I obliged, the old zipper catching a few times before it went all the way up.

"But why keep her around if you're not in love with her?" I asked.

She turned to face me and shrugged. "We understand each other."

"She has an unhealthy attachment to you. She needs therapy."

Ananda smirked. "Psychologists always say everyone needs therapy."

I shrugged. "Maybe everyone does."

"Maybe everyone just needs love." She picked up one of my eyeliner pencils and popped the cap off, then leaned toward the mirror on my wall and drew on her eyelids.

I chewed on a fingernail. I was still confused by their relationship. She hadn't cleared anything up.

"Ananda, there's another reason why I'm nervous about our show. I'm running out of graduation money. If we don't sell our art, I'll have to get a job, and I don't want to do that. I want to keep living our dream, to be artists."

She stopped for a moment, the eyeliner lowering slightly, then she continued. "We'll sell stuff. Don't worry."

"I hope so." I swallowed. Exhaustion tugged at my eyes suddenly. I sat down on the edge of my bed. "How long before people arrive?"

"A couple of hours?"

"I think I'm going to lie down."

She tossed my eyeliner on a shelf and pirouetted out of the room. "Sweet dreams." She closed the door firmly behind her.

I was disappointed she didn't stay with me, but not surprised. She was like a polyamorous muse, starting parties and projects everywhere, and leaving confusion in her wake. I knew I didn't have a chance with her, but no one did. Her sensuality was as uncontainable as the sky. She was going to do whatever she wanted and I couldn't change her.

I stared at the scarves billowing in the breeze and considered my choices. I could wait for her to come around, to want to be with only me, but something told me I'd be waiting forever.

I could share her with the world and try to be gregarious about whatever happened. But, no. I didn't want to share. I'd go insane with jealousy, just like Kitty did whenever Ananda butterflied here and there.

A third option crossed my mind. I could cut her off completely. No more intimacy. No more confusion. The thought of it made my heart tight. Could I say no to her?

And yet the alternative was torture.

I closed my eyes, knowing it was the right choice. I lay down. Sleep overcame me like a phantom. My last waking thought was hoping I didn't snore as loud as Kitty.

I awoke to the doorbell echoing through the house and stretched my arms over my head. A cerulean pre-dusk sky peeked through my curtains. How long had I slept?

Jared's nasal voice floated up from the foyer. My face scorched into a frown.

I often wondered what would've happened had we not seen Jared at the grocery that day. Ananda never would've invited him to the party. She probably would've forgotten about him. The tragedy that defined our time together and made us talk in hushed tones might never have happened. But she had invited him, and of course, he'd come.

More people would be arriving soon. I'd have to be congenial, even though I felt like crying instead. Then I remembered the extra pill Ananda had given me at the grocery. I reached into my pocket and pulled it out. It sat in my hand like a miniature egg in a nest.

I considered not taking it, but I needed to get through the night. Everything would be better after the party. We'd finish the collages, we'd sell prints, and we'd be artists.

I lifted my palm to my mouth. After a few minutes, the fog lifted and I could get out of bed. I ran my fingers through my hair and sauntered down the stairs.

Kitty posed for Jared in front of the flower altar while Blossom admired the collages.

Ananda stood in the center of the living room. When she saw me, she walked over and kissed my cheek. "Hey love. Sleep well?"

"Yeah. Where's the Swami?"

"He couldn't make it. It's just us." She picked up a wine glass from a nearby table. It was filled halfway with a frothy red liquid. She struck it with a chopstick so it clinked. The sound caught the attention of everyone in the room.

"Welcome to our temple," Ananda said, her eyes luminous. "I asked you here because we're on the verge of a new art movement. I want us to be immortalized. So if you're in, drink from my chalice. And if you're not, well, you're free to leave."

"What's in the glass?" Blossom asked.

"You'll see." Ananda winked.

The glass went around the circle. When it came to me, I hesitated. I had no idea what was in it. We didn't have any wine in the house. I lifted the glass and smelled vodka, lime, and pomegranate juice. I took a tentative sip and tasted cotton candy. Part of me worried about mixing alcohol with clemeral, but it was silenced by a burst of pleasure. I passed the cup to Jared.

"Thank you, goddess," he said, his smile saccharine.

124

I glared at him. All the clemeral in the world couldn't stop him from being a buzz-kill.

When the glass returned to Ananda, she downed the rest of it. "So, you're all in." She raised an eyebrow. "Follow me to my bedroom." She danced across the room and up the stairs.

Blossom and Jared shot up behind her.

Kitty threw an arm around my shoulders. "I love you Magdalene," she slurred, her eyes flushed with clemeral.

I looked at her warily, hoping the sentiment would last past the high. "I love you too," I said, mentally adding *when you're not a bitch*. "Hey, I wanted to ask you. What do you think about Jared? Do you trust him?"

She shrugged. "Sure, why not?"

"I feel like he doesn't belong here," I whispered. "He's so normal."

"Ananda likes him."

"That's what I'm worried about. She liked Brad, too, and he turned out to be an asshole."

Kitty stopped me on the stairs and looked into my eyes. "Ananda is different from you and me. We see the world for what it is. We know people are lazy, and what you see is usually what you get. But she sees the potential in people. She sees symphonies waiting to be written by a musician, choreographies inside a dancer, and art inside an artist. I don't know how she does it, but she's almost always right. Once she sees it in someone, nothing you say will make her change her mind."

I slouched. I'd hoped Kitty would side with me. "So I suppose she sees our potentials too?"

"Yeah, I know she does. Look, I have to apologize to you. I know I've been a bitch. I just get so confused about what Ananda wants, you know? One minute, she's in my bed, and the next, she's all over you."

"I know what you mean," I said, looking at the stairs as we walked up them. "But we're not romantic. We're not together."

"You're not?" Her face lit up.

I shook my head.

She smiled slowly. "Do you want to know what she sees in

you?"

My breath quickened, my heart stirred. I nodded. Of course I wanted to know.

"You're a healer."

My face scrunched in confusion. A healer? Was that all? What about my art?

We arrived at the top of the stairs. From our vantage, we saw into Ananda's room.

"Jared," Ananda said. "Take your shirt off. I can't stand to look at it anymore."

His eyes darted down to his striped shirt. "Seriously?"

"Yes. Try this on." She threw him a lavender t-shirt.

He winced, but took the shirt and walked away. I cracked a smile. I liked seeing him sweat.

Ananda held out a spring green dress to Blossom.

"Is this from one of your modeling gigs?" Blossom asked, her bubble eyes widening further.

"Yeah, most of the clothes in here are." Ananda rummaged through her closet again.

"Who made it? Do you remember?"

"Fendi, I think?"

"Cool." Blossom began to undress.

Jared raised his camera.

I walked over to him and put my hand over the lens, a venomous look in my eyes. "Maybe you should change in the bathroom, Jared."

He rolled his eyes and slunk away. I closed Ananda's bedroom door.

"Magdalene, catch." Ananda threw me a crinoline raspberry dress. "And Kitty, here's something for you."

The dress Ananda gave me was so long it pooled on the floor. I rifled through her closet for something else. It was impossible to tell what size anything was because none of the clothes had tags. I tried on four more dresses, but everything was too tight or too long.

I came across a cloud-white dress I'd packed when I helped Ananda move in. The dress seemed buoyed by its stitching and internal structure, as if it had half a lady inside it. Remarkably, there was a tag and it was my size. I tried it on and looked in her mirror. It fit my every curve.

"Can I wear this?" I asked.

Ananda grimaced and shook her head. "Anything but that one."

I shrugged out of the dress and hung it up. I took another one out and tried it on, even though I suspected it was too tight. When Ananda thought I wasn't looking, she shoved the white dress in the back of the closet.

"It's too hot in here." Kitty took off her blouse and fanned herself.

Jared opened the door a crack. I covered myself and let out a little yelp. Kitty went for the door, slamming it in Jared's face and turning the lock.

"That was my face," he said.

"We didn't say you could come in yet."

Blossom and I laughed. She looked radiant in the green dress. Ananda gave her a pair of long ivory gloves.

Kitty produced the pillbox from her purse. Everyone took another pill, including me. To my surprise, I found a dress that fit me — it was a little low-cut, and a slit went all the way to my panty-line, but it worked.

"I wish you had air conditioning." Kitty tore off her leather mini-skirt and fanned herself. She wore only her tiger-print lingerie.

I gasped. "Kitty, you need to find something to wear. Jared is going to see your..."

"My what?"

"Your underwear," I said, a blush rising to my cheeks. "He's taking pictures."

"I don't give a fuck."

"Are we ready?" Ananda asked, dressed in a red, jewel-encrusted gown.

We nodded and she threw open the door.

Jared shuffled into the room, eyes wary, as if Kitty might slam the door in his face again. "Sorry about that." He ducked his head. "I didn't know you were changing clothes." The nasal quality of his voice had softened. The lavender shirt made his skin look less mottled.

"It's okay," I said. "We're ready now."

Jared set up lights in umbrellas and a camera on a tripod. We play-acted storylines, posing with each other. Then we brought the mannequins onto the set and entangled our arms and legs in theirs.

Just when I'd figured out how to angle my limbs and head, Jared packed his camera away. He'd taken hundreds of photos, and his battery was dying.

We wandered to the backyard, where orbs of dandelion puffs and long grass shifted in the chilled night air. The moon was high in the sky, framed by stars and lacy clouds. It was as if the doors of some secret world had opened. Everything was saturated with beauty and poetry.

The darkness of night was palpable. I inhaled it, feeling the air swim in my lungs. Kitty passed her box around and we each took another. We meditated under the gnarled tree, the canopy of branches and leaves so thick and twisted, it looked like a stained glass cathedral. Somehow, in that moment, I knew we'd finish the collages in time. Everything would be alright.

"This is a house of enlightenment," Blossom said.

"It's a house of trance," I said, thinking about our collages.

"The House of Transformation," Kitty said.

Something in the air shifted, as if the house agreed with her. A chill raised the hairs on my arm. I looked around, expecting to see Rosie, but didn't see her anywhere.

Jared covered his face with his hands and groaned. Ananda placed a hand over his heart.

Blossom leaned close to me. "That's so amazing! It's like Ananda knew about his condition, but he hasn't told anyone but me."

"What condition?"

"He has heart murmurs. I think it makes him more special, don't you?"

I looked at Jared, hunched in front of Ananda. I hoped he

wasn't having medical issues. He could've been having a bad reaction. Ananda liked to lift people up from their mundane lives, but she wouldn't be able to save him from a real medical problem.

After a moment, she released him. He raised his head, wiping tear tracks away. Without his scowl, his face looked kinder, more open.

Blossom crawled to him and drew her arms around him. "Are you doing okay?"

Ananda sat beside me, eyes blazing and temples sweaty. One of her hands found my heart, while the fingertips of her other hand brushed my face, feeling like a thousand feathers. I closed my eyes and saw a rainbow of colors. She leaned close to whisper in my ear.

"All your fears are now replaced with love."

Her lips found mine again, but something was different. Her kiss didn't stir me.

I pulled away. Her gaze questioned me, but before I could say anything, Kitty butted in.

"Will you do me?" she asked.

I rose and walked to sit beside Jared and Blossom. They laughed at something, their fingers meshed.

"What's so funny?" I asked.

"The bugs." Jared smiled, his eyes watchful. "They're hilarious."

I looked across the lawn but didn't see anything. And then, suddenly, they appeared, their wings glinting in the moonlight before disappearing into the darkness.

"What happens when insects die?" he asked Blossom.

She shrugged. "They could reincarnate, or if they reach enlightenment, they could become one with God."

He ran his hand over the grass. "I want to reincarnate as a bug."

"Why?" I asked.

"Look at them. They're so free. It's like they're always dancing."

I exhaled deeply and nodded. I was beginning to see Jared as

Ananda did, as a lost soul, as someone who could be inspired to do great things if only he was given permission to do so.

"But you can dance too." I looked into his brown eyes. "You could be dancing right now."

"Yeah, but I have a heart thing. I can't overdo it. I can't even eat bacon."

"Ugh. I'd hate that." I grimaced.

"Yeah, I hate it too." He threw me a wicked grin. "So the next time you go out to brunch, you'll have to eat double for me."

I laughed. My smile grew tight as I looked at his black curls shining in the moonlight. I was ashamed to have misjudged him. He seemed so fragile in that moment. If Ananda saw something good in him, he had to be a decent person.

The rest of the night was a blur. We piled together under the tree. Ananda brought out her saffron robes and we huddled together beneath them for warmth. For hours, colors danced behind my eyelids like the aurora borealis.

I awoke at daybreak, shivering. Dawn's red smear marred the horizon. I wriggled out from under Jared's arm and limped to the back door. Once inside, I blew out the candles, turned off the stereo, and climbed the stairs to my bedroom, where I fell asleep instantly.

Chapter 16. Only Way Forward: excerpt from Analyzing Ananda

Several burned bridges line Ananda's past, which may be why she has virtually no friends from childhood, adolescence, young adulthood, or adulthood. Statements from past friends and allies (footnotes 58-73) show a pattern, in which Ananda befriends gullible suspects with flattery and sensuality, saps them of their resources, takes offense at the suggestion of compensation, and moves on to the next 'friend.'

The dual-victim deadlock she creates is an interesting psychological stance, because both parties feel hurt. Running away from relationships makes healing impossible, and recreates her feelings of helplessness and loneliness, which have been reinforced since adolescence.

To move past the point of dual-victim deadlock, each party would have to communicate past grievances and mistakes, and ideally, would forgive each other. However, since Ananda also displays a classic runaway mentality, her problems only compound.

I foresee a time when Ananda will no longer be able to run. Her problems will become insurmountable, creating a massive breakdown.

She'll have to face the truth and make peace with her history before she can heal old friendships or create beneficial new ones.

Chapter 17. Detox

The morning of Ananda's second day of detox, I bolted upright in bed, a scream lodged in my throat. In recurring dreams, I'd run from a vampire hunting me. Worst of all, in the last dream, the vampire morphed into Ananda. She was just about to gouge my neck when I woke up.

I dressed and tried to shake the nightmares off. I walked to the kitchen and made a pot of strong French Roast coffee. As it brewed, I peeked between the blinds. A couple of cameras snapped in my direction. I jerked back. We were still trapped.

I called John, listening to the rings with trepidation. Even though he was in the hospital, and he probably wasn't conscious, I wanted him to pick up. I never realized how much I needed my sessions with him. He'd probably say this was 'a test from the universe,' even though he knew I didn't believe in that crap. When the call went to voicemail, I threw the phone on the couch.

"Good morning, bitch!" Ananda walked in the kitchen, dressed in a t-shirt and leggings.

My heart stopped. I searched her face for any sign of animosity, but she just looked sleepy.

"Oh my Goddess," she squealed. "I can have chocolate cake for breakfast!"

She brought the cake onto the dining room table and cut a generous slice, then plopped it onto a dessert dish. She retrieved a fork from the strainer and dug in. "What's on the agenda today?" she asked with a mouthful.

"Uh..." I stalled, racking my brain. "Call John, get food, update your social media?"

"Okay. What else?"

"I don't know." I fidgeted with my favorite mug, my thumb caressing the blue divot on top of the handle. I wanted to tell her about my book but I hesitated. Maybe her second day of detox wasn't the right time.

She lowered her fork. "You're supposed to be helping me."

"Okay, with what? Planning for the Grammys?"

"You could give me therapy, like John was supposed to last night."

I took a deep breath. "Let's see how bad John is first."

She shot me puppy-dog eyes. "I thought you wanted me to be in therapy."

"I do."

"It doesn't seem like it." She took the cake into her room and closed the door.

I sighed. If only I'd slept better last night, I'd be more on my game. What did managers of pop stars do, anyway? I picked up my phone and called Kitty. She answered on the first ring.

"It's about time you called me back!" she said.

"Sorry, it's been busy. I wish you were here. When are you coming out?"

She breathed a ragged sigh. "I wish I could leave right now. But I have to stay until they finish editing everything. How's Ananda?"

"It's been pretty intense."

"Did she say why she came back?"

"She hit a low place. She doesn't even remember crashing into the Eiffel Tower. That's how messed up she is."

"Did you tell her about your book yet?"

"No." I cradled the phone against my ear and watched Ananda's door. "How can I do that when she's detoxing and her therapist is in the hospital?"

"As soon as this recording is done, I'll be there, if you can wait that long. Look, I have to go. I have to record chapter seventeen again. Apparently I was too sassy last time. But I'll see you soon."

I hung up. How long would it take for them to finish production and release her?

I called John again. I just wanted to hear his voicemail, but to my surprise, he answered.

"Hello Margaret. How are you?"

"John!" I imagined his body in ten different casts. My

problems instantly paled in comparison. "I was going to leave a message. I didn't think you'd pick up. Is now a good time?"

"I have an appointment soon, but I can talk for a few minutes."

"They said you were in a car accident. What happened?"

"I was on my way to your apartment last night when a car skidded through a stop light and T-boned me. The doctor thinks I'll be okay, but I need surgery. They gave me enough drugs to knock out a rhino!"

"I'm so glad it wasn't any worse."

"How's the detox?" he whispered.

"I don't think it's hit her yet — either that or xyritav detox isn't that bad."

"It's still early, I suppose. How did therapy go last night?"

I gulped. How could I tell him my guilt about writing *Analyzing Ananda* was ruining everything?

"I haven't given her any therapy." I slumped onto the couch.

"Why not?"

"I don't know, because she's so fucked up I have no clue where to start? Because I never studied addiction and withdraw? Because I always heard I shouldn't give my friends therapy, and maybe that's good advice?"

"But Margaret, she asked for your help."

"She doesn't know what she needs," I snapped.

"It sounds like you're still mad at her. Why is that?"

I glared at the window, fury and resentment bubbling up like molten lava. There were so many things she'd done over the years to make me mad. Where did I start? I sniffed back a lump in my throat.

"Come on," he said. "What's the first thing that comes to mind? Anything."

"Okay. When we lived together, she always promised we'd do things, but she never came through."

"Like what?"

"For one, she promised she'd show me around Europe, but it turned out she'd never even been there before."

John chuckled. "So she Aladdined you, huh?"

"What?"

"It's a basic con artist move. Aladdin tells the princess 'I can show you the world,' but he never does. I'm surprised you don't know it."

I threw a hand into the air. "See? This is why I can't work with her. I don't know anything about con artists!"

"Well Mag, as I see it, we can work through your anger this way, talking about every single issue, or you can transmute that anger by having compassion for her and what she's going through."

Rage fired beneath my skin. He should've been on my side. He knew about her lies, and yet somehow, she'd still blindsided him with her personality.

"Mag, will you think about doing just one therapy session with her? She needs you."

I huffed. "Fine."

"By the way, you should tell her about your book sooner rather than later. You'll feel a lot better. And you don't need my help with that."

"Yes I do." I gripped the phone tighter. "I need you to make sure she understands I regret it. Loyalty is really important to her, and once she knows about the book-"

"Okay, I believe you. We'll talk about it tomorrow. I have that appointment now."

"Okay. I hope they take good care of you there."

"Good luck kiddo."

As I hung up, I heard the foyer door shuffle open and Hayden stomp the snow off her boots. I took a calming breath and turned to greet her. She set a couple of bags on the floor before dashing back to the car. I took the bags to the kitchen and unpacked chocolate and fruit onto the kitchen counter. I smiled. Ananda would be so happy.

"I ordered business cards for us," Hayden said, carrying in the last load of bags and setting them on the dining room table. "They'll arrive in a couple of days."

"Great. So what's your title?"

She grinned. "*Personal Assistant to Ananda Dawn.* And you're

Ananda Dawn's Manager."

"Thanks for doing that." I smiled weakly.

Ananda emerged from her room and sat on the kitchen table. Her legs dangled as she watched us unpack.

"Someone's been shopping. Anything good?"

"I got all kinds of good stuff." Hayden pulled a notebook out of her purse. "I thought of a social media update too. How about 'resting up with my bestie before the Grammys'?"

Ananda pressed her lips together. "I don't like the word 'resting.' It sounds bad."

"Okay." Hayden sat at the table and crossed it out with a pencil. "Let's figure this out."

Eventually, they came up with 'taking it easy with a couple of old friends for the holidays.' Hayden posted it. Ananda was delighted when people liked it and left comments. The news latched onto it within a few hours and reported it verbatim. It seemed like they might even start talking about her as if she were a normal person.

I got out of giving Ananda therapy by saying I had a headache and I hadn't slept well. It was true, but in reality, I didn't want to give her therapy. If she despised me later for my book, it would set a bad precedent. She'd never trust a therapist again.

After Hayden left, I turned on Entertainment Tonight. Earlier that day, they'd announced Bertrand Le Fevre, the French officer who'd danced with Ananda, would be a guest.

I sat through several celebrities promoting new movies and television shows, then Bertrand walked onto the stage. He wore an impeccable suit, his black hair riffled with product. He shook hands with the host and sat. My finger tensed on the power button in case they mentioned my book.

"What have you been up to since that iconic dance with Ananda?" the host asked.

Bertrand flashed a smile. It looked like his teeth had been whitened since the Eiffel Tower. In fact, everything about him looked different.

"I have been learning English," he said, his French accent still heavy.

"Great. Can you tell us what happened that day?"

"I am called to the scene of a car crash, and the most beautiful woman in the world was there, acting like crazy."

"Yeah?" the host laughed. "Then what happened?"

"She grabbed me and said 'dance,' and so I did. She said she dreamed of it and kissed me. It changed my life. Now, I am going to ask Ananda Dawn on a date to prove I am the man from her dream."

"Ugh, really?" Ananda snorted from the hallway.

I jumped, my heart ricocheting in my chest. I'd been so distracted by Bertrand I didn't even notice her in the shadows.

"Desperation is so unattractive. Turn it off."

I pressed the button with shaky hands. The television blipped off and the room fell dark.

"Goodnight," she said.

"Night," I squeaked, all my senses on guard. I doubted I'd be able to sleep.

Chapter 18. Coming Clean

After barely sleeping again, I knew I couldn't wait another day. I had to tell Ananda about the book. The stress was killing me.

I picked myself up out of bed and walked to the kitchen. I knew what would make me feel better. I cracked open a tube of cinnamon rolls and set them into a pan. The doughy smell evoked so many weekend comfort food binges. I figured if detoxes were anything like reading rejection letters for my PTSD research, a heavy dose of fat and carbs would help.

After I slid the rolls into the oven, I texted Hayden.

Telling A about my book today. Come over after three.

I didn't want Hayden to witness my confession, but I wanted her to help with the aftermath if things got ugly.

I peeked through the curtains. Snowflakes swirled around the remaining paps and news trucks cluttering the avenue. I didn't see the fans anymore. The cold must have driven them away. I almost felt sorry for the paparazzi. The temperatures had to be near zero. Then I remembered why they were there — they wanted to capture Ananda in a compromising shot so they could scandalize her. Maybe they deserved to be in the cold after all.

I opened my laptop and checked my email. There was another bitter letter from Cleve. I was cc'd on several reviews of my book, too. People called it 'insightful' and 'personally revealing.' But I was also forwarded several new stories about how the publisher pulled the book from publication. Some speculated on the situation inside my apartment, especially with Ananda's benign social media update last night. Most of them called it 'yet another one of Ananda's publicity stunts.'

The timer rang. I leapt out of my chair, grabbed an oven mitt, and pulled the rolls out. The aroma of warm cinnamon and vanilla rose in the air, but it barely made me feel better. Being locked in my apartment with Ananda, the media encircling us, and not knowing what to do was beyond stressful. But it'd all end today once I came clean. It'd change things between us. All the work we'd done rebuilding our friendship would be erased. We'd start over with a new gaping wound in need of healing.

I slathered the rolls with cream cheese frosting and picked at one, but my guilt didn't let me enjoy the taste.

After a few minutes, Ananda's door creaked opened and she walked out in plush yoga gear. "Whoa, cinnamon rolls?" She picked one up and took a bite, her eyes closing in bliss. "I'd forgotten how good these are. But Mag, you're not eating this stuff all the time, are you? You know it's not good for you, right?"

"No," I lied, wiping my fingers on a napkin.

"Can I borrow your laptop? I want to shop for some new clothes for the Grammys."

I swallowed. "But John's supposed to call soon."

"I just want to look at a few sites. The screen on my phone is too small." She finished the cinnamon roll and reached for my laptop.

I put my hands on it. I couldn't let her use it. The ads for *Analyzing Ananda* didn't show up on phones, but they did on the laptop.

"I'm sorry, but I need it. I'm researching something."

Her eyes bugged. "Right now?"

"Yeah, sorry."

"Whatever." She shrugged. "I was going to ask Hayden to get me an ipad later today anyway."

When the phone rang, I leapt out of my chair. "Hello?"

"Mag, you sound flustered," John said. "Did you tell her?"

"No." I tried to sound casual. "But can we do that today?"

"Sure, I don't see why not. How about after her therapy? Is she free?"

"Yeah, hold on."

I handed the phone to Ananda. She took it to her room, but not before giving me a strange look.

An hour later, after their session was over, Ananda walked out of her room, pouting. When she saw me, she stopped and narrowed her eyes. "Are you okay? You look sweaty."

I wiped my palms on my pants. "I'm fine."

"He wants to talk with you."

I took the phone into my room and shut the door. "Okay, John. What's the game plan for the book reveal?"

"Before we talk about that, there's something that's troubling me."

"Really? What could be worse than my stupid book?"

"She's is doing remarkably well for someone undergoing detox. Has she thrown up?"

"No. I would've heard that. The walls are paper-thin here. Wait, what are you saying?"

"She used to take xyritav every day, right?"

"Right..."

"Any person who took it every day would've gotten very sick by now. I'm afraid she might have a stash."

My heart hit the floor. "Seriously? What should I do?" I whispered into the mouthpiece.

"Check her room. If she has a stash, she won't get the help she needs. There's the risk of overdose too."

I sunk my head into my hands. He was right. Xyritav wasn't like clemeral. Overdoses happened all the time.

"Do I really have to go through her stuff?" I whispered.

"Sorry kiddo. She asked for your help, and this is the best way to help her."

I couldn't help but think of the worst-case scenario: Ananda, dead in the snow, pills scattered around her like confetti. "What if she runs out of here and overdoses?"

"You have my permission to call the authorities. She claimed to be suicidal." He paused to cough. "Are you ready to talk to her about the book?"

I cringed. "I guess it's now or never."

"Let's do it. Put me on speakerphone."

I pressed the button. My stomach rolled over. This was it. I was about to tell Ananda the worst thing someone could tell her

— that I'd betrayed her trust and gave a piece of her to the media. My heartbeat chugged as I opened my bedroom door and walked into the kitchen.

She looked up from sipping coffee from my favorite mug.

I set the phone on the table with shaky hands. I couldn't meet her eyes, so I looked at the carpet. I wanted to run out or tell her it was nothing, but I had to get it off my chest.

Could this be the hardest moment of my life? Harder than defending my thesis? Harder than standing up to my parents?

Absolutely.

"Ananda," I said. "I have John on speakerphone. I have to tell you something."

"What's wrong?"

"I... wrote a book about you." My hands fluttered nervously in the air. "It's a psych evaluation, like I used to do in college."

Her eyes narrowed at me. "But I thought you weren't supposed to do that for your friends."

"Well, I started doing it for therapy, but then some publishers asked me to write something about you, and they egged me on, and before I knew it... it was out there."

Her eyes widened. "You published something about me? Why is this the first I've heard of it?" She whipped out her phone, her fingers racing.

"I think Mag is trying to say she's sorry," John said.

"Yes, I'm sorry. There are some unkind words in it. I don't mean them. The publisher twisted my words around."

Her eyes went cold.

I cleared my throat. "I- I asked them to pull all the books from the shelves."

"What did you say about me?" she asked, her voice sharp.

I bit my lip, my throat suddenly dry. I couldn't answer. I stared at the phone, hoping John would speak up and make the situation better, but he was silent.

She found the book online and clicked to read the sample chapter. Apparently it was still available to buy. I cringed, wondering how long it would take for the publisher to remove all traces of the book.

Her eyes darted back and forth and her mouth opened in shock. "Is this for real? '*Everything Ananda touches turns to gold, then brass, then corroded brass, and sometimes gold again. She never has to work too hard because she's used to getting everything she wants because she's beautiful. She doesn't know who she is because of that. It's that dark hole that keeps her running toward the next distraction, the next scandal, and the next fix. In this respect, she exhibits what is known as sociopathic tendencies.*'"

Her eyes burned with fury, her face red. I could barely look at her.

"Really? Sociopathic? What the fuck, Mag? I trusted you."

"I'm sorry. When I wrote it, I never thought I'd see you again. But like I said, they twisted my words around."

Her teeth clenched. She shot up from the table so fast my favorite mug crashed to the floor. "I guess I know how you feel now."

"Ananda," John said. "Mag just wanted to-"

She grabbed my phone and threw it against the wall. It shattered and fell to the floor. She stormed into the spare bedroom and slammed the door behind her.

"I'm sorry!" I shouted after her. "It's not how I feel now." I tried the handle, but it was locked.

"Go away," she said, her voice quivering.

I crumpled beside the door, my heart in my stomach. My book was off my chest, but I didn't feel any better. If anything, the situation was worse. I'd broken her trust and the tenuous friendship we'd built these last few days was gone. Tears washed down my face.

I picked up the smashed phone and the shards of my mug. I closed my eyes, wondering if Hayden would be able to fix anything about the situation.

Then I heard the staccato of pills shifting in a bottle from behind the door. Xyritav — the stash! I'd almost forgotten about it.

I leapt up and raced for the bedroom key in the bathroom bureau. I slammed it into the keyhole and threw open the door.

Ananda held a bottle in her hands. When she saw me, she

jumped. Pills flew everywhere. I crossed the room and clenched the bottle.

"Let go," she shouted, trying to pry the bottle from my hands.

"No." I pulled back. My hands were tinier, and I was able to wrap my fingers around the bottle. I yanked until it was free, then bent over, snatching up the pills from the carpet and the bedspread. I dashed out of the room, Ananda right behind me. Her fingernails clawed my back as I threw the pills down the toilet. My hand leaned hard on the flusher. They swirled as they went down.

"You little twat," Ananda growled behind me. "How am I supposed to do anything now?"

"I'm sorry. It had to be done. John was onto you. How could you lie to us? You're not even detoxing! I can't believe you were still taking them!"

"I was cutting back," she shouted, her lips curling in disgust. "You're such an ass!" She stomped back to the spare bedroom and threw clothes into her bag.

"You don't have to leave," I said from the doorframe. "I'm not kicking you out."

"I can't stay here anymore," she snarled. "And you're fired!" She slammed the door in my face and let loose a primal scream.

I bowed against the wall. I couldn't believe John was right. I hadn't wanted to believe him. I knew I should call him back on the landline, but I felt so hollow inside.

I wandered into the living room and sat on the sofa. I tried to breathe, but my chest was so tight. I hadn't expected her to take it well, but this was terrible.

Someone knocked on the front door. I glanced at it. Who on earth could it be? Hayden used a key. More flowers, maybe? I sat there, immobile. The knocking continued, more insistent this time.

I wrenched myself off the couch and tiptoed to look through the peephole.

Mrs. Gutesberg stood in an old housecoat, her arms crossed.

I closed my eyes and sighed. I wasn't in the mood to talk to her.

"I can see you through the peephole," she said.

I counted to five before unlocking and cracking the door. "What do you want?"

She glanced over my head, into my apartment. "What's going on in there? Did you get in a fight with Ananda?"

My posture went rigid. The paps must've told her Ananda was here. "Don't worry about it," I said icily.

"Well, the press is offering me money, and I don't know what to think. I'm just a widow trying to get by."

I gave her a tight smile and tried not to cry. "Please don't say anything. I'll write you a check. How much did they offer you?"

"A hundred dollars."

My breath latched. She'd considered selling us out for that little? "I'll give you two hundred if you sign a release form."

"Okay, but you need to keep her quiet. If she keeps this up, someone's going to hear. If not me, it'll be Sofia upstairs. She has mouths to feed, you know?"

"I'll talk to her too." I ground my thumb into my temple.

"You're lucky the apartment above you is empty."

I nodded and closed the door. I was pretty sure I wasn't lucky at all.

I retrieved privacy forms and checks, and went to Mrs. Gutesberg's door. After she signed, I knocked on Sofia's door. She took the money too.

Once home, I flung the forms onto the pile of receipts. I trudged to the sofa, threw myself on it, and stared at the ceiling. There was no telling how long Ananda would stay at my apartment. She might be gone in a matter of minutes, and all that hush money would've been for nothing.

After an hour of moping, I found the strength to call John back on the cordless phone.

"What's going on?" he asked.

I cringed. The concern in his voice made me feel weak all over again. "You were right about the pills. She had a stash. She fired me and she's packing her bags."

"What happened?"

"I heard her taking some, so I ran in and took them from her. I'm pretty sure I flushed them all."

"That's very brave of you, Mag. You did the right thing. But it comes down to this: are you still willing to work with her?"

I swallowed. It would be hard work, but setting her loose would be worse. She'd never improve without someone who cared. Besides, I had to make up for my book. "Yes. I still want to help her. I'll do anything."

"Okay. Maybe we'll get lucky and she'll stay. If that's the case, she'll be detoxing in a few hours whether she wants to or not. You'll have to be her friend."

I shook my head. "She called me an ass. I don't think we're friends anymore."

"Perhaps not now, but hang in there. I presume the paparazzi are still outside and you told her she could stay?"

"Yes."

"Good. Maybe that'll keep her there. And when she's ready to talk, she has my number."

"Thanks, John. I feel better knowing you're around."

"As long as nothing bad happens with my surgery." He laughed.

I half-laughed, half-sobbed. "Don't even joke about that. You'll get through it just fine."

"So will you. I have to go. More appointments."

I called Hayden next. I'd just sniffed back the torrential emotion when she picked up.

"Hello?"

"Hi. It's Mag. I'm calling from the land line."

"What's up?" The concern in her voice was audible.

Hearing her made me cry all over again. "Hey. Um." I set my head in my hands. "You should probably skip coming over today."

"What happened?"

"Well, Ananda wasn't actually detoxing, but she is now. I told her about my book. She smashed my phone and fired me."

"Shit. Is she still there?"

"Yeah, but I don't know how long she'll stick around. She's

packing her bag."

Hayden was silent for a moment. "Can I talk to her?"

I sat up, wondering if it'd be a good idea or not. If nothing else, it might give Ananda someone to talk with. I walked to Ananda's door. I could feel the fury emanating off it. I reached out and knocked.

Silence.

"Hayden is on the phone. Do you want to talk?"

At first, nothing happened. Then the door cracked open. Ananda's pale hand shot out of the darkness and took the phone. Then the door shut again.

I went back to my room and lay in bed. I wanted to talk with someone too, but I couldn't call anyone without either of my phones. It was just as well. I didn't have anyone to call, anyway. I couldn't trust anyone with what I knew.

I pulled the covers over my head and tried to sleep for hours before finally drifting off.

Chapter 19. Illusions

When I awoke, I felt the full weight of the Hanging Party later that night. We only had about ten hours to get everything ready. Despite Ananda's promises, we hadn't finished any more collages.

I sighed and rolled out of bed, looking at my wan reflection in the mirror. Last night's party highs were replaced by a low, dark feeling, like a shadow had taken residence in my brain.

I took a clarifying breath and washed up. I was determined to make my artistic career happen. We'd have to move out if we didn't sell any prints. Living at my parent's house again was not an option. It'd been years since I suffered through their early curfews and interrogations disguised as conversations.

I went downstairs to pick up the finished collages and saw two lumps snuggled together on the carpet. I looked closer and saw Jared's arm thrown over Blossom. Both of them slept hard. I didn't see Kitty and Ananda sleeping in the backyard anymore. They must've woken up and gone to Ananda's room. I didn't want to wake them. Kitty's moods were so sensitive.

As soon as I opened the front door, the heat of midday clung to my shoulders. I placed the collages in my backseat and drove to the copy place, prepared to flirt to get a discount, only the flirty guy wasn't working. In his place was a woman who looked like a bulldog. She didn't even say hi when I walked to the counter.

The prints and mat board total came to almost $100. I wrote the check in disbelief, a sinking feeling in the pit of my stomach. I told myself we'd sell prints, but I wasn't so sure. At least they were done, even if I couldn't do as many as I'd liked.

Once home, I found Ananda on the front porch with a mug of coffee.

"Thanks for printing the collages," she said as I heaved the packages onto the porch.

"I'm just glad they're copied."

"Me too." She smirked, holding up a sheaf of papers with a staple at the left corner. '*Glamour Becomes Us?*' You're a nut case, you know?"

She held up one of my old college papers. I laughed. "I was deconstructing fashion magazines for a class. Is Kitty inside?"

Her smile faded. "I don't think we'll see much of her for a while."

"Why not?"

"We had an argument. She got mad and left. She'll be back, though. She always is."

I started to ask what the argument was about, but stopped. If I never saw Kitty again, I wouldn't mind. "Is Jared still here?"

"No, he and Blossom left a while ago. They said they were going out to brunch. It might be a date!"

"Whoa. I didn't see that coming."

"Me neither. Let me see the prints."

We walked inside and I spread them on the carpet. There was my collage with the Cretan dancers, fireworks, and poppies; Ananda's water nymph one, with Monet, Waterhouse mermaids, and beaches; Isis with rainbow wings, time-lapsed stars, and the aurora borealis; and the one called *The Dance*, with people of all nationalities dancing, including a whirling dervish. Lastly, there was Ananda's collage of models with extra arms, like a Hindu Goddess. I made four copies of each, and mounted one of each on foamboard.

"They're perfect." She touched one tenderly. "But five isn't enough. We should do the one with woman's bodies and trees, the Machu Picchu one, and maybe the Green Man."

"But we don't have time or money. Unless you can buy the materials this time."

She was silent, chewing on her lip as if weighing something.

In the absence of words, she confirmed what I'd suspected. She was broke too. I started to calculate how much she owed me, but there'd been so many times, I began to lose count. It must've been over six hundred dollars. That much money could mean the difference between making it as an artist and having to get a job.

When she finally spoke, her voice gushed as if she hadn't heard my last statement. "These are a great beginning. They're perfect. I especially love the one you did of Isis. I bet we sell that one the most."

I couldn't meet her eyes, so I looked at the collage of Isis and said a prayer. *Please, Isis, make Ananda a better person. Please don't let the little things come between us. I love her too much for that.*

"The Hanging Party starts at nine," she said, "but we shouldn't get there until eleven or so."

"Why so late?"

"We want to make an entrance, of course."

I felt a pinch of trepidation. I never got along well with people who rolled into parties whenever they felt like it. I swallowed and counted my fears.

1. *Fear of being late*
2. *Fear of getting in trouble*
3. *Fear of not being an artist*

It was my first Art Party, but Ananda had done several of them. Maybe she knew how it worked. I decided I could trust her. After all, it was just the Hanging Party, not the actual show.

"Can you make the biographies and titles, since I went to the copy place? I don't know what they're supposed to look like."

"No problem."

When I checked in with her three hours later, she was sucking in her cheeks in front of a mirror, applying blush.

"Did you do the bios and titles yet?"

"No, but we have plenty of time. We don't even need them until tomorrow."

My jaw clenched. I walked out of the room to avoid rolling my eyes.

My stomach seethed with hunger. I went to the kitchen and opened the cupboards, but only found lentils, spices, and a pile of dirty dishes. Hadn't I just washed them? And yet, there they were, piled as high as possible.

A knock on the back door startled me. Jared smiled through the screen door, shirtless. His thin chest was golden beige. Black stubble covered his chin and cheeks like velvet.

"Hey. Ready for the Hanging Party?" he asked.

"I don't know. Ask me in a couple of hours. Want to come in?"

He walked in gingerly and stood in the kitchen, shifting his weight. "I wanted to ask you something. I'm living in the sticks right now, and my roommates are driving me crazy. I think we're about to get kicked out. I was wondering if I could move in here. I know you and Ananda don't have jobs, so I figured some rent money would help. Does six hundred a month sound okay?"

I looked at him. He seemed like a completely different person compared to the sniveling guy at the coffeehouse, as if he'd suddenly grown balls and become a man. And six hundred extra dollars every month meant I wouldn't have to give up so soon. I could be an artist a little longer. I felt a flutter in my spleen. I might be able to make it after all.

"Do you have a job?" I asked.

"No, but I sell prints sometimes."

"Do you have a job besides photography?"

"No, but..." He looked at the tile floor. "My parents help me out. It's just until I start making money. Don't tell anyone. People think it's weird, but I'm only twenty-five, you know? Anyway, I thought I could move into the attic and set up a photography studio."

I flinched. "Are you sure you want the attic? We have another room right beside Ananda's."

"Yeah. I think the attic suits me better."

"Okay." I smiled, joy rising within me. "I'll talk Ananda into it."

"Thanks, Mag. You won't regret it. Oh, and before I go, I wanted to tell you — I found your paintings the other night. The blue women."

I shrugged. It'd been weeks since I thought of them. "I don't really know how to paint. I don't know what I was thinking."

"I like them. They're really unique. But they don't have any depth."

"I know, that's the problem."

"I can show you how to contour. It's not hard, and it'll make their faces stand out more."

I took a little breath. "How do you know how to paint?"

"I had a good teacher in high school. Anyway, I'll see you later." He gave me a half-wave and loped off.

I watched him as he cut through the yard, his back glistening in the sunlight. I couldn't help but feel floored. The House of Transformation had changed him. I wondered — had it changed me as much?

I walked upstairs to Ananda's room and leaned on her doorframe. "Hey, Jared offered to pitch in rent money to live here. I think we should do it. We'll still have to pay some of the rent, but it's not much."

Her eyes widened and she embraced me. "Yes! We can be artists! Especially now that Kitty's gone. I couldn't get anything done with her distracting me. I want to make more collages with you."

I smiled back at her, but something had changed between us. Maybe she only said what she thought I wanted to hear. Or maybe I was no longer under her spell.

Something dark tugged on my mood, a palpable force that brought the energy in the room down. I wandered away and lay down on my bed. When I closed my eyes, I slipped into emptiness. A downward spiral of emotion came over me. I felt so heavy I could barely move like, a ghost of my former self, not unlike the ghost girl who lived with us.

When I opened my eyes, the sky through the windows was black. I sat up. How long had I been lying there? I walked out of my room. The house was dark and silent.

I walked down the stairs and saw Jared and Ananda hunched together in the living room, talking closely, a sole candle lighting the room.

Jared backed away, his hair falling in his face. He wore the lavender shirt Ananda had given him.

"You're awake!" Ananda said, clapping her hands together.

"Did I go to sleep?"

"Yep. You were out. We peeked in on you. Are you ready to go to your first Hanging Party?"

"I guess so." I looked for the bios and titles, but didn't see them anywhere. I clamped my lips shut and took a breath. I supposed we had one more day until the actual show. I just hoped Stevey wouldn't be upset we didn't have them tonight.

We loaded the prints into my backseat. Ananda sat awkwardly on Jared's lap in the passenger seat.

As soon as I parked, Jared opened the door and walked away from the warehouse. "I'll be back," he said.

"Where's he going?" I asked Ananda. "I thought he was coming with us."

Ananda shrugged and grabbed the prints. I cringed when I heard the edges of the mat boards bump against the car.

"So tell me," I said as we walked along the dusty hallway toward Stevey's door. "Why can't we just hang everything the day of the show?"

"Tonight is a pre-show party for us to hang up our pieces and mingle with the other artists. It's very low-key. Tomorrow will be a lot busier. We might make some sales tonight too."

People spread out all over the place, some attaching their work to the walls, some eating or drinking in the kitchen. We walked past an ancient Japanese woman hanging oversized photos of flowers, a man writing prices on the bottoms of clay sculptures, a red-headed teenage girl with miniature God's Eyes made from pins, two people dragging a hay bale into a showroom, and another group assembling a metallic construction over ten feet high. Ananda looked around, frowning.

"What's wrong?" I asked.

"Those people with the metal sculpture are in the room we're supposed to be in, remember? Stevey promised it to us."

I nodded, but it looked like they'd already put so much of their project together that it'd take a while to deconstruct and move it.

"Maybe we should have gotten here earlier," I said.

"I'm going to look for Stevey." She handed me the prints and walked through the hanging fabric.

The night wasn't starting off well. Instead of our breakthrough into the art world, it looked more likely that we'd fall on our faces.

A moment passed, and then another. I began to wonder if she'd return at all.

When she came back, her chin quivered. "There's only one place left."

"It can't be that bad, can it?"

She nodded. "It is. Follow me."

We walked through the hanging fabric, past a dimly lit area, and into a dark corner. To our left, a baby-faced girl displayed five paintings of horses, worse than my blue women, and to our right stood an old man in front of crayon drawings.

"Are you serious?" I whispered.

"This is all that's left," Ananda said.

"Wait. Did you see Stevey?"

"No, but someone showed me a map. We weren't even on it!"

"What?" My heart dropped a few feet. Our premiere show would be in a dark corner, sandwiched between two novices. I doubted we'd sell anything.

"Hi, I'm Pasha." The girl with the awful paintings held out her hand.

I shook it lightly, trying to conceal my disappointment. "I'm Mag. Have you seen Stevey?"

"He was here earlier. Do you need help? Wow, these are cool." She examined our prints. "How much are you selling them for?"

Ananda turned away, her eyes tearing up. "Um... no offense, but we really need to find Stevey right now."

"Nice to meet you," Pasha called as we walked away.

Ten minutes later, Ananda and I plopped onto a leather couch in defeat. We'd walked all over the warehouse. Stevey wasn't there. Everyone else had hung their art except for us.

People walked by with drinks in their hands, looking down their noses at their competition and fellow artists.

The lights went dim and someone cranked the music. A few people improv danced. One of them reached for me, but I threw my hands up. I didn't want a weird stranger touching me. He came at me again like it was a game. I glared at him.

I kept watching the door, hoping to see Stevey, hoping he'd tell us there'd been a mistake, that we had a great space somewhere. But after another twenty minutes passed without seeing him, my hopes deflated.

Ananda held her elbows tight against her sides, her eyes hollow. I was about to suggest we help ourselves to the cheap wine and food when she bolted off the sofa.

"Ricky!" She ran to the barista and threw her arms around him.

He gave her a hug and made eye contact with me. His jeans and messy brown hair made him seem less commercial. I rose from the couch just in time to avoid a wave of improv dancers, the collages in my hands.

"Hey you," he said to me.

I blushed and smiled. "Hey."

"Let's go," Ananda said.

"Where are we going?" I asked.

"You'll see." Ananda grinned.

I stashed the collages by the fridge and picked up a glass of wine. The three of us walked out of Stevey's warehouse and down the hallway. Ricky lifted an ancient wooden elevator gate and we stepped in. He shut the gates and pressed a button. It moved up slowly, past several floors with paint-splattered gates.

The elevator stopped on the sixth floor with a thud. He lifted the gates and we stepped out. He led us down a hallway and into a wide, dirty stairwell with black pipe handrails. Somewhere below us, women sang. The echoes of their voices were hauntingly beautiful, arresting me for a moment.

I looked up the staircase and saw Ricky and Ananda step through an open door into darkness. I followed and found myself on a cement roof with a brick ledge running around the perimeter. It looked like a swimming pool with all the water drained out.

I walked to the edge. The city spread out far below. Cars were the size of peas. People looked like ants. Ananda surreptitiously dropped a pill into my hand. My heart rose at the thought of it. I considered not taking it, but my dress had no pockets and I didn't have a purse. It sweated in my palm.

Ricky and Ananda ran off, laughing hysterically, dancing over the rooftop like the chimney sweeps in Mary Poppins.

I found my hand rising to my mouth. I swallowed the little piece of heaven and licked the taste off my palms. My mind crested with joy a minute later. I raced over the rooftop with them, the wind in my hair.

Ananda and Ricky looked like angels. Beauty lived in the arabesques of Ananda's hands, the tangles of her hair, and the shadows of Ricky's face. The sky looked like a jeweled silk veil above us.

The Hanging Party went on without us downstairs, but I didn't care. We had our own world on the roof. We existed in our own symbiosis, needing nothing, only each other, and yet...

I'd left our art by the refrigerator. Anyone could steal them or spill a drink on them. All our work would be for naught.

"Wait," I panted. "We have to go back."

"Why?" Ananda asked, her eyes luminous.

"Our collages are downstairs. We still need to hang them."

We took the stairs down. The girls singing in the stairwell were gone. Ricky reached for my hand. I held it, my nerves lighting up, a secret smile on my face. We rounded corners until we were in Stevey's warehouse again.

The trip-hop was so loud, my eardrums vibrated. With the dim light and thumping beat, it looked more like a sex dungeon than an art venue.

We wove through the maze of art and people to the kitchen. The collages were right where I'd left them. I picked them up and breathed a sigh of relief. Farther down the kitchen, Stevey stood near the sink, eating cheese and crackers with Barry.

"Hello ladies." He stuffed another piece of cheese into his

mouth. Barry smiled at us.

"Barry!" Ananda pointed across the room. "The metal sculpture people are in that room you said we could have-"

"Yeah, about that. I changed my mind." He brushed his hands off.

Ananda gave a helpless laugh. "What should we do with our collages?"

"Damien didn't tell you?" he asked, his eyebrows mussed.

"Who's Damien?"

"Damien, you know, the guy in charge tonight. Oh, look at you, poor things. You were supposed to hang them in the living room."

"But..." Ananda faltered. "The living room has no walls."

"I know. There are wires. It's the best place in the gallery. I thought you'd love it."

"Oh." Ananda let her head fall back. "Yeah, that's great. Thanks."

We exited the kitchen and walked into the living room. It was nearly pitch black except for a few streetlights shining through the second-story windows. I looked for the hanging wires, but they were nearly invisible. I bumped into a corner table and fumbled to turn on a lamp.

As the light clicked on, Ananda and I jumped back. A massive orgy writhed all over Stevey's couches. Men and women I'd seen earlier that evening wriggled in various states of undress and intoxication — a tangle of bodies and orifices thrusting and swaying. I turned, my stomach swirling.

The orgy didn't diminish its gusto after I turned on the light. If anything, it increased in fervor. Ricky and Jared appeared behind us, laughing. Ananda laughed too, and soon we all laughed so much, tears streamed down our faces. The fact that we had to hang our collages there was insane.

Ricky was the only one who could reach the wires easily, so we made him hang the art while we acted as a shield. It started well, but whenever someone moaned, we doubled over laughing again. An odor of armpits and genital funk hung in the air. Twice, someone pawed at my legs. I swatted them away.

After Ricky hung the last one, we raced up the stairs, giggling. On the rooftop, our private world opened up again. The clouds were tinged with silver and the moon had risen. In the distance, a train whistled and pounded the tracks. I danced like I never had before. My chance to be an artist was in proper order again. Everything had worked out.

Eventually, we all wandered to the brick ledge facing the city and stared at the ink-black buildings illuminated with yellow lights. The wind whipped through my dress and I shivered. A moment later, a warm body nudged toward me, blocking the wind. I turned. Ricky stared at me, his pupils dilated. He stepped closer and bent to breathe warmth onto my neck. I closed my eyes. His lips found mine. I melted into him, losing myself. After being flirted with Ananda for a month, I couldn't hold back. I breathed deep to keep from ripping his clothes off. After the moment subsided, he wrapped his warm hands in mine, and we turned to look at the city.

Ananda yawned and mumbled something about going home to bed. Jared had curled up against the brick wall, breathing heavily.

I clenched Ricky against me. I didn't want to go. I could've stayed on that roof until dawn. When I turned to say goodbye, he kissed me again.

"Get a room," Ananda said.

We parted, sleepy and smiling. He walked us to the parking lot, his hand in mine until the very last moment.

It was going to be an excellent art show. I just knew it.

Chapter 20. Art Party

The evening of the Art Party, Ananda and I dressed up and went to Ricky's coffeehouse. My heart rabbited just thinking about seeing him, but he wasn't there. Instead, a woman with a resting bitch face and a skunked pixie cut worked behind the counter.

I hunched over in my patio chair and sucked the last of my iced coffee through a straw. The memory of last night's monster orgy sent a shiver of revulsion through me.

"What if our prints got stained with orgy juices after we left?" I asked Ananda. "Or what if they smell like armpits?"

"You worry too much." She surveyed the sidewalk crowd through her sunglasses.

Maybe she was right, but rent was due in a week, our cupboard was bare, and my gas tank was almost empty. At least Jared was moving in. He'd spent all day unloading things into the house. We still didn't have furniture, but at least my artist dreams would hold out for another month or so.

I wondered about Ananda's job situation. I had no idea how being a model worked, but I needed her to pay me back. It was becoming a lot of money. It'd mean the difference between another couple of months of making art or having to get a job.

"Hey, did you ask your agent about any new modeling gigs?" I asked.

"Yeah, he's putting some feelers out there, but I don't know when I'll hear back."

"How is he going to get a hold of you? You don't have a phone, and we don't have internet at the house."

She shrugged. "He has Kitty's number."

"But you got in a fight with her."

She shook her head and smiled. "She'd tell me if I had a gig."

I sat back in my chair, wondering if she owed Kitty money too. "What time does the show start tonight?"

"Eight."

"I know you think I'm OCD, but the sooner we leave, the sooner we'll be able to tell if our collages were damaged. They might be crooked — Ricky hung them in the dark. And we still have to price everything and hang the biographies."

I looked at the matted titles and bios in the bag hanging on her chair. To my surprise, she'd spent all morning working on them, and they looked great.

She took her lid off and swallowed some ice cubes. "You're right. I do think you're OCD."

I salivated, imagining fruit and crackers heaped in giant platters. Not eating was doing wonders for my figure, but I was literally starving. I couldn't bring myself to buy groceries when rent was coming up so soon, and besides, the pastries Ricky gave us lasted a while. "Stevey might put out food again." My stomach let out a long growl.

She laughed and slugged her bag over her shoulder. "Okay, we can go."

We walked through the coffeehouse. I glanced at the counter again but still didn't see Ricky. Maybe he had the night off. We hadn't talked about whether he was going to the show or not, but I hoped to see him. Every time I thought of him, I found myself smiling. There was something about the way his eyebrows danced when he spoke, and his kiss was so soft and intuitive. It'd been so long since my last intimate experience. I didn't count Ananda. We had an intimacy, but it lacked substance. It didn't sustain me. She was like a rice cake. I needed a three-course meal. I told myself I'd take it slow, but my body was in overdrive. It knew exactly what to do with him.

We arrived at the warehouses an hour before the show. A few people rushed around, decorating and setting up.

Stevey wiped a leather couch off with a rag, a spray bottle in his other hand. Oversized fans blew air onto the couches. Our collages flapped a little in the breeze. I inspected each one and sighed with relief when I saw they were fine.

"Quite a party you had last night," Ananda said, clapping

him on the back.

He jerked his head up, his face red and dripping with sweat. "Those fuckers." His nostrils flared. "I can't believe they did that on my brand new sofas."

"That goes to show you," she said. "You can't trust improv dancers."

I stifled a laugh. "Is there anything we can do to help?"

"No, it's almost clean, thank God."

I mouthed the word *food* to Ananda. We walked into the kitchen. Barry, in a tuxedo with actual pants this time, arranged fruit and chocolate on oblong platters. Bottles of cheap wine lined the island like bowling pins.

"Barry!" I exclaimed, embracing him in a hug.

His face lit up and he set down a cluster of grapes. "Oh my God, it's Ananda and Magdalene. What have you been up to? Anything naughty? You look fabulous. Ananda, I can see part of your boobies."

"All part of the plan." She filled a small plate with crackers, cheese, and fruit.

"How are you?" he asked. "I saw your art over there. It's gorgeous!"

"We're good. How are you doing?" I asked.

"Fine. Just working a lot lately. The corporate life, you know? I'd give anything to live like you two. Your lives must be so amazing. I can only imagine."

"It's not all that," I said.

"Maybe not to you, but trust me, it's the lifestyle. The famous artists, Ananda and Magdalene..."

I laughed. "More like starving artists."

"It's still a glamorous life and I'm jealous as hell. But if you're starving, by all means, eat something."

I smiled at him and filled a plate with cheese, kalamata olives, and pita slathered with hummus. My mouth watered just looking at it.

"You're going to buy one of our prints, right?" Ananda asked.

"Of course I am. I just need to decide which one. They're all so pretty."

"You'd better do it soon. We're going to sell out tonight."

"Oh fine. Come help me pick one out."

As they walked out of the kitchen, Ananda threw a glance over her shoulder and winked at me. They returned a few moments later with an Isis print, which he asked us to sign and number. He handed me two crisp twenty-dollar bills, which I stuffed into my pocket.

"Thanks Barry." I kissed his cheek.

"Thank you girls. I'm going to put this in my car so it doesn't get damaged."

Ambient music played on the speakers.

Stevey appeared, chewing his nails. "The sofas aren't drying fast enough and people are already arriving. Those fuckers knew they were supposed to use sheets. I don't mind the orgy. God knows I've had my share, but I mean, have some respect. Those sofas cost five grand. Well, almost five grand. They're Italian." He poured himself a glass of white wine. "Where are your headshots and biographies?"

"Uh, in our bag," I said. "Where do you want them?"

"I don't know," he whined, storming off. "Just figure it out. I have more stuff to do."

I took them out of the bag and walked to the collages. As I clipped the last title up, Ananda arrived with a full bottle of red wine and a plate overflowing with hummus and chips.

"We're not starving artists tonight."

"Showtime," Damien yelled from somewhere within the warehouse. "Open the doors."

"Here, take some of these." Ananda slipped me two clemerals. "Jared's here. He's showing our photos from the other night. You're a model! Can you believe it?" She caressed me, a dopey grin on her face. She'd obviously taken hers already.

I thought about tossing mine in the trash when an unfamiliar pull told me not to.

Just one. Just take one. You're anxious, so you should take one.

I put one under my tongue and slipped the other in my

pocket. The heavenly dose seeped into my emotions. I leaned back on the couch and stared at Stevey's mobiles spinning in the air.

A crowd of people came through the doors and spread throughout the warehouse. An older man in a suit stared at us. I snapped out of my reverie.

"I'm going to pitch our plates." I collected everything in a heap and walked into the kitchen. I'd just thrown them away when I felt my heart flutter. I turned around.

Ricky set down a bag of day-old pastries on the kitchen counter. He looked even better than the night before, if that was possible. His hair hung in a funny way that made my heart leap.

"Hey," he said.

"Hi." Butterflies beat inside my chest. I didn't know what to say. I jammed my hands into my dress pockets and found the clemeral I'd slipped there moments before. I offered it to him without a word. His fingers touched my hand for a moment longer than necessary, and with deliberate slowness, he put it in his mouth, his eyes on mine. It was like we were past formalities and we knew each other on a soul level. After what seemed like forever, he finally spoke.

"Those photos of you and Ananda are pretty wild."

I drew away from him. "What are you talking about?"

"The ones Jared's showing by the entry door."

Dread rose like bile in my throat. Wild? I wondered which photos he chose. Some of them were pretty racy, with Kitty in lingerie, Ananda in a miniskirt and a halter-top, and me in that dress that revealed so much skin. I barely had any recollection of that night. Had I done anything crazy?

"What's wrong?" he asked. "You knew he was showing those, right?"

I shrugged, unsure what I knew.

"They're not so bad, but you should see them." He took my hand and walked me to the doors.

I tried to pull it together as I walked past the people filing in, but when I got to the entryway, my breath stopped. The pictures

Jared chose to blow up and print were the sluttiest from that night. In one, the four of us embraced, with skin for miles and lust in our eyes, touching each other's arms and necks. In another, we sandwiched the mannequins. My upper thighs jutted from my dress, and Ananda's chest fell out of hers. I swallowed hard. So that's what I looked like on clemeral. At least I'd kept my dress on. Blossom and Kitty posed in lingerie, their bra straps falling off like Victoria's Secret models.

"He's a genius," Ricky said, squeezing my hand. "Look at how beautiful you are, and look at how you're interacting. It's almost mystical."

More people entered the warehouse. They stopped, staring at the pictures and side-eyeing me.

The more I looked at them, the more I realized Ricky was right. For the first time ever, I looked beautiful. My face still looked mousey, but my cheekbones were as sharp as razor blades. I had a grace about me.

As if he sensed my worries, Ricky threw an arm around me. "Think of it as a fashion spread."

I leaned into him. What was it about clemeral that made everyone want to reach for each other all the time? Every time he touched me, rivulets of pleasure trickled up my arm, erasing my worries.

"How do you know so much about art?" I asked.

"I did some in high school — that and theatre. Now I'm studying to be a civil engineer."

"Theatre, huh? You don't strike me as the type."

"Yeah, I know. I'm a little shy. I always got cast as the villains. At first, I hated it. I wanted to be the hero. But after a while, I really got into the twisted roles. Iago, for example."

I laughed. "Maybe it's your brooding stare." I went on tiptoe and kissed him. He kissed me back passionately. I gave myself over to the taste of his mouth, his lips, and the edge of his teeth. When we pulled apart, Jared's camera flashed at us.

"Jared, please," I said, though I was secretly glad he'd taken a photo. I wanted to remember that night for the rest of my life.

"Excuse me," a woman said from the doorway. "Aren't you

Mag?"

I turned. The yuppie couple from the Swami's workshop stood in front of me, dressed as if they were going to the opera. The husband's eyes were glued to Jared's pictures.

"Hi!" I tore my hands off Ricky. He gave me a smoldering glance that said *I'll find you later.*

"Sorry to interrupt," she said. "Is this your work?" She gestured toward Jared's photos.

"No, these are my friend's. My collages are in the living room. I'll show you if you want."

They nodded and I led the way. I couldn't remember their names, but I was happy to see them. When we got to the living room, I gazed into the collages. Every nuance of the colors and curves resounded with meaning. I could barely believe Ananda and I created them.

"These are wonderful," she said.

I snapped out of the collage-world. "Thank you."

"How much are you selling them for?" the man asked.

"Which one?"

"How about one of each?" He pulled out his wallet.

"They're $50 each, so..." I faltered, doing the math on my fingers.

"$250." He handed me a wad of money.

A surge of joy revved within me. I'd just sold five collages! What had I been worried about? Selling our art was the easiest thing in the world.

"These are so beautiful," the woman crooned. "I'm sure they'll go up in value over the years. Will you sign them?"

I signed with a black sharpie, then flagged Ananda down and made her sign. Something in her eyes looked volatile. She wandered away as soon as she signed.

"Thanks again," the yuppies said. They waved, clutching their prints as they left. They made so much commotion, other people wandered over. I sold two more effortlessly.

When the crowd cleared and no one else wanted to buy, I looked for Ananda. I recognized a few people from the orgy the night before, hung over and doughy next to their work. I saw a few hipsters from the Arts District, a girl from the coffeehouse, and a guy who might've been in the gazebo, but I didn't know anyone.

I walked around and viewed the other exhibits. Some were interesting, but many of them seemed premature, not quite there. A few people got it, though. The metal sculpture guys who took our spot were amazing. I also liked the photographer who made mandalas and the mobile-maker, whose aerial art spiraled like ballerinas.

The installation rooms were another story. Much as Stevey described, they housed the weirdos and their deconstructed art. The first room was overcrowded with chairs, something different on each chair seat (a feather, a tea-light, a dead mouse). The second room had a funhouse mirror and carpet tacked to the walls in waves. But the third was the strangest. The room was filled with hay bales. Dozens of eggs lay scattered on them, while boomboxes blasted recordings of chickens clucking. I was turning to leave when I heard a shrill voice shout over the hubbub.

"Chicken vaginas! That's where eggs come from. Not just chickens."

My chest compressed. I knew that voice. I pushed past people and saw Ananda, clutching a young man's t-shirt. He brushed her off and backed away, laughing. She turned to a stout woman in the middle of the room.

"Do you know where eggs come from?" Ananda asked her.

The woman's face lit up, as if Ananda were part of the show.

"Hey." I caught Ananda's eye. "Let's get out of here." I threw an arm around her and started walking toward the door, but she stood, rooted to the spot.

"They don't care," she said.

"I know," I whispered. "But your mascara is running."

She allowed me to steer her across the room. I almost laughed at how easy it was to manipulate her when it came to her vanity, but her outbreak was no laughing matter. Why had she freaked out about eggs? We wove through the crowd, a few people glancing at us with concern.

Once inside the bathroom, I sat her in a chair and dabbed her eyes with toilet paper. She wouldn't stop crying.

"What happened out there?" I asked.

"I don't know. I saw all those eggs wasted on that exhibit. People in the world are starving! And then someone said they came from chicken butts, but they don't."

I tried to maintain eye contact, but her eyes kept drifting away.

"So you saw someone wasting food and you got upset?" I asked.

"Yeah..."

"Is this about something else?"

A girl our age walked into the bathroom. I gave her a tight smile as she went into a stall.

Ananda produced a compact from her purse and powdered her patchy face. "I'll be fine," she said. "I feel better already."

I peered into her eyes. "Are you sure you don't want to talk about it?" Her eyes darted to the bathroom stall and she nodded. "Did you see the photos Jared took? Don't we look awesome?"

A megaphone squealed. I opened the bathroom door and looked out. People crowded around the living room, watching a tall man in a white suit as he paced like a panther. He held a megaphone up to his mouth.

"Ladies and gentlemen, please step closer. You've got to see this amazing act! Come on in!"

Despite his clean appearance, an ugly shiver shot up my spine. I recalled his bulging eyes, the same smug grin smeared on his face. He'd reached for my legs at the orgy the night before. His fingertips had caressed my skin.

A crowd formed a circle around him and two clowns in full facepaint with red noses. Another clown walked into the circle, carrying a towering plate of sandwiches on white bread. My breath caught. Something about the clowns seemed off — they moved as if they were drunk. Several people backed away.

One of the clowns bit into a sandwich, then launched it high into the air. He held his hands out, but the meat, cheese, and bread landed at his feet. Another clown flung a sandwich over the audience's heads. They watched it fly until it hit the wall and fell, leaving a stripe of mayonnaise.

Then the clowns tossed the sandwiches like frisbees into the crowd, hitting people in the face, chest, and back. The crowd broke up, running from the food fight.

A slice of bread whizzed near our collages. Adrenaline fired in my muscles. I ran through the crowd toward our art, almost tripping on a piece of bologna smothered with mustard. I threw my hands up to guard our collages, but a slice of cheese sailed over my head and smacked the middle of a Kali collage. It slid, leaving a trail of ketchup.

Anger boiled inside me. I ran into the circle and grabbed the tray of sandwiches. The clowns tried to yank it back but I elbowed one of them in the face.

"This isn't art," I shouted. "This is bullshit. You just hit one of my pieces with your asshole show."

The megaphone squawked as the ringleader eyed me. His eyes were glassy, with a red glare that looked menacing. "Here's the voice of society, telling us what is and isn't art!"

I glared at him. "Fuck society, and fuck you."

I slammed the tray of sandwiches into the garbage can. Jared yanked the trash bag up, tied it, and hauled it out of the room. The few people who were left cheered. They probably thought my outburst was part of the act.

The clowns improvised with what they had, picking up the sandwich parts from the floor and rubbing them into their clothes.

I went back to my collages and cursed at a bright smear of mayo and mustard right over Isis' face. It was ruined. I tried to breathe through my clenched teeth.

Ananda walked out of the bathroom and looked around in surprise. She side-stepped condiments and sandwich parts on the floor and made her way to me. "What happened?"

"Sandwich explosions from those asshole clowns."

"We might still be able to salvage it." She picked up cocktail napkins from the coffee table.

"Oh... my... God," Stevey said behind us. He shook in barely controlled rage, his mouth a grimace. "What the fuck just happened?!"

I pointed at the clowns. "Those clowns started throwing sandwiches at everyone. Two of our collages are ruined."

"Hey," he snapped. "All of you clowns or jesters or whatever. GET OUTTA HERE. NOW."

The man in the white suit lifted the megaphone to his lips again. "Here's another voice of society telling us what to do!"

Stevey ran up to him and grabbed him by the white lapel. The megaphone fell to the floor and clattered. Stevey marched him to the door.

As they walked nearby, I mashed a piece of bread into his suit, leaving a bright trail of mustard. The clowns started to clean some of the mess up, but Stevey kicked them out before they finished.

He picked up the megaphone. It didn't squeal. "I'm going to press charges against those idiots. If you want to sue them with me, give me your contact info." He set the megaphone down and walked at a clip into the kitchen.

A few people cheered and clapped, but most just stared in awkward silence. After a few minutes, the warehouse was almost empty. The party was over.

Jared approached and handed me a wad of money. "I made rent money! I earned it all from selling prints. I can't wait to tell my parents. They're going to hate it so much."

"We sold some too," I said. "Did your stuff get hit?"

"No, I was too far away. Did yours?"

Stevey returned to the living room and crashed onto the couch with a bottle of white wine, looking miserable. He poured a glass and downed it in one gulp. His eyes were rheumy, his fists still clenched. Ananda sat nearby, barely able to keep her eyes open.

I sat down between them. "So, that was weird," I said, trying to diffuse the tension.

"Stupid fucking kids," he said.

"That collage has a stain," Ananda murmured, slumping

deeper into the couch.

"Where's Barry?" I asked.

"He just texted," he said. "He left after that fiasco. They got him pretty good with some ketchup, and he was pissed. What are you two on, anyway?"

My cheeks flushed. I didn't know what to say. Ananda dug in her pocket, withdrew two pills, and passed them to Stevey.

He popped them, washing them down with a healthy quaff of wine straight from the bottle. "Clemeral. I love this shit. I can't believe they gave it away for free in nightclubs when it first came out. It makes me wonder what else is out there I don't know about."

Ananda turned to him, her eyes half-closed. "You never know what you never know."

Something about the way she said it made me laugh despite the ruined collages, the freaks, and the smell of condiments in the air.

Jared took a picture at that moment. It's one of my favorite photos of that time. I just saw it recently, and it's incredible how young we all look. It captured the moment — Stevey's weariness of the art scene, Ananda's descent into more and more drugs, and me laughing, perched on the edge of a sofa, blissful and unaware.

That photo could've ruined my career if I had taken two pills instead of one that night. I would've been slumped along with Stevey and Ananda. Instead, I'm framed by them, leaning forward, looking into the distance as if I could walk away at any moment toward something better.

The rest of the night was useless. We stayed until midnight, but no one else bought anything. Stevey said someone leaked a video of the disaster, and that was why no one else showed up. He apologized over and over until he fell asleep.

I craned my neck, looking for Ricky, but I hadn't seen him since I sold art to the yuppies. I'd wandered to the roof three times, only ever seeing the moon.

We went back to the house with the prints that survived the sandwich attack. When I lay in bed and closed my eyes, a jumble of images danced behind them — Ricky's smoldering eyes, the clowns, Stevey's couches, Ananda freaking out, and the image of my face from Jared's pictures, so different from who I used to be. Maybe the house had transformed me as well.

Sleep descended upon me like vultures, with dark wings and no mercy.

Chapter 21. Trapped

The next afternoon, after recovering from the hangover, I sat in front of one of my paintings, a paintbrush poised in my hands. Jared had just taught me how and where to apply shading and light. So far, it worked. My blue woman's cheeks seemed to rise from the canvas, and she seemed alive, almost as if she could wink at me.

Ananda sprawled on the floor beside me, cutting up fresh magazines for our next batch of collages. The soft clink of silverware in water came from the other room as Jared washed the dishes. We'd taken clemeral in our coffee about an hour before. I knew I didn't have to — I wasn't addicted — but it made the work more interesting. Hell, it made the light filtering through the windows more interesting.

"Do you really think Stevey will sue those guys?" I asked, biting into a stale bagel.

Ananda cringed. "I don't know, but he said he'd never have another Art Party again. I don't blame him. Those people were insane."

"Where would we show our art if he doesn't have Art Parties?"

"We could get our own warehouse space. People would come to our parties for sure."

I nodded, even though I knew we couldn't afford both the house and a warehouse space.

Someone knocked loudly on the door. Ananda and I locked eyes. I wondered who it could be. I really didn't want to deal with a meter reader or a solicitor.

Another round of knocks came, louder. Jared appeared in the hallway, wiping his hands on his pants. I laughed — if it was a meter reader, he or she might have second thoughts about entering the house after seeing Jared with his shirt off and his hair wild.

He opened the door. Murmurs sounded from outside.

"Who?" he asked. "Oh yeah, she's here. Come in."

I rocketed up from the floor, my heart crashing in my chest. I hoped it was Ricky, that he'd somehow discovered my address, that he was standing there with a big bouquet of flowers. I was shocked rigid when I saw my parents standing awkwardly in the foyer.

I swallowed, adjusting to the reality of the situation. I assessed the house as they must've seen it — the collages, the rocks on the mantel, the nests of hair on the carpet. Shame rose in my cheeks.

I tried to think about my successes. I'd sold several pieces of art only the night before. But all I could see was the crack in my mother's smile and the bewilderment in my father's eyes. They stood like cardboard cutouts, and seemed just as flat.

My father stepped hesitantly into the living room, as if the floor might collapse from beneath him at any moment. My mother clasped her hands stiffly in front of her. She seemed ten years older than the last time I saw her.

"Hello Margaret," she said.

"Hi. Mom, Dad, this is Ananda and Jared."

Dad pumped hands with each of them while Mom nodded and whispered, "nice to meet you."

"I'm surprised to see you," I said. "I didn't know you were coming."

Mom simpered. "We left a message on your voicemail."

"But I don't have a phone anymore."

"Well, we called the last number we had for you. We thought you would've gotten a phone by now."

"I haven't gotten around to it. I've been too busy."

"You look so skinny," Mom said. "Are you eating enough?"

"I'm fine."

"No matter," Dad said. "Want to go to the old Brasserie for lunch? What do you say? You can bring your friends."

I looked at Ananda and Jared and saw them through my parents' eyes. They looked like washed-up survivors on a desert island. They both nodded, oblivious to the trap.

"Can we get cleaned up first?" I asked. "It was a late night and we're still in our pajamas."

"Your pajamas?" Mom exclaimed. "It's two o'clock in the-"

"Marjorie." Dad gave her a hard look, then turned his gaze back to me. "Go clean up. We'll wait for you."

I felt like I was twelve years old again, or perhaps eight. I ran upstairs, my heart thumping. I rifled through my closet but couldn't find anything appropriate for the Brasserie. Didn't I have anything nice?

I knocked on Ananda's door. She'd changed clothes and brushed her hair.

"Can I borrow a dress?"

"Sure," she said. "Your parents seem nice."

"Yeah, they're nice. They're just-" I stopped, not knowing how to describe them besides judgmental. "Just don't say anything too revealing around them. They think everyone has something wrong with them."

My parents played games with my high school friends, asking question after question. But the worst part was their conversation with me afterwards, where they'd play the game 'name the psychosis,' and goad me into participating. They'd examine my motives for being friends with them. They'd even told me to abandon friendships. Sometimes, they were right. I hadn't introduced them to any of my college friends for fear they'd tear them down too.

"Can I wear this one?" I asked, pulling out a velvet shrug dress. It looked like another sample dress Ananda had worn on the runway.

"Yeah, but it's hot out."

"There'll be air conditioning."

"Mm! I almost forgot what that's like. It's hotter now than the summer I was in Italy, and they're much closer to the equator."

Jared appeared in the doorway, freshly showered, in a white shirt and pair of khakis, which was at odds with his scrubby facial hair. We looked like a band of wanderers.

"Maybe this isn't such a good idea after all," I said.

"I'm ready for anything," he said with a relaxed smile.

"You're not ready for my parents. No one's ready for them."

"Come on, they can't be that bad," Ananda said, linking her arm in mine.

In the car, my parents grilled Ananda and Jared. Ananda said she just wanted to be an artist in a commune. Jared admitted his parents paid most of his bills. I leaned my head against the seat. They were doomed.

Once inside the restaurant, the aroma of fries and burgers drove me to distraction. We sat in a long booth in the back. I squinted, trying to focus on the menu, but clemeral blurred the words. I felt the weight of my parents' gazes on me and set the menu down. I knew what I wanted anyway.

"What've you been up to, Mag?" Mom asked.

"I had an art show and sold some collages."

"Really? Where?" Dad asked.

"Downtown, in a warehouse. We sold a lot."

"We? You and whom?" Mom asked.

"Ananda and I made the collages. Jared sold some photos too."

"You made collages together?" she asked, raising an eyebrow.

"Mm hm." I squirmed in my seat.

Mom leaned over the table toward me. "Are your friends dating?"

I looked at Jared and Ananda, giggling at the menu items, and shook my head.

"Well..." Dad said, resetting his napkin in his lap.

I frowned. Dad always said that when he didn't know what to say. I could tell he wasn't happy with me, but I didn't care. I dug my fingernails into my leg and made a pact that they couldn't take my art away. I wouldn't give in, not this time.

"We're going to make even more collages for the next show," I said, smiling sweetly.

"How much longer do you expect you'll do these collages?" he asked.

"I don't know. I might do it for the rest of my life."

"Being an artist is a fickle career," he said, his hands open like he was carrying something heavy in them. "You never know when it's going to leave you high and dry. Have you thought any more about going to grad school? You could always do art on the side."

"No, I haven't thought about grad school. Why would I want to repeat one of the most miserable experiences of my life?"

"Well, there's the money," he said.

Ananda burst out laughing and the focus turned to her.

"Creamed spinach? Is that a real thing?" she asked.

"Yes, and it's delicious," Mom said, signaling the server. "Order whatever you want."

After the drinks arrived, lunch went by a little smoother, though I couldn't help but feel sorry for Ananda as she had her turn under the spotlight.

The food arrived. The smell of my grilled chicken sandwich with pesto and fries intoxicated me. I tried to pace myself, but I wolfed it down.

My mother's face revealed a hint of shock. She'd barely touched her cobb salad.

"Sorry, I'm just- we haven't been to the grocery in a few days," I said.

"We could buy you some groceries on the way back if you want," Dad said. "By the way, how much did you make at your show?"

I smiled. "Four hundred dollars."

Seeing their eyes pop was worth the entire lunch façade. I almost laughed. It was proof I could make it as an artist if I tried hard enough. I didn't need to go back to college.

Then I realized I hadn't subtracted $100 for the prints, nor had I paid Stevey yet. Splitting the remainder with Ananda meant all my work for the past month had come to a mere $50.

"Maybe *you* should be paying for dinner!" Dad joked, elbowing Mom.

I rolled my eyes. He'd made his point. All at once, I felt tired. It was more than I could bear.

When we got back to the house, Jared and Ananda thanked them and got out of the car. Mom stopped me with a look. Her eyes, which had been soft and rejoicing at the restaurant, bordered on sharp.

Dad draped an arm around the seat and looked back at me. "Your friends are like the dirty hippie fairies you'd find in the woods–"

"I don't want to hear it," I said. "I'm sick of you ripping into my friends under the guise of caring about me. I can figure out my life without you telling me how to live it."

Mom laughed gaily, as if reiterating what they'd always told me – that I knew nothing, and they knew everything. I glared at the roof of the car to avoid rolling my eyes.

"Sorry sweetie, do we really do that?" she asked.

"Maybe if you look at your friends a little closer," Dad said, "you'd be surprised at what you'd find."

I turned my eyes to him. If he wanted to play dirty psychology, I was game. I could put the screws in too. "I need to make my own friends and decisions, unless you're saying you don't trust me."

"We trust you," he said. "We wouldn't loan you money or anything, but we trust you."

"So now you're saying I'm a failure?"

"We'd never say that, Squirrel," he said.

I fumed. He'd just used my childhood nickname. It was his trump card – the fact that he and Mom had raised me. And sure, they'd never say that, but they implied it. I sighed. "I like doing art. I like these people."

"No offense, sweetheart, but your friends–"

This time I let my eyes roll.

"Your friends are trouble. Capital T trouble. Neither of them have jobs, they're clearly on something or other, and they don't have a good grasp on reality. Do you remember the story about the ant and the grasshopper?"

"Dad. You don't have to diagnose my friends."

"I wouldn't have to if you had any common sense, but Maggie, it's like you're wearing horse blinders. I know this lifestyle is fun for you now, but you'll want more out of life than this."

176

"Whatever." I clasped the door handle. "Thanks for the food, and thanks for reminding me why I moved out."

"We're sorry," Mom crooned. "Bill, let's make a promise to Maggie. We promise to not talk about your friends anymore."

"But that chick's clearly–"

"Shh! Not unless Maggie asks us for advice. Does that make you feel better sweetie?" She reached for my free hand.

I sighed but slid my hand into hers. It felt like warm parchment.

"Take this," Mom said, handing me a folded up bill.

I resisted. I almost told her I could make it on my own. But on second thought, I took the bill and tucked it into my bra.

"Thanks."

"Love you," they sang.

"Love you too," I grumbled.

I got out of the car and stomped to the porch, watching until their car disappeared around the corner.

Chapter 22. Good Intentions

After my parents visited, I felt different about Ananda and Jared. I saw more acutely the dander in Jared's patchy beard and the grease in Ananda's hair. No amount of incense could cover the smell of overflowing trashcans, ripe bodies, and dirty dishes. A voice in my head that sounded suspiciously like my father remarked about the unkemptness of it all. As much as I tried to quiet it, it only got louder.

When we went to the grocery with the $100 from my parents, strangers asked us where we were from. Ananda spun a yarn about how we were only in town for the night, and did they have *halva?* The checkout clerk recoiled in fascinated disgust at our food. The tahini, figs, seaweed, chocolate, and coffee must've looked like a new fad diet amidst the cartons of eggs, gallons of milk, and shoulders of beef that populated other carts.

One evening, after the cupboards were bare again and my bank account dangerously low, I went to the backyard and ate bitter dandelion leaves and clover blossoms. I was so hungry I could barely focus. I considered calling my parents to ask for more cash, but I didn't want to admit defeat.

A car braked hard in front of our house. I peeked around the side of the house and saw Kitty step out of her Firebird. She picked up two loaded plastic bags and walked toward our front door.

I walked in the back just in time to see Kitty set the bags on the counter, a secret smile on her face. *Naan* flew through the air as she removed the contents of the bags. Ananda whooped, hanging on Kitty. The smell of curry made my stomach clench.

"What's going on?" I asked.

"The Swami and his assistant will be here in half an hour," Kitty said, a wild gleam in her eyes. "We're all going to get initiated. Do you have enough silverware and plates?"

I looked at the mountain of dirty dishes that'd piled up in

the week or so since Jared had done them last.

"Yeah." I reluctantly moved toward the sink. I ran the hot water, telling myself it'd be worth it to eat Indian food from real plates, though I was so hungry I would've eaten it from anything. Ananda sidled beside me, eyes twinkling, and dried dishes.

"I thought you and Kitty were fighting," I whispered.

"We were, but Kitty is seriously the best. I don't even deserve her."

"What changed?"

Jared and Kitty walked into the room, carrying a long rectangular table he'd found in the alley. Someone had taken the legs, so they set it up on the dining room floor like a Moroccan lounge table, surrounded with pillows. Jared took plates and glasses from our clean pile until the table was set. When we had enough settings, I hid the remaining dirty dishes under the sink.

I only had enough time to light incense and wash my face before the doorbell rang.

Jared opened the door for the Swami, Blossom, and a young monk dressed in saffron robes. Ananda had changed into her saffron robes too. The Swami laughed at it, picking up the edges and apologizing when it almost came undone. He radiated happiness. His presence in the room was palpable on a visceral level. The young monk behind him looked embarrassed and kept close to the wall. We each introduced ourselves.

"Thank you for welcoming me and my assistant Anjay here," the Swami said in a gravel-rough voice. He looked at our collages and decorations. "You have a nice home." I cringed as he lingered in front of the Green Man collage, with its phallus imagery and a print of a satyr dancing with naked women, but he merely smiled.

"This is where we do art," Ananda said, spinning beneath the branch-chandelier. "We also meditate and do yoga here — can you feel that? Do you feel things?"

It was obvious she'd taken clemeral. If someone didn't know the telltale signs, they might think she was just excited, but I could tell. Her jaw clenched, her eyes glossed.

The Swami nodded indulgently. Anjay handed him a small bronze bowl, and with ceremony, he rang it. The reverberations echoed throughout the house with gravitas. As the din died out, he offered it to Ananda, bowing slightly.

"This is a present for your temple."

"Thank you," she said, her eyes wide with surprise.

Kitty gestured to the dining room. "Dinner's getting cold."

The Swami looked at me. His eyes looked like shining brown marbles in the folds of his face.

"You sit beside me, please."

I nodded and smiled at him as we all sat at the table, although I didn't know why he chose me. Blossom and Ananda studied mysticism, and Jared was more talkative. Had he picked me because I was quiet? As if sensing my thoughts, the Swami patted my leg reassuringly.

Jared went to the kitchen and brought back a bowl of lentil soup and a ladle. When everyone had been served, I swallowed a spoonful, but something was wrong with it. The soup tasted sweet. I set my spoon down and shot him a questioning look. Jared's Cheshire cat grin faltered when he saw me.

I threw my napkin on the floor and stood up, nodding to the kitchen. He followed.

"Did you put clemeral in the soup?" I asked, arms crossed.

He giggled. "Just a little."

"But the Swami–"

"Don't worry. It's a tiny amount. It's only one pill for what, six or seven people? That's nothing."

I huffed. Was it really nothing? I couldn't tell. Had I thought he'd spike the soup, I never would've agreed to it. I couldn't believe he served it to the Swami and Anjay.

"Did you put it in anything else?" I snapped. "Any of the entrees?"

"No. Everything else is still in the packages. You can see for yourself."

I looked at the main courses in their styrofoam containers and sighed. "You'd better not be lying."

"I'm not. Don't worry, Mag. It's fine."

I returned to the dining room and sat down, still fuming. Jared served the curried vegetables, chili eggplant, samosas with tamarind sauce, and garlic *naan*. There was so much food, and it was so decadent. By the end of the meal, I felt pleasantly bloated, something I wasn't used to.

When we were done, Jared cleared the plates. Seconds later, the sound of running water and dishes tinkling softly against each other came from the kitchen.

Kitty slid a green pill into my palm and winked. "Have a mint."

I looked at it and considered not taking it, but after Kitty, Ananda, and Blossom each took one, I found myself wanting the cotton candy feeling. I slipped it under my tongue, but was surprised when it tasted bitter instead of sweet. Could she have given me a weird, bitter mint? It seemed unlikely. The Swami stared at me. I took a big sip of water.

"Swami, could you initiate all of us tonight?" Kitty asked.

"I will initiate only those who wish to be initiated. It is a serious matter."

"I'd love to be initiated," she said.

"Very well. We can start with you."

Anjay helped the Swami up to a standing position and handed him a tiny pot. The Swami closed Kitty's eyes with his hand, then chanted and anointed her third eye with red clay. After a moment, he bowed. She bowed too, her eyes watery.

Bliss rippled down my spine, but it was different from clemeral. Something spiked in my body, like rage, or excitement, or too many shots of espresso. I started to panic. I had too much energy — it was exactly how I imagined meth felt.

As the Swami performed the initiation on Ananda, she looked so high she could've pass for a junkie on a television show. I began to worry about her, and about the Swami and Anjay too. Did they feel what I was feeling? I glanced at the monks, but neither one was out of his element. I was glad they hadn't taken one of Kitty's 'mints.'

Waves of happiness crashed upon me, and I knew everything

would be fine.

"Wow," Kitty said, her eyes glowing. "I can feel what the Swami did to me. This is the first time in my life I feel like I should."

The Swami's chanting became fragmented, as if he forgot the words. He dotted Ananda's temple slowly, getting lost in her eyes.

"Sorry. I am tired." His eyes blinked slowly. "It is past my bedtime."

"*Do not go to sleep*," Ananda said, quoting Rumi. "*Enlightenment is waiting.*"

The Swami laughed and nodded. He teetered toward me. Anjay caught him and held him up. He looked at me questioningly, but I could only smile at him.

The Swami shut my eyes with his palm. When he chanted, his voice resonated in my heart. I felt as if I'd heard those words before, like an echo in my soul. Then I saw, in my mind's eye, a dirt-colored walls and bright sunlight shining through a window.

Saliva burst in my mouth. My stomach clenched and started to heave. I ran out of the room, out the backdoor, and threw up onto the grass. The spicy food I'd enjoyed so much landed at my feet in a red mess. I hurled again, then wiped my mouth and looked up at the weak stars, panting.

"Are you okay?"

I turned to see the Swami standing by the tree. He looked surreal, like an impressionist painting. "I just got sick, but I feel better."

"Do you want the rest of your initiation?"

I nodded. He smiled peacefully as he walked toward me. He closed my eyes again. His arms wove around me and he held me tightly, as if we were soaring and he couldn't let me go or I'd fall to the ground.

When he released me, all the winds of the world played on my skin. I opened my eyes. A white light illuminated him. He looked fragile, and yet so alive.

He stared into the depths of my soul. I stared back, feeling the layers of my ego shed, revealing a pureness and wholeness I'd never felt before. Whatever pill Kitty had given me, it was more than I'd ever taken. Part of me felt so heavenly nothing could bother me, but another part of me panicked. I wondered if I'd get sick again.

"When the mind is ready for enlightenment," he said, "it blooms like a flower. You cannot force a closed bud, but there is a shortcut. You don't mind shortcuts, do you?"

He pinched my ribs in what must've been an attempt to tickle me. I squirmed. He smiled, his eyes pure kindness. He embraced me again. His hands moved subtly, barely caressing me.

"You are so special," he whispered. "We should see each other again soon. I have something important to tell you. But if you are feeling better, we should return inside."

We walked back through the kitchen. In the living room, wild music played. Blossom and Ananda danced with Kitty. The Swami and I joined them. Even Anjay and Jared danced.

After a moment, Ananda dragged me into the kitchen. "I had a vision when the Swami initiated me."

"I got sick."

"Are you okay?"

"Yeah, but what did Kitty give us? I thought it was clemeral, but it tasted different."

"It's xyritav!" She grinned. "Can you believe it? It's so hard to get, but Kitty's prescription changed. Everyone's calling it the new clemeral!"

"Hm." Her bouncy excitement made me nauseous again. "Does it make everyone sick?"

"I don't know, but let me tell you about my vision. I was on a stage and I sang the most beautiful song. Hundreds of people cheered in the audience. It felt so real. It was like I was there!"

The image of the hut flashed before my eyes. Were visions part of xyritav? Maybe it stimulated that part of the brain. I started to ask something, but Ananda took my hand.

"I love this song. Let's dance."

We danced until I felt the tug of sleep. When Kitty offered

around the *Eat Me* box, I didn't see any clemeral, so I declined.
I didn't want to throw up again. I went to bed, but the bumping
beat of the party continued for hours afterward.

Chapter 23. Circumstances

The morning after the party, the House of Transformation was eerily quiet. When I opened my eyes, Rosie's lights churned at the foot of my bed. I fell back against the pillow, my head spinning.

The night before seemed like a dream. I only remembered bits and pieces, but everything had gone downhill after I took the xyritav. It was particularly embarrassing since the Swami saw me throw up.

When I came out of my room, Kitty was in the hallway outside Ananda's room, lacing up her boots. Her face looked pitted and her hair hung in unbrushed clumps. "I have to work in a few hours."

"That sucks." I yawned, stretching.

"Can you do my dishes today? In exchange for the workshop? You said you'd do them, and I really need it."

I took a big breath in and let it out slowly. The last thing I wanted to do was wash dishes hungover, but I also didn't want to be in Kitty's debt. She already looked at me like I owed her something.

"Yeah. Just give me a minute to clean up."

I brushed up and trudged down the stairs. Four people slept on the carpet. Anjay snored beside an upturned potted plant. Dirty dishes cluttered every surface, and spills stained the carpet. No one had closed the windows, and the frigid morning air made the chaos seem even dirtier. My father's voice spoke in my mind again. I walked out to the porch to wait for Kitty and clear my head.

I tried not to get sick on the way to Kitty's, but it took a lot of effort. I thanked my guardian angels when she finally pulled into a parking space in front of a lemon stucco condo. Kitty's manicured lawn, overflowing flower baskets, and cypresses in urns looked exactly like the pages in the Home and Garden magazines I saw at the thrift store. It made our place seem even rattier in comparison.

The inside of her condo looked like another magazine spread. Modern furniture was accented with rose and mint-colored pillows and curtains. Everything was made of sumptuous materials that made the place feel cozy.

She led me to her kitchen, which was also freakishly stylish, and to the Mt. Everest of dirty dishes. Plates and cups were covered in slime, mold, and crusts of former good times. They stacked in teetering towers all over — in the sink, on the counter, and on the floor. Kitty had a dishwasher, but it was full of other decrepit dishes. Several, if not all of them, would have to be soaked and scrubbed before washing. I swallowed and fought the urge to flee.

"You said you'd do my dishes a couple of times, but if you just do these, I'll call it even. I'll be in the shower. There's coffee in the cupboard."

My head ached, but I slogged forward and made a pot of coffee.

An hour later, dishwasher chugging, I scrubbed the last of the silverware. Kitty, refreshed from the shower and dressed in work clothes, stepped into the kitchen to survey my progress. She got a cup of coffee, poured cream from the fridge, and sat at the dining room table.

"Thanks again," she said. "Do you feel okay?"

"I'm still hung over." I shrugged, my voice flat.

She dug into her pocket and pulled out a couple of pills.

I looked at them warily.

"They're just aspirin," she said.

I dumped the last of the silverware into the strainer and took the pills with a glass of water. I leaned against the sink, regarding her. Her eyes had black half-moons beneath them. "Are you really going to work?"

"My credit card bills don't pay themselves."

"That sucks." I refreshed my coffee.

"You'll have to get a job soon too, right? Didn't you say this was just a break for you?"

I took my coffee to the table and collapsed into a chair across from her. "I still have some time. Jared is moving in, so that'll help with the bills, and I sold some prints at the show. By the way, why weren't you there?"

"Ananda and I were fighting, so I made other plans."

"Really? You seemed like best friends last night."

Kitty smiled and glanced at her lap. "I did something for her, something huge. Remember when I told you how the nudists took those photos of her? After I told you, I couldn't stop thinking about it. I was furious. So I staked out their place the night of the Art Party. I waited until they left to go to their backwoods excuse for a bar. Then I broke in and took all the pictures of all the girls they'd ever taken advantage of. I even took their computers and hard drives."

I gasped. "You broke into their house?"

She nodded. "It was for a good cause. Ananda was so happy. She'd always regretted those photos. I didn't get all of them. There are still a few prints that sold at an Art Party ages ago, but no one knows who owns those. If anyone asks, I was at the Art Party with you all night, okay? I doubt anyone will look for me. Bedlam is pretty far away, and those guys made a lot of enemies. I doubt they'd even tell the police."

Kitty was willing to do anything for Ananda. It made sense why they'd become friends again so easily. I never could've broken into someone's house.

Kitty looked at me, her eyes soft. "You and I are different from the rest of them, you know? We're the only ones who actually went to college."

"Yeah, but college isn't that special."

She smirked. "You don't see it now, but it is. Tell me what you think in twenty years."

"But Ananda didn't go to college, and she's one of the most fascinating people I know."

Kitty leaned forward. "She gets by on her looks. I've known her a long time. Since we were teenagers."

I blinked, dumbfounded. Why hadn't Ananda mentioned that? No wonder their friendship was so tight.

"She never told you?" she asked. "Figures. Let's just say she has a selective memory. You have a psychology degree – you could probably make sense of her. For instance, why'd she hate her name so much she changed it? I mean, I have a nickname, don't get me wrong, but it's because no one can pronounce Li Xia, much less write it."

I stared at her. "Ananda isn't her real name?"

"Oh, no. Her real name's Jennifer Clark. She didn't tell you?"

I shook my head. "She'd told me her parents chose that name because they were hippies."

"I'll tell you something else," Kitty continued. "Her family isn't wealthy. Quite the opposite."

"But she said–"

"I don't blame her for recreating herself, but the truth always comes out."

I swallowed. What else had been a lie? My heart thumped heavily. "What about her modeling career?"

"Ananda has never left the state of Minnesota, except in her mind, I suppose," she grimaced. "You don't know her very well, do you?"

I didn't know what to say. The person I thought I knew was a beautiful fabrication, the holes in her past like gaping maws. Her modeling career and her travels had been our first conversation. That was what made her so interesting to me in the first place.

Kitty looked at her watch and stood. "I gotta run. Can I drop you in the Arts District? It's on my way."

"Okay," I said, dreading going home.

"By the way, I know I have issues." She leaned on a chair. "I have September, October, November... I have problems. But I'll never lie to you about anything. I just can't say the same for Ananda."

The car ride to the Arts District was bumpy. Twice, my face shot toward the windshield. When we arrived near the coffeehouse, Kitty turned down a side street and stopped. I climbed out. She waved before peeling out down the road.

The world spun around me. My stomach protested, demanding food. I hadn't eaten anything since the Indian food the night before, and I'd thrown up most of that. I patted my pockets and felt the thick wad of cash from the art show. I was so relieved I almost thanked my guardian angels out loud.

I walked to the coffeehouse, pushed open the door, and felt my heart roll over when I saw Ricky working behind the counter.

"Hey you," I said, smiling up at him. I could almost taste his lips from two nights ago.

"Hey," he said, his eyes bouncing around the coffeehouse.

"How are you?"

"Fine."

I smiled. "That Art Party was fun, even though it got weird at the end."

He stared back at me as if he didn't know me. I wondered if I looked as hungover as I felt. I ran my fingers through my hair self-consciously. He was probably curt because his manager bustled behind him, making a sandwich.

The coffeehouse door opened, and a couple of businessmen got in line behind me.

"What do you want?" he asked me.

"Um." I looked around. I'd have to speak with him later. "A bagel with cream cheese and a large coffee please?"

He rang it up at full price. I handed him a few sweaty bills and he gave me change, all the while barely meeting my gaze.

As I pumped coffee from an air-pot and took a seat at a round metal table to wait for the bagel, I replayed our last conversation in the warehouse. Had I said something? I couldn't think of anything that would've made him act that way, unless he was mad that I stopped the sandwich clowns.

I rubbed my temples, trying to loosen the headache. The music in the coffeehouse hurt my ears, as if the speakers were made from aluminum foil. I wished I had another clemeral to sooth the pressure in my head.

What Kitty told me about Ananda came up in my thoughts,

but I wondered if I could trust anything she said. It seemed like she still had it out for me; like she was still trying to wrench Ananda back to her condo by any means possible.

Before long, Ricky plopped the bagel on my table and went behind the counter again. The line at the register kept getting longer. He avoided looking at me, and seemed pissed that I was even in the same room as he was. Where was the guy who'd kissed me on the roof and in front of Jared's photos?

Whatever was going on, I couldn't stand it. I grabbed everything and stomped out the door, letting it slam behind me. I was barely aware of walking until I found myself in the ornate, empty gazebo. Nearby, families played on monkey bars and swings. Homeowners trimmed bushes and mowed their lawns. I sank deep below the ledge and ate faster than I should have. When I finished, my stomach knotted. I pushed the plate and cup away and hugged my knees to my chest, hoping no one would approach.

So Ananda hadn't been to the Tate or the Louvre. Was that why I hadn't seen her in any of the fashion magazines — because she'd lied about being an international model? Were all her stories about living abroad false? And what about those sample dresses? Or had she cut the tags out to make the lie fit? The fact that she thought North Beach was actually a beach started to make sense too. But why did she feel she had to lie?

Another wave of pain and nausea quivered within me. I leaned against the cool brick ledge. I should've taken more aspirin. A moment later, my stomach rejected the bagel and coffee. I tried to keep the noise down, but someone near the playground gushed in concern.

Tears formed in my eyes. I sniffed and tried to clean myself up. It must've been the xyritav. I vowed I'd never do it again.

The stomach cramps lessened after a few deep breaths. I ducked out of the gazebo and walked back to the House of Transformation. If what Kitty said was true, things would never be the same. I was going home to lies.

"Hello?" I called into the house.

No one answered, but laughter echoed from upstairs. I walked up and peeked in Ananda's room.

Jared tickled Ananda on her futon as she laughed uproariously. She wore only a bra and panties.

"Hey..." I wondered what I'd walked in on.

She straightened. "Mag, where've you been? We looked for you."

"I went to Kitty's to do dishes."

She giggled behind her hand. "The Swami just left. He, um..."

"Should we tell her?" Jared asked.

"What?"

He laughed, exchanging a glance with Ananda. "Well..."

She laughed so hard she gasped for breath. "The Swami... and Blossom..."

"What?" A caustic sensation seared my throat. "They slept together?"

Ananda nodded, clutching her belly and laughing.

"They had sex?" I asked. "I thought he took a vow of chastity! And I thought she liked you, Jared!"

He shrugged. "I thought so too."

Ananda cackled, smacking the floor with her hand.

My heart clenched. We'd drugged the Swami. I hoped it was only a tiny dose, but what if he got the lion's share at the bottom of the bowl?

"Do you think it was because of the clemeral in the soup?" I asked.

Ananda and Jared laughed even more. Their glassy eyes confirmed my suspicion — they'd taken clemeral. I sighed, worried about the Swami. What if Kitty had offered him one of her 'mints'?

"By the way," Ananda said. "Jared's going to sleep in my room from now on. There's no reason he should stay in the attic or sleep on the carpet." She cozied into his embrace.

Jared smiled at me, smug as a lap cat.

I felt as if my brain would explode. Just a few days ago, that'd been our bed. We'd been inseparable. Now she was willing to sleep beside someone we'd just met.

"What about us?" I asked, my voice sounding like a squeak.

"It's Jared's turn now."

I nodded and walked to my room, closing the door behind me. A shadow crept over my heart. So this was the way it would be.

I fell onto my bed and let the tears come. I missed having her all to myself, but it wasn't just that. It was what Kitty told me, Ricky acting weird, my dad's voice in my head, and probably a good dose of PMS and insomnia. I couldn't even talk with Ananda because she was so messed up on clemeral or xyritav or whatever. I felt like shit, and I couldn't help it. I didn't want to breathe through the negative emotions. I could only feel the loss — the void in my soul — and I wanted to wallow in it.

Footsteps wandered into my room. I opened my eyes and saw Ananda, angelic, hovering over me.

She stroked my arm. "Why are you sad? We had such a great party last night."

I shook my head. Where would I even begin? Where does a list of grievances ever start?

She lay down, facing me. She embraced me and noodled her legs into mine, then brushed my hair away from my face and tried to look into my eyes.

I took a deep breath and wiped my face. When I looked at her, I saw the beautiful stranger I thought I knew intimately. I saw the person who'd lied to me for months.

She gazed back at me with pure love, maybe even longing. "Talk to me."

I blinked. "I liked it better when we didn't do any pills."

"What do you mean?" she asked, her eyebrows askew.

"I liked it better when we used to collage by ourselves, before Kitty or Jared. We were sober then, and it was fine."

She laughed. "Maybe you were sober, but I wasn't. I took clemeral every day, like usual."

My breath caught. "The whole time?"

"Yeah, what's wrong with that?"

"Well, you weren't prescribed it. It has a long-term effect."

She shrugged. "Don't lecture me. I like it."

I swallowed. "Kitty told me you lied about some things."

Her eyes flashed with surprise, and her grasp turned stiff.

I took a deep breath. "She said you lied about your name and traveling to Europe. Why would you lie?"

Her lips curled into a frown. She withdrew her arm as if she were burned. "What do you want me to say? That I hated my life? That I made up a more interesting life because my imagination did a better job of raising me? You know, not everyone has parents like yours."

"Wait. Can we talk about this?" I didn't know what I thought would happen when I brought up her lies, but I didn't think she'd get mad.

She got up and headed for the door, her eyes like ice. "I'm sorry I don't live up to your high expectations."

"It's not like that."

"You don't love me anymore. I can see it in your eyes."

I pushed up to a sitting position. "This is getting blown out of proportion. Let's take a step back and talk about it."

"What's going on in here?" Jared asked from the doorway. He was dressed in Ananda's harem pants. The glassiness of his eyes was visible from the bed.

"Nothing," I said.

Ananda sobbed against his shoulder.

He held her and glared at me. "What did you do?"

I rolled my eyes. "Kitty told me some stuff about Ananda, and I asked her about it. I guess she made up some of her past."

"The past doesn't matter," he said. "What matters is the present moment. People recreate themselves all the time. You need to respect her, not harass her about it."

"I'm not harassing her, I just—"

"Just drop it. Come on Ananda, let's go lie down." He led her to their bedroom.

I stood up and went after them, but the door closed in my face. I stared at it, my confusion peaking. Was this really happening? The whole day seemed like a nightmare.

I threw myself on my bed. Tears welled up again. Their hushed voices floated through the walls. He probably consoled her just as I had after we moved her stuff out of Brad's apartment. I huffed, wondering bitterly if she'd ask him to do a naked cleansing ceremony too.

I closed my eyes. This time, no lights moved behind my eyelids. Darkness enveloped me, and I let it take me away.

Chapter 24. Detox Redux

The morning after my huge fight with Ananda, I awoke to a silent apartment. I lay in bed under the covers and held my breath, my ears straining for any sounds that meant she hadn't taken the first plane back to LA. I only heard a cardinal chirping outside.

It was torture not knowing if she was in the next room or halfway across the world. I could imagine her stumbling through the paparazzi late last night, getting into her rental car, and taking off to God knew where. I listed my fears on my fingers.

1. *Fear of losing Ananda*
2. *Fear of failure*
3. *Fear of the future*

Then a racketing cough and the slosh of vomit hitting a bucket erupted from the next room. I cringed, but my chest filled with light. She was still in my apartment! Maybe she knew I was there for her, that I still wanted to help her despite the harmful words I'd written about her.

I got up and made coffee. Ananda didn't emerge except to use the bathroom. She refused to look at me, which was understandable. My book was pretty disparaging. I couldn't help but think things would've gone a lot smoother if John wasn't in the hospital; if he could've been here to mediate the conversation and take away her stash of pills.

My phone was smashed beyond repair, but the sim card was okay. My favorite mug, however, could not be replaced. The shards made clinking sounds as I brushed them up. As I tipped them into the trashcan, the memory of when I'd received it flashed back to me. I'd seen it at a coffeehouse and remarked on it, and my boyfriend had bought it for me on the spot. It was such a warm time of my life, even though it was brief.

I picked a big blue shard out of the trashcan and ran it under the tap until it was clean. My fingers curled around it.

The edges cut into my hand, but I didn't let go.

I glanced outside my apartment. We were still surrounded. I worried they'd heard us arguing last night, or that someone snitched on us, but as each hour passed and no new speculations or news about Ananda hit the internet, the butterflies in my stomach subsided a little.

Hayden arrived around eleven with the latest phone the young people were using. We sat at the dining room table while she loaded apps I'd never use onto it. We tried to ignore Ananda's heaves.

Hayden wrung her hands. "What are we supposed to do about her?"

"She needs to get it out of her system. Detoxing from xyritav isn't too bad. People get sick for a few days, and they crave it, of course."

"I can't imagine what she's going through." She shuddered. "Hey, did you hear Cypress tweeted something at us?"

"Really? Ananda loves her. You should tell her."

Hayden shook her head. "It's not good." She held out her phone.

@AnandaDawn Why are you hiding out? Can't decide what to wear to the Grammys?

"Well that's sort of rude," I said. "Why does she care?"

Hayden ran a hand through her curls. "I don't know, but I'm not going to respond. I don't think we should tell Ananda either."

"She'll find out sooner or later."

"Maybe later is better. Hey, there's a drug that'll make her stop puking. I have some pills leftover from the last time I had food poisoning. I'll go to my place and get them. Can you think of anything else I should get?"

"Yeah, groceries." I gave her a list. "Also, magazines — fashion, travel, nature, a little of everything. Take the rental. Your car looks like it's falling apart, no offense."

"I know. It's a piece of shit. I hope I can afford a new one after working for Ananda for a few months."

I smiled tightly. "We don't know how long she'll be here.

But that reminds me. Let me write you a check for your second week. Sorry I've been so bad about that."

"Why are you still doing it?" she asked sheepishly. "Ananda fired you."

"Well, maybe she'll change her mind." I handed her a check.

Hayden forced a smile, but she didn't look optimistic. "You should charge your phone." She slipped on sunglasses and her coat.

I watched through the blinds as she cantered down the front steps and into the crowd of paps. The Greaseball hounded her, shoving a microphone in front of her and following her to the car. A couple of paparazzi even snapped photos. She remained stoic and didn't respond. It lifted my heart that she was so good about it. Hiring her had been the right thing to do.

My phone lit up with another email from my former publisher. I cringed as I opened it. My book had been a bestseller in twenty-two countries when I pulled it.

When I'd written it, I didn't care if Ananda's feelings were hurt. It was my way of talking back. I now saw it for what it was — a childish retort with big words. Even though I'd apologized, I knew how harshly Ananda took criticism. She held onto grudges like they were superglued to her psyche.

Deep down, I probably wanted some kind of confrontation, like a child acting out, not caring if the attention was a reprimand or affection. But how had I let myself become so bitter? What did I think the book would solve? It exposed, more than anything, my terrible wound from her absence. She was right. I had given up on my dreams. I'd faded like a plant without light because no one had believed in me like she had.

I knocked on her door, my heart heavy. "It's me." Hope made the pitch of my voice higher. I had a flashback of being a teenager, my mother on the other side of the door, trying to get me to talk.

"I don't want to talk to you," she said.

"Is there anything I can get? You sound miserable."

"No."

"Some filtered water?"

Silence. It'd been a couple of hours since she'd last ventured out. I went to the kitchen, poured a glass of bottled water, brought it to her door, and knocked.

She cracked the door. Shadows lined her face and she looked sweaty. She was surely detoxing this time. I was so stupid to think she was detoxing before.

She took the glass, snapped the door shut, and retched again.

"I'm here if you need anything."

Kitty emailed. Her flight was scheduled to arrive in a week, on Christmas Day. I started an email back to her.

Kitty,

I'm so glad you're coming. Please plan on staying at my apartment. I wish it could be sooner too. We're still holed up here.

Ananda is doing okay, but she's detoxing from xyritav and is pretty sick. She's been puking a lot. It should be over by the time you arrive. I probably don't have to say this, but please don't bring any drugs into the apartment.

I told her about my book. She didn't take it well. I asked my agent to withdraw it from stores, but it's too late. The damage has been done. I wish I'd taken you up on your offer to proofread the contract. In any case, I'm trying to make up for it now.

We have an assistant to run errands, and buy groceries and take-out. I've known her for years. You'll like her. I look forward to your visit. We wish you were here.

Love, Mag

I pressed send and googled 'how to manage a pop star,' but every page was riddled with legal terms and taxes. It was clear I had no idea what to do. Since Ananda wasn't talking to me, I had no way of knowing if she was serious about firing me. In the meantime, I was going to do everything I could for her.

Ananda's door creaked open and she walked into the kitchen, dressed in blue flannel pajamas, her arms crossed and her face puffy.

"Hey," I said.

She breezed past me as if I hadn't spoken at all and pulled a cereal bowl from the shelf.

"Hayden is picking up groceries. Kitty will be here Christmas day."

"I know," she croaked. "I spoke with her last night."

"Do you need anything?"

"A notebook."

I went to my bedroom bookcase and drew a blank book I'd always intended to write in, but never had. In the corner of my room, I saw the vintage blue suitcase with my collages and hundreds of images. I hadn't opened it in years. Not so long ago, Ananda and I created art so seamlessly it felt like a mystical relationship. Now we were both at low points. Who would've thought we'd be going through deceit and detoxes?

I walked back into the dining room and gave the book to Ananda. She took it and retreated toward her room.

"Do you feel like talking?" I asked.

She hesitated in the doorway and looked at me for the first time, her eyes stinging red. "No. I'm basically trapped here, which is ironic because I'd rather be anywhere else."

My head sank into my chest a little. "I'm sorry about the book."

She rolled her eyes and slunk into her room, closing the door behind her.

At least she didn't slam it.

Hayden returned, loaded with bags and a huge box. "I had a great idea," she said once everything was inside. "I bought a juicer! It's supposed to be great for detoxing. I also got some vitamins and detox herbs."

"Where'd you get detox herbs?" I asked, looking at the bottles.

"I used the self-check-out at a fancy grocery store like 20 miles away. No one followed me."

"I'm so glad you're helping. I couldn't do this without you." Tears pooled in my eyes again.

She gave me a hug. "It's going to be okay."

Ananda's door squeaked open. "Hey girl," Ananda said to

Hayden.

She'd cleaned up a little — with her brushed hair and a little bit of makeup, she didn't look as wretched.

"Did I hear you got me detox herbs? You're so sweet. Come here and give me a hug."

Hayden went to her and they hugged. After they broke apart, Ananda picked up the juicer box and read the sides.

"I hope you like carrot juice," Hayden said. "I'm going to make some right now."

Ananda laughed. "I hope I like it too."

Our eyes met for a fraction of a second, then she looked away.

"Oh yeah," Hayden said. "I scheduled a yoga instructor to come over tonight."

"How'd you know?" Ananda asked, rubbing her shoulder. "I totally need a good session."

"It's going to be for all three of us. If we're going to work this close, we'll need to do some bonding activities."

Ananda's face scrunched. She retreated into her room without another word.

"Are you sure about that?" I whispered. Hayden and I might be the only ones to show up for it.

She shrugged and started unpacking the juicer. "We'll see."

I called John on my new phone. It rang several times before going to voicemail. I'd hoped his wife would've picked up to tell me how he was doing, but I supposed she was busy.

I thought about calling Mary, but I couldn't trust her not to tell Caroline. I'd never called Caroline about my position because I still wasn't sure whether my job with Ananda was secure or not.

I called Kitty. She answered on the second ring.

"What's up?" she asked.

I went into my room and collapsed my head into my free hand. "I'm just overwhelmed."

"Mag, you can't take things too seriously right now."

"She hates me," I whispered.

"I wouldn't say she hates you. It's good you got it out in the open, don't you think?"

Tears rose to my eyes as I tried to breathe. "The thing is I was wrong. She doesn't have sociopathic tendencies. She's so much more than that."

"Just keep telling her that. She might start to believe it. I gotta go. The engineer is calling me back to the studio. We're trying to get this audio book ready for Christmas Eve sales. They won't let me leave LA until they're done editing, just in case they need me to re-read something. It's bullshit, but I'll be there in a few days, and I'll be able to help then. Just hang in there."

"I can't wait to see you."

"Me too. Good luck."

I hung up and lay down on the bed. Talking with Kitty wasn't the relief I needed, but it helped. My heartbreak diminished a little. I wiped the tear tracks from my cheeks.

Between cracks in the curtains, snowflakes swirled around the naked branches of the trees behind a brilliant blue sky. I counted the paparazzi on the street. One more had packed up and gone home. They dwindled in number, but that just meant the most ferocious ones stayed. I wondered if we'd ever be free from them, or if this was just my life now.

The collage suitcase looked forlorn in the corner. For the first time since the House of Transformation, I had free time. I could collage. Maybe that's what Ananda and I needed, to come together with our creativity, just like the old days. Though I doubted Ananda would want to make art with me right now.

I unlocked the suitcase and threw back the lid. On top was the last collage I'd made at the House of Transformation. A raven stood on the world, stars and nebulae behind it. I tossed it aside and dug deeper, finding ones Ananda and I had created when the House of Transformation was at its peak. They were so familiar it was like seeing old friends.

I took the suitcase into the living room and hung our old collages up. When I finished, I took a step back. A tiny chill tickled up my spine. It was like the House of Transformation had risen again. All that was missing was the green carpet and Rosie. It was a little spooky, seeing them all on the walls, but also refreshing. The old soulful rumblings of art and beauty stirred within me again, even amidst the chaos and despair. How had I stared at the white walls of my apartment for so long?

When the yoga teacher showed up that night, I could barely concentrate. I forgot about the non-disclosure form until Hayden reminded me. Ananda joined us, but she didn't look at me. If she noticed the collages on the walls, it didn't show.

At the beginning of the class, my heart thudded. I was half-afraid Ananda would attack me in downward dog. But after a while, I lost myself in the breathing, the movement, and the music. For a moment, something eternal resounded within me. A little of my sorrow drained away, and peace took its place.

After the last pose, Ananda shot up and slid back into her room. Before she left, I felt the energy shift between us. Maybe it was the collages on the walls, or the yoga, or the sandalwood incense, but something was different.

Hayden scheduled another appointment with the yoga teacher. We needed all the help we could get.

Chapter 25. Best Laid Plans

Hayden insisted we take part in Ananda's detoxing activities so she wouldn't feel isolated. I initially declined. Juice fasting never seemed like my thing. Besides, I didn't think anything would heal the rift between us. Hayden didn't give me a choice.

The first day of our juice fast, she made us celery-beet-carrot juice. I stared at the purplish-brown concoction and almost vomited, but I held my nose and drank it. By lunchtime, my mood was darker than molasses. I stayed in my room to avoid snapping at her.

On our second day of juice fasting, I sweated and felt spacey. It was better than feeling bitchy, but I was still miserable. I never realized I needed detox too — not from prescription pills, but from years of eating junk food.

Hayden constantly worked on her new laptop, scheduling some activity that was supposed to help Ananda create new mental connections and heal her dependence on xyritav. Once, when I asked what she was doing, she hid the screen and mentioned something about research before going into the next room. She started a calendar on a whiteboard. She wrote '3 days sober!' and 'you're doing great!' Every day, we had a meditation or yoga class. Hayden bought new clothes for Ananda and flooded the apartment with lilac and jasmine oil diffusers until we were in a wash of scent at all times.

She hired a cleaning lady, which was another miracle. Despite my best intentions, I couldn't bring myself to wipe counters or sweep floors. I diagnosed myself as depressed — I had all the symptoms. I could barely keep up with my own hygiene, let alone a whole apartment. The cleaner apartment lightened the mood a few degrees.

Hayden found a new massage therapist who carefully read the confidentiality agreement before signing. I'd never had a massage before because I'd thought they were a waste of money, but Hayden insisted I have one, saying she'd already paid for it.

I surrendered to the strange customs of oil, music, and being touched without clothes or judgment. I was shocked at how relaxed I felt when it was over.

I thought of calling Darren, but froze up whenever I lifted my phone. I had no idea what to say to him. Later that day, he texted.

What's up?

I felt so guilty about having ignored him that I gave in.

Not much, you?

He replied with three texts about work drama. I skimmed the messages and tossed the phone onto the couch. Something kept me from reaching out to him. Maybe I had a different perspective since Ananda crash-landed in my life again. Even though she'd been a false friend at times, she knew me so deeply. She knew my thoughts, how I felt, and what I loved. She was art, soul, and dreams. Darren barely knew me at all, only that I liked mozzarella sticks and Monty Python. He had no dreams or hobbies, 'unless you count watching tv,' he'd said with a guffaw on our first date. He was a safe bet, and before Ananda showed up, we were on a similar path. Now everything about him felt so wrong. What was I doing with him? Why was I stringing him along?

Ananda started to feel better after the third day of juice fasting. She'd stopped puking and started looking normal again. Hayden prepared an anti-oxidant diet for us, with avocado, quinoa, berries, and steamed vegetables. My skin looked clearer, and I lost a couple of pounds, so it wasn't all bad.

Hayden managed Ananda's social media like a pro. Every couple of days, she made Ananda dress up and take photos. She posted the best one with an update. I joined social media on my phone and saw the updates. It was surreal, of course, but they were perfect — normal and sweet, as if Ananda had recaptured some of her innocence.

Hayden and Ananda's friendship blossomed. They often disappeared into Ananda's room for several hours at a time, emerging only to go to the bathroom or to do our communal scheduled activity. From behind the door, laughs punctuated the air while I worked on spreadsheets and ideas for the Grammys. I wanted to be in there too, but I was never invited. I began to feel like a ghost in my own apartment, almost as if I didn't exist at all.

Letters arrived from Bertrand. He wrote that he wanted to take Ananda on a date and asked her to write back. He signed his letters 'your boyfriend.' She never wrote back, of course. I couldn't help but empathize with him. I, too, had written her, asking her to write back and she never did. But this was different. I was her friend before she was a superstar, whereas Bertrand knew nothing about her. He was in love with the idea of her.

I missed working at the New Beginnings Center, missed my office and my girls, but most of all, I missed my schedule. I missed watching the sun come up over the city with a cup of coffee on my desk, going out to lunch with Mary on Tuesdays, and the Center dinners of lasagna, pizza, and meatloaf. I missed spending time alone in my apartment as I prepped for the next day, when the television wasn't covered with a tapestry.

I eventually gave in and called Mary. She was less bitter than the last time I spoke with her, but still not warm. She didn't have anything to report besides a new girl in and an old girl out. Apparently, the money Ananda donated went toward buying better bedroom furniture for New Beginnings. I wanted to see it for myself, but I couldn't brave the paparazzi that still choked the sidewalk. Hayden breezed through their shouts and questions several times a day, but I'd look guilty if I went out there because that's exactly how I felt. When I caught sight of myself in the mirror (slouched, brows drawn, head hung), I could barely meet my own eyes. I inevitably found myself lying in bed, curling into a fetal position.

Eventually I got out of bed and called my parents' landline. They both picked up.

"Honey! How are you?" Mom asked.

"Is Ananda taking over your life again?" Dad asked.

"It's messy," I said. "I'm hanging in there."

"You sound awful," she said.

"Thanks, Mom."

"You're setting boundaries, aren't you?" he asked.

"Yes, I'm trying. How are you?"

"Doing well. I just retired!" Dad said.

"Maggie," Mom sighed, "can you believe the Psych Center is making me work three days longer than your dad before I can retire?"

My jaw hit the floor. I thought they were too young to retire.

"You're both retiring before Christmas?" I asked.

"Yep," he said. "The deal changes every year, and it's going to screw over the people who retire next year, so we're calling it quits."

"Congratulations. Are you going to have a party?"

Dad laughed. "The rest of our life is going to be a party. Your Mom and I decided to move to San Francisco. We'll pack up the house after Christmas."

I almost dropped the phone. "Seriously? Why haven't I heard of this?"

"We thought retirement was years away," Mom said, "but it just happened. And we love San Fran. The weather will be so much milder. Do you want to come home to Eau Claire for the holidays? We can have one last time in the old house before we sell it."

My breath caught. I never expected my parents to sell my childhood home, much less move to California. I wanted to run through the paparazzi and drive to see them right then and there, but I couldn't leave. I had to be here for Ananda in case she needed me.

"I'm stuck at the moment," I said.

"Why do you have to stay there?" Mom asked. "Are you afraid of the paparazzi?"

I exhaled a big breath. How could I tell them I was so depressed I could barely get dressed in the morning? "We're preparing for the Grammys."

"How exciting!" she said.

Dad laughed. "Don't let her go naked again."

"I won't."

"I hope you're taking care of yourself," he said.

"I am. I miss you."

After I hung up, I wondered if they'd heard the despair in my voice. If so, they didn't mention it.

A few days into Ananda's detox, the actor George Brasso died at the age of 75. Everyone was in mourning. The same social media accounts that lambasted Ananda for all her crazy stuff sniffled for Brasso. Although I was sad he passed, I was ecstatic the limelight shifted away from Ananda. That same day, the number of paparazzi in front of my apartment dwindled down to five.

John was recovering from surgery, and held phone sessions with Ananda every other day. I talked with him twice a week, a towel stuffed under my bedroom door like I was a paranoid teenager. I mostly talked about Ananda-drama and my depression.

He said he might be out of the hospital in a few days, then he'd be able to have sessions at my apartment again. I secretly did a little dance when he said that. I couldn't wait to see him again.

My relationship with Ananda got the slightest bit better every day. We said hi to each other in the hallway and when we happened to be in the same room. A week later, we branched out into short sentences.

"How's it going?"

"Good, you?"

"Fine."

"See you."

"Later."

I had doubts about whether she'd forgive me for my book, but things were getting better.

When Christmas was only nine days away, Hayden made us promise not to get each other presents, which was just as well, because Ananda wouldn't have gotten me anything anyway. She hauled in a Christmas tree and decorations. She and Ananda decorated the tree for hours with eggnog and Christmas carols.

That was the day I finally gave into thoughts about collaging. After seeing the collages hanging all over the apartment, I was inspired to make new ones. I opened the suitcase and spread the cuttings out on the floor, but something didn't feel right. The images were dated. Just like fashion magazines from seven years ago, the colors were passé, the themes trite, the emotion a little less fresh.

I started going through the magazines Hayden brought in, taking time to perfectly cut every image. I let my mind go blank and spread them on the floor with the old ones, just like I used to, but the collages didn't rise from the chaos. They were missing a vital link or two, or three. Inevitably, after working on them for several hours, I'd slip the images back into the suitcase, unglued, unmanifested.

One morning, Hayden burst through the apartment door, out of breath, her brows furrowed. "Mag, the press knows," she panted.

I looked up from a pile of receipts. "What?"

Ananda peeked out from her room and joined us.

"They know I've been doing Ananda's social media updates. They're questioning everything I wrote."

My pulse quickened. "What? How? Did you tell anyone?"

"No, it's a math thing. Here, let me show you." She opened her phone and played a video.

A sharp-featured blonde reporter from NBC News interviewed a Yale mathematician with curly brown hair lacquered with product. He pointed to a graph with two squiggly lines on it.

"If you look at Ananda Dawn's messages before the Eiffel Tower crash, there's a 1:3:5 rhythm. After that, there's a 2:2:8 pattern, which is a 96% difference. This is definitive proof that something is going on."

The reporter nodded. "But what's really happening? Who's doing this, and is it with her permission? What's your opinion?"

"There are several possibilities. She could've had a brain injury during the car accident in Paris, or a fan may have hacked into her account. Maybe someone's covering for her. It's even possible another personality has taken over and wrote in this new pattern."

"Another personality would certainly explain the lack of newsworthy events since the Eiffel Tower crash," the interviewer said. She turned to the camera. "What do you think? Contact us at–"

I stopped the video. I felt lightheaded all of the sudden. I couldn't believe anyone could talk like that on national television. And even worse, the mathematician was so handsome, the public would eat him with a spoon. He was bound to get air time on all the major news centers. I sighed. Weren't there more important things to do besides hassle celebrities?

"Great," Ananda said. "The media still hate me."

"They don't hate you," I said. "They're fascinated by you."

She pouted. "They're fascinated by my demise."

I pursed my lips. I wanted to tell her it wasn't true, but she was right. Ananda's life was like a car crash, and the whole world was rubbernecking. It was almost like they wanted her to fail.

"Are you going to fire me?" Hayden asked.

"No. It's not your fault," I said.

Ananda sniffled. "We had no idea this would happen. But what should we do?"

Hayden glanced at both of us. "We should give them what they want. You should make a press statement."

I turned my gaze to Ananda. Dark circles still lined her eyes. Though she was better, she was on the verge of tears.

Ananda shook her head. "I can't do a live interview. Can't I just write something on social media?"

"I don't think so." I slumped into a chair. "The social media thing has been blown out of proportion. They'll be analyzing every message for those stupid patterns."

"I have an idea," Hayden said.

Hayden first came to the New Beginnings Center when she was sixteen, tagging along with one of our residents for a warm meal. Winter came early that year, and October was crisp. Hayden only stayed long enough to eat a burrito. Legally, we couldn't hold the girls, so we tried everything to entice them to stay, including pizza nights, jars of chocolate and candy, and even personally funding a cat that lived there, but Hayden wasn't swayed. For weeks, she popped in now and then for dinner and took off.

Two months later, she came in with the flu. She was dehydrated and shivering. She put up little resistance about staying. A medic came by on a housecall and hooked her up to a saline bag. I ran a humidifier I'd bought with my own money and slept on the sofa in my office, checking on her every couple of hours.

To my relief, she got better. She stuck around for Christmas and opened up slowly in therapy, sometimes preferring to stay silent rather than talk. After a few weeks, she told me about a troubling foster care situation in a drug den, where she and her brother sometimes ate paper because there was no food in the house. When her brother didn't come home one night and things got sketchy, she took off too.

After a few months of investigations, I busted her former foster parents. They got sentenced to ten years in prison.

Hayden thrived. She got her GED and went to a community college. She got a fast food job and helped make dinners at the Center. After she found her brother again, they moved into an apartment together. She's been independent ever since.

She looked so grown up these days. All traces of her baby fat had been contoured away by Ananda's makeup skills. The dark circles under Ananda's eyes were covered with layers of concealer and powder. They sat on my couch in the trendiest clothes, facing a video recorder.

"Ready?" I asked.

They nodded. I pressed the record button and gave them

two thumbs up.

"Hi everyone. I'm Ananda! I'm starting a new vlog, and I wanted to let everyone know so you can subscribe to my feed. I want to stay in touch with all you adorable fans because the media is saying a lot of crazy stuff about me right now."

"It's insane," Hayden said from the couch beside her.

"I know! It's so weird. People can say whatever they want about me on the news — it doesn't even have to be true. So today, I want to talk about the new mathematical pattern in my social media posts lately, and explain the reason why. This is Hayden, my new personal assistant."

"Hi!" She waved to the camera.

"I've been busy working on my new album. I don't always have time to keep in touch with all the emails, phone calls, letters, and comments, so I asked Hayden to help me out. Like, the other day, I said, 'Hayden, tell my fans I'm recording my new single, I love them, and I'm eating chocolate cake for breakfast.' And Hayden does it, but the words come out a little different. Could you read the message you wrote?"

"Sure. 'Eating chocolate cake for brekkers and recording my new single. Love you!'"

Ananda's eyes crinkled. "So, you see, it's not that different."

Hayden shook her head. "Not at all."

"These news people are talking about me having a split personality or brain damage, and it's not true. Here's the thing. People want to know how I am and what's going on in my life, and that's so sweet. But the people who run the news think you just want to hear bad news, so they make things up and try to get a rise in me. Like, they post a picture of me when I'm blinking and say I have problems, and it's just not true."

"That's the reason we're making this video."

"Yeah. I want to give you firsthand information, so you can decide what to believe."

Ananda smiled slowly and laughed. Hayden tried to contain her smile.

"I think that's all for this video, but Hayden and I will post more. And don't believe the hype. Merry Christmas and happy holidays."

Ananda blew a kiss while Hayden waved again.

I stopped the recording and sat back in my chair. It was perfect. It was exactly what we needed to combat the crazy rumors.

Hayden posted the video on Ananda's social media and it went viral. Fans left comments in support of her, and the media discontinued the mathematician story within a few hours.

The next day, a sound engineer installed a temporary recording studio in Ananda's room. For the next few days, she recorded while I did the bills, and Hayden ran errands and posted. Every night, we had yoga, massage, or meditation. I ticked off the days until the Grammys.

Ananda and I still didn't have what I'd call a friendship. She tolerated me, but we rarely exchanged more than a dozen words every day. I wondered what I could do to change that. Hayden said she just needed time, so I cut and collaged in my room while they laughed in her room.

One night, after Hayden left, Darren called. I almost didn't take it, but at the last second, I picked up. I hoped I'd be able to sort out my feelings if I talked with him.

"Hey," I said sheepishly.

"Hey you! I've been trying to get a hold of you."

I bit my lip. What a dorky thing to say. Maybe I should've just let it go to voicemail like the other three times he'd called.

"Sorry," I said. "I've been so busy lately, you know, being Ananda's manager."

"Oh yeah? What do you do all day?"

"There aren't enough hours in the day," I said, even though it was a lie. Though I updated spreadsheets, scanned receipts, ordered groceries, and managed Hayden, several hours of my day were as blank as a canvas, and about as meaningful.

"The holidays are coming up," he said. "Any chance you'll be free?"

"I don't know if I can leave the apartment."

"Are you afraid of the media?"

"Yeah."

"Well, I'd really like to see you. Could we have dinner at your place?"

"Here?" It was already awkward enough here. I couldn't imagine having a romantic dinner with Darren in my apartment while Ananda traipsed around in yoga pants.

I sighed, wondering if I should just break up with him. It always came down to this moment, because no one compared to 'the one who got away.' Darren wasn't even a quarter of the man he was.

"Darren, the thing is—"

Then my synapses fired and a brilliant thought entered my mind. Ananda's star qualities always came out when she met strangers. If I had a dinner party at my apartment, some of her kindness might rub off on me. I knew I'd be using Darren, but it'd also help me decide once and for all if I liked him or not.

"What are you doing on Christmas Eve?"

On Christmas Eve, the dining room table was resplendent with a crimson tablecloth, white candles, and my good plates. The Christmas tree sparkled and flashed in a rainbow of colors. Holiday jazz crooned from the speakers. Carryout from our favorite gourmet grocery warmed in the oven, the savory smell making my small apartment feel homey.

Hayden and her brother, Justin, would arrive any moment. With several bottles of wine and two men added to our company, I hoped Ananda would be dizzy with good graces.

Darren arrived first, just as I took the casserole out of the oven. His knock was instantly recognizable.

Dun dun dun-dun-dun. Dun dun!

I set down the entrée, then threw a glance at Ananda's room. Her door was closed. I breathed a sigh of relief. I wanted to have a moment alone with him before anyone else arrived.

I opened the door and saw Darren standing in the foyer, wearing a brown tweed coat and hat. All my mixed emotions rose to the surface again. Did I like him? Could I be with him for the rest of my life?

He pulled a bouquet of red roses and baby's breath from behind his back. I smiled and embraced him, catching a whiff of his enticing toasty smell.

"Thank you Darren. Please come in."

"How are we tonight?"

"We're... alright." I hoped he didn't catch my pause, the cue that any smart psychologist knows is either a lie or an omission.

He walked inside and took off his coat.

"I'll take that," I said.

"No need." He pulled a hanger from the closet and hung it up, as if he'd performed that act a hundred times. He flashed me a frozen smile, his eyes darting around my apartment like a frightened rodent. "It looks different in here. I like it."

"Thanks. I'll go put these in water." I went into the kitchen and unwrapped the plastic from the flowers. As I slid them into a vase, he crept up behind me.

"Is she here?" he whispered.

I turned. "Yeah, of course she is. We can't leave, remember?"

"Oh. Well, I didn't see her, so I didn't know."

"She'll make an appearance later. She likes to primp before social gatherings."

He gave me a livid smile. My heart sank a little. It was like he was already in her pocket, and he hadn't even laid eyes on her. I took a deep breath and gave him a fresh confidentiality form.

"You'll need to sign this before we have dinner."

He scribbled his name at the bottom and handed it back to me.

I steeled myself. He hadn't read a word of it. "So, you won't talk about your experience with Ananda? Because that's what this form you didn't read says." I smiled, trying to keep my voice light, but a little of my annoyance crept through.

"Of course." His eyes bugged out a little. "How are you, Mag? It's been a while."

"I've been busy. You?"

"Okay." He leaned in for a kiss.

I startled. I felt like I hadn't seen him in months, but it'd just been a few weeks — that's how much my life had changed. In perspective, he seemed chubbier, less polished, and way more mundane. How had I snuggled up with him on my couch and let him into my bed?

My mind flashed back to that night. His bulk rocked over me. We'd each had a single orgasm, and then there was an awkward silence, some customary words, and sleep. The following morning, I'd showered and watched television for hours before he rose. He'd waddled into the living room, my sheet wrapped around him like a toga, and asked if I wanted to go to McDonald's for breakfast. Had that been the moment I recoiled from him?

He puckered, waiting for me to kiss him. I gave into a brief kiss, but I felt nothing but his slimy lips. He smiled in a nauseating manner, his hands finding my hips.

"Hello lovebirds," Ananda sang from the kitchen door.

Darren whipped his head around. His eyes traveled up her body even though she wore a somewhat unflattering velvet tracksuit.

I sighed. It was in men's nature to observe female body dimensions. But when his gaze remained on her for longer than a moment, whatever feelings I had for him shrank. I wondered if I'd ever find a man who loved me more than he liked gawking at Ananda.

"Hi," Darren said to her.

"Darren, this is Ananda. Ananda, Darren."

"Pleasure to meet you," she said, her million-dollar bullshit smile sparkling.

"Wow. I can't believe this is real."

My brows furrowed. It was one thing to be star struck — it was another to act like an idiot. Had I thought this would happen, I never would've invited him over. Ananda's eyes widened for a moment before she walked into the living room.

He gaped at me. "Wow."

"Yep," I said, my teeth grinding.

The front door opened with a whoosh. Hayden's timber floated in the room. I sighed with relief and walked into the living room.

"I can't believe she's dating a bobblehead," Ananda whispered to Hayden.

They laughed, though Hayden straightened when she saw me. A tall young man stood beside her. He looked like Hayden, but taller, a couple of years older, with muscles clearly defined beneath his flannel shirt. His eyes were a darker shade of brown too — hers were like autumn leaves, but his were chocolate.

"Mag, Ananda, this is my brother Justin."

"Hi." He reached out to shake our hands.

"Hi. I'm Ananda." She took his hand with hers on top.

He smiled back at her.

Darren appeared behind me, a glass of wine in his hand.

"Everyone, this is Darren," I said. "This is Hayden and Justin."

"Hi," he said, taking a nervous gulp.

An awkward silence filled the room.

"Who else wants wine?" I asked. I knew I did.

Throughout the meal, Darren and Justin stared at Ananda, but she was either blithely unaware, or maybe she enjoyed it. When she playfully swatted Justin's arm and erupted into giggles for the third time, I cleared my throat. I had to draw boundaries for her. Physical contact was a precursor to her manipulations, and I couldn't let that happen.

"Justin, could you please help me in the kitchen?" I asked.

He rose from the table and followed me. When we were alone, I shut the door and faced him. I felt bad, making him uncomfortable, but I had to level with him.

"Look, Justin. You seem like a nice guy, but Ananda does this to everyone. Don't take it the wrong way, okay?"

He shifted. "What do you mean?"

"She flirts with everyone. It doesn't mean she's into you. It's just what she does."

"She can make her own–"

"She makes her own decisions, but she confuses everyone in the process. You heard about the French guy, right? She danced with him under the Eiffel Tower and told the world she dreamed about marrying him. It's the most romantic thing that's happened this decade, but she hasn't spoken to him since she got out of the police station. This is just what she does."

The kitchen door swung open and Ananda walked in. My heart stopped for a second. I hoped she hadn't heard our conversation. Her top was unzipped slightly lower than it was just a moment ago. I cringed. I knew she loved attention, but this was blatant.

"Need another hand?" she asked.

"Sure, Ananda, you can pour the milk. Justin, could you please take the cake out of the refrigerator?"

Justin opened the refrigerator door and Ananda went to get the milk at the same time, and they bumped into each other. Ananda giggled and batted her eyelashes.

"Go ahead," he said.

"No, you."

He took the chocolate cake out and into the dining room. Ananda got the milk out and started to pour it. Justin was there again almost instantly, gazing hungrily at Ananda.

"Put these on the table please," I said, giving him the silverware.

He was back in no time again. "Do you need help with the milk?" he asked Ananda. She laughed.

"Justin," I interrupted. "Could you reach the top shelf and get down five plates?"

"Sure," he said.

"Great. Let's go." I gave him a pointed look.

We walked into the dining room together, where he set the plates down on the table and turned back.

"I'm going to help Ananda carry the milk out," he said.

I rolled my eyes and sunk into my chair.

"Are you okay Mag?" Hayden asked.

I gave her a pained look. "I warned Justin to not be too taken with Ananda, but he's not listening. She's such a flirt. I'm just worried he'll get the wrong idea."

Hayden smirked. "I know. She flirts with me too. It's kind of hot."

I took a deep breath, not even knowing where to start, but Hayden beat me to it.

"I know how she is. I read your book. It's just weird to see it in action."

"What? You read my book?"

"Yeah. I have to say it's pretty accurate. It sounds like you guys had a pretty fucked up time in that house. I can't believe how many drugs you used to do."

Darren's eyebrows shot up. Apparently he hadn't read my book.

I waffled. "It wasn't always by choice. I mean, you have to know — I never would've started doing clemeral if I hadn't been drugged by Kitty."

Hayden's eyes popped. "The same Kitty who's coming here tomorrow?"

I nodded. She leaned back, her face a mask. Maybe it wasn't such a good idea to invite Kitty over.

Another peal of giggles cascaded from the kitchen. I groaned, pushing up from the table, and stormed into the kitchen.

Ananda leaned close to Justin and whispered, their faces animated with glee. Glasses of milk stood on the counter.

"Well, these glasses aren't going to carry themselves," I said.

Ananda caught my arm, laughing. "Justin just told me about the time he snuck into a golf course at night and made snow angels in the sand pits."

He smiled, dumbstruck that Ananda was making a big deal out of him. I smiled stiffly back at them. On one hand, that was the longest sentence Ananda had spoken to me in weeks. But on the other hand, she was flirting with him. It made my stomach sour. I gave him a warning glare.

Justin cowed slightly and scooped up three glasses at once. "I'll get these."

Ananda picked up a glass and followed him. One glass remained on the counter, presumably mine. I picked it up and went back to the dining room.

The lights had been dimmed. Several candles shone on the

cake. The glow made everyone look rosy and warm.

"Let's hold hands." Hayden reached out.

Her hands were warm. I struggled to hold Darren's clammy hands.

Hayden looked around the room. "I've only known Ananda for a couple of weeks, but she's changed my life. She made me believe in transformation, creativity, and inspiration. It's been so great getting to know you."

She turned to me. "Mag, I've known you for years. You were there for me during the roughest patch of my life. I just want to say I truly appreciate you from the bottom of my heart."

"Thanks," I whispered.

She turned to face the guys. "Justin, I love you. We've been through so much together, and now we're on the other side. And Darren, it's nice to finally meet you."

She swallowed and looked around at all of us again. "So, Ananda and I were talking about how we don't have much of a family. Mag, I know you can't see yours right now. That's why I was glad when you said she wanted us to get together, because at least we have each other."

My heart warmed. Darren squeezed my hand, and despite my mixed emotions, I squeezed it back.

"Now, if Ananda would do the honors and blow out the candles, we can eat this cake."

"You want *me* to blow out the candles?" Ananda asked, disbelief making her voice an octave higher than normal.

"It's all you."

Ananda looked tentatively at the cake, then took a deep breath and blew, just like it was her birthday. It struck me that she might never have had a birthday party like this. In a way, Hayden created a sense of family for her. My heart softened. All my remaining frustrations with Ananda dissipated. This must've been what John meant by transmuting negative emotions.

Justin sliced massive pieces of chocolate cake and handed them out. No one could finish them, even though it was the best cake I had in my life — better than wedding cake, better than any of my own birthday cakes.

I sat on the couch with Darren as Ananda and Justin cleared plates and started washing the dishes. Ananda still giggled, but I didn't mind. Maybe it was the wine, but I was happy she was having a good time.

Darren smiled at me blankly. He'd barely spoken a word all night, and worst of all, I didn't know what to say to him. I wondered if he felt as uncomfortable as I did.

"Hayden, did your brother sign the non-disclosure form?" I asked.

"Yep." She didn't even bother to look up from texting as she lounged in the armchair nearby.

"You really do think of everything."

She huffed. "I forgot to get a salad tonight, but I don't think anyone noticed."

"No, it was perfect." I was so proud of her at that moment. She had overcome so much.

"Well, I'm stuffed," Darren said. "And we might have to buy a treadmill for Mag if she keeps eating this well."

I shot him a confused glance. What on earth did he mean? It didn't make sense — I'd lost weight since I last saw him. Was it his way of reaching out to me? Was he passive aggressive because I hadn't called him for a couple of weeks?

Hayden gave me a strangled look. A silence hung in the air, one Darren didn't seem to be aware of.

He bobbleheaded in my direction. "You're squinting at me again."

I looked away. I didn't know how to respond. The tension snuffed all the air out of the room. Hayden must've felt it too, because she got up and walked into the kitchen.

"Darren, are you mad at me?" I asked.

"No. If I was, I'd tell you. 'No mind games,' remember?" he quoted from my SoulM8 page.

I nodded, but I didn't believe him. His body language was edgy even though his face was calm.

Ananda walked into the room. "Do you want to hear the new song I've been working on?"

"Sure." I wiped moisture from my brow. I was happy to focus

on anything besides Darren.

"Just a sec." She went into her room.

Justin appeared in the doorway of the living room, drying his hands with a towel. His smile was as satisfied as a cat's. "The dishes are done."

"Thank you."

"Thanks for having me. It's a nice place." He looked at the collages appreciatively.

Ananda emerged and hooked up her ipad to my stereo. Electronic music filled the room, Ananda's voice drifting over it. It sounded different from her old music — less produced, more heartfelt. I could only imagine what it'd sound like once she got into a studio. I hoped it kept some of the same tenderness.

"It's not done yet. I'm still working on some parts."

"I love it," I said. "It sounds like Cypress."

Hayden and Justin nodded.

"I have a name for the new album," Ananda said. "I'm going to call it 'I Am Art.' What do you think?"

"I like it."

"Play it again."

After Ananda played the song three times, I yawned. Hayden and Justin rose to say goodnight. When they got their coats from the closet, Darren leaned close and snuck a kiss. I jumped back as if he shocked me.

"Did I surprise you?" he asked.

"Yeah, sorry."

"For what?"

"Um..." I stalled. I knew why I was sorry — it was because I didn't love him. I didn't even like him, but I didn't have the courage to tell him. So there I was, playing mind games after all. "Never mind."

"I'll call you tomorrow, but you should try to relax, Mag. I know it's hard for you to take time off work, but it might be good for you."

My mouth popped open. He didn't know me well enough to say that. It didn't matter that we'd been on three dates. That kind of talk was reserved for my parents and long-time friends only.

"Goodnight." He gave one last bobble of his head before slipping out.

"Bye, everyone." Ananda waved, then slunk into the bathroom.

"Mag," Hayden whispered, her brow wrinkled.

"What's wrong?"

Hayden and Justin exchanged a look. My thoughts raced. Did Hayden hate Darren? Did Ananda make out with Justin?

"Tell me!" I said.

Hayden pressed her lips together, then swallowed. When she looked at me, her eyes were watery with tears.

"Ananda asked Justin to get her xyritav."

I shook my head, my fingers finding my temples. I thought we were doing so well. Apparently, I was wrong.

Chapter 26. Kitty for Christmas

On Christmas morning, I rose early. Hayden had the day off, though given last night's circumstances, when Ananda asked her brother for xyritav, I doubted she had the heart to come in today anyway. I wanted to tell Hayden her cheerleading and long talks with Ananda hadn't been for nothing, even though she might've seen it that way. I wanted to call John and hear what he had to say about it, but it was Christmas, and I knew I needed to respect that boundary.

I'd just taken a sip of spicy holiday-roast coffee when Kitty texted me.

"I'm here!"

I peeked through the curtains and saw her wrangling a suitcase out of a rental SUV. I yanked on my snow boots and coat, effervescent happiness bubbling within me. I ran out to meet her, momentarily forgetting about the paparazzi. They perked up for a second, but as soon as they saw I wasn't Ananda, they lowered their cameras.

I ran up to Kitty and hugged her, inhaling her ginger perfume. She shivered in her leather jacket. "Kitty, why didn't you bring a coat?"

"And ruin this silhouette?"

I laughed. She was the same as she ever was.

We walked through the snowdrifts and into the apartment. I closed the door behind us, stomped the snow off my boots, then gave her a real hug.

"Merry Christmas," I said.

"Merry Christmas. It's so nice to be back in St. Paul. I missed you."

"I missed you too. Phone calls aren't the same as seeing each other." I couldn't believe it'd been four years since I last saw her. She'd barely aged, but she looked more sophisticated, as if her haircuts cost more these days.

"Whoa. Your apartment looks like the House of

Transformation."

"Hopefully without the same consequences." I laughed and instantly regretted it. Kitty and I had both lost friends that night. "Do you want some coffee? How was your flight?"

She followed me into the kitchen. "It was fine. Where's Ananda?"

"Sleeping. She likes to sleep in." I poured coffee and cream into a cup and handed it to her.

She wrapped her hands around it. "Is your assistant here?"

"No, Hayden has the day off, but you'll meet her soon enough."

I leaned against the sink, taking her in. "So, what do you want to do while you're here?"

"Can we go out? I mean, are we stuck here?" She slurped her coffee.

"We're pretty stuck. The paparazzi really want a picture of her, but we don't think it's a good idea. She's getting better. She doesn't look like she's detoxing anymore. But last night, she asked Hayden's brother about scoring some xyritav, so the cravings and impulses aren't under control yet. But how was your recording? Did you finish in time for Christmas?"

"Yeah, but I'm pretty pissed. The producers knew we had a deadline. They dicked around for weeks, then made us work overtime. I'll never work for that company again."

"What book is it?"

"The Carnal Valle."

"Any good?"

"Yeah. Shouldn't we wake Ananda up?"

"I think it's best if we let her sleep. She'll be up pretty soon. By the way, she and I are still patching things up. We're not exactly best friends right now. I think we made some progress over the last few days, but it's hard to tell."

"She's still mad about your book?"

"Yeah." I dug my hands into my pants pockets.

"I'll try to help out. She's easier to manipulate than you think," she said with a vicious smile.

"Thanks. Hey, you don't have any xyritav or clemeral, do

you?"

She glared at me, silent.

"Kitty, if it wasn't necessary, I wouldn't ask, but you have to get rid of them or keep them locked up in your rental car."

"You know I'm on meds."

"Those are fine."

"That's... all I have."

I narrowed my eyes at her, catching the pregnant pause, wondering if it was true.

Ananda's door opened. She bounded out and embraced Kitty tightly. Kitty teared up a little.

I decided to give them time to catch up. I snuck out of the room and called my parents.

"Margaret! How are you, squirrel?" Mom asked.

"Good, Mom. Merry Christmas. How's retirement?"

"This is the best Christmas ever. Your dad got me a high-tech blender and I got him an ipad. He loves it. He's playing on it like a little boy. How's living with Ananda? Still driving you crazy?"

"Yeah. She's so-" I stopped myself. I wanted to talk about us, not Ananda. "What are you two doing for New Year's Eve?"

"We're going to the Pallin's party, like usual. Then on New Year's Day, we'll drive the moving truck to San Francisco. We picked out an apartment in Oceanside — it's supposed to be an up-and-coming neighborhood."

"That sounds so exciting. I wish I could help."

"What's new with you, Margaret?"

"I started collaging again, and I got my first massage."

"It sounds like you're retired too. Bill, say hi," Mom yelled.

Dad emitted a faint "hello!"

"Tell him I say hi. I wish I could be there."

"We wish you could too, but we understand you can't leave the apartment. We're going to start packing things up tomorrow! It'll be a real Boxing Day."

I blinked back tears, imagining them taking down my framed crayon drawings. I wished I could help them pack up, but leaving Ananda alone with Kitty sounded like a bad idea. "Can you visit me some time this week?" I asked.

"We're pretty busy with everything right now. Why don't you come visit us when this blows over."

"Okay," I said, wondering when that might be. "I love you."

"Love you too."

Kitty knocked on my door. "Ananda's going to play her new song. Do you want to hear it?"

"Yeah." I shuffled into the living room and plopped onto the couch.

Ananda pressed a button, and the song played. It sounded even better than the last time.

"That was gorgeous," Kitty said when it was over. "Are you going to perform that at the Grammys?"

Ananda shrugged. "I guess so."

Kitty's head jutted forward. "You guess so? Isn't it only a month and a half away?"

"I haven't planned it out yet."

Kitty shot me a look. I didn't know what to say. I'd started planning for the Grammy performance, but so many other things had come up, like her detox, my book, my depression...

"It'd be a great song for the Grammys," I said.

"Thanks." Ananda's eyes met mine for a moment.

"I want to do something," Kitty said. "Let's go to the Arts District."

"We can't leave the apartment," I said.

Kitty raised a finger in the air. "What if I drive my rental up to the apartment door and you both hop in?"

I shook my head. "They might get a picture of her."

"Not if I drive to the back door. We can drape a sheet over Ananda so no one can tell it's her."

Ananda laughed. "I'll be the Ghost of Christmas Present."

"It's not a good idea." I shook my head. "Besides, everything is closed. It's Christmas Day."

"That Chinese place is always open on Christmas. And the park is always open."

"Please Mag?" Ananda asked.

I considered it. It sounded like a terrible idea, but I wanted to leave the apartment too. It'd been weeks since we got trapped, and I could barely stand it anymore. And who knew? Maybe an adventure would make my situation with Ananda better.

For whatever reason, Ananda hadn't named Kitty in any of her books, so she was considered 'a nobody' to the paparazzi. Kitty used to be furious about it, especially since she'd known Ananda longer than I had, but I always thought Ananda might've been protecting her from unwanted media attention.

Kitty walked to her SUV rental, stirring no attention from the paps, and drove around the block. She cut through a lawn and pulled up to the back.

Ananda stumbled by the back door, wrapped in one of my sheets. I caught her. She held me for a second, and then, as if remembering she was still mad at me, pulled away.

"Come on," Kitty yelled.

I held the back door open as Ananda dove into the back seat. I squeezed in after her and slammed the door.

As Kitty drove over the snowy lawn and sped onto the road, paps scrambled behind us. Part of me wondered if we should be doing this. We'd have to go back, and who knew what they'd do to try to get a picture. But the paps hadn't expected our getaway, and we lost them in no time.

Kitty drove to the Arts District park. It was empty except for snowdrifts and denuded trees. Weak winter light shone on my face, and the fresh air smelled of cider and balsam fir.

We sat down on the sun-splattered wall of the gazebo. It was more beautiful than I remembered, with ornate arches and a roof made of oxidized copper. This was where I'd first hung out with Ananda, and where Kitty had picked me up the day after the House of Transformation went down. I still loved it, even as the ghosts of friends and acquaintances drew near and chilled me even more. I inhaled deeply and watched my breath form a cloud in the air before the wind whipped it away.

Kitty tsked, looking at her phone. "The restaurant doesn't open for another half hour. I wish a coffeehouse was open."

Ananda opened her studded Karl Lagerfeld purse for a piece

of gum. "Maybe a gas station is open. They usually have coffee."

I shook my head. The thought of bad coffee was only marginally better than no coffee at all. The effort to get it would be significantly more work than it was worth. I wished Hayden were with us. She'd know what to do. "I should've packed a thermos."

"Do you want to walk around the neighborhood while we wait for the restaurant to open?" Kitty asked.

"I don't know. Do you think that's safe?" I asked Ananda.

"What's not safe about it?" Kitty asked.

"You haven't seen how people behave around Ananda. It's insane."

"It's fine." Ananda lit up. "I doubt anyone will even recognize me."

"But at the Indian restaurant, people were all over us in an hour. It was like they knew you were going to be there."

As I said the words, my brain noticed the gap in logic. How did the paparazzi get there so quickly? Ananda was recognized by the servers — that was inevitable — but how did a crowd of news vans, photographers, and journalists get there so quickly?

"Wait a minute," I said. "Did you tip them off?"

"Yeah," Ananda said softly, looking at the ground.

"Oh my God." I stood and faced her. "All this time I thought you were hounded by the media, and you told them exactly where you'd be? Was it all a set-up to stay at my apartment?"

"I'm sorry Mag. I needed to show you what my life was like. But I really do need your help." She reached for my hand, a blush of embarrassment on her cheeks. It was a new look for her. I'd only ever seen her angry or spacey when confrontations arose. She'd just owned up to it, and had even apologized. Maybe she was growing after all. I nodded and tried to let my anger dissipate. Rising above it. John would be proud.

"It's okay," I said. "I understand why you did it. You're right, it's one thing to see a video of you on TMZ. To see all those paps in real life is quite another experience."

"Thanks," she said. "By the way, I'm not angry about your

book anymore, either. You were right about a lot of stuff. I'm trying to own up to my past, and I was just mad because that book was like a detailed list of my faults. A 130-page list."

"I'm still so sorry about that."

"It's okay."

"Guys," Kitty interrupted. "I'm freezing. Let's walk."

I shook my head. "You were the one who was too cool to wear my old winter coat."

"That lumpy trashbag-looking thing from God knows where? You're right, I'd rather freeze."

The sidewalk was only wide enough for two of us to walk side by side, but we linked arms and squeezed together as we crunched through the snow. Wreaths and ribbons adorned the houses and iron fences. The Christmas lights, both inside and outside, were radiant. Although we passed a few people, no one recognized Ananda. I wished we'd made a trip outside sooner. I never realized how starved I was for nature and scenery.

We walked into the steamy Chinese restaurant just as it opened and huddled into a booth. The tea was weak, and the food too oily, but it was perfect. Ananda kept her sunglasses on the entire time and wasn't recognized.

After lunch, we drove around St. Paul until we found an open gas station. Kitty bought three bottles of wine and terrible coffee. By the time we got back to the apartment, we were exhausted. It was another debacle getting Ananda in the back door, especially with the paps on the back sidewalks and street corners.

After dropping me and Ananda off at the back door, Kitty parked the SUV on the street. This time, instead of ignoring her, the paps hounded her. I watched through the blinds as they took her picture and pelted her with questions. She took her time, facing the cameras and answering them. She breezed into the apartment a moment later, her cheeks pink with the wind.

"Why were you talking to the paps?" I asked.

She gave me the bag of wine and hung up her jacket. "They just wanted to know who I was."

"But we haven't been talking to them. Talking encourages

them."

"You always worry too much. It's not a problem if I tell them my name, is it, Ananda?"

"I suppose not," she said, her face impassive.

I pressed my lips shut. I hadn't even considered the confidentiality form for Kitty, but now I wondered if I should have. But Kitty wasn't dumb. She wouldn't sabotage Ananda. Her conversation with the paps couldn't have lasted more than thirty seconds. It was probably nothing.

I looked at my phone for the first time in hours and saw I had three missed calls from Darren.

"What kind of wine do you want, Mag?" Ananda asked, smiling.

All the remaining weight from the past couple of weeks fell away. "I'll do the Cabernet."

We talked and laughed until all three bottles were empty and it was so late it was early. I offered Kitty the couch, but she slept in Ananda's room. Their relationship was still an enigma to me, even though I was probably the closest one to them. For the first time, I didn't care.

The next day, Hayden arrived at the apartment early. My head pounded from the wine. I lingered in bed until I couldn't sleep anymore. When I came out, Hayden cleaned the living room. Empty glasses clinked in her hand.

"Let me help you with that," I whispered. "You don't have to clean. We can call the cleaning lady."

"It's okay." She pouted.

She clanked the glasses on the counter, not seeming to care if she woke Ananda and Kitty.

I wondered if she was still upset about Ananda asking Justin for xyritav. Then I smelled the black oily coffee and swooned. "You made coffee? You're an angel." I poured a cup, got some ibuprofen from the cupboard, and threw back the pills. "How are you, Hayden?"

She frowned. "I thought Ananda was getting better, but it's like everything we did was for nothing."

"She is getting better. It's just a slow process."

"Then why did she want more xyritav?"

I put a hand on her arm. What Ananda did was typical addict behavior, but she didn't know that. It must have felt like a betrayal. "That's just how detox works, but the important thing to remember is she's still sober. You have a big role in that. You should feel proud."

She eyed the empty wine bottles and raised an eyebrow. "Still sober?"

"Not alcohol, obviously, but she hasn't had any xyritav."

"Does it work that way?"

"We're not the twelve-step program. She never overindulges in alcohol, so I don't think it's a problem."

She breathed out forcibly and crossed her arms. "Maybe she should follow the twelve steps. It works for other people."

It was clear she still had a lot of qualms about Ananda. I wondered if they'd ever be as close as they were before.

"Let's update the whiteboard," I walked to where Hayden had written '20 days sober!'

Hayden uncapped the marker. She slowly erased '20' and wrote '22.'

"Kitty is staying with us. She's sleeping in Ananda's room right now."

"Is she nice?"

I hesitated. "Most of the time, she is. Once you get to know her."

"Great," Hayden said, the tone of her voice implying otherwise. "So, what do you need today? More groceries?"

"Um... What was the last social media post you made?"

"I posted a Happy Holidays message yesterday," she grumbled.

"Okay. We'll let that breathe for a while. I have another shopping list for you."

"Should I still use your credit card?" She dug in her purse for it.

"Yeah. Another one should be arriving soon."

"Is that all for today?"

"Yes. By the way, I have another check for you. I know Ananda appreciates your time, even if it doesn't seem like it. She gave you a Christmas bonus."

"Thanks." She stuffed the list and check into her coat pocket, then walked out without another word.

I stared after her, my heart heavy. Ananda never realized how mad she made people. At least she'd started to take responsibility for her actions. Her apology to me was a huge breakthrough, one I couldn't wait to tell John about.

I picked up my phone and called him, but I heard the familiar babbling of his voicemail. I left a message, whispered what happened, and asked him to call back.

Kitty came out of the bedroom stretching. Ananda's keyboards sounded shortly after.

"Please tell me there's coffee. Oh thank God." She helped herself. "It's so good to be here. I'm glad I finally made it."

"I'm glad you're here too. I think it's good for Ananda to see you."

"Thanks for not kicking her out when things got rough. It must've been hard. But there's something I've been dying to ask you. Why do you think she went to you and not me?"

I braced myself. I didn't want to make it sound like Ananda liked me better, because it probably wasn't true. I figured it was because Kitty was still surrounded by the xyritav lifestyle. Only a year ago, she told me she took it on New Year's Eve. I was probably Ananda's only clean friend.

"Maybe it's my psychology background?" I said.

"Yeah, I guess. I didn't realize how much I missed her. It's like there was a giant hole in my life."

"I know, me too."

"Is the assistant here?"

"No, she just ran out. Why, do you need something?"

"Not really. I guess I don't know what you guys do around here. What are we going to do for the next three days?"

I counted the days on my fingers and my pulse quickened. "You're leaving before New Year's Eve?" I'd read online that holidays were hard for recovering addicts, and the more friends they had to distract them, the better.

"Yeah. I already RSVP'd to a party in LA."

"You should stay. It'd be so much fun. We do yoga, get massages, drink juice."

"So it's like a spa?" She brightened. "I've never been to a spa. I get manis and pedis, but I always wanted to check into one of those places. I could really use a massage."

"I can arrange that. Today or tomorrow?"

"Today. What else do you do? Just hang out? That sounds boring."

"Yeah, we hang out a lot. Ananda writes music, I do collages and plan stuff, and Hayden shops for us."

She leaned close to me, her mouth twitching. "Are you and Ananda together? I can't tell. She's still so confusing."

I gave her a small smile. She was caught up in Ananda's emotional whirlwind again. "No, we're not a couple."

"Cool. But why doesn't she know what to do for the Grammys? You need to get on top of that. People plan that stuff months ahead of time, and you have, like, a month and some change. Does she have any idea what she wants to do?"

I shook my head. "I don't know. You'd have to ask her."

"You're her manager. You need to keep her on track."

"Do you know anyone in LA who could help?"

"No, but Ananda has tons of friends in the business."

I poured myself more coffee, turning my back to her. "It might be hard to find someone who doesn't use, though."

"Is it really that bad if she uses a little xyritav?"

I faced her. It looked like the old Kitty was back. "You didn't see her when she was in the worst part of her detoxes. The vomiting, the shakes — they're real. She was a mess. Maybe you can do it now and then and not be addicted, but her brain is different. You do understand that, don't you?"

"I guess, but I don't think she needs it. At least, I never saw her like that."

"Unfortunately, that's how it is. She wants it so much she asked a stranger for it the other day."

"Okay, fine, I get it. But I'm going to need to leave this

apartment again. I can't stay cooped up in here all day."

"Why don't you go out now while she's playing music?"

"Can't we go out to dinner or something? We were fine last night."

I shook my head. "Nobody was out yesterday. It was a holiday. People will recognize her now, and she doesn't have bodyguards anymore."

"Do we really need them? Or can't we hire some?"

"I don't know. Let me think about it."

"Fine. I'm going to the bookstore." Kitty sashayed out of the apartment. She talked to the paps and gave them more face time before getting into her SUV.

I grimaced, knowing I'd have to tell her to stop it. I started to wash the dishes. Last night's hangover still pinched my head.

"Where is everyone?" Ananda asked. "Did we scare them all away?"

I rinsed the suds from my hands. "Yep. I'm afraid no one likes us at all."

"Good," she said, hugging me. Her body felt warm against mine.

"What do you want to do for the Grammys?" I asked.

"I'm not focused on that. I'm focusing on my new song."

"I know, but you signed the contract to perform at the Grammys, and if you don't go through with it, there's that five million dollar penalty."

The money wasn't all I was worried about. If she skipped her performance, the press would read into her seclusion. Stories about her addiction might rise again. We needed to be careful.

"Well, I can't afford to pay five million dollars, so we'll have to figure something out."

I was embarrassed I hadn't watched many of those awards ceremonies. "What do people usually do?"

She shrugged. "All kinds of things."

"We can watch videos of past awards. Maybe it'll inspire you." I flipped open the laptop and searched for recent performances. Of course, Ananda's nude xyritav-crazed moment was there. I scrolled past it, looking for a dance number, but she touched my hand.

"Go back. I want to see it."

I searched her eyes. "Are you sure?"

She nodded. I didn't have a good feeling, but I scrolled back to it. "You know this might be painful."

"It's okay. I need to see who I was back then."

I clicked on the video. The camera panned over a theatre packed with people in glittering gowns, designer clothing, and punked-up hair, like a sea of strange and beautiful creatures. Red velvet curtains opened. Ananda walked out. From the distance, it was hard to tell if she wore a nude-colored leotard or what, but as she crossed the stage, the crowd hushed. She was clearly wearing only Louboutin heels. Her body bounced with each step until she reached the podium. Her eyes shone like diamonds. She read the award nominees from the teleprompters as if in a dream, not looking into the cameras once.

I paused the video. "Are you okay?"

Ananda had the same spacey look in her eyes, as if she were there. She snapped back, met my eyes, and nodded. I pressed play.

"The award goes to..." She tore the wrapper, but fumbled with the card. The camera cut to the crowd. Some people snickered. Others gaped in shock.

"Cypress," Ananda said.

Cypress broke into a grin and walked onstage. Ananda walked back to the curtain without congratulating her, her soap-white butt jiggling all the way. The camera cut to Cypress, making a pie face and shrugging at the camera. I pressed pause.

"You okay? That must've been hard to watch."

She sighed. "It's weird. I feel like it wasn't me up there."

"In a way, it wasn't. Things you did on xyritav don't come from your authentic self, because your brain was sort of hijacked."

"Yeah. I can't believe I did that to Cypress, too. She's one of my favorite musicians."

"Don't worry about her. She sees a naked woman every time

she takes a shower."

"But I left her hanging there. She probably thinks I'm a total ditz."

I took her hand and squeezed it. "It's more important what you think of yourself in the present moment."

"Yeah, I guess so."

"Do you want to watch some more videos? Maybe some with dancers in them?"

She stood, her posture stooped. "If it's alright with you, I think I'm going to lie down for a while. I don't feel so good."

"Sure." I gave her a quick hug. Reliving that moment couldn't have been easy. "If you want to talk about it, I'm here."

"Thanks." She sidled into her room.

Kitty brought up a good point — we had about a month to figure out Ananda's performance at the Grammys. That meant making a lot of appointments.

When Hayden returned from the grocery, she called a couple of massage therapists for Ananda and Kitty, then left for the day. I declined a massage this time, and instead focused on the growing pile of receipts on the kitchen counter. I'd have to ask Ananda for another check to cover all the expenses we were putting on my credit card.

I'd just started entering the receipts into a spreadsheet when the massage therapists arrived. By the time they exited Ananda's room, I was still hard at work. I wrote each of them a check with a large tip, as usual, and walked them to the door. I worked on the spreadsheet a while longer, but my eyes were so heavy I could barely keep them open.

The apartment was quiet. The lights were off in Ananda's room. Maybe they were knocked out by their massages.

I went to my room, slipped under the covers, and fell asleep almost instantly.

The next morning, the sound of Hayden unlocking the door woke me. I threw on a robe and went out. She stood by the door with her arms crossed. She still had her coat and boots on, which was strange. She usually took her boots off to avoid tracking snow into the apartment.

"Is something wrong?" I asked.

She began to crumple, tears circling her eyes. "You don't know?"

"Don't know what?" I asked, my heart clenching hard.

"Ananda and Kitty left last night."

"What? Are you sure? How do you know?"

"It was on the internet. I have a Google search set up to email me every four hours so I can see what Ananda's fans and the news are saying about her." She gasped for breath between her tears.

"So they went out for the night?" I asked.

She looked at me piteously, silent.

I walked to Ananda's door and tried to open it, but it was locked.

Hayden's mouth opened, but she didn't say anything.

I started to panic. I grabbed the key to Ananda's door, shoved it into the lock, and turned it.

The room was empty. All of their clothes and bags were gone.

"They got on a plane to LA," she said.

The world dissolved beneath my feet. I stared at the room, willing it to be untrue, wanting them to be hiding in the closet. Of course, they weren't.

I collapsed onto the floor. Hayden went down beside me, holding me. I reached out for her, tears running down my cheeks.

Ananda had left me again, possibly forever.

Chapter 27. Total Eclipse

Ananda was still mad at me because I confronted her about her lies, but she had Jared to distract her. They did everything together. He had quite the bank account — he took Ananda and Blossom out to meals and drinks at the fanciest places. I wasn't invited to these occasions, but he said it wasn't about me. It was for his new photo series he called Nouveau Art, which he derived from 'Art Nouveau, but with a twist.' He insisted Ananda wear stage makeup and her best dresses when they went out, just in case the moment was right to photograph her, and so she did — to the coffeehouse, to restaurants, to the park, and on the street. She donned headbands and scarves, and was more beautiful than ever. She wasn't a model before, but she was now.

Blossom also starred in these works, as she had long hair. I didn't, and that was Jared's excuse for not inviting me. The one time they invited me out to dinner, I couldn't afford wine. They rejoiced in having a designated driver and each drank four glasses.

Several times, when I accidently walked onto the 'set' in the living room or in the hallway, he told me to move out of the way because my hair 'modernized the image too much.' I wanted to point out that his digital Nikon was also out of place, but I kept it to myself.

Jared wanted his next set of pictures to be his everlasting glory. He'd already contacted several magazines and bragged that they were all interested. I didn't believe him, but Ananda and Blossom did.

More often than not, I'd wake and find myself in the house alone. Jared and Ananda would return with full tummies and a full filmcard. Blossom stayed at the house sometimes, sleeping in a corner of the living room, in a place we affectionately called 'Blossom's room.' I never asked her what she did with the Swami. I didn't want to know.

One night, the front door squeaked open and a stampede pounded up the stairs. I rose and dressed quickly. Jared, Blossom, and Ananda laughed so hard they couldn't even stand up straight. They took one look at me and burst into a new round of laughter.

"I'll be right back." Jared bounded up the attic stairs two at a time.

I tried to catch his eye, but he ran off too quickly.

"Hi," I said to the girls.

Ananda mumbled something about changing clothes and slipped into her room, but Blossom perked up.

"Hi Mag. We're going to the dance club. Want to come?" she asked, her eyes blurry with clemeral.

"Sure. Can you wait a few minutes? I just need to put on makeup."

"Got it," Jared yelled, thundering down the stairs.

"I think we're leaving now. Just meet us there."

"Well... Can you wait a moment?"

Jared ran down the stairs toward the front door, but Blossom dawdled, looking deep into my eyes.

"If you're meant to be there, you'll be there. Everything happens for a reason." She caressed my arm, then traipsed after Jared.

Ananda came out of her room and tugged down a minidress that barely covered her ass. Her eyes were so glassy they were tinged with blue.

"Who's driving you guys?" I asked.

"What do you care?" she snarled.

"Maybe you shouldn't get in a car with them."

She screwed up her face. "Don't should on me, Mag, and I won't should on you."

"I just worry about you."

She stormed down the stairs and slammed the door.

One evening when I was by myself, someone knocked on the front door. I peeked through the beveled glass and saw the Swami, looking out of place in his flowing white robes.

"Hello, Mag. How are you tonight?" His eyes twinkled.

I smiled, impressed he'd remembered my name. "Hi. I'm good. How are you?"

"Well. Is Tiny Blossom here?"

I shook my head. "No, it's just me here tonight."

"Do you know where she is?"

I shrugged. "I have no idea."

He stared at me for a moment, then extended a hand. "Then you shall come to dinner with me. My treat."

I hesitated. I didn't want to give him the wrong impression, but I was so hungry I would've eaten anything. Maybe I could also explain what might've happened that night with the clemeral. It would put those guilty feelings in my mind to rest.

The Swami led me to an old Buick parked in front of the house. He held the back door open and I climbed in. He sat beside me, closing the door with a quiet thud. Anjay nodded at me from behind the wheel and pulled away from the house.

"So, tell me about your family," the Swami said.

"My parents live in Eau Claire. They're psychologists."

He nodded. "Still together. So rare for this country. You went to college?"

"Yeah, St. Anne's."

"And your degree?"

"Psychology."

"Just like your parents. I bet they are so proud of you."

"I guess, but I really just want to be an artist."

"Your art, yes, I remember. Tell me more about that."

I explained my idea about combining color, texture, and movement. He listened raptly, and before I knew it, we arrived at an Indian Restaurant. As soon as we parked, Anjay leapt out of the car to open my door, and then the Swami's.

"I think you will like this restaurant," the Swami said, his arm on my shoulders.

We walked in and sat in a booth. The smell of curry and fresh cilantro made me lightheaded. Anjay sat at a different table, cracked open a book, and started reading.

"Sit with us," I said to him.

He shook his head and threw up a hand to deflect me.

"He's fine by himself," the Swami said. "He sees me so much, he's probably sick of hearing me talk."

"Okay." I swallowed. "About what happened a weeks and a half ago at the party, I just want to say-"

"It was magnificent. I had an awakening that night."

"You did?"

"Absolutely. Thank you again for having me in your home. It's a special place. And your art is very enlightened. May I purchase some for my meditation room?"

"Of course." I hadn't expected to sell art while dining out. He was so sweet. It made me feel even worse for what'd happened with the soup. It was hard to talk about, but I knew I had to tell him what happened.

Before I could speak, the server arrived. The Swami took the liberty of ordering for both of us, which turned out to be a feast. Not only did we have soup and entrees, but also fried appetizers, chutneys, a bottle of wine, and two baskets of bread.

"Why were you all alone tonight?" he asked between bites of appetizers.

I looked at my lentil soup. I could've told him my friends left me because I wasn't cool enough or rich enough to go out to dinner with them, but I didn't. "I thought I'd work on a collage for the next art show," I lied.

"You're a true artist. You have a gift. Everyone else in your group goes through the motions of spirituality, but you live it. That is why I wanted to talk with you. You are the most spiritual one in your group."

My jaw dropped. I finally got recognition for my dedication. "Thank you. But I have to tell you something. I'm afraid someone put something — some prescription drugs in the food the other night. So, if you experienced anything strange, that may have been why."

He shook his head. "The only thing I felt was nirvana. It was a magical night, one I will never forget."

I bit my lip, unsure if I should press the issue. But he didn't seem concerned.

The entrees and bread arrived and we ate in silence for a moment. After I'd eaten my fill of *saag paneer*, I wiped my mouth and set my napkin on the table. I was stunningly full. The Swami stood and helped me up, leaving Anjay to pick up the tab.

"Come with me," he said. "We will wait in the car. We can talk more about your art."

I walked with him to the car. We sat in the back seat and he leaned toward me.

"Thanks for dinner," I said.

"You're welcome. May I embrace you?"

I nodded and leaned in. His arms encircled me, smelling like warm sandalwood. I let myself dissolve in his embrace. His fingertips caressed my back. Only Ananda had ever caressed me like that.

I kept waiting for Anjay to emerge from the restaurant, but I didn't see him.

The Swami's long strokes went lower, until he touched the middle of my spine to the nape of my neck. When his hands ran down my legs, I pulled away.

Under the streetlights, we looked into each other's eyes. His face peaked with desire, his eyes burning. He touched my face, my lips.

I shook my head. "I can't do this with you. You took a vow of celibacy."

He withdrew his arms and bowed his head. I looked around the parking lot and saw Anjay sitting on the curb near the restaurant. As soon as he saw my face, he walked over, opened the driver's door, and started it without a word.

We drove home in silence. I tried to think of a topic of conversation and failed. Instead, I watched each streetlight, shining like a sentinel, bringing me closer and closer to home.

When we got to my street, the Swami took my hand, his eyes watery. "I meant what I said. You are special."

"Thanks," I mumbled.

Anjay opened the door for me. I stepped onto my street. He closed the door and glanced at me, a hollow look in his eyes.

Then they drove off into the night.

I trudged into the empty house, walked upstairs to the bathroom, and removed every article of clothing. I felt dirty, as if the Swami's intentions festered on my skin. I stepped into the tub and turned on the tap. Warm water sloshed around me. I leaned back against the porcelain as the tub filled.

Where were my friends? I couldn't believe they excluded me, and all because I'd asked Ananda about her past. The more I thought of it, the more it seemed like Kitty had known my inquiries would go awry. I wondered if she knew Ananda would shun me as she shunned other people from her past.

And then there was Ricky. I didn't understand why he was so rude to me. Maybe he had a clemeral hangover. That was one thing I didn't miss — the black mornings.

I sloshed the water around me and tried to clear my mind, but I couldn't. I was so lonely it hurt.

Rosie appeared by the bathroom door, her cluster of lights swaying. I smiled at her. I figured she could use a friend as much as I could.

"So you're still here too, huh?"

Her lights bounced.

"Well, today sucked. My friends ditched me, and someone I looked up to..." I couldn't even finish the sentence.

Her lights seemed to spiral.

I squinted at her. I couldn't tell what she was trying to say. Was she happy? Angry? Sad?

"Rosie, what's it like where you are?"

Her lights fell in slow motion to the floor and faded until I couldn't see them anymore.

"Rosie?" I asked, rising.

But she was gone.

I fell back against the edge of the tub. I hadn't thought it possible, but I felt even more alone.

I lived without roommates for a few days, the house as silent as a library. I was so lonely I drove to the coffeehouse, hoping to find Ricky in a better mood than the last time I saw him. I came prepared with an apology, even though I didn't think yelling at the clowns who'd destroyed my art was a bad thing.

I walked into the coffeehouse, inhaling the smell of espresso and caramel syrup. The wheezing sound of milk being steamed pervaded the room. Ricky stood behind the espresso machine. When he saw me, he turned off the steamer wand but avoided my gaze. I walked to the counter. This time, his boss wasn't there. No one waited in line behind me. Only a couple of people sat at tables.

"What's going on?" I whispered. "Why are you treating me like this?"

"Medium latte," he said, setting a cup on the counter.

A man in sweats walked up and took it.

"Did I say something to upset you?" I asked.

"Mag..." His eyes darted around the room.

My heart cried out. Where was the guy who'd kissed me on the rooftop? What had happened?

"I–" He looked me in the eyes. "I don't date girls like you."

I narrowed my eyes at him. "What do you mean by that?"

His palms turned up as he walked down the bar. "I don't judge you. It's fine. It's just not my thing."

I paced after him. "Just what do you think my thing is?"

"You know, the House of Transformation stuff."

"What stuff?"

"Mag, you gave me a pill the other night. I thought it was a breath mint. The next thing I knew, I was tripping my balls off."

I gasped. Hadn't Ananda gotten the clemeral from Ricky? Hadn't he taken one the night before, when we ran over the rooftop in my Mary Poppins dream? I'd just assumed he'd want one. I hadn't even asked.

"I'm sorry," I blurted. "That was an accident. I don't do any drugs anymore."

A couple of people in the coffeehouse turned to look at us.

He moved in closer. "It's not just that, it's the other stuff too."

"Like what? The rituals?"

"Rituals?" He shook his head. "The orgies. I just don't–"

"What are you talking about? I was never in one of those."

"You don't have to deny it. And everyone's talking about you and the Swami guy."

"That wasn't me, it was–" I stopped myself before saying her name.

"It was someone else."

"Well, I heard it was you, but really, it's everything about you. I might run for an office one day, and you just don't fit into what I want out of life. Look, I have to make a sandwich for a customer."

I shuffled backwards in disbelief, my stomach clenching in guilt. An ocean of tears pooled just behind my eyes. I'd drugged someone, just as Kitty had drugged me. I could barely believe it.

I felt as if all my friends had turned against me at the same time. Ricky, Ananda, Jared — even Blossom couldn't bring herself to talk for more than a couple of minutes... all of them except Kitty. She was the only one who remained constant throughout the whole ordeal, the only one who was up front about her emotions and her motivations. And she was right — she'd never lied to me.

"Can I use your phone please?" I asked.

Ricky winced like I had leprosy, but he handed me the phone.

I dialed Kitty's number. It rang twice before someone answered.

"Hello, Kitty's phone," Ananda said.

I slammed the phone down, left the coffeehouse, and went home, even though I knew I didn't have anything to look forward to there.

28. Space

The next morning, I awoke and wandered through the House of Transformation. I hadn't seen my roommates for a week. It felt as empty as when I'd first moved in, except infinitely dirtier. The house seemed bigger, more alive, and yet silent as death. I kept seeing shadowy movements from the corners of my eyes, but when I turned to look, the shadows retreated. Not even Rosie made an appearance that morning.

I tried to tell myself the solitude was nice, but I missed everyone. I was mad at Ricky, even though he had good reasons to disengage from me. I wished Ananda would talk with me, but she seemed as remote as the next galaxy.

On the bright side, my distractions were gone. I could prepare for the next art show in the hopes of selling some collages and making rent money. I still wanted to try to make it as an artist.

I ploughed through two new collages, one that might be good enough for showing. I couldn't figure out how to make the other one complete. Nothing I tried worked.

That afternoon, Jared came home, this time without his usual entourage. He had a new haircut that made him look less bedraggled and more sophisticated, like a renaissance painter.

"Hey," he said from the foyer.

I stood up and brushed the tiny paper cuttings from my sundress. "How's it going?"

"Great. I've been staying at Blossom's. We're getting ready for the next Art Party. I just came back for my thumb drive." He walked to the mantle and retrieved it, then dawdled by the door, glancing at my finished collage. "That's a nice one."

"Thanks. I'm doing that show too."

"I'll be showing my Nouveau Art series. It's going to be huge. So I guess I'll see you tomorrow at the Hanging Party."

"Yeah, but if it gets weird like last time, I'm leaving. Hey, did you hear a rumor we're having orgies here?"

"What? Weird," he said, looking not entirely displeased.

"Will Ananda be there tomorrow?"

"I don't know. Why?"

I frowned. "You know why. She's still mad at me for bringing up her past. She thinks I'm judging her, but I'm not. I miss her."

"I know what you mean. She's like a drug. I miss her too when she's not around. You were closer to her than anyone, except maybe Kitty." He shifted his weight and started walking toward the door. "I should get going."

"Wait. I need a favor. Tell her I never meant to hurt her feelings. I just want it to be like the old days."

He shrugged. "I don't know where she is. I haven't seen her for a while."

"She's at Kitty's. Whenever you see her, could you put in a good word for me?"

He nodded and left. I wondered if he'd actually talk with her about me. No one liked to ruffle Ananda's feathers. She made examples out of people who were on her bad side.

I turned back to the unfinished collage and tried more images, but none of them worked. Ananda would've known what piece was missing.

I dragged myself to the Hanging Party at Stevey's warehouse, almost against my better judgment. I had to, since my work would be on display and I needed the rent money.

As soon as I got there, Pasha directed me to a shadowy corner on the far side of the warehouse. She was in charge this time.

"Sorry," she said smugly. "There's nowhere else."

I sighed. Hardly anyone would make it that far. Without Ananda to pull strings for me, I was a nobody, and nobodies don't get good places to show their art.

After hanging my collages, I walked around. Ricky and Jared talked in the kitchen. I snuck past so they wouldn't see me. My heart still burned. I still liked him. I wished Jared would talk to him about me, but I knew better than to hold my breath for that.

I sat on a couch next to a mohawked girl and a guy with pink hair. I listened in to their conversation and nodded a few times, but they ignored me. After ten minutes, I gave up.

I got up and climbed the dusty concrete stairs, recalling the ethereal music I'd heard just a few weeks ago. I opened the crusty door at the top of the stairs. A cool breeze brushed through me. The starry sky yawned overhead as the sun went down behind the city.

I went to the edge of the roof and looked down at the parking lot. Kitty's car wasn't there. I'd hoped she and Ananda would be here. Maybe Kitty could talk some sense into her. After all, if Kitty knew all her secrets, what was the harm in my knowing them too?

I picked up a pebble and pitched it with all my strength into a copse of trees. Fuck everyone and their stupid ways.

Farther down the roof, a tall man in a loose suit jacket smoked, watching the sunset. The wind played with his medium-length straggly hair. He noticed me watching him, then reached into his coat pocket and produced a white pack of cigarettes, opening the top with his thumb, as if to ask if I wanted one.

I shrugged and walked toward him. I pulled a cigarette out of the pack. He struck a match on the ledge, cupping the flame against the wind. I inhaled until an ember formed.

"Thanks," I said, exhaling smoke from my nostrils.

Closer up, I could see his eyes were hooded, like a scholar, and blue as lapis. He said nothing, only turned to face the sunset again. Lights snapped on inside office buildings. The cityscape was coming to life.

I took another drag. We watched the colors and clouds drift in silence. Not talking was comforting, almost like I'd known him for years.

When the cigarette was a stub, I brushed it on the outer ledge of the roof and watched the sparks fly as they fell stories below. Only a faint red glow remained on the horizon.

"Are you showing anything at the Art Party tomorrow?" I asked.

"No. It's not really my thing. I have a studio on the fourth floor."

"What do you do?"

"Music."

I nodded. I didn't mind he was terse. I didn't feel like

talking either.

"Perhaps I'll see you tomorrow." He gave me a half-smile before walking toward the door.

I nodded and turned to watch the dying sunset.

Chapter 29. Art Party II

This Art Party would be different from the last. With no clowns to ruin the show, I might be able to sell prints later into the night. I might have repeat customers, like Barry and the yuppies, even if I was in the darkest, farthest corner.

Months ago, when we were 'besties,' Ananda had told me I could wear anything from her closet, so I sort of felt like I still had permission, even though she wasn't talking to me. I needed to stand out to attract people to the prints. I wanted something high art yet understated — something that would enable me to feel confident.

When I opened the door to Ananda's room, the emptiness was eerie, almost as if someone watched me from the shadows. I leafed through her dresses and skirts until I found what I was looking for — the cloud-white architectural dress I'd admired weeks ago. Though she hadn't let me wear it for the photo shoot, she might not mind now. After all, I'd just be wearing it at the Art Party. Any sign of the mayonnaise bandits and I'd be out the door. I'd return home, hang up the dress, and she'd never know.

As I applied mascara, I thought of the strange man on the roof. He'd just stood there beside me as I fumed. I didn't know why I felt so comfortable around him. I didn't even know his name. Maybe I was lonelier than I realized.

By the time I arrived at the Art Party, it was in full swing. People cluttered every walkway and danced to the strange music, which sounded like slowed down techno with several effects. Art lined all of the walls.

I went to my homely corner and watched moneyed people walk by, clutching art.

"These are my collages," I said.

They walked on. People glanced in my direction, but most skipped my corner. I didn't recognize anyone. I yawned. It was going to be a long night.

A flapping sound erupted from the center of the party. Several people unrolled yoga mats in a flash mob, Blossom among them. They raised their arms and moved in synchrony from one pose to another. My heart fluttered to see her, and I waved. She smiled, but she was focused on teaching and didn't wave back.

A few people looked at my work, but mostly, people got tipsy on the free wine and beer. Jared's large photos of Ananda were set up on the other side of the room, creating a bottleneck in the crowd.

After three hours of standing around with no one stopping to look at my collages, I grew as annoyed as I was bored. I wondered about the man on the roof. I thought I would've seen him by now. I considered taking a break to go to the roof when I saw him entering the party through a door across the room. His suit was so wrinkled, it looked as if he'd slept in it. We locked eyes and a shiver of electricity sparked within me.

He walked through the masses until he stood in front of my work. For the first time that night, I was happy to be in the corner because we had a modicum of privacy. In the light, I could see his hair was dirty blonde, his skin a light olive color. He gazed at them without a word.

"I thought you didn't like Art Parties," I said teasingly.

"I don't. I get curious sometimes, though. These are good–"

"Thanks."

"–but if you scan them and tweak the colors, you'd get rid of things like this." He touched a photocopied crease.

"I know, but I don't know how to use Photoshop. Do you know?"

"Yeah, it's easy. I can teach you."

"That'd be nice." My heart beat a little faster at the thought of a Photoshop date.

"If you want, I can show you now. This party is about to get crazy again." He glanced back at the door he entered from, his mouth twisted.

"It can't be worse than last time."

"I saw those guys outside — the ones that had the sandwiches. They have a bunch of dildos. I'm not sticking around for whatever's happening next."

My eyes popped. "Are you serious? Why'd Stevey invite them back?"

"I'm sure he didn't. They're probably crashing the party because he kicked them out last month." He raised his brows at me. "So do you want to get out of here or what?"

I looked around the room. Anyone with an ounce of money to their name had left. Maybe it was too late, or maybe the Art Party wasn't publicized enough. Maybe the bologna frisbees and chicken vaginas at the last Art Party drove away anyone with a shred of class. Even though I desperately wanted to sell a collage, I also didn't want to be there when the bandits went crazy.

"Help me get these down," I said, removing the collages from the wall.

"Ugh. They just walked inside."

"Hurry." We tore them down and ran.

"Follow me," he said.

We shouldered our way through the crowd. As we exited, a bullhorn whistled with feedback.

"This way," he said.

We ran down dimly lit corridors painted in 1960's hues, then trekked up four flights of stairs. We rounded a corner and went down a long hall. He unlocked a door painted with gears and wires. We walked in, breathing heavily.

The room had a futon in the corner and an enormous desk topped with a computer, printer, and several other gadgets. Two walls of windows overlooked trees.

"Do you want me to show you now?" he asked.

I shrugged. So much for a romantic date. I gave him a collage and looked at him sidelong as he scanned it. He opened Photoshop, then walked me through airbrushing a crease out and changing an image's color.

"Should I be taking notes?" I joked.

"You only need to remember a couple of things. You can

always look online if you forget."

He handed back the collage and our fingers touched. A tingle passed between us, so intense I almost dropped it. I leaned forward, my hair falling in my face, and set the collage down with the others. When I straightened, I caught him staring at me. He turned away shyly.

"I can leave if you're busy," I said, disappointment starting to deflate me.

"That dress." His face clenched. "Where did you get it?"

I looked down at the white dress. Fear flashed through me — did Ananda steal it from someone? Was that why she didn't want me to wear it? A sheen of sweat formed on my skin.

"I borrowed it from a friend. It's not mine."

"What friend?"

"Ananda."

He nodded. "I thought I recognized it. I bought her that dress. She begged me for it, but she never wore it. Now I can see why. It probably didn't fit her." He looked at my curves and raised his eyes slowly to meet mine.

"How do you know Ananda?" I asked.

He kissed me before I knew what was happening. I breathed in his scent — evergreen, cumin, and ozone. The kiss was without conflict, without thought. It was better than Ricky's. It was sensation and soft lips. The world faded to black. He moved closer to hold me. The heat from his body enlivened mine. Our hands travelled to each other's shoulders, necks, and hips.

An eternity later, when we broke away, cool air rushed between us, charged with electricity.

I stifled a yawn. "Sorry. It's late."

"You can stay here tonight if you want. We don't have to do anything."

I gazed at him. There was something trustworthy about him, something constant and secure.

"Okay."

His eyes smoldered as he picked up something from the floor and tossed it to me. I caught it. It was a t-shirt, one of his own presumably, for how large it was.

"I'll show you where the bathroom is."

We walked down the hallway until we reached a room with a couple of sinks below a long mirror with black splotches.

"I'll give you some privacy," he said. "Remember, I'm the circuit door."

I changed into his shirt, which came down to my knees. Then I scrubbed my teeth with my finger and some toothpaste from the sink. In the antique mirror, my cheeks looked flushed, my lips a shade darker than normal. I looked like someone in love. I couldn't believe I'd met someone, that I was sleeping over, that I wore one of his shirts. And that kiss was so intense, like he knew exactly how I wanted to be kissed. I didn't even know his name. We'd never introduced ourselves.

I padded back to the room and slipped in. He was out. I furtively looked for mail with his name on it, but didn't see anything.

When he returned, we lay down together on the soft futon. His pillows were heavenly, and his bed smelled like him. We gazed into each other's eyes. He clasped my hand and wove his fingers through mine. He turned out the light with his other hand, and we were bathed in darkness. I kissed him again, tasting the peppermint of his toothpaste.

"You didn't tell me your name," I said.

"Brad. And you're Mag, right?"

My heart stopped and I flashed hot and cold, my muscles stiffening. It was Ananda's Brad, the guy she'd lived with. No wonder he'd looked familiar. I'd called him an asshole! Did he know who I was? Or was this his idea of getting revenge on her?

He kissed me again. I hesitated, wanting to ask him about Ananda. I never heard his side of the story. She might have lied about him just as she lied about virtually everything. I wanted to ask a million questions, but I didn't know how to begin.

But more than anything, I wanted to release the tether Ananda still held on me. I decided it would be my revenge against her, against her teasing sensuality, against her icy withdraw. I kissed him and lost myself in sensation.

Daylight lit up the studio with crisp lines. I arose before Brad and looked out the window at the trees covered in dew. He got up, dressed in the same rumpled suit, and ran product through his hair.

"Let's get breakfast," he said. "I hung your dress up last night, so it should be fine."

He left for the bathroom while I dressed. When he returned, I went to the bathroom and ran a hand through my hair and resmudged my eyeliner. My reflection gazed back at me — not so moony or wan. Something was different. There was a purpose behind my eyes, a confidence I'd lacked before. Maybe I really had put Ananda behind me.

I walked back into his room. "Where are we going?"

"You'll see."

He drove me to an upscale breakfast place, the kind with real maple syrup, wood paneling, and a window view of a small waterfall. It was by far the most elegant place I'd ever been to without my parents. Even though we were surrounded by silver-haired couples, I felt more at home than I had in a long time.

After we ordered, I stared at him. "So. Did you know I was the one who helped Ananda move her stuff out of your place?"

He shook his head. "Not at first. You look different. But I recognized the dress. After you told me it was hers, I figured it out. I should thank you, by the way. Her stuff had been sitting there for months. I almost moved it out myself. So, you drove the getaway car?"

"Yeah. Sorry I called you an asshole."

He laughed. "You did? I didn't know that."

"Ananda told me you were an asshole, and I believed her. Ironically, now I'm on her shit list. She doesn't even live at my house anymore, but her stuff is there and she isn't paying rent. She isn't even talking to me anymore."

He shook his head. "Sounds like Ananda."

"Tell me what happened with the two of you." I steeled my jaw, hoping it was something I could live with.

His hooded eyes clouded. "Why do you want to know?"

"Because I can't figure her out. I thought we were friends,

then I found out she lied to me about all kinds of things. I have no idea what the truth is."

He took a deep breath and glared at the ceiling. "I met Ananda through a mutual friend at the dance club. She was into music, I was into music. I needed a vocalist for a song I wrote, and she said she'd do it. Then she needed a place to store her stuff, then she stayed at my apartment... We went out a few times and she always forgot her purse. That's how I ended up buying that dress. When I asked her to not sell drugs out of my apartment, she got mad and stayed at Kitty's. She only came back when I wasn't there. Once, when I went away on a business trip, I came back and my apartment was trashed. My neighbors said she threw quite the party."

"Wait, do you work for the Department of Motor Vehicles?"

Brad laughed heartily. "No, what gave you that impression? Oh wait, let me guess. She told you that?"

"Yeah," I said, feeling sheepish. Another lie. "What do you really do?"

"Automotive engineering, the design and testing sector."

"Oh. That's pretty different."

"Yeah." He laughed.

"She also said you walked in on her changing clothes."

"That happened, it's true, but her door was wide open and I didn't stick around. She's not my type."

I leaned back in my chair, masking my face. Who wasn't attracted to Ananda? I thought no one was immune to her charms. "She also said you punched a wall." I cringed.

He shook his head. "I've never punched a wall in my life. Scout's honor. As a musician, my hands are pretty important to me." He spread his fingers out. They were unscarred.

"Wow, the things she makes up about people." I gulped.

"Yeah. Do you ever wonder what she's saying about you?"

My stomach sank. "I hadn't thought of that."

Brad templed his fingers and leaned across the table toward me. "What I don't understand is why you're hanging out with her. I heard you have a BA in psychology."

"How'd you know that?" I smiled. Had he asked around

about me?

"I had to see who Ananda suckered. No offense."

Our food arrived and we were silent for a moment. I recalled the night before, kissing until we were exhausted. I bit my lip, wanting to crawl into his lap and kiss him again, right there in the restaurant, amidst the servers and the septuagenarians eating their eggs.

"So why are you hanging out with her?" he asked again, raising his knife and fork.

"I asked her to move in with me because–" I faltered. Why had I asked her to move in? Was I seduced by her flattery, her grandeur, her lies? And then I remembered. Beneath everything, she could be a good friend.

"She believed in my dream to be an artist. No one else has ever supported me like that. It was like having a live-in Life Coach. She got me the first show at Stevey's."

I repressed a sigh. Last night had been a bust. I hadn't sold any collages at the Art Party. "But now, the dream is over. I'll have to find a job with my degree."

"You know, psychologists with only bachelor's degrees have some of the lowest paid jobs in this country. I heard it on NPR."

I smirked. "I suppose I could go to grad school, like my parents want me to."

He lifted his mimosa flute and gazed into my eyes. "To the future, whatever it may hold."

"To the future."

We clinked glasses and drank. I never wanted to go home again.

30. Lost

After Ananda left my apartment on that cold wintry day, the paparazzi left too. The street looked empty without their clunky white vans.

I ventured out of the apartment, bought my own groceries, and ran my own errands. I found out my bank account was dangerously low and my credit card almost maxed out. I'd never gotten another check from Ananda for everything Hayden and I had bought. All the food, massages, vitamins, therapy sessions, the cleaning lady, and Hayden's hours added up to $9,000. We'd blown through cash. Without a job, I faced a cold winter indeed.

My publisher made good on his threat to block my royalty checks. At the time, I hadn't cared. Ananda gave me a job making $500,000 per year. But since she was gone again, I was financially and spiritually bereft.

I went through the first stage of grief — strong denial. I was certain Ananda would come back with shopping bags, giggles, and a pile of receipts. As time went by and it didn't happen, I entered the second stage.

I was furious she'd done it to me again. She'd completely sapped me of my time, money, and resources. As I cleaned up 'her bedroom' and set up my office again, I cursed at every article of tiny clothing she'd left on the floor. I cursed at the mess in the kitchen. I raged about Hayden — she'd quit her job to work for Ananda, and Ananda had thrown her away like leftover ramen. I called John and vented for days.

And then the bargaining stage came on. If only Kitty had never come. If only I'd monitored them like a mother hen. If only we hadn't drank wine. If only we hadn't gone out. *If only.*

To make matters worse, the Minnesota Board of Psychologists sent me a letter stating my license was suspended indefinitely. It was because I'd admitted to using clemeral and xyritav in my book, and because I diagnosed Ananda's disorders publicly. I read the letter twenty times, the words not registering. I tried to call the Board, but their offices were shut down for the holiday. That letter must've been the last thing they did before departing for vacations.

Then I hit full depression. My life had a flatline quality, like a black hole consumed me, even with the twinkle and bustle of the holiday season. Darren texted a few times but I ignored him. He was too needy, too expectant. I knew better than to think he could cheer me up. If anything, I'd transfer all my anger at Ananda onto him, and he didn't deserve that. So his calls went to voicemail until I could deal with it. Only I wasn't dealing with it very well.

Mary called to ask if we could meet up. I showered for the first time in days. We met for lunch on a Tuesday, just like when we worked together. I picked at my sandwich, barely able to eat. A box of my old office stuff sat below our table, my San Francisco picture on top.

"The new guy is settling in really well," she said. "He actually likes your red walls."

I half-smiled. "What else is new?"

"Not much. Same old, same old. What about you?"

"Well, you know Ananda left." I sighed. "I don't know what I'm going to do now."

Mary looked at her sandwich and swallowed. "I heard your license got revoked."

"You did? How?"

"Caroline got a letter."

I ground my teeth. Was public shaming part of the board's mission? But I kept my mouth shut. In truth, I wondered what options I had.

"I wish you the best of luck, Mag."

"Thanks."

On New Year's Eve, Darren texted again, and said I 'wasn't the only girl on the internet.' At first, I was pissed that he thought *he* was breaking up with *me*, but as the night wore on, I began to feel relieved. At least I didn't have to worry about that problem anymore.

I watched the Times Square New Year's Eve countdown in my pajamas, drinking sparkling wine from a chipped coffee mug. I'd never felt more alone than I had at that moment. I checked my phone compulsively to see if Ananda texted, but either my phone wasn't working or no one was texting me.

Somewhere, Ananda and Kitty were living it up, wearing short skirts and dancing on tabletops. I pictured them, ravenously drunk and high, laughing about me and my sad apartment.

I texted my parents *Happy New Year* but didn't hear back. I imagined their phones buzzing in their coat pockets as they drank from crystal flutes and ate crostini with their friends.

When it was almost midnight Central Time, the crowd on the television was loud and happy. Couples looked hopefully at each other. Then they counted down. My heart raced as if I were there.

When the year rolled over, all I felt was my broken heart. I looked at my phone. No one had called or texted. On the television, people kissed and cheered. Noisemakers went off and people popped streamers out of miniature plastic bottles. They sang *Auld Lang Syne*, but there were no kisses for me, no sing-a-longs.

I watched as the world celebrated, wanting to curl into the fetal position and sleep for days. I downed my mug of sparkling wine and poured another. Everyone else was celebrating. I just wanted to be obliterated.

My phone flashed. I snatched it up.

Happy New Year. <3 u

I sighed. At least Hayden had reached out.

Happy NY

I pressed send before correcting it to *NYE*. Oh well. She knew what I meant, right? *Happy New York*. I laughed and facepalmed.

I passed out, unable to keep my eyes open as the countdown and celebrations continued in other time zones.

On New Year's Day, I awoke on the couch. The morning news rattled in the background. I turned off the television and made coffee. A thick pounding reverberated in my head. I looked through my wide-open blinds and glared at the world.

I wasn't sure what I'd expected when Ananda hijacked my life, but I didn't expect to feel this abandoned. In hindsight, I should've seen it coming. She was selfish, rude, and deeply disturbed. I'd joked about her being a sociopath for a good reason. Why did I think she wanted to turn her life around? How had I been tricked again?

The worst part was how miserable I felt. Everything I used to love no longer made me happy. Was it because I'd glimpsed a life outside of my preconceived boundaries? Maybe I'd grown numb to taking chances. I wondered bleakly if I was moving into the acceptance stage, but I didn't know. I was still depressed, not to mention hung over.

I made myself wash up, made myself go out. I knew I'd feel more normal once I was surrounded by other people. I went to the Chinese Buffet in the Arts District, even though it reminded me of a week earlier, when I ate there with Kitty and Ananda. Someone once told me it was good luck to eat Chinese food on New Year's Day, but that wasn't why I went. I didn't believe in luck. I went because it was the perfect place to be alone. Aside from the occasional plate whisked away, I could gorge to my heart's content and not be bothered by anyone. The rag-tag clientele of hood rats, foreigners, overactive children, and dazed parents would be too preoccupied to bother with a middle-aged woman fiddling with her phone and eating plate after plate of *lo mein* and *kung pao* chicken.

I sipped the hot, weak oolong tea and scanned my texts. My parents hadn't even texted back yet. Some parents they were. I shoved a pork bun in my mouth and thought about my fears with a deep sigh.

1. *Fear of being alone*
2. *Fear of failure*
3. *Fear of spiraling down into the pits of depression*

A moment later, my phone lit up. Mom was calling, as if she'd finally remembered she had a child. I thought about taking the call, but I wasn't sure if I could talk without crying. I pressed decline. Seconds later, a text appeared.

Happy New Year! How are you?

I set down the pork bun and wrote back.

Fine. Miss you. Can't talk. You and Dad have fun last night?

Yes. Had a late night. ;)

I shoved my plate away, trying not to think about my parents doing it.

Saw Ananda on the news. Mom texted. *Not living with you anymore?*

No, why? What was she doing?

Public intoxication, not sure if alcohol or what.

My heart raced. It couldn't be anything good. I scrolled through the internet news on my phone and soon enough, I found a video taken last night. Ananda staggered out of a club, alone, her limbs moving unnaturally, her eyes shining. She tripped and stumbled. People nearby jerked away, as if she had a contagious disease. She fell to the concrete, but caught herself with her hands and uprighted. She glared at the camera for a second before stalking away, weaving a crooked line down the sidewalk, leaving gawkers and catcallers in her wake.

That poor girl, Mom texted.

I sighed. I couldn't tell if Ananda was using xyritav again or not, but it certainly looked like it. Moreover, all the health benefits from the last few weeks looked like they'd been scraped off her. She was gaunt again, with hollowed cheeks and eyes. The video was only a few seconds long, but it was enough to let me know she was alone, and her addict brain had won again.

I left a twenty on the table and ran out of the restaurant.

Back at my apartment, I threw clothes in a bag and speed-dialed Hayden. She picked up after one ring.

"Is she back?" she asked, breathless.

"No. We're going to find her. Can you leave tonight? Or tomorrow morning?"

"Yeah! Are we really going to LA?" she shrieked.

"You bet we are."

We caught the first direct flight out of the twin cities that night. The whole time we were airborne, I couldn't read, couldn't watch a movie. My mind kept replaying Ananda falling and lurching, like a slow-motion video. I glanced at Hayden, asleep beside me, her mouth open like a lamb.

By the time we touched down five hours later, I had a plan.

"This is heaven!" Hayden threw her arms out into the balmy air outside the airport. "Happy New Year to us."

I walked to the nearest taxi with a light on. The driver leapt to action and muscled our bags into the trunk. He opened the back door and I slid in. Hayden climbed in next to me.

"Beverly Hills, Metcalf Hotel, please."

We started to move and my heart enlivened. We were in the same city as Ananda, and soon enough, we'd find her and help her. We rode past palm trees silhouetted against the smeary sunset.

"Mag, there's no snow, no parkas, no snow boots, no warming up the car!"

I nodded. The escape from the dark St. Paul apartment into the warm, humid air made me feel like summer had never ended. People walked by in open-toed shoes, and there wasn't a dirty snowbank in sight. As we passed the 'Welcome to LA' sign, I crossed my fingers. I hoped we would be welcomed, and that we'd find Ananda before it was too late.

Our adjoining rooms in the hotel weren't fancy, but they didn't need to be. We just needed a place to crash.

After throwing our luggage into the rooms and changing, Hayden and I met up in my room.

"What's your plan to find Ananda?" she asked.

"We'll hit up all the hot spots — all the places Ananda has been to in the last four years."

"It might take me a while to find all of them."

"I know. Let's start with the one she was at last night."

"Okay, but if we're going clubbing, you need to change. You can't wear that out."

I put my hand on my hips. "What do you have against turtlenecks and chinos?"

"Don't worry, I'll fix you up."

"We should hurry." I looked at my watch. "It's getting late."

She cocked her head. "We'll obviously need an energy drink for you too, because ten o'clock is early. Come on."

She placed her hand on my back and guided me into her room. She rummaged in her bags and threw an orange printed dress at me. "This is a loaner. Try it on."

At first glance, it looked too gaudy, too bright, and far too young for me, but when I put it on, something magical happened. I no longer looked like an old-lady-in-training. It was as if years of emotional baggage lifted off me. Hayden nodded her approval.

"Now, let's do your makeup."

We stepped out of the hotel looking like different people from the ones who came in. I hailed a taxi while Hayden fidgeted on her phone.

It took us twenty minutes to get to the club where Ananda was last night, but once we were there, elation made my skin prickle. I recognized the place she'd tripped and the stretch of sidewalk where she'd lurched away. The club pounded beats. Well-heeled people wove around us, oblivious.

"Here's the plan," I said. "One of us goes in, and one of us waits outside. If you see her, call me. I'll do the same. Whoever's inside will talk to the bartenders and ask them to call us if they see Ananda. Do you have your phone on vibrate?"

Hayden grinned. "Look at you, all technologic."

"Can you look up the next club to go to?"

"Sure," she said, her fingers already flying over her phone.

I approached the door. A bouncer with bulging neck muscles threw up his hand. "Twenty."

I passed him a twenty-dollar bill and he opened the door. The bar took up the entire right side of the club. Laser lights pivoted over an empty dance floor. I looked in the lounge area, but didn't see Ananda's lanky frame. Maybe Hayden was right — maybe it was too early. I took a seat at the bar.

A bartender chatted up a couple seated near me. He poured them shots and then walked toward me, smiling like a game show host. "And what can I get for you?"

I hesitated. What did people drink these days? I was feeling adventurous. "Could I have a fireball?"

"Sure." He lifted an amber bottle from the back of the bar and poured a generous shot.

"I'm looking for Ananda. She was here last night."

His gaze flicked to me, all humor gone.

I tapped my business card on the counter. "Will you call me if she comes in here? Please?"

His mouth was a smug line. "Are you a fan?"

"I'm her manager. My name is Mag. I'm tr–" I stopped. The couple nearby had stopped talking. I leaned in closer. "I'm trying to help her, to make sure she doesn't get in more trouble."

"Oh yeah?" He set the drink down in front of me. "How much is it worth to you?"

"Two hundred?" I hadn't meant for it to come out as a question, it just had.

He glanced down the bar and took my card. "Yeah, I'll call you if she comes back, but I don't think it'll be anytime soon. She got kicked out last night for being too drunk."

I nodded. I doubted she was drunk, but if he wanted to call it that, I wasn't going to stop him. "Do you know any other clubs she goes to?"

He shrugged and looked at my purse. I ferreted out two fifty dollar bills from my billfold and slapped them on the counter, then lifted the shot glass and drained it. I gasped. The cinnamon liquor burned the inside of my mouth. The bartender pretended not to notice.

"She likes dance clubs, but she doesn't arrive until 1:00 am at the earliest. Try the Milk Bar. My friend works there and said she used to come around."

"Thanks." I ambled off the chair. My vision was woozy for a second, but I made it outside to Hayden. She took one look at me, threw an arm around my shoulder, and hailed a taxi.

We went to the Milk Bar and several others Ananda had supposedly visited, but we didn't see her at any of them. We continued until after 3:00 in the morning. My stack of business cards dwindled down. No one had called yet, but we'd made progress. We now had nine bartenders looking for her.

The next afternoon, I woke up with a hangover. We lunched at the hotel restaurant. That night, we hit up ten more bars, and the following, twelve.

Two weeks and two days after Hayden and I landed in LA, while I was waiting for a bartender at our fourth club canvas of the night, my phone lit up with an LA area code. I fumbled to answer it and ran outside. Hayden's eyes grew wide when she saw me on the phone.

"Hello?" I asked.

"Hey," a masculine voice said. "Ananda's here at the Warp. You said two hundred, right?"

"Yes! Thank you so much." I hung up the phone and grabbed Hayden. "She's at the Warp!"

"Let's go!"

We arrived at the Warp in twenty minutes, just after 2:00 am. Blue neon lights rimmed the two-story building, and dance music pounded.

"Wait here," I said to Hayden.

"Are you sure?" She caught my arm. "Wouldn't it be better if it was me?"

I hesitated. "I'm a therapist."

Hayden nodded, eyebrows raised. "Good luck."

A line of people waited to get into the Warp. Some of them eyed me as I walked to the bouncer.

"Who does she think she is?" someone hissed. "We've been waiting for an hour."

The bouncer crossed his arms and fixed me with a glare.

"Hi. I'm Ananda's manager." I pulled a card out of my bag and offered it to him.

He didn't take it. "So what?"

I leaned in close. "I'll pay you two hundred dollars to get in. I have to see her."

His face remained impassive. He shifted his gaze to the street.

"Five hundred," I hissed under my breath.

I dug the cash out and furtively held it against his meaty leg. He palmed it without a word, though his face cracked with a smile. He pushed open the door for me. People in line complained, but I rushed in.

Beautiful people packed the club, lit by pendulous Edison bulbs. The same blue neon piping ran inside the bar along the brick wall. The bartender who'd called met me at the end of the bar.

"Where is she?"

"Beats me," he said, his palm open.

I evaluated him and took a deep breath. He seemed honest enough. I handed over the cash. He walked away without thanking me.

I made my way through the club, trying to blend in, scanning the crowd for Ananda. When I didn't see her on the first floor, I climbed the stairs, which was no easy feat in my new heels. I watched the people dancing, my back against the wall.

After ten minutes, I could tell none of them was Ananda. I'd been punked.

I walked to the bathroom and sat down on a toilet seat, trying to figure out what to do. I pulled out my phone. No calls. That meant Hayden hadn't seen her, either. I wondered if Ananda had snuck out the back door.

I slumped forward, letting my head fall into my hands. On the floor of the stall beside me lay a studded Karl Lagerfeld purse. I perked up and peered under the stall. Matching black heels.

My breath caught. It could be Ananda, or it could be someone else entirely. I didn't know what to do. I couldn't call her name out. She might run, and I didn't want to chase her down. There was only one thing I could do.

I steeled myself. It was now or never.

I crept under the stall.

A blonde bent over, snorting lines of white powder from the toilet tank lid. When she finished, she threw her head back.

My heart lifted. It was Ananda.

She saw me and jumped back, her mouth flying open.

"It's okay," I said, adjusting my dress.

She backed against the stall. A halo of powder crusted around one of her nostrils. She looked worse than she had in the video. Her skin had a gray tinge, and her eyes were glazed beyond anything I remembered, besides the night when the House of Transformation changed everything. My heart clamored for her.

"This can't be real," she said. She reached out to poke me. "Oh, God. How is this real?"

I bit my lip. I'd planned what I'd say when I found her, but I never imagined it'd go down like this, with me crashing her bathroom stall.

"Ananda, I'm here to help you."

She embraced me in one of her death-tight grips. I was surprised, but my arms flew up to hold her back. My heart thundered. I could save her, and this time, I vowed I would. I'd make sure she never backslid into the pits of addiction again.

"How'd you know?" she asked, tears forming in her eyelids. "How'd you know I was here? Are we psychically linked again?"

I nodded, even though it wasn't the truth. "I knew you were here. It was like you were calling me."

Her eyes bugged out and she clutched me harder. "Yes, I was. But..." She gazed at the floor as if she felt sleepy all of the sudden.

"What is it?"

She closed her eyes and collapsed. I tried to hold her up, but she was too heavy. Her head sank onto my shoulder, then she shuddered and something warm ran down my back. I tensed. She'd just thrown up on me.

"I was going to go back to Paris..." she murmured. "But I changed my mind. I tried..."

"You're tired?"

"I tried to overdose." Tears streamed down her face, then her eyes rolled back into her head.

I fumbled for my phone. With trembling hands, I texted Hayden.

Call 911. Upstairs women's bathroom.

268

Hayden responded immediately.

On it.

Ananda had gone limp. Was she dying in my arms? I knew she didn't want to go to the hospital, but I didn't give a fuck. If we didn't get her to a hospital, she might die. I wanted her to live, to survive this. She shivered beneath her minidress. I held her as she blinked and came to.

"How many pills did you take?" I asked.

"Seven, but I have eight more. I can't take the rest..."

"Why? Is it because you want to live?"

She looked at me piteously and nodded.

"I want you to live too." I stroked her hair.

Her body convulsed and she threw up again, this time on the floor.

I looked around, panicked. Where was the ambulance? What was taking so long?

I tried to focus. I wadded up toilet paper and cleaned her face. She was still. I couldn't tell if she was breathing or not. I slapped her cheek and she inhaled sharply.

To my surprise, she laughed. I started laughing too, despite the tears flowing down my face.

"Don't make me slap you again," I said.

"You're so abusive," she croaked, the hint of a smile on her lips. "Why do I keep going back to you?"

"I love you. I always have. Even when you thought I was against you, I loved you so much. I just want you to live."

She looked at me through slitted eyes, as if to say she'd try, then they clouded over. I slapped her face again, only this time, she didn't respond. She just lay there.

Paramedics ran into the bathroom, shouting. I unlocked the bathroom door and they charged in. They tried to talk with her. One of them shone a flashlight in her eyes. I stepped back, unable to say a word. It was almost like before, seven years ago, only I wouldn't let her out of my sight this time. I knew the paramedics recognized her, but I didn't care about her secrets now that her life was on the line.

They lifted her onto a stretcher, her body jostling like it was weightless. I followed them through the club, opening doors as we went. The bouncer regarded me sorely as I passed him. A few people in line said 'Oh my God!' Camera phones lifted in our direction.

Hayden ran out to meet us. An ambulance revved nearby on the sidewalk. The doors opened and they loaded Ananda into it. I followed, but a medic kept me from getting too close. When I tried to enter, he put a hand on my chest.

"I need to be with her!"

"Only a family member or a spouse can ride in the back." He tried to shut the doors in my face, but I pried them open.

"I'm her manager," I squeaked.

"Ma'am, I just said only a family member or a spouse-"

"She's my girlfriend!" I shouted. I shoved him aside and climbed into the back, finding a cramped seat next to the other stunned paramedics who'd obviously just heard what I shouted. I didn't care about the ramifications, about what the media would say. I was all Ananda had, and I was going to come through for her. I reached for her hand.

"Let's go!" someone said.

The siren wound up. I clutched a rail as the doors closed and we took a wide turn.

Hayden stood on the sidewalk, looking at me through the ambulance doors. I hoped she'd catch up to us.

The medics worked on Ananda in a frenzy. One of them injected her with a shot, another put a saline drip in her vein.

"She's going into cardiac arrest!" one of them shouted.

They pulled out the paddles and charged them. I watched, breathless, feeling like my own heart had stopped. I squeezed her hand, willing her to stay. She couldn't leave now, not after all she'd been through.

They jolted her heart.

Nothing happened.

Again.

Nothing.

The last time they jolted her, she jerked up, eyes wide. She fumbled with the straps as if she could escape. But when our eyes connected, something changed in her. She relaxed, or maybe she resigned. The medics pushed her back on the bed and stuck her with another needle.

We gazed into each other's eyes. My world was right there. She didn't have to talk. Her eyes said it all. How sorry she was, how she knew she'd made a mistake, how terrible she felt. And maybe even how relieved she was.

When we arrived at the hospital, the paramedics rushed her into the ER. I had to stay in a waiting room, but a nurse told me they pumped her stomach and put more saline in her system. Once she was stable, they moved her to a private room in the ICU. The doctor put her under for a couple of days until her organs could recover from the shock.

The next day, she was moved to a non-ICU area. She slept like Sleeping Beauty in a hospital bed, her face filling out by the hour with the rich hospital tube-food. Hayden and I took turns holding her hand, sleeping, and ordering food from the hospital cafeteria. We memorized the nurses' and doctors' names. Her room had a bathroom, so we never had to face the mob of press and fans just outside the door. We'd have to sooner or later, but I was too angry at the moment. The media were still demonizing her.

I needed time to calm down and write a statement. I had a couple of days before Ananda was scheduled to wake up. Then, it would be time for her to face the truth.

Well, almost the truth.

Chapter 31. Regeneration

I stood before a wall of cameras and reporters. There were so many blinding lights behind all the photographers and videographers, I felt as if I were in a pressroom instead of a hospital hallway. Countless microphones clustered in front of me like a bouquet. A sea of faces pressed forward, waiting for my statement. It'd been two mornings since Ananda was moved from the ICU into a regular hospital bed.

I cleared my throat and looked down at the words I'd written on my paper.

"Good morning. My name is Margaret Woods, and I'm Ananda Dawn's manager. I want to reassure everyone that Ananda is going to be just fine. Two nights ago, she combined alcohol and xyritav. The effects of that combination can be very dangerous. As soon as she felt ill, we called an ambulance. Doctors expect her to make a full recovery."

I took a deep breath. "She wanted me to relay an important message to all her fans." I swallowed and turned the page.

Of course, none of it was true. Ananda didn't have a message — she was still knocked out. But John and I decided to come clean for her so she didn't have to lie anymore. The duality had gone on long enough.

"Ananda has had a problem with drugs for quite some time. Her message is simple. They aren't the solution to life's problems. She's going sober. With your love and support, we can get through this together. Thank you."

I turned to leave, but a clamor erupted of a hundred people asking questions all at once.

I faced the crowd, my neck and shoulders tense. I could answer a couple of questions, but that was all my nerves could handle. I pointed to a pasty journalist in the middle with a raised hand. The room hushed.

"When will Ananda herself make a statement?"

"She's taking a break from the spotlight right now, so I can't answer that."

"Will she still perform at the Grammys?" another reporter asked.

"Yes." I hoped it was true.

"Did Ananda try to take her life?" someone shouted.

I shook my head. John and I decided we wouldn't tell anyone she was suicidal. We didn't think anyone deserved to know, except the people who could help her with it. The media might use it to destroy her even more than they already had.

"Ananda behaved recklessly, but no, she wasn't suicidal. Before the ambulance arrived, she told me she didn't want to die."

"Isn't this just another stunt for publicity?" a man with greasy hair asked.

My eyes narrowed in on him. I recognized him from outside the Indian restaurant and from my lawn. He was the paparazzo that drove Ananda crazy, the one who'd taken photos of her naked without her consent. Anger seethed inside me as I stared him down.

"This is a very serious event, and we're taking it very seriously. That's all the time I have. Thank you for coming."

I turned on my heel before they could ask anything else, stormed past our newly hired enormous bodyguard, and slipped into the hospital room. I closed the door and leaned against the wall, trembling with fear. Public speaking had never been one of my strong points.

Ananda lay there, still in her induced coma, surrounded by several vases overfilled with roses. A monitor nearby beeped with her subdued heartbeat. She was scheduled to wake up sometime soon.

"You did great," John said, cupping my shoulder. "You hit all the right points."

Hayden nodded. "Now we just have to deal with the dust settling. People are bound to talk. I'll rally the fans."

After a few minutes, Ananda stirred and opened her eyes. She looked at the tubes in her arm and her eyes grew large.

"Hey." I reached for her free hand. "It's okay."

Ananda had been afraid of having a hospital record, no matter how confidential it was supposed to be. Now, it was all out in the open. My speech to the paparazzi ended her lies and the shame that came with them.

She blinked slowly, as if resigning to this outcome. Perhaps she realized she'd pushed it to the limit, right to the cusp of death. What would've happened if I hadn't found her that night? What if she'd stayed home instead of going out?

A moment later, the nurse walked in, a placid smile on her face. She reached for the clipboard and marked Ananda's vitals.

"I see you've woken up, dear," she said loudly. "How are you feeling?"

"I'm-" Her voice cracked. She cleared her throat. "I'm not deaf. I can hear you just fine." Ananda winked.

Despite the grim surroundings, Hayden and I both cracked smiles.

"You're lucky to be alive," the nurse said. "Do you know where you are?"

"Hospital."

"Well your vitals look pretty good. I'll let the doctor know you're awake." She hung the clipboard onto a hook and left the room.

Ananda's bleary eyes met ours. "I'm sorry."

"I know," I said. "It's okay. We're here for you, but..." I glanced at John. "Hayden and I are going to give you some time with John. We'll be back in a little bit."

We gathered our purses and laptops. As I closed the door, I heard John ask how she was feeling.

The hospital hallway had been almost completely cleared of the news junket that was present just moments ago, but a couple of reporters remained. One guy with a camera approached us, but our security guard blocked him as we shuttled past.

"Where are we going?" Hayden asked.

"Cafeteria. I need coffee."

We walked in silence for a while. She looked at me from the corner of her eye.

"What do you think John is saying to her?" Hayden asked.

"He's probably trying to get an idea of her mindset. He's also going to tell her the press knows about her addiction, so she doesn't have to hide it anymore. I hope he can put a positive spin on everything she's been through."

"I can't believe he cancelled all his other appointments for the next week," Hayden said.

We picked up orange trays and started down the cafeteria line.

I eyed a hairnetted attendant and picked up a salad. "We have to whisper."

"What do you think Ananda and Kitty did when they ran away?"

"Besides lots of xyritav? I have no idea. I only hope Kitty isn't in the same predicament."

I had mixed feelings about Kitty. I was still mad she got Ananda back on xyritav and basically led her toward rock bottom. On the positive side, there was nowhere else for Ananda to go but up, at least, that's what I hoped. I couldn't imagine anything lower than this, except dying, of course.

Hayden and I ate but didn't talk. Without even asking, I knew she was committed to this. She was loyal — one of the reasons why I loved her. When we were done eating, I pulled out a folded piece of paper from my pocket and laid it flat on the table between us. It was a schedule, with a column of events. GRAMMY was written at the bottom next to the date.

"I have a plan," I said. "I'm warning you, it's intense. If we figure Ananda will need two weeks to suss out her performance, the stage, her dress, and her makeup, that leaves her two weeks to get better and finish her single."

"But we don't know how much longer the doctors will want to keep her," Hayden said, her lips pursing.

"I know. That's the scary part."

"What else do you have planned?" She craned her neck to look at the paper.

"Now that she's awake and doing okay, I can hire the choreographer and the background dancers."

"Okay. I can work on the dress and makeup appointments

for the day of the Grammys.”

“I hope we can pull this off.”

“We will.” Determination straightened her features. “Whatever she does will be epic, as long as she remains sober.”

“Right,” I said. “We’ll do our best. The rest is up to her.”

“Now that she’s awake, I can update her social media. I just have to figure out what to say.”

“Maybe you could say ‘Feeling lots better. Thanks for the support’?”

She tilted her head and made a face. “Too cheesy. It’ll need to be good. I’ll work on it.”

“Hayden.” I took her hand. “I know you sacrificed a lot to do this.”

“You mean my fast food job?” She laughed. “I wouldn’t call that sacrifice.”

“I mean — you’re good for her. Whatever happens, just remember that.”

Fear flashed in her eyes. We both knew what could happen to Ananda. She already broke away from us once to find xyritav. What would stop her from trying again? Sometimes a bright flame burns down the whole candle, whether it wants to or not.

I hoped Ananda would be strong and survive, but I knew we could only monitor her so much. In reality, once we were out of the hospital, she’d be surrounded by gaggles of people. It’d be hard to keep track of her all the time. I had to trust things would work out without helicopter-moming her.

We returned to the hospital room just as Ananda and John appeared to be finishing. She looked radiant despite her red eyes.

“There she is.” Hayden leaned down for a hug.

“Hi,” I said, hugging her.

Ananda held us tightly, just like the old days. My nose burned and I blinked away tears. When I pulled away, tears shone in her eyes too.

“Are you having a breakthrough?” I asked.

She nodded weakly, sniffing back tears and looking at the ceiling, eyelids fluttering.

John nodded toward the door. I followed him out. He pulled out a prescription pad and scribbled on it.

"How is she?" I asked.

"She knows how lucky she is. It sounds like she was in pretty bad shape, but she's recovering. The doctor came by. He still wants to keep her on anti-psychotics."

"For how much longer?"

"I don't know. They want to observe her a little longer before they release her. In the meantime, Hayden should pick up these prescriptions. I'm going to see her every day now through next week. I'll be back tomorrow." He patted my shoulder as he left.

I walked back into the hospital room.

Ananda sat up in bed. "John told me about my new 'transparency.'"

"Truth is a good thing."

She looked down at her blanket. "I guess you didn't have much of a choice, since several people saw me leave the club in a gurney. I feel a little relieved, actually. Can I just ask one favor?"

"Sure, what?"

"If the paparazzi get a photo of me leaving the hospital, it'll all be over. They'll tweak the picture to make me look worse and run the story for months."

"She's right," Hayden said. "A photo like that would set us back."

"Okay, so you're saying we have to think of an escape plan? I think we can handle that." I gave Hayden a sly look.

She smiled. That was another thing I loved about her — she was game for anything.

Hayden and I tried to make the extended hospital stay fun. We bought matching pajama sets, binge-watched movies and television, ate bonbons, and played board games. Ananda couldn't wait to get out of the hospital, and I didn't blame her. I'd started to dream about the long tiled corridors and fluorescent lighting.

By the time Ananda was allowed to leave, nine days after being admitted near death's door, she'd overcome all her detox symptoms and was almost as healthy as when she lived at my apartment.

I'd been working on our escape plan for a few days. All the entrances and exits were monitored by the media — every one except the kitchen delivery door. I borrowed a dining cart, the kind with metal doors to keep food hot or cold. Ananda tried to fit in the box and found it to be cramped, but doable. The plan was for us to whisk her through the hospital, into the kitchen, and to an unmarked van with a private driver. It was ridiculous, but Ananda agreed it was better than walking through the lobby doors.

At 11:00 pm on the night of the escape, Hayden and I donned starched nurse scrubs and mouth guards. Ananda changed into a hoodie and yoga pants, then contorted into the cart. I tried to close the door and bumped into her legs.

"Ow," she said.

"Can you tuck your legs in a little more?" I asked.

"Yeah. How long do I have to be in here?"

"Ten minutes? Fifteen?"

Ananda sighed from within the cart. "Just don't waste any time, okay?"

"Everyone ready?" I asked.

Hayden nodded. "Let's go."

We wheeled Ananda out of the hospital room and past the security guard. We'd filled him in an hour before. I'd asked him to stay behind to preserve the illusion that Ananda was still in there. He winced as we walked by, as if to say 'you're making a terrible decision.' I frowned at him behind my mask. What did he know?

Hayden ran ahead to scope out the hallway, her curls bouncing. I pushed the cart and discovered one of the wheels was flat. I hadn't noticed it earlier, but now that Ananda was in there, I saw how bad it was. It thumped loudly as I speed-walked toward the elevators. I turned a corner, pushing hard.

Hayden waited by the elevator, her foot tapping nervously. Numbers lit up above the elevator doors, but I was too agitated to pay attention.

A muted metallic bang rang out as Ananda shifted in the cart. A middle aged man and a woman in her sixties glanced in my direction. My heart hammered hard. I turned my eyes toward the wall and pretended to be interested in the wallpaper, afraid if I looked them in the eyes, I'd give away our secret.

At last, a resounding ding announced the elevator's arrival. The doors floated open. I went in first and faced the rear. Hayden came in, holding the other side of the cart.

The doors closed and we started moving, but I nearly jumped when I realized the elevator was going up instead of down. Hayden freaked out too, her eyes wide as she jammed the button for the ground floor.

Ananda shifted noisily again. I felt the heat of gazes on me. I pretended I'd made that sound by hitting my leg against the box, only it didn't make the same sound. The man eyed me suspiciously and tapped on his phone. Surely everyone knew Ananda Dawn was staying here. Did they recognize me from the teleconference, even with the mouth guard?

The woman got off on the tenth floor, where we picked up a young mother and a child. On the fifteenth floor, we picked up a couple of teenagers. The man got off on the twenty-first floor.

Thankfully, we started to go down again. I tried to breathe, but the air seemed to have been sucked out of the elevator.

We waited through several more stops before finally arriving at the ground floor. The bell rang and the doors rolled open. I pushed hard and wheeled Ananda out, breathing a little easier.

"Which way?" Hayden whispered.

I twirled, looking at the signs. There weren't signs for the kitchen, and neither of us remembered which way to go. To the left were more hospital rooms. To the right, administrative offices.

"I don't know," I said, my eyes crimping with worry.

"The right?"

"Okay." I took a deep breath and pushed the cart, but the

flat wheel stuck to the ground. Hayden got behind the cart and both of us pushed. The flat wheel finally rotated with a loud smack.

We walked down the hallway and finally saw a sign for the kitchen, pointing us ahead. Hayden beamed at me. We were going in the right direction. We ran down the hall.

As we passed a nursing station, a mass of reporters and paparazzi lurked behind thick glass exit doors. I stopped and backed the cart into an alcove, nausea rising in my stomach. They hadn't seen us yet. But to get to the kitchen, we'd have to pass right in front of them.

"What are we going to do?" Hayden whispered.

I shrugged. What option did we have? Backtrack and find the kitchen another way?

Ananda bumped again within the cart. My watch said twenty minutes had passed, much longer than we'd promised. I doubted she could last much longer.

"Maybe they won't recognize us with the mouth guards on," I said.

Hayden nodded.

We put our heads down and pushed. My heart throbbed with adrenaline as we walked past the glass doors. Hayden was so hunched down, she looked like a turtle. I turned my head away from the doors, pretending to talk to Hayden in the hopes that our faces would be blocked from the reporters.

We'd just passed the glass doors when Ananda shifted again. A loud bang resounded from the cart. Several people looked in our direction, including the Greaseball. He locked eyes with me for a terrifying moment. I pushed past the doors and ran toward the kitchen, panting.

The glass doors opened with a whooshing noise behind me.

"How much longer?" Ananda asked from the cart.

"Shh!" I said, pushing harder.

I looked back. A trail of people with cameras followed.

"Shit," Hayden said.

The doors of the kitchen were in sight. Hayden ran ahead, swiped a key fob, then opened the doors as I pushed the cart into a room. We slammed the doors shut behind us.

I bent over and caught my breath.

Hayden shook her head.

A woman with hair the color of rusted steel looked up at us from chopping carrots.

"Hold it. What're you doing here? I don't recognize you."

"We're new," Hayden chirped, her hands fluttering up. "Is Jerome here?"

"He clocked out half an hour ago," the woman said, hands on her hips as she stared Hayden down.

"Time for us to leave then!" Hayden said. She nodded toward the back of the room but my knees locked.

"I'll just- return the cart." I pushed until the lumpy wheel gave.

"Let me see your key fob," the woman said to Hayden.

"Sure." She shot me a glance that said *get Ananda out of here!* "It's right here in my pocket. Or maybe the other pocket?"

"You just used it to open the door. Where is it?"

I pushed the cart into the back room. It was a maze of aluminum sideboards and hanging pots and pans. Where was the back door? I walked past pots boiling on burners and tureens stacked beside a double sink. One guy scrubbed dishes absent-mindedly while another mopped the tile floor.

Finally I saw the back door. I kept my head down and pushed.

Ananda shifted again. The cart tipped on the bad wheel. It started to roll. I took my hands off just in time. The metal doors flew open with a metallic bang and Ananda tumbled out, right at the feet of the mopper.

The old man jumped back, his mouth open. Ananda got up slowly, almost slipping on the wet floor. He caught her hand, staring in stunned awe.

"Thank you," she said.

"You're welcome."

I read his name badge. "Hey, Harry, we have to go out the back door without anyone seeing us. Can you help us?"

He was dazed, but he nodded.

"Hayden!" I called.

She rushed into the room. The old woman followed behind her, rattling off a battery of words, but when she saw Ananda, she stopped.

Harry held open the back door. We skated over the wet floor toward it.

"Oh my God," the woman said. "I can't believe Ananda Dawn is in my kitchen. I have to get an autograph."

"What're you talking about?" asked the dishwasher, shaking the suds from his gloves.

"We don't have time," I said. "We have to get out of here!"

I started to push Ananda toward the open kitchen door, where our van waited in the dark night, backed up to the door. I could see the open back doors and the red glow of the taillights.

"Of course we have time," Ananda purred. She walked toward the woman, her head held high as the woman gave her a yellow notepad.

I was impressed. It was as if a whole other personality came over her. It was the most confident I'd seen her since Christmas Eve. However, as proud as I was, the press was trying to find us. I knew the Greaseball recognized me. His eyes were too sharp, too intense.

"Ananda, we have to get out of here. The press knows we're leaving. Some of them saw us, including that one that doesn't like you."

"We're clear for now," Hayden said, peering out the back door.

I shot her a look. She shrugged.

"Can you make it out to Debbie?" the woman asked before turning to Hayden with an admonishing look. "You should've told me it was Ananda Dawn. I would've let you do just about anything."

"Will you sign this for me?" the dishwasher asked, holding a receipt.

"Of course." Ananda scribbled on it.

"Uh oh," Hayden said. "We have company!"

I looked out the door. Headlights illuminated our van.

"Let's go!" I yelled.

"Bye." Ananda waved, lifted her hood up, and ran for the door. I ran after her, but we were too late. The Greaseball and his crew ran toward the van, flashes popping and video cameras streaming. Ananda jumped into the back of the van with a thump. Hayden and I ran in after her, the paps right behind us.

"Go!" I shouted to the driver.

I held onto a seat and reached for one of the open doors right as the driver punched the gas. My hand slipped and I was thrown toward the open doors of the van. Fear jolted through me. Asphalt rose before my eyes, except I stopped — something had caught me. I looked back and saw Ananda holding onto my scrubs with her death grip, her other hand firmly on the metal brackets below the seats. She pulled me toward the front of the van.

The doors flapped wildly. Hayden held onto a seat belt, but couldn't reach the doors to close them. I extended my arm, but the van swerved. One of the doors banged near me. I stretched my arm out, grasped the cold metal of the handle, then slammed the door shut. We swerved again and I caught the other handle and closed the door.

I looked through the tinted windows at the photographers scrambling in the distance and sighed with relief.

"Well, we almost got away with it," Hayden said.

"If it wasn't for that stupid wheel." I laughed despite everything that had just happened.

"That was amazing," Ananda said. "I feel so exhilarated, like I'm a new person!"

"But we got caught," I said. "They have pictures of us, and they're probably harassing the kitchen staff now. And they know we're on the move. I just hope they're not fast enough to follow us."

"I know they took pictures," Ananda said. "But they can't be great. I had a hood up and I was moving pretty fast. They'll probably be too blurry to use. So we did it. We got out of there without getting a hospital photo. I'm so relieved."

"I think you're right," Hayden said. "They only really got a good shot of me as I jumped into the van."

"I'm surprised they were smart enough to find us at all." Ananda laughed. "Usually someone has to tell them every detail, and even then, they still get it wrong."

"Do you think they're evolving?" Hayden asked in mock horror.

"Whatever happens, it'll be fine," Ananda said. "Maybe it was my time in the hospital, or maybe it's because everything is out in the open, but I feel like I can deal with things better now."

I smiled at her and squeezed her hand. It was a nice juxtaposition — her reassuring us, instead of the other way around. I liked this new Ananda.

"Ugh," Hayden said, looking at her phone mirror. "My hair is a mess."

I squinted at her curls. "Doesn't your hair always look like that?"

She cocked her head at me. "Thanks Mag. You really know how to make a girl feel better."

"I mean it always looks good. You always look good."

"Hayden, you look fine," Ananda said, "but if you have a problem, you'd better fix it now. They're probably following us."

The paparazzi were waiting for us at the new hotel I'd chosen for our crashpad. I'm not sure how they knew. Maybe someone working at the hotel tipped them off.

We walked out of the van and into a dozen cameras. We pushed them out of our way as we walked toward the hotel.

"Ananda Dawn! Over here!"

"Ananda, how does it feel to be sober?"

"Ananda, you look beautiful! Over here."

"Ananda!"

We kept a fast pace, our heads down. From the corner of my eye, I saw Ananda break away from us, face the cameras, and wave. I shot her a questioning glance. She jogged back to us.

"What?" she asked. "I've missed this."

I shrugged, running to keep up with Hayden as we strode into the hotel doors.

"Finally, a real bed again." Hayden fell back onto her bed.

I smiled and unpacked my clothes into the drawers. Our suite had three bedrooms and a common room. It wasn't the biggest suite in the hotel, but it was the best I'd ever stayed in.

"Hayden, could you get me some organic strawberries and hemp milk?" Ananda asked before stepping into her bathroom. Seconds later, she closed the door and the shower hissed.

Hayden rolled over and typed the items into her phone. "What else do we need?"

"Let me give you a credit card," I said.

"Make sure Ananda pays you back for last time," Hayden said. "Don't let her sneak out again."

"I hid her purse. She isn't going anywhere. But be careful out there."

"Don't worry about me. Worry about those deadlines. They're going to be here before we know it."

"Yeah, I know."

After Hayden left, I looked at the schedule. I'd crossed off a few dates, but we had less than two weeks until her Grammy performance. There were so many things to do — people to call, appointments to make...

But before I delved into that rabbit hole, there was something I needed to do. I picked up the letter from the state board of psychologists, opened my laptop, and begin writing.

To whom it concerns,

I am writing to ask for the reinstatement of my psychology license. I'm aware my book about Ananda Dawn diagnosed her with a disorder publicly, but I need to tell you my publisher and agent changed the book to be more sensational. Attached is the last version I sent them, without any diagnosis.

The book also revealed personal drug use from my history with her. Several other psychology professionals have similar situations, only their histories aren't public. I stopped doing drugs of any kind seven years ago, and I've been giving back to the community ever since.

I feel the decision by the Board to revoke my license was hyperbolic and myopic. My work at the New Beginnings Center has improved the lives of many people, and one day, I may wish to continue that work. Please reconsider my situation.

Sincerely, Margaret Woods

I took a deep breath. The letter contained a lie. I'd used xyritav in the past seven years — when Ananda drugged me — but they didn't need to know about that. As long as they didn't demand a drug test, I'd be safe.

I sent the email and said a little prayer.

Chapter 32. The New Future

After my romantic breakfast with Brad, he suggested I stay at his warehouse. I agreed to it. The House of Transformation was too dreary. Living there alone was bringing me down, and it didn't look like Ananda and I would ever make up. With him, I wouldn't be alone, and I could work on my collages using his computer.

We stopped by the House of Transformation on the way back to the warehouse so I could pack a bag. Brad waited in his car.

"Hello?" I called out.

I hoped Ananda wasn't there so I could return her dress and escape, undetected. No one was there except Rosie, dancing at the top of the stairs. I walked right through her as if she weren't there and threw clothes into a backpack. I wanted nothing more than to get out of the house as quickly as possible. I practically ripped the white dress off and hid it in Ananda's closet. I never wanted to wear another piece of her clothing again. I threw on a vintage polyester dress, tossed my toothbrush and make-up in the bag, and ran out of the house.

Brad and I luxuriated in each other's company. We walked to parks, lounges, and took elevators to the tops of skyscrapers to look over the city. I was nervous when he wanted to go to the Arts District coffeehouse, but Ricky wasn't working, and I didn't see Ananda or anyone else I knew there either. It'd be awkward to explain to Ananda that I was dating him, or whatever our relationship was.

When we were in line at the coffeehouse, my eyes wandered to the locally made mugs on the back wall.

"They're the same color as the sky today," I said, squeezing his hand.

When we ordered, Brad asked the barista to put my coffee in one of those mugs. It was over thirty dollars, but he didn't bat an eye, just laid down his credit card.

He handed me my steaming coffee in that perfect, hand-thrown mug. "For all the blue skies ahead."

After three days filled with adventure, he went back to work. I uploaded more collages and edited out the folds and bruises, playing with the colors and adding textured overlays. It was a redefinition of my art. It made them even sharper, even more striking.

I was still surprised and sad that being an artist hadn't worked out financially, but at least I had Brad. He uplifted me as much as Ananda's curt remarks and searing gazes punched my spirit down. He joked we were both survivors of Hurricane Ananda. It made me laugh, though I still felt devastated. I missed her.

After a week, I ran out of clean clothes and collages to tweak. I had no excuse not to go back to the House of Transformation. I drove there and sat in my car. The house looked ominous from the street, as if something inside looked back at me through the dark windows. I took a deep breath and opened the door.

I wandered through the house. I heard no one, saw no one. After climbing the stairs to the second floor, I heard a conversation coming from the attic.

"Hello?" I called out, walking up the creaking attic stairs.

"So, the prodigal daughter returns," Jared said. Someone laughed.

My eyes adjusted to the bright lights. Ananda sat on a stool, wearing a gown and long gloves. She sneered at me before turning away to face the wall.

My chest and limbs felt weighed down. I wondered if Jared had said anything to her about how sorry I was. If so, it didn't seem to have worked.

"We haven't seen you for a while," Jared said. "Where've you been staying?"

I scoffed. "Like you guys care where I am?"

"Of course we care," he said, fiddling with his camera.

"Whatever. I just came by to grab some stuff. I'm moving out."

"Are you sure?" he asked, his face troubled. "Things are just starting to get interesting."

"Well I can't afford to live here. I'm broke. I didn't sell anything at the last Art Party."

He shook his head and sighed. "Stevey said he's never having another Art Party again after that last fiasco, and he means it this time."

"What happened?"

"The same people who crashed the last one scared everyone away with some adult toys. Stevey called the police on them. The rest of the night was dead. Hey, who was that guy you left with?"

"No one," I lied, feeling my face turn scarlet.

Ananda turned to me, her eyes suddenly alert.

"Come on, who was he?" he asked.

"I didn't know who he was." It was partially true. I hadn't known who Brad was when I left with him. But I didn't want to talk about him. It'd only alienate me further from Ananda. Besides, if my relationship track record held up, it would fizzle out in a week or so anyway.

"I wish Stevey's Art Parties hadn't gone down that way," I said.

"Yeah. I can't say I'm surprised, but it's sad. It's the end of an era, but a new one is on the horizon. The next Art Party will be here, at the House of Transformation. You should come. The theme is 'Spirits in the Material World.' Ananda remade the song and she's going to sing it."

A ghostly shiver walked up my spine. I looked around the exposed rafter beams, expecting to see Rosie, but I didn't see her anywhere. I wondered if it was another ghost. My fears rose to the front of my thoughts.

1. *Fear of the unknown*
2. *Fear of the supernatural*
3. *Fear of losing my friends.*

"Are you sure you want to have that theme in a haunted

house?" I asked.

Jared shrugged, lifting his camera to snap a few pictures of Ananda. The silence between clicks was thick.

"Hey, Ananda?" I asked, facing her.

She looked straight at the camera, silent.

"Are we okay?" I asked. "We haven't talked for a while."

"Whatever," she muttered.

I side-stepped until I was between her and Jared. "Ananda, tell me how I can make it up to you."

She looked up at me, her mouth a slash. "Why should I bother? You don't believe in me anymore. You just want to knock me down."

"That's not true. Kitty told me all those things about you, so I asked you about them. I don't care if you lied. I really don't. I miss you."

She lifted her chin and sighed. Something shifted behind her eyes. "Well, I didn't lie about everything. It's true I've never been to Europe, but I read books about it. I really did stare at that Bosch painting for hours when I was little, only it was in a book too. And my mom wasn't a Stepford wife, but she tried to be one before she went crazy."

I nodded. It finally made sense. She'd lashed out to protect herself. She'd become so enmeshed in the fabrication of another past, she was afraid of anyone who threatened to expose the truth.

"I'm sorry I asked," I said. "I didn't know it was a sensitive subject."

She sighed. "Just don't tell anyone else about it. I think I'd lose my mind if the whole city knew."

"I won't tell anyone... So are we good, then?"

"Yeah. You don't have to move out." She gave me an apologetic smile.

My chest swelled with hope. I might have friends again. I hugged her and felt her warm arms encircle me.

"You should come to the party," she said.

"As long as you don't invite the Mayonnaise Bandits." I laughed.

"We won't. I'm really excited to sing for everyone. It'll be like my vision."

Jared arranged Ananda for the next picture. I could tell the conversation was over. I waved to them and walked down the stairs.

I opened the door to my room. Clothes were strewn everywhere and the bed was unmade. After staying in Brad's warehouse, my room seemed foreign, as if someone else had been living there. I grabbed more clothes, slung the bag over my shoulder, and went down the stairs.

The first floor of the house, once so warm and inviting, seemed cold and hollow, even in the late summer heat. The carpet was covered in lint and hairballs. All the plants were dying. The branches and pinecones Ananda and I had lovingly brought into the house were disintegrating. A layer of dust clung to everything.

My old collages hung on the walls. I touched some of them, remembering the golden days when Ananda and I had created them. They exuded a weak light now, much weaker than before. I took a few down for scanning. Maybe I could breathe new life into them.

I walked out of the house and felt the real world slide into place around me. I became aware of birds chirping, people mowing lawns, and cars cruising by. I hadn't heard those noises inside at all. It was as if the house was enclosed in a bell jar, alone in its own little realm.

I got in my car and started it. I'd made up with Ananda. Our friendship might never be the same as it was, but we were past the bad part. That meant a lot to me.

I drove to the Santa Clara coffeehouse, bought a small coffee, and scanned the want ads. Nothing interested me. I thought about calling my parents to ask for help but decided against it. I didn't want to get into another heated conversation about my future or my choice of friends.

Brad and I met up for dinner that night at the warehouse. He boiled pasta on a single burner while I chopped basil and vegetables on a tiny table. He ran to the bathroom to strain the pasta.

"Thanks again for dinner," I said once it was plated. "I feel bad that you're always paying for it, though. I wish I could take you out."

"It's no problem." He forked a summer squash. "I enjoy it. But if you really feel so bad, you can give me one of your original collages."

I laughed. "That'd barely cover one meal."

He looked at me across the table, suddenly serious. "What are your plans for the future?"

My fork hovered over the pasta. "Well, I looked at the want ads today, but all the jobs sucked."

He waited for me to continue. I took a deep breath, knowing the death knell of my artistic career had rung. It was time to give up. I'd given it a shot, had shown my collages, and received a little acclaim. I felt the rest of my life and my student loans looming over me.

"I'm going to apply to grad school," I said slowly.

"I think that's a wise decision."

"Yeah. I just wish I had a little longer to be an artist."

"You had a good run at it."

"Yeah, I guess."

"Would you have changed anything this summer?" he asked, bringing his wine glass to his lips.

"Yeah. I wouldn't have waited so long to meet you." I thought back to the night before. Waves of pleasure undulated down my body.

Brad smiled and reached for my hand. It was a perfect moment, if those existed — a moment I knew I'd hold onto for the rest of my life.

"Hey, I have to tell you something." He frowned. "My work is transferring me to New York."

And the perfect moment shattered. At first I didn't comprehend what he said, and then it dawned on me. He'd be leaving.

My heart clenched for several seconds, then limped into an erratic beat. I breathed somehow, and nodded. I knew going back to school would be hard for our relationship, but I never thought this would happen.

"How soon?" I asked, my voice a whisper.

"Three weeks from today. I just found out." He gazed at me soulfully, his eyes pleading. "I don't want to go."

"Did they give you a choice?"

"If I want to keep working for them, I have to go. In this economy..." He squeezed my hand.

I blinked back tears. It wasn't fair. We'd just found each other. "Maybe I can apply for grad school in New York."

"You should, but you still have to take the GRE, and you don't have a lot of time."

I nodded. I pushed my plate back, feeling too sick to eat any more. My future had changed 180 degrees. It was all so last minute. I'd have to scramble to get ahead. I doubted I could get into any NYC school on such short notice, not that I could handle the prices for an out-of-state student.

"Don't worry," he said. "Whatever happens, you'll be fine."

I shook my head. I couldn't help but think it was a lie to make me feel better.

"You're a strong person," he continued. "This time with you has been amazing."

I stared at him, shocked by his frankness. "Are you breaking up with me?" I gasped, a tear streaking my face and falling onto my plate.

"No, no," he laughed. "Not at all. I think we should stay together until one of us has to move, if that's okay with you."

I nodded. He got up to embrace me and I rose to meet him. I needed the comfort and the contact. He'd be gone so soon.

I led him to the futon and pulled him down with me. If he had to leave in three weeks, I was determined to have as much of him as I could.

Ananda became friends with a girl with dirty blonde dreadlocks and a spritely face. I first saw her in the Santa Clara coffeehouse, where I studied with my table-sized GRE book. She and Ananda traipsed in, a study in contrasts. Ananda had switched out her Nouveau Art couture for earth tones and natural fibers, but she still sparkled like a diva, while the new girl dressed in patchwork that appeared to be made from repurposed rags. They slid into a table across the coffeehouse. Ananda gave me a tiny wave, but the new girl was either so self-absorbed or messed up, she didn't acknowledge me.

Jared walked in a moment later. Blossom followed, her face buried in a yoga magazine. Her eyes looked juicy with xyritav. To my surprise, she sauntered to my table and sat down.

"Hi," she said. "How've you been? I've missed you."

My heart melted. She was always so kind, even if her brain was on another planet. "I've missed you too. I'm studying for the GRE."

Her eyes passed over my book dully. "Mm."

"Who's that girl with Ananda?" I asked.

"Clary. She's from Colorado. She just moved into the House of Transformation."

"Really? When?"

"I don't know, maybe a week ago? What have you been up to?"

"Well, I have a boyfriend now." I swallowed, pressing my lips together. "But we're breaking up in three weeks."

"That's too bad. Why?"

"He's moving to New York, and I'll be in grad school, hopefully." I bit back my tears.

"Everything happens for a reason." She touched my arm. "Sometimes we don't see it, but someone's looking out for us."

I managed a smile. I hoped she was right. "How are things with you?"

She paused thoughtfully and looked at the table. "I'm going through some transformations. The House of Transformation has changed me. I don't know how to explain it, but I don't think I'll ever be the same again."

"What's different?"

"Everything. The whole world. I have a completely new perspective on life." She glanced at my book. "But I don't want to interrupt your studies. It was nice talking with you." She tiptoed to the other side of the coffeehouse.

I tried to study, but the air felt charged with Ananda's presence. I found myself reading and re-reading the same sentence without understanding it. It was just as well. My brain was full for the day.

I stood and glanced at my former gaggle. Blossom had her back to me, deeply entrenched in her magazine. Clary looked at me with malicious eyes, then whispered something into Ananda's ear. She threw her had back and laughed. It was clear from their body language they weren't interested in a visit from me.

I gathered my things and pushed through the door and onto the sidewalk, breathing in the hot, humid air. A hand touched my shoulder and turned me around.

Jared cocked his head and held his arms out. "Hey. No love for me?"

His patchy beard had grown since I'd last seen him. It made him seem wiser, like a stained-glass apostle. I clasped him in a light hug.

"I talked with Ananda about you," he said.

"Thanks. I guess it worked. I'm not on her shit list anymore. How've you been?"

He hooked his thumbs into his belt loops and gazed at the sky. "Mag, I just have to thank you so much."

I blinked. "Why?"

"I've read books about people coming of age. It's usually when they're in their teens. And here I am, at twenty-five, just now realizing who I am. It feels amazing, like the summer of my life has finally begun." He squeezed my hand. "I'm just so grateful for everything you and Ananda shared with me."

I smiled weakly at him, but a combustible rage seared my heart. It wasn't fair. It should've been *my* coming of age, the summer of *my* life. Instead, he was getting everything he ever wanted, and I was on the outside looking in.

"Please come to the party," he said. "It's going to be great."

I sighed. "That's the day before my GRE test. I should probably stay in and study."

"That's understandable. You have to think of your future. I guess I'll see you around." He turned and walked back into the coffeehouse.

I adjusted my bag, watching as he joined the others. I wanted to go in and hang out, but I also felt a sense of finality. We were moving in different directions, whether I was ready to, or not.

Chapter 33. Art Party III

The night before the GRE test, I dropped my book to the table with a thud. I thought I could pull an all-nighter, but after thirteen hours, I could barely concentrate on all the useless words I was trying to learn.

Chilly night air blew in through the warehouse windows. Tree leaves waved in the wind.

I thought about the Art Party at the House of Transformation. Jared's new photos had to be gorgeous. Ananda probably primped for hours for her performance. I wondered if Blossom might lead another yoga flash-mob. My heart thudded heavily. I missed them. It was strange to be outside of the House of Transformation. At one time, I was such a part of that scene. Now, I was moving onward and upward. Hopefully, I'd be at a graduate school next month. This time between college and university would be like a crazy dream in my rear-view mirror. I imagined I'd tell my kids about 'the summer I tried to be an artist.'

I felt I should say goodbye to that world and my illusions that I belonged there. If I got accepted into any of the ten colleges I applied to, it might be one of my last chances to see my friends.

Brad worked on a music program on his computer, staring at a moving screen with different tracks. When he saw me, he slipped off his headphones and raised his eyebrows.

"Do you feel like getting out for a bit?" I asked.

"What about studying for your test?"

I stood up and stretched. "I need a break."

"Okay. What do you have in mind? The coffeehouse?"

I held my breath. "Do you feel like going to the Art Party with me?"

He frowned. "I thought you were done with that scene."

"I am. I just want to pop in and say goodbye to everyone."

"You do remember Ananda doesn't exactly like me, right?"

I walked over to him and sat in his lap. My hands massaged his shoulders as I gazed into his eyes. "I don't care what she thinks. I love you and I don't care who knows."

He smiled. "I love you too, Mag Woods."

We kissed. Everything else faded away, our world enveloping us.

"I promise to make it an early night," I said.

"Okay." He smiled.

Hazelwood Road was clogged with cars. We parked one street over. We walked in silence, my hand in his. The House of Transformation stood out like a Candyland among the trash and boarded-up houses. Christmas lights and colored bulbs illuminated every room. Thumping music drifted out the windows.

We stopped on the porch. He faced me and took my other hand.

"You ready?" I asked.

He took a deep breath. "Yeah."

Branches cluttered the foyer, like a small thicket had grown there, extending along the walls. A green light strobed randomly.

In the living room, hundreds of blue Christmas lights looped around the branch-chandelier. A mass of people bobbed to reverb-reggae, their eyes shining, their pupils dilated so much their irises were obscured. The music and lights made me feel funny, as if my consciousness was altered somehow. I pulled Brad closer.

"Nice house," he said.

"It was nice once." I looked at the art on the walls. Most of the collages had been taken down. Paintings were hung in their place. I walked past a few rudimentary flower paintings and beginner landscapes, and then stopped, a flush of heat rising in my face.

My blue women hung on the walls. No one had asked me if that was okay. I wasn't ready to show them yet, but there they were, for the world to see.

"What's wrong?" Brad asked.

"Um... These are my paintings." I shook my head.

"I didn't know you painted. Is that why you wanted to come tonight?"

"No, I wouldn't show these. They're not ready."

He peered at them. "They're pretty good."

I looked at them in the dim light. Faces rose from the canvas with a life of their own. Even so, I wanted to take them off the walls. "Let's find Ananda and Jared."

"Lead the way."

I led Brad into the red-lit kitchen. It was packed with people. Pasha gave me a strange look and returned to her conversation with a hipster guy. In the sink, dirty dishes piled six feet high, like a disgusting game of Jenga. The remains of Indian food take-out sat on the counter in scraped-out Styrofoam containers. I picked up the last piece of *naan*, dipped it in a smear of curry, and bit in. It tasted creamy and spicy at first, then a metallic taste coursed through my teeth, like shredded foil. I spit it out into my hands and threw it into the overflowing trashcan.

"That tasted funny. Ugh." I spit into the garbage. "Let's look upstairs."

We stepped over several people making out and talking on the stairs. On the second floor, a dog-eared Dylan poster peeled from the spare bedroom door. Clary's room.

I opened my bedroom door. A circle of people sat on the floor and on my bed. A cloud of pot smoke escaped a dready guy's mouth. Anjay, the Swami's assistant, sat among them, dressed in street clothes. I shot him a questioning glance, but he looked away.

Brad and I met eyes. He must have seen the panic behind them, because he nodded.

"Everyone out," I said.

"Aw man," a guy in patchwork said.

"Sorry, I need to pack. I'm moving out."

"Can I move in?" he asked.

"Um... check with Jared."

Anjay stood up last, a disquieted look in his eyes.

"Anjay?" I asked.

His mouth turned down, then he walked past me and down the stairs as naturally as if he were in his monastery.

A stomach cramp doubled me over. I felt like I'd been kicked. I groaned.

"What's going on?" Brad asked.

I stumbled to the corner of the room and threw up, tears shooting in my eyes. I recognized this feeling. I'd felt like this when I'd eaten Kitty's green pill. I pounded my fist on the floor. I hadn't wanted to take anything. My test was only a few hours away, for Christ's sake!

Brad brushed the hair out of my face. I almost cried with how tender he was.

"Are you okay?"

I shook my head and leaned into him. "I get sick when I take xyritav."

He tensed. "When did you take that?"

"It was in the Indian food." Another wave of nausea made me lurch forward again. I choked as vomit came up and splattered the floor.

He smoothed my shoulders with his broad hands until my stomach calmed. The xyritav connected to my neural receptors and a volcano of bliss erupted within me. I sat up and took a breath.

"Can you handle packing some stuff?" he asked.

I laughed, nodding. Could I handle it? I could handle anything.

He tossed trinkets into my luggage while I stripped the sheets off the bed and piled my clothes on top. After fifteen minutes, the only things left were the dresser and the naked bed.

I looked at my nearly empty room. Even in my blissful state, a lump of sadness welled in my throat. It was all gone, almost as if it'd never happened at all.

Brad opened the bedroom door. Music and pot smoke wafted in. The stoners had moved to the hallway. We shouldered past them, carrying bags, almost tripping over people on the stairs. We pushed through the throng in the foyer and out the front door.

Once outside, the beauty of the night made me feel electric. We walked down the sidewalk, loaded with my belongings. I looked at Brad and laughed. He shook his head and cracked a smile.

"What's so funny?" I asked.

"You were puking just twenty minutes ago. Now you're really happy."

"I am really happy."

He laughed, leading me toward the car. As he packed my things in the trunk, it reminded me of my first encounter with him, when I'd taken Ananda's belongings from his apartment and packed it in my car. We'd come full circle.

He smirked at me. "We should go home. You have an early morning. I just hope you have enough time to sober up."

I shook my head. "I have to get my art."

He hesitated as if he wanted to say something, but didn't.

I took his hand. "Please? I just want to get my artwork, and then we'll leave."

He sighed and ducked his head into my neck. "Okay, but I'm going to park closer. I saw an open spot."

A few minutes later, I took my paintings down. No one noticed. People slumped on the floor, deep in conversation. The dready guy gathered hairballs on the carpet.

Brad removed the Borscht painting from the mantle and looked at the corners.

"That's not mine," I said. "It's Ananda's."

"Actually, it's mine. It disappeared from my apartment after one of her parties. I thought she'd sold it for drugs."

He looked at the paintings in my hands. "Do you have all of them?"

"Yeah, but I don't know where the rest of my collages and my suitcase are. They have to be here somewhere. Let's find Jared and Ananda. They'll know where they are."

"I'll put these in the car." He took the paintings from me.

I went upstairs and checked Clary's room first. Apart from a pile of clothes and a sleeping bag, it was empty. Ananda's room was completely dark. As I reached for the light switch, my fingers ran across the scratched wood.

Help Me.

I shivered as I flipped on the switch. The light revealed several people huddled in the center of the room, hands and elbows lifted to shield their faces. Everyone was clearly wasted — their eyes were sweaty, as if their brains boiled. Jared smiled like a mad hatter. Ananda and Blossom were painted blue, just like my paintings.

I shook my head and took a step backwards. The House of Transformation thing had been taken too far. They weren't raising consciousness if no one was conscious. All the same, I felt the urge to sit with them, to join in the tea party.

I clawed my fingernails into my leg to keep me focused. I needed to get my artwork and leave. The GRE test was tomorrow.

Jared popped up. "I was just about to suggest we go downstairs. Ananda will be performing soon."

Everyone got up, filing out like zombies. Brad crested the stairs and stood beside me in the doorway.

When Ananda saw him, she startled back as if she'd seen a viper. "What are you doing here?"

"It's okay," I said. "He's with me."

She shot me an incredulous look and ran down the stairs. Kitty ran after her.

Jared thrust his chest out, his smile verging on manic. "We've been opening portals to other dimensions all day. We just opened up a giant one. I think we'll actually see Rosie tonight!"

I took a tentative step toward him. "Why would you want to see her?"

"Proof of the afterlife. We're going to find out what really happens when someone passes through that gate."

He started to breeze past me, but I caught his shoulder. "Where are my collages? I can't find them."

"Maybe they transcended." He brushed past me and walked down the stairs.

My face flushed. "Let's look in the attic. It's the only place we haven't looked yet."

As we climbed the squeaky attic stairs, my unease grew. A lone, bare bulb lit the mostly empty room, making the shadows long and dark. I felt as if we were being watched, even though we were the only ones in the room.

"Aha!" Brad lifted a pile of collages from the floor. My suitcase was beneath them.

"Thank you so much." I kissed him. Trickles of pleasure flowed over my lips.

He kissed me but pulled away. "This place is creeping me out. Can we go?"

"Yeah. Let's go home."

We walked down the stairs to the living room. Dance music blared. Everyone writhed to it except for us.

I hesitated. "I'm going to say goodbye. Will you wait for me?"

"Sure. I'll put these in the car." He kissed the top of my head. "Be right back."

I walked into the throng. Blossom swayed with glazed eyes. Barry pumped his fists. Ricky staggered into the room, his eyes blazing.

My pulse dropped. He must've eaten the Indian food, unaware of the xyritav it contained.

He grabbed Blossom and held her close in a slow dance. "I can't decide who I wanna fuck first." He stared at me as he mashed his body against hers.

"Ricky, are you okay?" I asked. "Do you want me to call someone?"

He kissed Blossom's neck and ran his hands over her, his eyes focused on me.

The music climaxed. Stevey rocked in a corner, covered in sweat. Anjay danced mindlessly. Kitty paced like a caged tiger. Everyone was in their own realm — not connected, not spiritual, not transforming into anything positive. The House of Transformation had become something different, something uglier and debased. It was like the Hell panel from The Garden of Earthly Delights had come to life in three dimensions, in the house I used to call home.

I stepped over people lying on the carpet and walked into the kitchen. Ananda and Jared argued by the sink. As soon as she saw me, she became livid. The tendons in her neck were stretched tight, her breathing animalistic. Her eyes were so glossed that she looked unreal, like one of my paintings. She was more messed up than I'd ever seen her before.

"Why did you invite Brad here?" she snarled. "Is that where you've been all this time?"

"Yeah, but he's actually a really nice person. You should give him another chance."

She poked a finger at me. "I can't believe you betrayed me."

I shook my head. "What did he do that was so bad?"

"He walked in on me when I was naked." She crossed her arms.

"He admitted to that, but said he walked away. What else?"

"He invaded my space," she said through gritted teeth.

"You're the one who moved in with him." I ran a hand over my forehead. "You know what? Never mind. I was just coming to say goodbye. We're both moving out of this town."

"You two deserve each other," she said.

"Maybe you should see someone about all that fear and rage within you. It'll eat you up if you're not careful."

Her eyes went cold for a moment, then she stalked off.

I closed my eyes. Why did I react to her malice? I hadn't meant for our last interaction to be so confrontational. I should've known what would happen. She couldn't handle dealing with her past.

I shook my head. "I don't understand why she's so stuck on being a victim all the time."

Jared collected me into a one-armed hug. "Well, she's fragile, and no offense, but you're sort of klutzy. You're right though. She should see someone. I mean, therapy helped me."

"You've been to therapy?" I asked, dumbfounded. Poor Jared. I'd misjudged him for so long, and now I was leaving.

He tucked his dark locks behind his ears. "Yeah. I went through a breakup and started flunking out of law school. I turned it around and graduated, but I was pretty depressed."

"I never knew you had a law degree. Why didn't you tell me?"

"Mag..." His mouth twisted. "When've we ever had a conversation about anything besides art or Ananda?"

I was speechless. Had it truly been that way? "Jared, how come you look more sober than everyone else?"

He shrugged. "I had a little bit, but I'm the master of ceremonies. I'm here to make sure things don't get too far out of hand."

"Did you put xyritav in the Indian food?"

"Yeah, but we ate it hours ago in a ceremony. How did you know?"

My breath came ragged. "It wasn't all gone. I ate some and I didn't know. Ricky had some too, and he doesn't do *anything*. That's why he was mad at me — because I gave him a clemeral and he thought it was a mint."

"Oh. I guess we didn't throw away the containers. Oops."

"I'm worried. Do you know what xyritav overdose looks like?"

"No, but we'll be okay. This house is protected. The Swami blessed it, remember?"

I stared at him. That was xyritav logic, not real-world logic.

All of the sudden, the music dropped. Chatter ceased. The house was silent for a moment. Then the chords from *The Universe is Sound* played over the stereo.

In the living room, Ananda sang over the song, dancing and stretching her arms out to the people gathered there. Brad fumed in the hallway, his mouth turning down. Clary approached Ananda and they danced together, arms flailing like aquatic creatures tossed by the ocean. When Ananda nuzzled her neck and the kiss traveled up to Clary's lips, the crowd catcalled.

My heart sank. Just like that, I'd been replaced by another person willing to take on all her crazy dreams and not ask too many questions.

The music cut out before the song was over. Ananda glanced

around the room, confused. Kitty threw the stereo cord on the carpet, tears streaming down her face. She held something the size of a baseball, which I realized was the crystal cluster she'd bought for Ananda.

Ananda untangled herself from Clary, her eyebrows mashed together. The whole room held their breath. Not even the hippies joked.

"What's wrong?" Ananda asked.

"You're such a fucking asshole!" Kitty's eyes lit with fury.

"What are you talking about?"

"You bitch! I'm in love with you and you're making out with her!"

Ananda's lips fluttered, as if to conjure an excuse, but no words came out.

Kitty raised her arm and threw the crystal at the nearest window. Broken glass sprayed across the room. The crowd shielded themselves and backed away. People spilled out the front door.

Ananda glanced around at the remaining people. It made her look desperate, like she was looking for an escape route. She put on her bullshit smile and walked over to her. "We were just dancing, that's all. Calm down. Besides, you and I aren't even together."

"That's not what you said last night," Kitty said, a fresh torrent of tears falling.

Ananda reached for her, but Kitty flung her off and stormed outside.

I shouldered through the crowd, chasing after her, Brad right behind me. "Kitty, wait!" I yelled, running down the sidewalk.

She spun around, her face monstrous in anger.

"Let me drive you home," I said. "Please. You're in no shape to drive. Let me take care of you."

Her features crumbled. She melted into my embrace and handed me her keys. I helped her into her car and raced back to Brad.

"Follow me to Kitty's. When we stop, look up the signs of

overdose on xyritav."

He nodded, his eyes cloudy with resignation.

I climbed into the Firebird with Kitty and started it up with a loud rumble. I'd sobered up, but I still didn't know what to say to her. Pills and tormented emotions were a bad combination. I couldn't help but think it could've been me making a scene, had I tried to cling to Ananda instead of letting her go.

I made a few turns and pulled onto the main road. "Do you want to talk about it?"

She scrunched down in the seat, hiding her face against the window. "No."

I drew a deep breath and turned onto another road.

"She's just the worst!" she shouted, gasping for breath through her tears. "We've been together for a year, and she still tells everyone we're just friends."

"She isn't very good at relationships."

"You can say that again. I hate her."

"How much xyritav did you take tonight?"

Kitty didn't answer, just stared out the window. Finally, she spoke. "I took three from my own prescription, but everyone else ate the food. I saw Jared dump it in. Did you know he bought a bag of powder from a chemistry student at the community college?"

My heart beat irregularly. "No."

"Well, I don't trust a chemistry student. Who knows what's in that powder? Plus, who knows how much they actually took? My pills have fillers and binders. The amount of xyritav in the pill is much smaller than the size of the pill. He put so much powder in that food..."

I gasped. I'd only eaten a swipe of the curry, and I'd spit it out, but I was so affected, I'd puked. Who knows how much the others ate? I pressed hard on the gas, every red light feeling like an eternity.

When we finally arrived at Kitty's condo, I helped her walk through the door. I took her to the bedroom and sat her down on her four-poster bed.

"Do you need anything?"

"Water," she croaked, pulling the sheet over her.

I ran to the kitchen and got a glass of water. When I got back to the room, Kitty's eyes were closed and her breathing deep. I set the water on her nightstand.

"I'll call you tomorrow," I whispered.

On my way out, I threw her keys behind the sofa, just in case she tried to go back to the House of Transformation. I locked her door from the inside and ran back to Brad's car.

"We have to go back to the house, now!"

The Swami rose after having knelt prostrate since sunrise. His knees pinched and his back cramped, but he knew he didn't deserve relief. He'd questioned his beliefs, who he was, and even the brotherhood. He'd dishonored his monk's vows. And now, he couldn't feel the warmth of God's love anymore. Where it was once as omnipresent as oxygen, it was nowhere, not in his meditations, the monastery, or the sunset.

He recalled that night at the House of Transformation with darkest remorse. How lovely everyone had been, how strange and beautiful the house was, and then the meal, which contained too much cream, but was otherwise delicious. And then the mark on his soul.

A demon had risen within him, a lecherous imp that bade him to touch flesh, to worship the goddess within the women there, especially the one like the Goddess Lakshmi. She was so beautiful he couldn't take his eyes off her, and she was so kind. Their innocent gestures became lustful, and as if in a helpless trance, he'd become possessed with urges. Her compliance complicated matters even more. She showered him with soft kisses and pressed herself against him, all the while smelling like jasmine. He could smell it even now, could see her lithe body as she writhed on him, then under him, and then all over him as he helplessly plowed into her flesh over and over.

To make matters worse, he'd tried to do the same thing with the other girl, only she'd shamed him, like a slap in the face. But she was right.

He'd hoped the prostration would assuage his shame, regret, and fear at his own powerlessness. He wanted a ray of God's love to shine upon him again. But he felt nothing but the depth of despair and solitude, like a cold pit, deep in the earth, like a cancer eating his heart.

He walked to an old wooden desk and fell into a chair. He stared at the single flickering candle until the world faded away. He thought of the House of Transformation and its denizens, its madness, and the girl, who was so good, and yet so terrible. It was an evil place disguised as a good one. It had to be dismantled.

When the energy spiraled up, he whispered an incantation with all the ferocity he felt at the failure his life had become.

"Scatter. Scatter to the winds. Scatter."

"But you have your test tomorrow," Brad said. "Shouldn't we go home and let you sober up?"

"No, drive. They could overdose. They bought a bag of xyritav powder from a chemistry student."

Brad drove as fast as he could. When a red light stopped us, he swung around and took another way.

I took his phone and read the overdose section of a xyritav webpage out loud. *"Overdose of xyritav may be difficult to diagnose due to its stimulant and depressive qualities. Signs to look for include shallow breathing, no response to stimuli, blue lips, and the appearance of sleeping."*

My lips trembled. "Brad, there were people lying on the floor!"

"Maybe we should call an ambulance."

I bit my lip. We were almost there. Maybe everyone knew about the xyritav in the food and had shown restraint. Maybe everyone would be fine, and I'd walk in on them singing Kumbaya. I decided to wait until I saw what was going on for myself.

As soon as Brad parked in front of the house, I ran inside.

The music had changed to what sounded like Philip Glass on morphine. The energy, once buoyant, now felt vacuous, as if frost had fallen or Rosie had invited all her ghoulish friends to the party. The colored lights barely illuminated the rooms. I batted a light switch, but nothing happened. Somehow, it was freezing — a cold sweat covered my skin. I ran my hands down my arms, but nothing made me feel warm. I turned off the stereo and the house dropped dead silent.

I tripped over something and looked down to find Ricky, curled up near the wall. Stevey lay passed out nearby. Brad looked around the room, his eyes wide.

"Call the ambulance. Now!" I shouted.

"I'm on it." He tapped on his phone and walked outside.

Blossom stood on one foot in a yoga pose, sweat covering her trembling body. Something looked different about her, but I couldn't pinpoint it. Then I realized — it was her chest. When I'd first met her, her chest had been so flat, I'd laughed when I hallucinated her nametag read Tiny Bosom. Now, her breasts were engorged to the size of melons. Her formerly concave tummy sported a tight protrusion. My breath caught. Could she be pregnant?

"Blossom?"

Her eyes reflected back at me without seeing me, then she collapsed. She sputtered, her lips quaking. She reached up and clutched my shirt roughly.

"My new name..." Her cornflower eyes bored into mine. "My new name is Yes. Call me Yes."

"Okay." Tears pooled in my eyes.

"I've been transformed. I'm saying yes to life."

She mumbled something, but I couldn't understand her. Was she chanting? I looked around the room. Ricky's lips were turning blue.

"Ricky?"

I touched his shoulder. He flopped over, one arm splaying on the carpet, his eyes clouded like old fish. I backed away.

More people lay on the dining room floor, some still, some moving. I searched among them for Ananda.

"What's the name of that drug again?" Brad asked from the doorway.

"Xyritav."

I clamored up the steps, hoping against hope Ananda hadn't eaten too much. She deserved better. I needed her to live. I needed her in my life.

I found her at the top of the stairs, leaning against the wall, her face slack. She'd changed into a gown and had re-done her makeup in bold blue and white strokes. Her cheekbones were so highlighted, it looked like real bones protruded from her face. Her lips were dark blue, though I couldn't tell if it was makeup or if it was an overdose symptom. I'd never seen her so messed up before. It was like looking at a ghost.

"Ananda, are you okay?"

Her eyes flickered in my direction. She murmured something I couldn't make out.

I leaned close. "What'd you say?"

"*I am the cerulean doll*," she intoned, her voice otherworldly.

My chest tightened. She must be hallucinating. Where were the paramedics? I prayed for the sound of sirens. "Did you eat the Indian food?"

Her head lolled on her neck and her eyelids fluttered shut.

"No, stay awake!" I shouted, shaking her icy arms.

Her eyelids cracked open and she looked at me through slits. "Let me go."

"I'll never let you go."

She became limp in my arms.

"No, Ananda!"

She didn't respond.

I shook her again, a storm of tears streaking down my face.

From the corner of my eye, Rosie's lights hovered in the air, as if she too, were holding her breath. I shook my head. I didn't have time to indulge her. Ananda was fading away and there was nothing I could do about it.

"Help me, Rosie." Tears washed out of me. "I don't know if she's going to make it. *Help me, please.*"

Ananda's head fell forward. I cried out. I was going to lose her.

A flash of white popped. It lit up the room for a second

before darkness fell again.

Ananda's eyes flew open with a jolt. She grasped me, as if she just realized what was happening. She convulsed, her body arching. She threw up again and again, choking between the pulses.

I held her throughout her heaves. Even though I was repulsed by the vomit and bile drenching my shirt and the floor, a bubble of hope rose within me. She might be okay — she might live through this.

"Did you do that, Rosie?" I whispered. I looked for her lights, but didn't see them.

Sirens wailed outside, first far away, and then close. Red and blue lights flashed through the window. Then paramedics shouted and stomped into the house.

"Up here!" I yelled. "Hurry!"

Two paramedics pealed up the steps.

"Step back." One of them crouched over her and took her pulse. The other prepared a shot. Ananda reached for me, but I backed away until I was against the wall. The paramedic administered the shot. "Get her to the ambulance."

I ran down the stairs, kicking paraphernalia and rubbish as I went.

In the living room, paramedics swarmed like angels over the lumps on the floor. A gurney lifted and they rushed someone out. Another kneeled over Blossom, whose head waved back and forth. He called for help, and soon Blossom was encircled by them. Ricky lay against the wall, still and silent, ignored.

My legs grew weak as I realized he was gone. The worst part was that he never saw this coming. He never would've taken xyritav willingly. Our conversation at the coffeehouse told me that much. He'd just eaten the tainted food. Now he'd never be an engineer or run for office. All those dreams were gone, snuffed out like a candle.

As the paramedics moved from one body to the next, I realized several people were too far gone to save. I cried, my heart aching. There was nothing I could do but watch as they pronounced more and more dead.

I gazed at the window, where the flower altar had been just a few weeks ago. My tear-streaked face looked back at me, transformed with grief. But there was also something behind it, something outside. My eyes shifted focus.

Jared stared at me from the backyard, his eyes haunted.

"Jared!" I shouted.

He turned and ran into the dark night.

I raced through the kitchen and burst out the back door. I whipped my head around. My blood boiled with rage. I wanted to ask him why he thought buying powder from a chemistry student was safe, and why he dumped it in the food. I wanted to ask why he'd poisoned everyone at the party. But he was gone.

I walked to the front of the house and found Brad. He embraced me. I pressed myself against him, as if his touch could erase what I'd seen. My clothes reeked of Ananda's vomit, but he held me close.

Ananda lay still in an ambulance. I pressed my face into Brad's chest, fearing the worst. I tried to take a breath, but it came up jagged. Ananda's hand made a small gesture, a little wave. Relief crashed over me. At least she was alive.

"She's in good hands now," he said.

I nodded, unable to speak.

"It's a good thing we called them when we did. One of the guys told me if we'd waited half an hour longer, they'd all be dead."

Tears seared my face. "I wish we called them earlier. We could've saved more of them."

"You can't blame yourself. We didn't know how bad it was."

I nodded, but couldn't resist thinking that we did. Kitty told me as much. My stomach wrenched. If only I hadn't fallen out with Ananda, or if I'd just lived there, I could've stopped the whole thing. I never would've let Jared do it. No one would've died.

He looked at me, his face concerned. "Are you feeling okay? Do you want to get checked out?" he asked as the paramedics loaded another body-strewn gurney into the second ambulance.

"I'm fine."

"Miss Wood?" a police officer asked.

"Yes?" I wiped the tears from my face with one hand, still holding Brad close.

The officer's badge shone in the darkness. "I have a few questions for the report. Do you live here?"

I staggered and sniffed back tears. "My name is on the lease. But I've been staying with my boyfriend for the past three weeks."

"Were you aware this party was going on?"

"Yeah, but it was just supposed to be an Art Party."

"An art party," he repeated.

"Yeah, an art show."

"How'd you know they were on xyritav?"

"Someone told me."

"Do you know how the drug was administered? No one said they took anything."

I shook my head. So Jared hadn't told anyone, the stupid fucker. "It was in the food."

"What kind of food? Brownies? Cookies?"

"Indian food."

"Really? And everyone ate it?"

"I don't know. We got here late." The night winds had picked up again, and a chill ran through me.

"Who put the drugs in the food?"

I swallowed. Jared's pale face, escaping into the night, loomed in my mind. Should I name him? It'd put him behind bars for life, maybe several lifetimes, depending on how many people died. Just thinking about it made me cry again. All those bodies in the dining room...

"I don't know how it got in there."

"Who else lives here?"

"Ananda Dawn, Jared, and Clary. I don't know their last names."

"Who else was at this party?"

"Um, Kitty, but her real name is Li Xia. I don't know her last name either. Stevey, Pasha, Ricky, some hippie guys..."

I tried to think of Blossom's name but I couldn't remember.

All I could think of was her new name.

Call me Yes.

"Can you think of anything else that might help us with our investigation?"

I shook my head.

"Where can we reach you?"

"Here." Brad gave him a business card. "My number is on there. Do you need anything else?"

"Not now, but the detective might call you tomorrow. Here's my card. Call me if you think of anything."

Brad took the card and put it in his pocket. "She has a test tomorrow morning, but she'll be free by two o'clock."

I looked at him, silently thanking him as the officer strode away to interview the survivors. I'd finally stopped crying. I felt hollow, like a piece of my soul had been carved out.

"There's nothing more we can do here," he said. "We should go home."

I knew he was right, but I didn't want to go. I wanted to stay longer, to know that Ananda would be okay. I wanted to stay until all the people were helped, but I let him lead me away from the House of Transformation. He opened the passenger door to his car. As I was about to step in, someone yelled.

"Where'd she go? She was just here."

A paramedic stood in the middle of the street, looking around. The ambulance they'd loaded Ananda into was empty.

I looked around the dark streets.

"Mag," Brad said.

I ran around to the side of the house, into the backyard, and into the alley. Stray cats leapt out of my way as I raced past trashcans and spare tires.

"Ananda!" I screamed into the darkness.

No one answered.

I cursed and squeezed my eyes shut, willing her to come back. My eyes fixed on the alley as I bent to a squat, salty tears running down my face. After a minute of silence, I trudged back to Brad's car and fell into the passenger seat. The police would never find her. She wanted to be gone, so she was.

In front of us, the House of Transformation looked like a giant severed head with the blood drained out of it — the open windows like eyes, the front door like a grotesque mouth. Maybe it was the xyritav, but a wave of nausea rose within me again. I tucked my head into Brad's shoulder, wishing it would stop. He kissed the top of my head and started the car.

As he drove us away from the house and the monstrosity it had become, I expected to feel relief, but I didn't.

I slept in nightmarish fits for minutes at a time before waking with a start. In one of my dreams, the house moved into the tree branches in the backyard, and an old woman who lived in it tried to kill me. In another, the house was underwater. People swam into it and floated in and out of rooms. They wanted me to breathe underwater and join them, but I kept choking.

When my alarm went off, the tears started again. Brad held me, but it was no good. There was only one thing that would make me feel better. I needed to know if Ananda made it out alive.

I called the hospital to ask about her, but I couldn't remember her real name. 'Jennifer something or other' didn't get me anywhere. I asked about the other people at the house, but the attendant refused to release information to anyone who wasn't family.

Brad made eggs for breakfast, but I could barely eat. I felt thousands of miles away from him. He was kind, of course, but no matter how closely I held him, or how many kind words he spoke, there was a space between us. He was letting our breakup happen. He didn't have to go to New York — he could stay and get a job somewhere else. He wasn't fighting for us, and we both knew it.

I packed a bag for the test. I knew it'd be horrible. I felt like I had ten hangovers, despite having taken several ibuprofens. Brad drove me to the test site. I kept crying along the way.

"Good luck," he said, kissing me.

I'd need more than luck to get a good score. I'd need a miracle.

I tried to focus on the test, but I kept picturing Ananda lying in a gutter. Then I remembered Blossom's delirium. And Ricky, who was so blasted out of his mind he'd tried to start an orgy. I shook my head and looked at the anagrams again. As I blinked back my tears, the words dilated into Rorschach patterns.

I bombed the test. My score was abysmal and there was nothing I could do about it. I supposed I could take it again, but it was the last thing on my mind.

Brad picked me up. We went straight to the hospital. When he told the staff we were the ones who'd called the ambulance, they let us know about the situation. Several people didn't make it. They didn't say who. They led us to Stevey, in critical condition in the ICU. I felt a stab of horror, seeing him hooked up to tubes, needles, and a breathing apparatus. But even though he lay there motionless, his steady heartbeat on the monitor reassured me.

An orderly asked if we could identify bodies. I didn't want to go to the morgue, but he insisted we might know someone, and anything would help.

We walked through countless hallways, then boarded an elevator down to the pits of the hospital. Finally, we walked through the stainless steel doors of the morgue.

The air was heavy with formaldehyde and rust. The orderly pulled back the sheet from Ricky first, and my heartbeat stopped.

"That's Ricky," I said, my voice a whisper. I'd liked him, and there he was, pale and lying on a slab, his lips parted for a last gasp of air.

"What was his last name?" the orderly asked.

"I don't know. All I know is he works at the coffeehouse in the Arts District."

He pulled back another sheet. I stared down at Yes, her angelic blonde hair spilled on the slab. My throat swelled up and tears overflowed my eyes. I hadn't wanted her to die. She was so young. She was the best of us, the most optimistic, the kindest. Brad drew me into his arms.

"It looks like you know this one," the orderly said, looking at his feet. "I'm sorry for your loss. What's her name?"

"Blossom. I don't remember her birth name, but she was a yoga teacher."

He wrote on a clipboard and pulled back another sheet, and then another, and another. I could scarcely believe what I saw. Eight people were dead. Anjay was among them.

The orderly walked us out of the morgue in silence. He rode the elevator up with us to the main floor, where he pointed out the exit. Brad and I walked in a daze. The smell of the morgue seemed to follow us, lingering on our clothes and hair.

Once outside, I gulped in the fresh air and squinted at the sun. It seemed wrong that the sun was so bright, wrong that birds sang and flocked in the trees. It seemed wrong that people laughed and talked about the weather. It was definitely wrong that Brad and I were no longer as close.

A spark of hope nudged me. If those were all the bodies, that meant Ananda, Clary, Pasha, and Barry might not be dead. But if that was the case, where were they?

We went to the warehouse. I called the detective and numbly arranged to meet him at the warehouse tomorrow, after Brad left for a weeklong work project.

That night, after dinner, I got an email accepting me into the University of Kensington's Graduate School of Psychology. Despite my late application, they offered me the last opening in their department for a teacher's assistant.

I knew I wouldn't get into the New York schools. At best, I'd be on a waiting list until they saw my GRE score, then they wouldn't want anything to do with me.

I wrote U Kensington back and accepted the position, my heart thudding in my chest. When I pressed send, I felt a brighter future begin to close in around me. I'd be at the University of Kensington! But I'd be far away from Brad. Everything would change.

We celebrated that night with real Champagne, but it was bittersweet. It was the end of our era, which was obvious in so many ways, even as we smiled and clinked glasses. Perhaps he sensed the distance looming between us too, because we made love for hours — sad love, make-up love, goodbye love. All the love we ever had, or ever would make, all at once.

Chapter 34. What Remained

Detective Smith pounded on Brad's warehouse door at nine the next morning. I let him in. He hunched over his notepad like an obese weasel and evaluated me with the distaste of someone who would rather be doing anything else. After we got through the preliminary questions, he chewed his pen and squinted at me.

"Where were you last night?" he asked.

I blinked, confused. "Last night? You mean the night of the party, two nights ago?"

"No, not the night of the party. Where were you last night?"

"I was here with my boyfriend. Why? What happened?"

He shrugged, brows knitting together. "Can he confirm this?"

"Yeah, call him. He'll call you back as soon as his flight lands."

"And you were here all night?" He looked around at the messy studio.

I wished I'd cleaned up, but it was all I could do to make coffee. Tears sopped my eyes again.

He leaned close to study me. "What's wrong?"

I looked at the ceiling, hoping the deluge would hold off.

"You going to tell me, or what?" he asked.

The wall of tears behind my eyes burst. "Three of my friends died. I saw their bodies, and the bodies of the other people from the house, and my boyfriend and I are breaking up." I sobbed into my hands. I knew I looked hysterical, but I couldn't help it.

"You should see a grief counselor," he said flatly.

"What?"

"You need to see someone about that. The sooner the better." He glanced at the ceiling. "Do you know who would've set fire to your house last night?"

"What?!"

"Who might've set fire to the house you lived in? Anyone

come to mind?"

I gasped. "It really caught fire last night?"

"Yeah. It almost burned to the ground before the fire department got there. All the evidence is gone. We're lucky we moved the bodies before it happened."

"Oh my God." I sat on a bar stool and tried to breathe.

He looked at the piles of my belongings. "It looks like you moved some of your stuff out of there."

"It wasn't me."

"Who was it?"

I swallowed and shook my head.

"Look." He got up. "I can see you have a lot on your mind. Before I go, did you think of anything you didn't tell the police?"

"No. But have you heard from Ananda — I mean Jennifer? She's the one who ran out of the ambulance that night."

He closed his writing pad. "No. Tell you what. When you move, email me your new address. If I need you, I'll be in touch."

As soon as he left, I picked up the phone and called Kitty. Between sobs, I told her everything — the overdoses, Ananda out of her mind, Rosie, the ambulances, Ananda's escape, Yes and Ricky on morgue slabs, and finally the fire.

She was livid. "I can't believe that about Ricky and Blossom — I mean Yes. It's so sad. And Rosie really did that? And the House of Transformation burned down?! That's insane!"

I trembled. "It's all so much."

"What would've happened if you hadn't gone back? You saved Ananda's life."

"If she's still alive." I wiped my eyes. "I keep thinking of her dying in an alley or a gutter somewhere. I can't believe she ripped out the IVs and ran out of the ambulance. She could be anywhere. I just wish I'd called the ambulance earlier. Eight people are dead! What if you hadn't told me about the powdered xyritav? I might not have gone back."

"I can't believe Jared spiked the food and then ran off. I wonder where he is."

"The last time I saw him, he was running away from the cops." I thought again of his ghostly face in the window and shuddered. A quiver of guilt struck my chest. "I didn't tell the cops it was him."

"Hm. I doubt we'll see him again. I just wonder where Ananda is."

"I know." A chill raised the hair on my arms. "Do you think Jared set the place on fire?"

"Hold on. I have a call from an unknown caller. It might be her!"

I looked at the heap of my belongings from the house lying by the door. My collages were on top. I turned away. I couldn't think of them at the moment.

Kitty clicked back. "That was the detective."

"What did he want?"

"He's coming over in twenty minutes."

"Are you going to tell him about Jared?"

She sighed. "I don't know. I'll have to figure that out."

I held my breath. I wasn't sure if Jared deserved our mercy or if he deserved to go to prison.

"I can't find my car keys. Where'd you put them?"

"Oh, sorry. They're behind the couch. I put them there in case you tried to drive back to the House of Transformation that night. I should've told you. Just with my test and everything else–"

"It's okay. It was smart. I actually did try to drive back that night. I tore my condo apart looking for them." She laughed a little. "You really do know me, don't you?"

"Speaking of smart," I said, trying to sound hopeful. "I got into the University of Kensington even though I bombed the GRE." I should've been happy, but all I could feel was shock and dread. I wanted to wake up and have it all be a nightmare.

Keys jingled on the other line. "Congrats. Do you want me to pick you up after the detective leaves? We can look for Ananda together."

I looked around Brad's loft. I didn't belong there. I was a temporary visitor, and I'd be leaving all too soon. "Sure. Let's meet at the gazebo."

When I left Brad's, a cool rain pelted me. I didn't bother going back for my raincoat. It felt good on my face. It distracted me from feeling anything else. I wandered around the gazebo for a while before Kitty arrived.

Even though I was sopping wet by the time I climbed into her car, she was silent. Maybe she understood. She drove slowly for once. We searched the streets, neither of us speaking. It was our first shared silence. I was sad it came on the heels of a tragedy instead of a shared joy.

"How was the detective?" I finally asked.

"Fine. The video cameras at the condo backed me up. Even though I was alone at the time of the arson, I'm not a suspect. He was curious why you didn't tell him you drove me home, but it wasn't important."

"Ugh. With everything else, I guess I forgot."

"It's okay. I don't think you're a suspect either." She cast me a sidelong glance with red-rimmed eyes.

A cold lump swelled in my chest. "Brad and I are breaking up."

She exhaled through her nose. "You really like him, don't you?"

I nodded, unable to say anything else.

"Is there any way you can work it out? Like a long distance relationship?"

"Not the way he talked about it."

"That's too bad. By the way... I didn't tell the detective about Jared spiking the food."

I nodded. Neither of us could implicate him, even though he'd killed eight people that night. In my heart, I didn't think Jared was cruel. Stupid, yes, but not an intentional murderer. As shady as his actions were, he'd never intended to harm anyone.

We drove through back alleys and side streets, but didn't see Ananda. After an hour of looking, Kitty turned down Hazelwood. I steeled myself, my breath hard in anticipation. I needed to see the burned house for myself, to know it was actually gone.

Smoke hit my nose, and then I saw it. What was once the House of Transformation was a smoldering rubble of blackened wood. Ashes spread everywhere, like shrapnel. Smoke trailed on the wind. The kitchen sink and the fireplace still stood, and the tree in the backyard was blackened, but everything else was gone.

We stared at it in disbelief. There really was no more House of Transformation. It was surreal, as if someone had tried to erase the house, and a black smudge was all that was left.

I wondered how the fire started. Did Ananda come back to do it? I doubted it. Kitty couldn't have — she was stuck in her condo. I wondered if Jared had the capacity. But the police already had the empty containers of Indian food. There was no evidence left for him to have to burn down a house.

What about Clary? I hardly knew her, but she seemed the type. She'd looked at me with unmasked contempt and righteousness in the coffeehouse, the same way I'd once looked at Brad before I knew him. But what would she gain from setting it on fire? All of Ananda's belongings burned, and probably hers too.

A thought crossed my mind — one so terrible I could barely think it before shoving it into the recesses of my mind. Maybe the house had set itself on fire. Maybe demons danced through Ananda's portals and up the walls, and the hell fire from their hands and feet made the house catch flame.

A patch of darkness hung over the house, like a tear in the fabric of the sky. I wasn't sure what I was seeing, if it was an illusion, the smoke, or if it was real.

"What is it?" Kitty asked.

"The portals are still open. I think that's why the house burned down."

She stared at the sky, her forehead wrinkled. "How do you close a portal?"

"I think I know how."

"What about Yes and Ricky?"

"They can stay if they want. This isn't about them. Will you help me?"

She nodded. We stepped out of the car. The rain had let up, but the sky was still gray. As I circled the house, I imagined the spirits flying back into the portals, going back to where they came from. On our second time walking around the house, I imagined the portals closing. On our third rotation, I could no longer see the dark tear, but I saw something else floating above the wreckage and smoke. I squinted and saw a cluster of twinkling, bouncing lights. My face tingled with wonder.

"Rosie is here."

The lights expanded until two other forms flanked her. A mother and father? Or was it Yes and Ricky? I gasped. It was. They held Rosie, like a family, like it was always meant to be that way. Rosie was happy. She danced and turned. I felt the love emanating from them, as if they felt fine and they wanted me to be fine too.

I blinked as tears swam into my vision, then saw nothing but the faintest of glimmers in the sky. "Thank you, Rosie, whoever you were. Goodbye Ricky. Goodbye Yes."

Kitty glanced at me, her breath caught. "You didn't see Ananda's spirit, did you?"

I shook my head, feeling dizzy all of the sudden. A piece of half-burnt paper flew against my leg and flapped. I bent to pick it up. It was typewritten, with a professor's red ink and a torn edge where a staple had been. On the back was Ananda's scrawl in water-bled cursive. Kitty leaned beside me to read it.

Portal Magic
The Other Side
Revelations
Books by Ananda Dawn

I glanced up at the sky, wondering if Rosie or Yes saved this for us. If they did, what did it mean? *The Other Side* was particularly cryptic. Was Ananda still alive? Or did this mean she was dead?

Kitty bit her lip and glared at the rubble.

"She's still alive," I said without thinking. She had to be.

Kitty turned to me, her eyes tortured. "How do you know? Can you sense it? Like you sense ghosts? Where is she? Will you look for her?"

I held the paper in my hands and thought about Ananda, her acid green eyes, and her flowery black perfume. I didn't sense her around the house, though several other ghosts were there, hiding behind trees and playing on the roofs of nearby houses. I wondered if they were the newly departed or if they'd been there for a long time. I was relieved I didn't see the shadowy, lurking spirits. I hoped that meant we delivered them back to wherever they'd come from.

I closed my eyes and thought of Ananda's orange hair, our collages, and those dreamish moments when we slept beside each other.

Ananda, where are you?

I rocked forward. A two-lane road cut through the darkness. Yellow dashes zipped by like blips. My vision rose skyward, and I saw flat land with heavy cloud-cover, like Kansas or Iowa. I opened my eyes.

"What?" Kitty asked, her face creased with worry.

"I think she's on the road."

A teenager approached us on the sidewalk. He had shaggy hair and a trucker hat. I thought I recognized him from the time my car ran out of gas and some guys pushed it to the house.

"It's weird, huh?" he asked, lighting a cigarette. "My dad said that house used to be a funeral home, with a morgue in the basement. A daycare too. Someone even said it was a Mosque."

I looked at the House of Transformation. In its last incarnation, it was all of those things and more.

"It burned for a while before the firefighters came," he said.

"Do you know who burned it down?" I asked. "Did you see anyone?"

"Nah. Prolly a candle."

"We have to go," Kitty said, her jaw clenched.

We drove down more alleys and roads, Kitty asking me if I felt anything every couple of streets. I didn't. We looked everywhere, but didn't even find a scrap of Ananda's clothes. It was like she'd vanished.

By the time she drove me back to the warehouses, powdery dusk had fallen. We'd been silent for at least an hour. We were both thinking the same thing — Ananda was gone, and there was no way to get in touch with her.

Kitty parked in front of the warehouse, but left the motor idling. It was clear she wasn't interested in coming in. Whatever friendship we had, Ananda had been the heart of it, and now that heart was gone.

"Maybe she'll reach out," I said.

Kitty said nothing at first, but after a moment, she nodded, her chin quivering.

I'd barely closed the door when she sped off, probably to look for Ananda again.

I knocked on Stevey's warehouse door. No one answered. He was most likely still in the hospital, but I expected someone to be there, perhaps Barry or another one of the bears. I dug in my purse until I found a receipt. With a pencil, I wrote *Hope you feel better soon!* and slipped it under the door.

I was so tired, I felt like I walked through water. I climbed the stairs to the roof and smoked, looking at the buildings, cars, and people in the distance.

If my vision was true, Ananda would be among strangers. She'd be charming them and laughing and exclaiming in delight and touching their arms. She'd be fine. I just didn't know if I would.

The next morning, I awoke to bird songs. I threw the U Kensington brochures on the kitchen table and resisted cracking them open until after I had coffee. Slowly, I opened each one. I took in the photos of attractive lawns, ornate architecture, and students cheerfully studying together.

I received emails from the head of the graduate teaching assistants and the housing department. My room would be in West Hall, a graduates-only dorm, known for its quiet times. It was a gray-bricked building with turrets, surrounded by a lawn peppered with junipers, cypresses, and ancient oaks. It looked like Hogwarts. Ananda would have loved it — she would've wanted to take photos everywhere. I imagined her leaning in one of the Gothic arched windows as Jared snapped away.

Later that day, I loaded my car with my belongings. It wasn't hard. Everything was already packed. I drove the two-hour jaunt to the university. When I entered the sleepy college town, I was surprised at the lushness. The grass was greener, the air cleaner.

After getting a little bronze key from a laid-back guy in the housing department, I took a bag up three flights of stairs to a cream-colored room. It was smaller than Brad's loft, and cozy, with a desk, a bed, and a closet. I set the bag down and looked out the leaded windows. The front lawn sprawled before me.

I brought up more bags until my car was empty. It was strange to hang my clothes in the closet and dress the bed with my sheets. I finished as the sun set. The lights of the campus came on, making it look like a fairy village. I leaned out the window and smoked my last cigarette, gazing at the beauty.

In this new place, something shifted inside of me. I started to look forward to my time there. I'd left so much behind, but I'd arrived at a destination with so much potential. It was a beginning. The days would tick off like minutes. My new life would roll out like a fine carpet.

To my surprise, the Bosch painting was packed among my things, wrapped in a sheet. I hadn't realized I'd taken it. I stashed it in the back of my closet, planning to give it back to Brad the next time I saw him. I couldn't bear to look at it. It reminded me of everything I'd left behind.

I thought about Ananda in the days following. I imagined her life would change for the better. She might meet another soul mate, or have an adventure that would change the course of her life forever. Since the twin cities were full of her broken friendships, I wondered if the road offered her another chance to reinvent herself yet again.

I went through a reinvention too. After one last weekend of bliss with Brad, with longing looks and kisses that lasted hours, I dropped him off at the airport. He promised he'd be back if it didn't work out. I told him I hoped it didn't. I hoped they'd fire him, or he'd hate the new job, or he'd think the city was too noisy and busy. More than anything, I hoped he'd miss me and have to move back.

But as time wore on, none of those things happened. He wrote me every day, telling me how much he liked his new boss, subways, bodegas, and street vendors. I wrote him back about my meetings with professors and registering for Statistics and Abnormal Psychology.

Grad school was the opposite of art. It was the realistic continuation of my career in the path I'd acquiesced to several years ago, when my parents informed me I couldn't be an artist.

They were elated I 'quit that art thing' and was back in school. Seeing them after the fall of the House of Transformation was comforting, though I wanted nothing more than to regress back to childhood — no job, no school, just baking cookies with mom, playing checkers with dad, and stomping in puddles with rain boots. They knew I was disturbed, but I wasn't talking about it yet. I was still processing everything. I didn't even know where to begin.

The landlords of the House of Transformation were furious. They wrote me several emails, demanding to know what happened. I never responded. What could I say? We unleashed demons? Ghosts came out of portals and took people with them?

Detective Smith contacted me again, asking if I remembered Jared's last name. I didn't. That was the last time I heard from him.

The day before classes started, Kitty called to tell me she was moving to LA. She said she'd find better vocal work out there, but I wondered if she'd heard the same rumor I had — that Ananda took off with Clary for LA. No one knew the origin of the rumor, but it spread like a fire across our community. People I didn't even know asked me if I'd heard it, including the new barista at the coffeehouse.

Kitty and I met for one last hurrah at The Wolf, a bar at the end of the Arts District known for its black walls and low lighting. I arrived early and sat in my car, trying to decipher my Statistics textbook. Kitty drove up in a brand new red mustang. I wasn't surprised. She seemed like the type who'd squash her grief with shiny new possessions. She got out of her car and rapped on my window.

"Come on, I need a drink," she said, though from her bleary eyes, it looked like she'd already been drinking.

We walked into the bar and sat on stools. The day-drinkers barely glanced at us. Kitty ordered two LA sunsets. They came in martini glasses and tasted of strange fruit.

She gulped hers as soon as it arrived. "I'm so glad I'm leaving the twin cities. It's hard to make a living and I can't stand the art scene." She lifted a finger to the bartender.

I took a tentative sip. I didn't want her to move to LA. She was all I had left of those magical, horrible days. I knew she was impatient and catty, but I'd grown to love those things about her, just as she probably loved my worrying, OCD nature. We understood each other despite our differences, and we'd both survived the fall of the House of Transformation. I thought our friendship would've continued for years. I never thought she'd move across the country.

I ran my fingers over the wood grain of the bar. "Did you find a place to live in LA yet?"

"Are you alright?" She squinted at me.

I met her eyes. "I guess. I'm sad you're leaving."

"Come on, it's not that bad." She threw an arm around my shoulders. "You act like I'm breaking up with you."

I smiled but it fell from my face. "I'll just miss you, that's all."

"I need to explore the world, you know?"

I nodded, a pinprick of fear stifling my throat as I toyed with the glass.

1. *Fear of abandonment*
2. *Fear of social ostracization*
3. *Loss of support network*

"You'll be fine," she said. "Besides, doesn't school start soon?"

"Yeah. Tomorrow."

"You'll get busy. Things will get better. Don't worry."

I took another sip of the martini, but it was too sweet. It reminded me of clemeral. I pushed it away.

"Did you go to Blossom's- I mean Yes's funeral?" she asked.

I glanced at her, shocked. "No. I didn't hear about it."

"I didn't go either. I just wondered if Ananda was there or not. I thought about going, but Yes's family is really closed-minded. They didn't get her at all. She was happy in life, and she's probably happy now too, if what you saw was true."

I stared into my drink. I wanted to tell her seeing Yes floating in the sky was just my imagination, but then again, I wanted to believe she was happy too.

Kitty snickered. "I just had a crazy thought. Wouldn't you just hate it if Ananda became famous?"

I laughed, much to my surprise, and nodded. "Let's make a pact," I said, "If you find her or if she reaches out, give her my email address. I'll do the same."

"Okay."

Kitty rummaged in her purse and laid down enough money for the drinks. We embraced. When we drew apart, I was surprised to see tears in her eyes. She dashed them away.

"Study hard. Make me proud."

"I will. Take care."

She gathered her purse and sashayed out the door, disappearing into the bright day.

My first couple days of school were so different from my previous life that I had culture shock. I was scatterbrained during my meetings with the faculty. None of them offered to take me on as a student, which meant I'd have to work myself sick to impress them.

My office was in a windowless basement room slopped with white paint so long ago, it looked ivory. The dampness and faint whiff of something rotting never went away. The fluorescent lights flickered, sometimes flashing in spasm-like strobes. Spiders took up so much real estate that whenever I dropped my pencil and it rolled under the desk, I left it there.

In my first month, I was given more homework than I'd seen in my entire four years of undergraduate study. I barely interacted with the other grad students — we were like rats in a maze, with hangovers from studying too late into the night.

Where was the artful life I'd dreamed of? Where was the *joi de vivre*? I'd lived life to the fullest and did what I loved, yet the money hadn't followed. I'd never be an artist. My parents had been right all along. I resigned myself to living on the outside of the artistic world, always looking back at what might've been, at the life I might've led. I tried not to think about Brad, but my heart ached at the thought of him walking beneath skyscrapers, eating hot dogs from street vendors, and not missing me enough to move back.

In my second month, I was assigned a tight schedule of social work assessments. In the bombshell of my broken dreams, my life purpose shifted to help people with real problems restore their sanities.

I tried to create collages again in those rare hours when my homework was done and no test or ten-page paper loomed, but none of my pieces seemed to fit together. I was left with a jumble of random images that I eventually packed into the old suitcase along with the other collages. Every time I looked at that suitcase, it was a reminder of how little art I actually had in me. Was it because Ananda was my fountain of inspiration? Was it because I wasn't at the House of Transformation? Or was it because so much of my time was taken up with the incessant chore of learning that I couldn't focus on anything else besides sleep and food?

I thought often about the House of Transformation. It came to me in dreams and when I was trying to pay attention in classes. If only things hadn't gone sour. If only my art career had taken off, I could have bought the house, mowed the lawn, and cleaned up the street. I would have taken care of Ananda and Jared. We would've revolutionized the art scene. But things had started to fall apart long before our falling out. I felt a constant pang of regret about Yes and Ricky. The image of them embracing each other with Rosie floated into my vision every time I closed my eyes.

I tried to put those thoughts out of my mind. They were of no use to me anymore. The American Board of Professional Psychology didn't accept the paranormal, due to lack of scientific evidence. I came to the conclusion I hadn't really seen ghosts. Xyritav was a hallucinogen. There must've been residuals in my brain when I'd 'seen' those lights. I was a fool to think otherwise.

The days turned into weeks, then months, and before I realized it, I'd been there two years. I finished my thesis — a fifty-two page paper entitled Preventing Depression in Young Adults. I touched on my experience as a 16-year old runaway and supported it with over a hundred articles.

After I graduated, I sent my resume to several private practices, but was never called in to interview. I only had my graduate work as a relevant job. I moved back in with my parents for two months, then scored an interview at the New Beginnings Center. The director, Caroline, had attended a psychology conference where I'd presented my research, and she was impressed. She said I was over-qualified for the job, and they couldn't pay me very much. But I accepted the position. I had to start somewhere.

Working at the New Beginnings Center was everything my social work internship was not — it was younger, homier, and a hell of a lot more hopeful. I became absorbed in work and my successes. I received grants to continue the work. We added more rooms in my second year. I didn't think about my social life because work was my life. I gained several pounds thanks to the desk job. My hairdresser said he didn't think women past thirty should grow their hair past their shoulders, so I let him cut it off. It was the most unflattering look I'd ever had, but everyone else seemed to like it, so I kept it.

I thought about those old times, when the House of Transformation was alive with art and what seemed like happiness. But either those memories never happened, or happened for mere moments before evaporating.

The older I got, the more ridiculous and unsustainable that artsy life seemed. My desire to change the world, to heal people with art... my downfall was inevitable. And yet the spurring desire to do good and create more love in the world stayed with me. I put it to use at work. I told myself I was making a difference, but when I was alone, it wasn't enough. Sure, I'd saved those girls who cycled through the Center, but I wanted to save the world. Everywhere I went, I saw them — the wounded, the desperate. I wanted to do more.

I started going to therapy, to a woman with long red hair. She told me to let it go, to not try so hard, to enjoy the pleasures of life, to try new things and make new friends. She basically told me the same things I told other people. Nothing she said helped me understand myself or my burning desire to change the world. I stopped seeing her.

I kept in touch with Kitty. During her first year in LA, she scored three national commercials and several radio shows, but she still hadn't found Ananda. After a while, I stopped asking. We talked almost every week but had little to report besides the usual. The space between our conversations stretched out until a month passed between calls, then longer.

During my second year at New Beginnings, when every tree seemed to drop copper leaves on my drive home, I heard *Fire in my Heart* on the radio. Ananda's voice came through my car speakers, instantly recognizable. I pulled into a parking lot, my heart drumming in my chest. Could it really be her?

She sang wordless sounds, breathy vibratos. The beats worked into a climax, her voice guiding me, reaching into my heart and pulling me into the wondrous spaciousness of *her*.

I fumbled with my phone to google her, and with a start, found her on Wikipedia. Her hair was bleached to an almost white-blonde and her eyes were enhanced to be even greener than real life. She looked supernatural, like a Goddess.

The world dissolved as I read about her. She was discovered at a dance club and recorded the track I'd just heard in one take. I found a fan page and read that, and then another, and then another. Her facebook page had over a million fans. Famous photographers had shot her, and she was beautiful in each photo. I read everything I could find until my phone died.

I raced home, downloaded her album, and listened to it on repeat. All her songs spoke to me. I found myself singing along with her. It was almost like being close to her again. Warmth flooded throughout my body. It was as if the world had shifted and she was in my life again. I emailed her, overjoyed she was alive and thriving. I told her about graduating and my work. I asked if she wanted to meet up and reminisce.

I cancelled my appointment with my hairdresser and started growing my hair out. I painted my office raspberry red and hung fabric on the walls. I felt expansive, as if my life was more than just my career, as if possibilities were on the horizon again, and if I went out and sought them, they might be mine.

Ananda's first song was only the beginning. *Fire in my Heart* reached number eleven on the charts, and sat just below the top ten for three weeks. You know the song, I'm sure. It's a household song. Little kids turned it into a patty cake song. Several people parodied it. Talk show hosts made fun of it.

What followed was a pile-up of fame — more songs, interviews, concerts, magazine covers, and advertisements. The world became infatuated with her.

I checked my email several times a day for her response, checked my junk mail folders, and wrote again to tell her I hadn't heard from her yet. Still no response.

After weeks of dashed expectations, I became withdrawn. I took lunch by myself instead of with my coworkers. I went home instead of having dinner with the girls. I took down the fabric from the walls of my office and deleted her album from my playlists. When she came on the radio, I changed the channel.

Mary asked me what was wrong. I laughed, but I don't think I convinced either of us. It was obvious something was wrong.

I started seeing a new therapist named John. He helped me realize I was still furious at her for our estranged past, but that I also missed her terribly.

A week later, as I was making progress in therapy, her biography arrived at my house. I called in sick and binge-read it. When I came to the chapter about the House of Transformation, I was shocked.

Ananda and her girlfriend Magdalene (Mag) Woods rented a house where ritualistic drug-induced orgies were commonplace. Visitors to the 'House of Transformation' called it a wonderland of decadence, drugs, and lust under the guise of spirituality and art. Ananda and Magdalene initiated friends and strangers into their cult of sensuality. Magdalene, trained in psychology, used her knowledge to brainwash as many people as she could into the cult.

I was so furious I threw the book against the wall. I pounded out an email, demanding her to remove the false part about me. Still no response.

Eventually, someone figured out I was the 'Mag' in the book. I got calls for interviews. John helped me through it. I tried to cover it up, but I was falling apart.

One day, Mary plopped the book on my desk and asked me if it was true. I took a deep breath and looked up at her. John had warned me about this. People would want to know our history. He and I had rehearsed my line until it sounded natural, and not like I was still furious with her.

I shrugged. "She and I lived in the same house, but there was no cult. It's just Hollywood sensationalism."

Mary wanted to know more, but I refused to talk about it.

In therapy, it was another story. It was all we talked about. I couldn't believe Ananda had allowed people to think we had orgies. No one had sex in that house, except for Yes and the Swami, and maybe Jared. I wanted to scream it all over the internet, but I kept my mouth shut. I didn't want the attention. At the end of every therapy session, John and I repeated the mantra we came up with for avoiding more scandal.

'Don't poke the bear.'

Time passed. When my student loans kicked into repayment, I applied to jobs that paid better, but no one would even interview me. They'd heard about me — the psychologist who'd abused the trade. A google search of my name showed Ananda's book excerpts for the first couple of pages of results before my thesis or anything about the New Beginnings Center popped up. Also before my accomplishments were powerpoint presentations from psychology teachers who used me as an example of 'what not to do.'

When Ananda's second album, 'The Moth and the Flame,' was released, it was received well, but it wasn't as strong as her first album. The hits weren't as likable.

This is when the first cracks began to show in Ananda's starry facade. She was on xyritav in public more often. She presented the Grammy award nude. She wandered onto a live SNL skit. She became known for doing crazy things, which created more controversy. She rode the wave of the media's love-hate relationship and got sicker. I watched it from my St. Paul apartment like it was pay-per-view, unable to take my eyes off her, unable to reach her no matter how many times I tried, each time, growing more bitter at the lack of response.

Then anger got the better of me. Against John's advice, I responded to the voicemails and emails I'd been receiving for years. I vented to them. I explained how wrong her biography was, how that portrayal wasn't who I was. I wrote diatribes against her, against everything she'd lied about in her book, against everything she stood for. I wanted something in print defending myself, and the only way I could present it was to demonize her. *Analyzing Ananda* was born.

In the end, the publishers used my words to paint her as a fame-hungry, mood-swinging diva who'd do or say anything to get what she wanted, regardless of other people's feelings. I should've known better. I should have gotten a lawyer to check the paperwork, but I signed away most of my rights and didn't know what was printed until it was too late.

Chapter 35. Release

The morning after we escaped the hospital, Ananda and Hayden recorded a vlog on the balcony. I sat in my hotel room at a fancy white desk and made spa and salon appointments for her. We ordered room service for brunch and discussed my plans for the Grammys. Ananda was on board with all of it. I'd hoped she'd have suggestions for a choreographer or a dance group, but she didn't. I spent the rest of the day compiling a list of dance companies and called around to inquire if they were available. I finally booked a group, six hours after I started looking.

That night, while Hayden watched bad reality tv, I asked Ananda if I could speak with her alone. We went into her room, and I shut the door.

"So let's talk," I said. "I know you still have therapy with John, but is there anything you wanted to talk with me about?"

She sat on the edge of the bed and took a deep breath. "Yeah. You were right about John being good. He brought up some issues I never cleared with you. I wanted to talk with you about them."

"Okay."

She bit her lip. "I know my boundaries are pretty bad. It's something I'm working on. I shouldn't have come to your apartment without calling. I definitely shouldn't have put xyritav in your tea. I'm sorry."

I gave a tiny shrug and closed my eyes for a second. "Apology accepted."

She laughed nervously. "Pshew. That was easy." She paused, her face straightening. "Now here's the hard one."

I sat down in a chair and nodded.

She swallowed. "I know I confused you when I kissed you seven years ago."

"Oh." I hadn't expected we'd talk about that.

"I don't know why I do things like that. John said I have

poor impulse control. I just see something and I want it. I don't think about implications or consequences. And that's what I did with you."

I squinted at her. "What did it mean to you when you did it?"

"Um...I guess I just felt so happy and I loved you."

"That's usually something you do with people you're in love with," I said. "At least, that's what's recognized by society."

"But Mag, I've never been in love. I've tried, but it gets mixed up with my other emotions. That's something John and I have been talking about."

I kept my face neutral, trying not to show how surprised I was. "I see how that could be confusing for you."

"Yeah, and my confusion confused a lot of people. I can't handle relationship expectations, because I don't feel what other people feel. You know, everyone wanted me to be something for them. Except for you. You always just liked me for who I was, so I felt safe. Sorry if I confused you."

"That's okay. It was a long time ago. But it sounds like you're figuring out who you are and what you want."

"Do you think I'll ever be able to fall in love?" she asked, crystalline tears shining in her eyelids.

"Maybe one day."

She sniffed. "I really did believe in you. I still do. You're one of the artsiest people I know."

"Thanks."

"Can I have a hug?"

I hugged her for a long time. She breathed through her emotion. I was so impressed with her apologies, I almost laughed. It was one thing for her to go to therapy, but it was a whole other thing to turn her life around with the lessons she learned. It was like she was reinventing herself from the inside out yet again.

The next day, we uploaded Ananda's new song to itunes, since her Grammy contract said her performance song needed to be available to buy online. Even though the track sounded rusty, there was warmth to it, like a live album.

"One more thing down," Ananda said, hugging me and Hayden.

I leaned into their embrace. Our plan was working.

After Ananda left with a new bodyguard for the spa, Hayden and I hit the streets. Being near LA was so liberating. We were nobodies again, and we navigated the streets with ease. Semi-famous people surrounded us everywhere. No one paid any attention to us.

"Come on, I want you to shop with me." Hayden pulled me into a beachy clothing shop.

"But I want to see the ocean," I said, pulling back.

"Trust me, you need new clothes. You have to look like an LA manager. They eat outsiders alive here."

I frowned as she pushed me into a changing room.

"When was the last time you actually bought clothes at a real store?" she asked.

"Do snuggies count?"

"No, they definitely do not."

"I was joking."

She threw a magenta dress into the room. I took off my clothes and stepped into it. "So what's the plan for tonight?"

"Practice for Ananda's big interview. I still can't believe that was in her contract."

"Me neither." I walked out and showed her the dress.

She shook her head. I went back into the changing room, slipped it off, and tried on the next one.

"Whoa. Ananda's already making waves in LA." Hayden thrusted her phone into the room.

I looked at a photo of Ananda walking from our hotel to a taxi.

Ananda steps out in LA with new single.

"That was fast," I said. "Hey, are we E-listers, or what?"

"You're probably on the F-list, especially with your current wardrobe. But I might be an E-lister. Someone asked for my autograph."

"Why? Did they think you were someone else?"

"No, they knew who I was. They recognized me from the vlogs I do with Ananda."

"Oh," I said, wondering at how little I understood celebrity culture. "Are you going to do the whole 'try to be a celebrity' thing?"

"Nah, I'd rather be Ananda's assistant. I can't do what she does — the way she works a crowd and the spotlight. It's too much work."

"And working for her isn't?" I laughed. I stepped between the curtains to show her a red dress.

She looked me up and down approvingly. "You're getting that."

"No way. It's $300. I can buy ten dresses for that much."

"Ananda's paying for it," she said, a glimmer in her eyes. "She told me to buy you some clothes in LA so you don't stick out so much."

"I don't stick out."

Hayden handed me a pair of studded ballet flats. "Trust me Mag, you need help." She held out her hand.

I begrudgingly took off my sneakers and handed them over.

"Can't I just watch interviews instead of being coached?" Ananda whined. She was back from the spa, her roots touched up, her face fresh from a peel.

"We don't know this interviewer," Hayden said. "He could ask anything."

"Brase Legal?" She snorted. "Is that an elf name or something? Did you look him up online?"

"Yeah, there's no record of this guy anywhere. I don't know what the Grammy people were thinking when they put this interview clause in your contract."

Ananda's face cracked. "Do you really think he's going to ask me about xyritav?"

"Yeah, and when he does, you should have an answer, and look like you believe it."

"Fine." She rolled her eyes.

I left to pick up dinner. When I got back to the room, they

were still at it.

"Again," Hayden said. "*You had a problem with drugs, didn't you?*"

"Yes. It was prescription pills, but now I'm clean, and I feel great."

"Good, I actually believed you that time. Okay, so next, he's probably going to ask you how long you've been clean. Do you know how long it's been?"

"Two weeks?"

"Say it again."

"Two weeks!"

"Don't look so astonished when you say it. Put your guard up. One more time. How long have you been sober?"

"Two weeks."

Hayden grimaced. "We'll have to work on it."

The next morning, while Ananda slept in, Hayden and I checked to see how many people bought her single. Only a few thousand sold. I figured there was a lag time between the purchase and the reporting of sales, but Hayden mumbled something about real time data and left the room. Worse still, the song had an average rating of 1.5 out of 5 stars. Reviews included 'worse than her techno-pop shit,' 'sounds unfinished,' 'bad quality,' 'boring,' and 'bitch can't sing.'

When Ananda walked out of her room in a terry-cloth robe, she saw my frown. "Not good? Let me see." She reached for my laptop.

"No," I said. "I'm not going to let you read mean comments before your interview today."

"Mean comments? What are they saying?"

Hayden walked into the room again and took Ananda by the arms. "Haters gonna hate. You need to stay positive."

Ananda set her hands on her hips. "I have a smart phone, you know? I can find out what they're saying."

Hayden ran to her room and snatched Ananda's phone from the charger.

"Give that to me!" Ananda said.

"I have an idea," I said. "Hayden and I can write positive reviews. That'll make the average go up."

"It doesn't really work that way." Hayden looked at me like I was from a different planet.

"Are the reviews that bad?" Ananda asked. "I thought my fans liked me."

"They do," I said. "These people are trolls. They just get off on saying negative stuff. Trust me. The tide will turn. Sometimes a song isn't popular at first, but then people realize it's good. Anyway, you need to get ready. Your interview is in three hours."

Ananda whimpered. "I try to do something from the heart, and they treat me like this?"

"Don't take it personally," I said. "Artists need thick skin. You're fabulous, remember? Look at me, sweetie. Where's my Ananda?"

She looked at me and became more focused. I smiled. She was getting so much stronger. The old Ananda would've lashed out or crumpled.

"You're right," she said, sniffing. "I have to get ready."

After she walked out of earshot, I turned to Hayden. "What the hell is up with these bad reviews?"

"I don't know. I'm starting to worry we messed this up. The sound quality isn't the greatest."

"I know, but we never had time to re-record her song."

"I can't believe some people want to tear her down," Hayden said. "I mean, over five hundred one-star reviews? They say she's inferior because she doesn't write all her songs, but when she does, they hate that, too. Some people don't like her because she lightens her hair... some of them don't even need a reason — they just don't like her. I wish I could do something."

Tears pooled in her eyes, just like four years ago on my sofa at the New Beginnings Center.

I held her and took a deep breath. At that moment, I wanted nothing more than to be out of Hollywood, out of LA, and back at the Center. At least there, I knew how to fix things.

Chapter 36. The Interview

The interview was rolled out as a low-key deal: no cameras, no audience, and no photos. The producer said Ananda could wear sweat pants if she wanted, and it would take an hour tops. However, once our taxi arrived at the warehouse, we saw things were much different. A crowd of people stomped around with signs, like the hoard of villagers in Frankenstein.

"This isn't right." Hayden's face flushed as she looked through her emails. "There aren't supposed to be any people here. They said it would just be you and the interviewer."

"Wait a minute." Ananda rolled her window down. As soon as the crowd saw her, they ran toward us. I shrank back in the taxi, but as they got closer, I saw they didn't have picket signs — they were fans. Their signs had supportive messages.

I love Ananda!

Ananda Rocks!

"They don't hate me?" she asked.

"Of course they don't," Hayden said, the relief visible on her face.

"I have to talk to them." She stepped out of the cab and was immediately given books and CDs to sign, and was hugged by fan after fan as they gushed over her and took selfies.

I sat there in disbelief. It was the exact opposite of the paparazzi. Instead of negative comments and demeaning questions, they yelled they loved her. It made me wonder where the bad press from her single came from.

Hayden took a call and climbed out of the car. I followed Ananda into the hot LA sun, walking around until I got a good shot of her surrounded by her fans. As soon as I posted it to her social media page, my phone lit up with hundreds of responses. At first, I flinched, afraid it was the trolls again, but most of them said good things.

Hayden ran back to the car and glanced at me nervously.

"Who was on the phone?" I asked.

She squirmed. "Do you really want to know?"

"Yes, why? Who was it?"

"Ananda's old friend Jared Kieran. You know him too, right?"

"What? Why were you on the phone with him?"

"He's going to look into the bad reviews and see if her former label is responsible for them."

"Really?"

"Yeah, he called me this morning. He said he saw the same pattern with other artists who went off their label. He wants to represent us at no cost, because he knew Ananda from that house you guys lived in."

I bit my lip, wondering how much Hayden knew about Jared. Probably not much. I didn't know if anyone ever told Ananda what Jared did, either.

"Does Jared really think Yellow Records would give her bad reviews?" I asked. "They're one of the biggest record companies out there. Why would they care about her new single?"

"Maybe because *they* could have made that money. Ratings are different these days. There's a new formula that makes the songs go on the charts. It's not just about how many albums sell. There are also videos watched, requests at radio stations, and plays from online stations. It's complicated. It might be in their best interest to make her look bad, especially if they have another singer they want to promote."

"How do you know about all this?"

"What do you think I do when I'm not working?" she asked.

My mind raced. I knew record companies had odd practices, but this was weird. The possibility of seeing Jared again was even stranger. I never knew what had happened to him after the House of Transformation burned down. I'd barely thought of him, but when I did, I imagined him in a posh city like Brooklyn, debating the merits of light roasted coffee with other hipsters. I couldn't imagine him wearing a suit and showing up for court.

"That's not all," Hayden said. "I wanted to tell you... I asked your ex-boyfriend Brad to remix her song."

"What?" My face blushed hot and cold. "Why?"

"He remixed some of her old songs and they sold pretty well, so we're hoping we can get a dance remix. I didn't think it was important, but I talked to some studio execs, and now I wonder what we were thinking, letting her record herself without any production help."

I surreptitiously frowned at my reflection in a nearby window. I looked like a sleepy mouse, even after I opened my eyes wider. My cortisol levels skyrocketed just thinking about Brad.

"You okay, Mag?"

I shot her an uneasy look.

She caught me by the shoulders. "Tell you what. How about you and I make appointments at that fancy salon Ananda went to? Would that make you feel better?"

I nodded, but my mind was already wondering if Brad had a girlfriend. The last I heard, he was dating a girl in a band. How could I compare with that?

One of the rusted doors to the building opened a few feet in front of us. An overweight guy in black poked his head out. "Ananda's supposed to be on stage soon," he said.

"Wait a minute," Hayden said. "We were told this wasn't going to be a stage interview."

He shrugged. "I just do what I'm told."

"Can I speak to Bobby?" she squeaked.

"Bobby doesn't work here anymore." He turned to leave.

"Okay, great," Hayden said, her face frozen with frustration. "It's a stage interview."

"At least Ananda didn't wear sweat pants. But you're right. Something weird is going on here."

We ushered Ananda away from her fans with promises she'd see them on stage. She shot us confused looks, but she went along with it.

We told her what happened in the dressing room, which was murderously hot and humid. While she fixed her makeup and Hayden tried to call Bobby, I wandered out the door.

On stage, people maneuvered cameras and carried lights.

Around the next corner, someone received star treatment in front of a vanity with mirrors and lights. One person applied makeup, another worked his hair, another shined his shoes, and yet another lint-rolled his suit. I peeked out from behind the corner until I saw a sliver of his face. Then I froze, rooted to the spot.

It was Richard Trucco, the same paparazzo who'd camped out in front of my house for a month and yelled lewd things at Ananda, the one who took photos of her in her underwear and sold them to the Enquirer, the one who caught my eye when we left the hospital, and the one who worked with her ex-manager when xyritav was slipped in her bottled water. No wonder the interview seemed like a set-up. The Greaseball was behind it.

I ran back to the greenroom and threw open the door. Ananda had just cracked open a bottle of water and was about to take a drink. I slapped the bottle from her hand. It fell to the floor, gushing onto the carpet.

"What the fuck, Magdalene?"

"The Greaseball," I panted. "He's here. He's going to interview you."

She rose from her chair. "Are you serious?"

Hayden's eyes flashed wide.

"I wouldn't joke about that."

Her shoulders tightened. None of us expected this to happen. The interview was supposed to be a cakewalk.

A stagehand peeked in. "You're on in three minutes."

"I can't do this." Ananda breathed hard.

"It's in the contract," Hayden said. "If you don't do this, you'll have to pay the penalty. I'm sorry."

Ananda shook her head, her eyes wild.

"Look at me, Ananda." I knelt before her. "You can do this. Just get through this interview, fulfill your contract, and we'll leave. Play to your fans in the audience. Paint yourself as an ingénue, just like before."

"You'll be great," Hayden said. "We'll be in the audience to support you."

"What if I'm going out to an execution?" she wailed.

"Screw them," I said. "You got this. Just be yourself."

She gritted her teeth and took a hard breath. "So it's finally come down to this. *Mano a mano*. If it's a fight he wants, it's a fight he'll get."

Hayden and I walked to the audience area and sat in our reserved seats in the front row, getting a few nasty looks from the people behind us. No one smiled, and the air was still and hot. The audience was as nervous as a pen of cows in line at the slaughterhouse. I didn't see any of the fans from outside.

"Does this feel like a set-up to you?" I asked Hayden.

"I don't know, maybe. They weren't supposed to have video cameras here."

"How can they get away with this? They lied."

"I don't know. There were so many clauses and references in the contract I didn't understand." She bit her lip, her face pinched with worry. "I feel like this is all my fault."

"It's not. Don't worry. Ananda is amazing. She will rock this interview."

More lights popped on. Camera crews hustled to their places. Hayden grabbed my hand as they counted down from ten. I tried to still my breathing but my heart beat too fast.

Cheesy music played over the speakers and the Greaseball strode onto the stage. He had the same shit-eating grin on his face. He wore a nice suit and his hair was so pomaded it shone.

"Thank you, thank you," he said at the few audience members applauding. "Thanks for coming out tonight. You know our guest as the princess of pop, with eleven 'top ten' songs over the last five years. She's had an intriguing history, including her nip slip at the recent inauguration, her arrest for disorderly conduct at SeaWorld, and dancing under the Eiffel Tower with a police officer. Let's give a warm welcome to Ananda Dawn!"

My heart thudded like an alarm clock as I waited for Ananda to come out. She slipped through the curtains like a ray of sunshine through clouds, her smile radiant. Hayden and I clapped franticly. Much to my surprise, the crowd went crazy with applause too. Despite my worry, I found myself smiling. She shook hands with the Greaseball.

Hayden yelled out, "We love you, Ananda!"

The crowd echoed her. Ananda looked into the audience and beamed, taking it all in.

"Welcome, Ananda," the Greaseball said. "Please have a seat."

"Thank you."

"How are you?"

"I'm great. How are you?"

"Fantastic," he smiled slimily. "Ananda, you've just come out with a new single called *I Am Art*, but the reviews say it's not up to your usual hit status. People are saying it's underproduced, and quite frankly, underwhelming. What can you say about that reaction?"

Ananda faltered, but caught my eye. I nodded. She righted herself almost immediately.

"This song is different from my usual songs. I actually wrote this one myself. I've never released any of my own songs, so this is my most personal song ever. It's straight from my heart."

He shook his head. "There's not a lot going on. It's not something you could play in the dance club. Care to comment?"

"That's true, but how much of our lives are spent in the club? I listen to music all the time, when I wake up, shower, when I relax at night... It's not always about the dance beat. Sometimes life has more mellow moods, you know?"

"Yes. Now, you've been single for quite some time."

"Yes, I have." She shuffled her hands as if she didn't know where to put them.

"Why is that?" He leaned in.

She paused, glancing at the audience. Her smile started to slip. I could tell she was trying to turn up the charm, but she was thrown off by the Greaseball.

"I suppose I haven't met the right person yet. It's hard to meet people when you're as busy as I am."

"Well, I know someone who's been dying to see you again. Let's bring him out. Here he is — Bertrand Le Fevre!"

Music played as the cop who danced with Ananda under the Eiffel Tower walked on stage, carrying a bouquet of purple roses. He was immaculately groomed and dressed in a sharp suit. The audience gasped and applauded ecstatically.

I gritted my teeth. It was a dirty trick.

Bertrand stopped in front of Ananda and knelt as if proposing, offering her the flowers. With trembling hands, she accepted them. The Eiffel Tower dance played on a giant screen behind them.

The Greaseball gave her a cruel smile, obviously enjoying it. "Ananda, you said Bertrand was — and I quote — 'the man from my dreams.' So how about a date with this handsome guy? It's on us. An all-expense-paid date just before the Grammys!"

The audience exploded in applause and catcalls of delight. Ananda smiled weakly and nodded. Bertrand gave the audience a goofy grin. He was so relieved he was almost dancing.

I felt so bad for her. What could she do? She was trapped.

"I wonder," the Greaseball continued. "Can we see the two of you hold hands?"

"Jeez," Hayden said. "He's really laying it on thick."

I nodded. Bertrand reached for Ananda's hand. She gave in. Even though she wore her million-dollar smile, she was resigned, shocked into submission. Bertrand looked genuinely happy, though. He raised their hands into the air and gave them a massive shake. The audience responded with awws and a smattering of applause again.

The Greaseball babbled something about being out of time, and the music played again. Ananda blew kisses to the audience with her free hand and exited the stage with Bertrand.

"What the hell!" Hayden said.

"I don't know."

We ran to the exit doors and through the backstage hallways to Ananda's room. She stood awkwardly next to Bertrand. As soon as she saw us, relief washed over her face. She held out her arms to embrace us. "Wasn't that just the weirdest?"

"I couldn't believe how rude he was," Hayden seethed.

"Hello," Bertrand said. He looked nice enough, but there

was something off about him, as if his Hollywood groomers had somehow buffed out his soul along with his blemishes.

Someone knocked on the door. The Greaseball walked in, belly first, and stood before us, smiling a greasy smile.

We gasped. Hayden's jaw almost hit the floor.

"What did you think of the interview?" he asked.

"What did I think?" Ananda yelled. "*I think* I have a restraining order against you."

"Those expire, my dear." He eyed the room. "Uh oh. It looks like you spilled some water."

She snarled. "I couldn't take the chance of you poisoning me with xyritav in my bottled water again."

"Me? What do you mean?"

"I know you and my old manager Jerry used to put it in my bottled water. Were you hoping I'd be tripping for the interview?"

"Of course not. I'd never do that." He picked up a bottle of water from the table, cracked it, and took a swig. "That wasn't me — that was Jerry."

"You can say whatever you want, but we both know what you do. You try to ruin careers, only I'm beating you at your own game. And another thing — who is Brase Legal and why didn't he interview me? Did you pay him off?"

He flinched. "I thought you'd realize that's an anagram for your favorite term for me, although I'm not fond of being called a 'Greaseball.'"

I shook my head at the ceiling. So that was why it looked so familiar.

"I'm not your enemy," he said. "I've been trying to help you all these years."

Ananda huffed. "I don't believe it for a second."

"My darling Ananda, where do I begin?"

Hayden and I crossed our arms as he dawdled. I wondered if there was another hidden camera in the room, if this was some clever way to catch Ananda being furious. I wondered what he could possibly say to change the unpopular opinions of everyone in that room, except perhaps Bertrand.

"That interview was engineered for your approval ratings to go through the roof, just as everything I've ever done was. The photos of you in your hotel room, bringing that audience that loved you, bringing Bertrand here — it was all to rebrand you as a success against the crushing tide of fame."

Confusion scrambled Ananda's features, then she shook her head. "No, I don't believe it. You're just trying to save face for what happened out there. My fans love me."

"If you remember, the interview was supposed to be just you and me, but then you released *that song*. You really needed the support, so that's why we brought your fans here. It was a lot of work. We emailed everyone who bought your album in a 60-mile radius, though it appears one person bought five hundred copies, strangely enough."

Ananda looked sidelong at him. "Why should I believe anything you're saying?"

"You don't have to believe me. I'm just happy you're on the right path. You're doing great! You just have to keep going. And I simply adore your new single. It's so earthy."

Ananda made a face. "Why the hell didn't you say that on stage?"

"Look, I know I insult you, but it's all part of the shtick. Think about how terrible I seem compared to how lovable you are. Of course people are going to take your side. That's the magic of Hollywood! Jerry knew that too, and he was just putting the finishing touches on it when you fired him and decided to do your own thing."

She crossed her arms. "I find it hard to believe Jerry had any good intentions when it came to me. He just wanted to make a fool out of me."

"Ananda, who do you think paid for this? Who paid for all the workers and flew Bertie out here? Who put that interview in your clause? Of course Jerry cared about you. He wanted to do one last thing for you before he's gone."

"What are you talking about? Is he sick?"

"He has pancreatic cancer. He isn't expected to live much longer. The doctors gave him two months."

"Oh God, poor Jerry." Ananda sat in a chair and covered her mouth with her hand.

"Wait," I said. "How do we know you're telling the truth?"

The Greaseball shrugged. "I took pictures when I saw him last. See for yourself."

He passed his phone to me. Sure enough, there were pictures of him with a sunken-eyed man in the hospital.

"I even asked Cypress to tweet at you and pretend you had a spat, though that's more for her career than yours."

"You're behind that?" I asked.

"She's not really mad at me?" Ananda asked, her eyes brimming with hope.

He shook his head. "No, in fact, she adores you."

"Wait, if you're really on my side, why did you always ask me if I was sober? What was the point of that?"

Something resembling a smile broke across his features. "Ananda, dear, it was clear you were using. I was trying to inform you of what everyone else already knew — you needed help. It worked, didn't it? You finally got some help."

He looked around at our flabbergasted faces, then straightened his tie. "I have to run, but good luck, kid. It's been an honor working with you. It's all you from here on out. This is the last time you'll see me. Believe me, even if you wanted me around, I have plenty of other starlets to put through the rigmarole. Whatever you choose to do from now on, you'll be golden." He winked before exiting the room.

Hayden and I stood in stunned silence.

Ananda shook her head. "All this time I thought he was out to get me, and it turns out he was working for me? I don't even know what to think anymore."

"Can I do anything for you?" Bertrand asked Ananda. He reached out and put a hand on her back, but she shifted away. Optimism slowly faded from his features.

I felt sorry for him. Did he realize Ananda and the Greaseball had used him? I thought he was in on it, but maybe he was a patsy, just like Ananda had been at the beginning of her music career. We met eyes for a second. I gave him the

House Mother look. I'd have to deal with him, and I wasn't looking forward to it.

"I want to see the fans that stuck around," Ananda said, getting up.

Hayden nodded, moving toward the door. Bertrand attempted to go too, but I stopped him.

"Go ahead ladies," I said. "I have to talk with Bertie here."

Hayden gave us a piteous glance, most likely remembering the talks I had with her boyfriends when she lived at the New Beginnings Center.

"Have a seat, Bertrand. I have a few questions for you." I pulled out a non-disclosure form from my purse and slapped it on the table in front of him. "What's really up with all this? Are you here for money? Did the interviewer bribe you?"

He gaped like a fish out of water. "No, I am in love with Ananda."

"But you don't really know her. She's complicated. She's bossy and greedy. She's insane sometimes. She runs hot and cold. Why would you want to be with her?"

"We had a romantic day. I want to get to know her to see if it's real."

I stared at him. "Do you do any drugs?"

He shook his head.

"What if someone offered you money for information about Ananda?"

"I will say no."

"Never?"

"Of course, very yes," he said, his jaw set and his eyes serious.

Against my will, I cracked a smile. Some things don't translate to English very well.

"Okay. Here's the deal. You can stick around, but Ananda's really busy right now. She has a huge performance at the Grammys in less than a week, and we're way behind schedule. She'll be working fifteen-hour days. She might not be able to go out with you for a while. Is that okay?"

"Absolutely," he nodded enthusiastically. "I will wait."

"Well, my name is Mag, and I'm her manager. I'll have my

eye on you. If you hurt her, if you tell the media anything about her, or if you mess her up any more than she already is, you'll have to answer to me and my lawyers. I need you to read and sign this form. If you don't understand something, I can get a translator."

He read the document and signed. His eyes pleaded to me. "If there is anything I can do to help, please tell me. I want to help her."

My heart warmed a little. She could've picked a worse looking policeman, that's for sure.

If only the Grammys were as easy.

Chapter 37. Performance

The week of the Grammys, we rehearsed during our allotted times. Hayden and I watched Ananda like referees in case anyone tried to slip her any xyritav. We ordered all her food and personally brought in all her water bottles. We even installed a deadlock on her greenroom door that only we had keys to, so no one could change out the bottles.

However, xyritav was the least of our concerns.

The dancers I'd hired whined and missed cues. They looked as lifeless as old carrots. When I saw their dance, I was shocked when I realized they were rehearsing the same tired shuffle in expectation of performing it at the Grammys. It certainly wasn't worthy of a Grammy performance.

"It doesn't have to be good," Hayden said after one particularly bad performance. "It just has to happen."

I chewed a fingernail. "But we don't want her performance to be a joke."

"Well, do you want to talk with Madame Butterfly over there?"

I looked at the choreographer, sitting in the audience in dark cat-eye sunglasses.

"I suppose I will."

"Good luck," she huffed.

"Hey Gloria," I shouted, striding toward her.

She remained impassive. I stopped in front of her and waved.

Her head snapped toward me. "What is it?"

I hesitated. I'd barely spoken twenty words with her, but she'd promised a dynamite show.

"The dancers... they're missing cues and they don't look very animated. Could you talk with them to get... I don't know, more energy into the performance?"

She tsked and turned away from me. I leaned forward and waited, hoping she'd answer my question.

"You give me a week to put this together," she said, her Eastern European accent clipping the words. "And you want perfection?"

I shrugged. "Technically, you had a week and a few days."

Her eyebrows shot up. "We are still in rehearsal."

"But the performance is tomorrow."

She stood up and looked at me as if she might spit on me, then turned and walked away.

I rolled my eyes. Great. If she was going to take another smoke break, I wouldn't see her for an hour. "Okay, thanks," I called after her.

I walked backstage and sat down in one of the cushioned chairs. Hayden frowned, tapping out an email on her phone. Ananda was trying on her white sequined costume with a seamstress who had several pins in her mouth.

"Let me guess," Hayden said. "It didn't go so well?"

"Nope."

"Well, I have worse news. I just got an email from the sound guy. He said we can't use the recording Ananda made at the apartment. It's too low-fi. Apparently, he's been waiting for us to give him another one, but I never received the message."

"But the song sounded fine during dance practice."

"He said through the high-quality amps, it sounds like a giant refrigerator was running offstage. He said our only solution would be to have Ananda play the song live."

Ananda cringed. "I don't know if I can do it live. I never play my own instruments when I perform."

"The Grammys are tomorrow," I said. "Why did he wait so long to tell us?"

"I'll look into other options," Hayden said.

"We'll figure something out," I said to Ananda.

She nodded, but the look in her eyes said she feared the worst.

The day of the Grammys arrived. Ananda tried playing her music with a drum machine and a keyboard, but it was clear she hadn't practiced in a long time. She kept missing beats. The dancers were a little more animated, but they lacked zeal, and still didn't have the choreography down.

After the twelfth run-through, Ananda walked off the stage toward us, her head in her hands. "This isn't working."

"You just need more practice," I said, smoothing her shoulder.

"I don't have time. I'm supposed to perform this song in eight hours. I need a break." She uncapped a water bottle and took a swig.

"Take ten everyone," Hayden shouted.

The dancers walked to the buffet table, complaining and shooting us dirty looks.

"What's really bothering you?" I asked.

Ananda held her head in her hands, her eyes quivering with tears. "The dancers are going to make me the laughing stock of the Grammys again. Can you just make them get it?"

I looked at them, wondering what I could do. When I didn't answer right away, she stormed off to her greenroom.

"She's PMSing," Hayden said. "She just needs to get through this five million dollar price tag on her performance. Otherwise, it'd be another slam to her reputation. The critics would eat it up, especially with the hospitalization and drug confession earlier this month."

My brows furrowed. "Hayden, I'm afraid I pushed her too hard. She said she performed well under pressure, so I thought it'd be okay. But I think I screwed this up."

"I'll find out what she wants to do," she said, running after Ananda.

I nodded. If it came down to it, maybe Ananda's sanity was worth more than five million dollars. I sat in an audience chair, running my hands along the red velvet on the armrest. Some coiffed celebrity would sit in this same chair in their best attire in just a few hours, watching Ananda's performance, or whatever we scrambled together.

"Uh, hey," said a dancer from another crew. "It's our turn on stage,"

"Fine. Take it." I waved.

Ananda's dancers glared at me. "What are we supposed to do?" one of them asked.

I walked over to them. They were getting on my nerves. "Just hold on a few minutes. We'll figure it out."

I piled a plate with a croissant, fruit salad, and dark chocolate, and sat down in the velvet seat again to mindlessly shovel food into my mouth. It was another bleak morning, just like every other morning this week.

I'd hoped today might be different, that we might have a breakthrough, but it was worse. More critics had come out with scathing reviews of Ananda's single, and it wasn't just Yellow Records. Magazine reviewers, radio hosts, and bloggers all over the world spoke out about how much they detested her new song. Ananda's fan base was split in two. There were the people who loved her new experimental, ambient sound, and those who thought she'd gone off the deep end. I found it hard to believe anyone detested her music, but hundreds of one-star reviews said otherwise.

"Mag? Is that you?"

I dropped the croissant to the plate and saw Brad, standing in the aisle beside me. I threw the plate on another chair and stood to face him, taking in his deep blue eyes and graying hair at his temples. He'd gained some weight, but it looked good on him, making him seem more solid instead of the toothpick-thin silhouette I remembered. My heartbeat increased. Suddenly, I was glad Hayden insisted on getting our hair cut at the salon last week.

"What are you doing here?" I asked, licking the chocolate from my fingers. "Are you meeting someone?"

I went through the list of starlets going to the Grammys, and tried to figure out which one he was with. Probably one ten years younger and a thousand times richer than I was.

"I'm here to see Hayden Madden, actually. She emailed me about a remix. Then she emailed again last night, saying things weren't going so well. I was already in town, so I thought I'd drop by with it."

"Really? Do you have it with you?"

"Yeah." He patted his briefcase. "How have you been?" His hooded eyes glinted in a way that warmed my heart.

I hesitated. I wanted more than anything to catch up with him, but Ananda needed a solution, and fast. "Would it be possible to listen to it right now?"

"Sure. My schedule is clear."

"Great. Follow me."

I walked with him to the backstage area, past snide glances from our dancers and murmurings of the other dance troupes. When I held open the backstage door, his hand brushed against mine for a moment. My fingers tingled. I felt myself flush and smile, despite my predicament.

I knocked on the greenroom door. It opened a crack and Hayden poked her head out. Her eyes flicked to me, then Brad.

"Hayden, this is Brad."

"Oh, hi!" She opened the door and shook his hand.

"Hi," he said. "I have that remix if you want to hear it now."

"Yeah, come in."

Ananda turned around from the vanity, a tube of lipstick frozen in her hand.

"Hello Ananda," Brad said stiffly. "Long time."

I realized they'd never made up all those years ago. I rolled my eyes. Enough was enough.

"Ananda, it wasn't just me that saved your life at the House of Transformation. It was Brad too. If he hadn't called the ambulance, you would've died, so I don't want to hear about any imaginary problems you thought you had in the past. You guys are friends now, okay?"

Hayden went stiff, looking across the room at our faces. She didn't know about our weird past, and I wasn't in the mood to relate it to her at the moment.

"Actually, Brad," Ananda said, setting down the lipstick. She met his eyes. "I want to say I'm sorry. I was incredibly stupid when I was younger. I never should've been mad at you. All you did was try to help me. I just didn't know how to take it."

I inhaled sharply. Another apology! She'd made so much progress lately I felt giddy.

Brad put his hands in his pockets. "It's okay. It's in the past."

An awkward silence permeated the room until Hayden stepped forward.

"I invited Brad here," Hayden said, "because he has a remix of your new song. It might help us with our dilemma tonight. Can we hear it?"

Brad unlocked his phone and played the song. Beats started up, then chords materialized. When Ananda's voice came on, the lyrics were out of order, but they were all the better for it. He'd even created a hook that wasn't there before.

I gazed at him. I couldn't believe I was in the same room as he was, after all these years. With a rush of pleasure, I noticed he didn't have a ring on his left hand.

"Oh my goddess!" Ananda clutched her heart. "This is it! This is the song I want to do for the Grammys."

He flinched. "Wait. Aren't the Grammys tonight?"

We all nodded.

"Okay," he said. "I guess I have some editing to do, then."

"It's perfect the way it is," Ananda said.

"There's just one thing," Hayden frowned.

"What?" Brad and I asked at the same time. We glanced at each other for a second.

"The song has to be available for purchase by the time of the performance. It's in the contract. Can you upload it?"

"Sure," he said.

"And can you email the song to me and put both mixes on a thumb drive — one with her voice and one without? They want to use the track for an intro later on." Hayden cringed. "Sorry."

"Wow. I'm glad I didn't stop for lunch," he said.

"There's a buffet," I said. "It's for people working on the Grammys. Technically, you're one of those people now."

"I have to make a few calls," Hayden said, rushing out of the room.

"Thank you so much Brad," Ananda said, exhaling deeply. "Now I just have to find the dancers. Excuse me."

Brad and I both moved to walk out of the door at the same time. We both stopped. I knew he was pressed for time, but he made no movement to leave. We gazed into each other's eyes and I felt my breaths shorten, just as they always had in his presence.

"Thanks for doing this," I said.

"Not at all. I guess I'll see you in a couple of hours."

Two and a half hours later, Brad knocked on the greenroom door. I opened it with a little smile. Hayden leapt up from the couch.

"I came as quickly as I could," he said, passing a thumb drive to Hayden.

"Thanks again," she said. "I'm going to get this to the sound guy."

Brad turned to me. I found myself holding my breath.

"Do you really think Ananda can pull this off?" he asked.

"I hope so. She's working on it with the dancers."

"But she only has a few hours before her performance. Doesn't she have to do hair and makeup, and sit in the audience and stuff?"

"I guess. I'm just glad she isn't presenting naked this year."

"Yeah. That was pretty weird." He laughed.

"Apparently, she was mismanaged for a while. Her bottled water was spiked with xyritav."

"I'm glad she's recovering. I think you're really good for her," he said, sitting in a chair nearby.

"When she listens, I'm good for her." I laughed, sitting opposite him. "But what's new with you?"

"A lot of work, not a lot of music. That remix was actually fun. I uploaded the song on itunes, by the way. I distorted her voice so you can't really tell it was a bad recording. I can't believe she's going to perform my remix for the Grammys! I guess I should be happy about it, but it's also a little unnerving."

"Why is that?"

"You know me, I'm a perfectionist. I always feel like there's something else I could've tweaked. I wish I could've re-recorded the vocals, you know?"

"Yeah. Maybe for the next song?"

"Sure. By the way, Hayden and I never talked about my cut of the profits."

"I can take care of that. I'll look up typical remix percentage cuts, and give you a little more than the high end. I'll also make sure you're well compensated for everything. Just give me a while to cut the check. I might need to lie on a beach for a week or so after today."

"Okay." He ran a hand through his hair. "So what have you been up to lately? I mean, I know you've been helping Ananda. That must be cool."

"Yeah, but... I've been thinking about getting out of the entertainment business."

"Already?"

"Yeah. It's too fast-paced for me, and the problems are so stupid. The whole frenemy thing is just awful. I'd rather be dealing with real problems, like the runaways at the New Beginnings Center. At least there, I actually feel like I'm making a difference. Here, I feel like a misshapen cog in a factory that makes nothing."

"Well, a lot of people love Ananda. You're helping them, and you're definitely helping her."

"Thanks. I just don't love it, you know? Don't say anything to Ananda or Hayden about it. I want to wait for the right time."

"Sure. Do you want to grab dinner?"

I gazed into his eyes. I couldn't tell if they smoldered with affection or if it was just my reflection. I sighed. "Any other night than tonight. Rain check?"

"Okay. I'll see you around."

I watched him leave, then let myself smile. He'd asked me out to dinner! I wondered if anything would come of it. I wished I could've gone out right there and then, but Ananda needed me, and I couldn't let her down.

I turned back to the task at hand: getting Ananda to live through this Grammy ordeal by whatever means possible. I couldn't imagine the pressure she was under. There'd be hundreds of cameras and millions of people watching tonight.

I wove my way through the techs and backstage people and went to the stage. I found everyone in the stage pit. The scantily clad dancers encircled Ananda and Hayden.

"I don't care. You're all fired," Ananda said.

The dancers gaped from Ananda to me. "Ms. Woods, can she do that?"

"Uh." I looked at Ananda. Her eyes were set. She looked livid. Hayden shrugged helplessly beside her.

"Sorry," I said. "We'll mail you a check, I promise."

"But I told my mom I'd be on tv tonight!" a girl whined.

"Well, we don't always get what we want," I snapped. "I wanted to be an artist, but my parents practically made me study psychology, and here I am, cleaning up after Ananda!"

The girl crumpled into herself, pouting.

"Just please go," I said. "Everyone, please leave. NOW."

I turned to Ananda as the dancers filed away in disbelief.

"So, it'll just be you up there on stage?"

She collapsed into my arms. "I can't do this. I can't memorize the new lines in this short time. What am I going to do?"

I looked at my watch. We had two hours until she had to be in her seat in the audience with Bertrand.

"Would it help if we made you cue cards?" I asked.

Ananda nodded, a spark of hope in her eyes.

"Let's go," I said to Hayden.

We raced to the nearest drugstore on foot, my heart nearly exploding with adrenaline. We bought two markers and all the white poster boards they had, then ran back to the greenroom and started writing the lyrics onto the posters while the hairdresser fussed with Ananda's locks.

As I wrote, I thought about calling John. It'd been so long since we last talked. I wanted to tell him I started having panic attacks again, only I didn't have time. The irony wasn't lost on me, but I resolved it wouldn't happen again. After the Grammys, I'd quit working for Ananda. These past several weeks had been rewarding and uplifting, but also punishing and degrading. I missed using my brain for work. I missed the raw emotion and helping people. Ananda was worth it, but I couldn't sustain it. Working for her was like running a marathon. I wasn't cut out for it.

It was only then, within hours of the Grammys, that I allowed myself the luxury of thinking about quitting. Ananda needed someone trained in this. This last minute scramble was just another brick of proof in the house of my ineptitude.

We finished the cue cards just as the beautician finished Ananda's makeup.

Bertrand came into the room and leaned in to kiss her. "You look beautiful."

She pushed him away. "You'll smear my makeup." She sidestepped him to look at herself in the mirror.

Bertrand slumped away and pulled out his phone again.

"Shit." Hayden looked up from her phone. "You have, like ten minutes until you have to sit in the audience."

Ananda's hands trembled as she smoothed flyaway hairs. "Any last thoughts?"

I faced her and smiled. "Your new song is great. You just have to do it."

She nodded and took a deep breath. Tears sparkled in her eyes.

"What's wrong?" I asked.

"Just stress." She wiped her eyes and clutched her purse so tightly, her knuckles were white, then she tucked it under her arm. She gave me a false smile that slipped off her face.

Everything stopped in my mind — the room went quiet. She was holding the purse too tightly. She didn't need it. It could only mean one thing. I tried not to let the suspicion show on my face.

I pretended to look for something in my purse as Hayden said something encouraging to her. When I saw my opening, I reached out, snatched her purse, and wrenched it open.

Lying in the shell of her purse were her lipstick, her compact, and three green pills.

Ananda scrambled, trying to take the purse back, but I held on. She pulled hard. The seams ripped, making everything fly.

A xyritav landed right in front of Hayden's feet. She bent down to pick it up and shuddered. "Ananda, what the fuck is this?"

Ananda's eyes filled with tears, but she didn't say anything. She just stood there looking defeated.

"I thought you were over this!" Hayden said, her nostrils flaring.

I wanted to tell Hayden to back off, but I also thought Ananda deserved being lectured by a twenty-one year old. She deserved to know how her actions affected other people. I shot Bertrand a sharp look. He shrugged and stepped out to the hallway.

When Ananda didn't answer, Hayden gave me the pill and stormed out too, slamming the door behind her. Ananda cried in earnest as I collected the two other pills and flushed them down the toilet.

"Where'd you get them?" I asked, searching her eyes for glassiness.

"A dancer," she whimpered.

"Did you take any?"

"No, but everyone hates me. I might as well take them if it helps me get through the night."

I shook my head. "Nobody hates you."

"The critics hate me. I have one of the lowest ratings ever for a new song."

"They're critics. They hate everything. They don't know you, though. I know you, and I know you're bigger than this. I know we've been on a breakneck schedule, but you can do this performance tonight without xyritav. You're stronger than you realize. You're Ananda fucking Dawn!"

After a moment, she looked at me.

"Here's what I want you to do," I said. "Put on your headphones, listen to the music, and get your game face on. I'll get you when it's time for your performance, okay? Can you do that?"

She nodded, and we embraced.

"Do it for me and Hayden. We'll have your cue cards in the

pit. You can do this! You just have to survive tonight. After this, you can do whatever you want, okay? So think about that too."

"Okay." She sniffled.

On my way out, I saw Bertrand in the hallway. He staggered toward the door, as if to join Ananda. I put my hands up.

"You're not going in, and she's not coming out until she has to perform."

He looked affronted. "What should I do? Sit in the audience without her?"

"I don't care. You figure it out."

He simpered, but I had bigger things on my mind. I just hoped Ananda's star quality would rise to the top for this performance.

I walked to the buffet table backstage and found Hayden shoving cake in her mouth. A television nearby showed the celebrities on the red carpet, arriving and giving face to the cameras. I sighed. Ananda should be among them, throwing her head back and laughing, Bertrand on her arm. Instead, she wailed in her greenroom, trying to find her inner peace.

I took a deep breath and named my fears. Today, they seemed bigger than ever before.

1. *Fear of failure*
2. *Fear of not making it through this ordeal*
3. *Fear of the unknown*

I closed my eyes for a moment. I told myself after a few hours, it would all be over — the Grammy performance, my job, and the mega stress. I could get through the night. I repeated it like a mantra.

Hayden turned to me, her eyes bleary. "The press knows she fired her dancers. One of those little tutus ratted us out. Everyone's waiting for Ananda to fail. I feel bad for what I said, but really, after all we've been through! And she goes and gets it from a dancer! It's only a matter of time before one of them leaks it to the press. It's a disaster."

"Take a deep breath," I said. "Neither of us can control her and we can't blame ourselves."

Hayden nodded, her chin quivering.

"I gave her a pep talk," I said. "She might come through. She has that super-power, you know?"

Stagehands ran through the backstage area, walkie-talkies crackling. "Places, everyone. We're live in ten! Get all the celebs in their seats now!"

"Hayden, if you want, I can do the cue cards by myself. You can sit in the audience with Bertrand."

She snapped back to the present moment and shook her head. "No way. He gives me the creeps. I mean, who breaks up with their girlfriend of two years for a pop star? Plus, he never talks. He just sits there and sulks on his phone."

"Yeah, he's weird," I said, taking a breath. "So you're still in?"

"Absolutely."

"I'm so glad to have your help. I couldn't- I wouldn't do this without you. Ananda's my friend, but you're the reason I'm still here."

She clasped me in a hug and I hugged her back. I didn't have the heart to tell her I was going to quit after the performance. I just wanted us to get through the night. Hell, after tonight, she might quit too. Maybe we both missed our sanities.

I wondered where Brad was. I wished he were nearby to be a sane voice, to hold me and tell me something nice. Wherever he was, I hoped he was watching.

A few minutes later, the music swelled and the announcer listed the upcoming acts. Finally, the host, a middle-aged comedian, walked through the curtains and swaggered onto the stage. He received applause and started making jokes. One of them was about 'what crazy thing Ananda was going to do tonight.' When the camera cut to her seat, not even Bertrand was there — some nobodies sat there instead. Hayden frowned and shook her head. I bit my lip, my pulse racing. I kept glancing at my watch to make sure I'd get Ananda onstage in time.

About two hours later, just before it was time for her to perform, I knocked on her door. When there was no response, I opened the door with my key.

Ananda tugged earbuds out and stood up from her chair. I scrutinized her to make sure she was sober. Her eyes were clear. There was something different about her — her posture was confident, yet resigned.

"I finally found the strength to do it."

"Something's different about you," I said. "What is it?"

"I understand it all now. I wrote those lyrics when I was first sober, and they didn't make sense at the time. Seeing them in this new order makes it clear. I don't need xyritav anymore."

"Good. I'm so glad. Are you ready?"

"Yes."

I took the cue cards and we walked to the edge of the stage. I turned to her. "I'll be right in front with Hayden. You're going to be great."

She gave me a gorgeous, real smile. She was electric, just like the old days, but this time, she was lit up from within, without any external assistance. It was amazing. For the first time that day, I felt things might actually work out.

Hayden and I crouched in the pit with the cards. Several front-row celebs looked at us askance, but I was beyond caring. My heart beat in my chest so rapidly that I sweated armpit stains in my dress as we waited for her to be announced.

"Ladies and gentlemen," the host announced from the side stage. "It is with great pleasure that we give you... Ananda Dawn."

The house lights fell. Smoke obliterated the stage for a second as Brad's music began to play over the speakers. It sounded so rich and big, with huge crescendos.

The smoke dissipated and Ananda stood there, looking fabulous, gazing into the audience. She walked to the center of the stage. When it came time for her to sing, she missed the cue.

My breaths quickened as I tapped the cue card at the point she should be singing, but Ananda just looked into the audience like a statue.

Hayden scrambled up and waved to get her attention, but Ananda had a faraway look in her eyes. If I hadn't checked on her just a few minutes ago, I would've sworn she was on clemeral or xyritav.

The beat went on, and still, she didn't sing.

"Stop the music," Ananda said into the microphone.

The audience shifted uncomfortably.

"Stop the music!"

The beat dropped. Dead silence stifled the atmosphere. The guys behind the cameras looked at each other. Ananda cleared her throat.

"What's going on?" I whispered to Hayden.

She shrugged, as alarmed as I was.

"Oh my God," one of the celebrities gawked. "She's doing this on live tv?"

Ananda shook her head and gazed into a camera. "This isn't me. This isn't who I am. You might think you know me, but you don't."

I looked around. Mouths gaped as far back as the balcony. No one in the audience even breathed.

"These awards," she said, "the singing and pageantry, this whole thing just isn't me. When I did the *Eiffel Tower* thing and presented the award naked, that wasn't me either. That was the xyritav, but this is who I really am. Take a good look."

She walked to the other side of the stage.

"I know you've all heard about my addiction. There was even a joke about it tonight." She looked at the host, whose face had turned sour.

"It's not a joking matter to me. My childhood was a disaster. I never should've made it, not in Hollywood, or anywhere in this world. I thought about ending it several times. You could say I lucked into this job. I mean, I can't even sing that well! But I got discovered, and I wanted to be loved *so much* that when my manager pressured me to do crazy things to be in the spotlight, I let it happen. He gave me endless bottles of xyritav. He knew I was addicted. When I refused it, he put it in my water. That's why I did so many crazy things."

Hayden reached for my hand. I could barely believe my ears. From the corner of my eyes, I saw star-studded celebrities horror-struck, fingers touching parted lips, eyes wide.

"I've been off xyritav for three weeks now, and I'm trying to become the person I always wanted to be, but it's hard, especially with the whole world watching." She sniffed back tears.

"So I'm going to take a break. I'm going to sort myself out. I arranged to get help at the Beverly Hills rehab center. I'll be going there right after this. My friends Mag and Hayden helped me through so much." She glanced at us, tears shimmering in her eyes. "And I really appreciate it, but I need more help to get me through this addiction."

She took a deep breath that was picked up by the microphone and carried throughout the whole arena.

"I'm retiring from the music industry. Thank you all for your love and support over the years."

She blew a kiss, took off her microphone, and set it on the floor. Then she walked off the stage.

There was a moment of stunned silence. Hayden and I looked at each other, breathless. What had just happened?

Everyone in the audience looked around, shrugging, mouths still popped open.

Then the crowd erupted in thundering applause. One row at a time, every single person in the room stood up and clapped. Some people even wiped tears from their eyes.

As we rushed backstage to Ananda's dressing room, I had an inkling of what happened. Ananda had shed another layer, had become reborn, just like the phoenix I always knew she was.

The audience was still clapping by the time we reached her dressing room.

"I'm sorry," Ananda said to us. "I just realized I need more help than either of you can give me."

"It's okay," I said. "We understand."

Hayden cried and nodded.

"I really love you guys," Ananda said. "I'm sorry I put you through so much."

"I'm sorry I yelled at you," Hayden said.

"It's okay."

We embraced. Ananda squeezed us tightly. I shut my eyes

and felt tears sting, then sniffed them back and looked at her.

"Are you sure about this? Rehab?"

"Yeah. I'm going to talk Kitty into going too. She talked about it before, and she needs this as much as I do."

We broke apart. Ananda wiped her eyes with a tissue.

"Wait, what happened to Bertrand?" I asked.

"He's long gone," Hayden said. "He's been texting his old sweetheart. He's about to get on a plane right now."

"How do you know that?"

"I cloned his phone and I've been reading his messages."

"You did what? That's illegal!" I said.

"Anyone can do it, it's not hard. Anyway, he wrote her yesterday, saying LA wasn't what he expected and he's coming back to her."

"That's a relief," Ananda said.

I looked into her eyes. She'd just thrown away her entire singing career, and she seemed more sane and more certain of herself than ever before.

"What you did out there was amazing," I said. "It must have taken a lot of courage."

"Yeah. Well, I learned something when you put my addiction out there. All the pressure is gone, and I'm free now."

"What the-" Hayden said.

From the other side of the door, we heard the familiar thump of Brad's remix.

"Why are they playing your song?" I asked.

"I don't know, and I don't care." Ananda threw makeup and clothes into her bag.

Hayden switched on the television in the room. On stage, the dancers we'd fired earlier that day performed the routine to Ananda's new song, but this time, they leapt with impassioned faces, kicked with determination, and twirled with zeal. I was shocked. Why hadn't they done that when we were practicing?

When the song ended, the dancers posed in a formation. Every member of the audience stood again, and deafening applause rang out for what seemed like an eternity.

The host came on stage, a sheepish look on his face. "A

brilliant tribute to Ananda and her new song, possibly her last song ever. I think I speak for everyone when I say this: Ananda, we all love you, and we want the best for you. You're a superstar, and you always will be."

The applause carried as the camera panned over the boisterous crowd. A few people lifted lighters in the air. The camera cut to the front row, where the most famous people cheered and wiped tears from their eyes.

A rising starlet gulped at the camera. "We love you, Ananda."

A diva in her fifties nodded. "Take care of yourself. Call me."

More people down the line waved and clutched their hearts. The host continued.

"Every once in a great while do we meet someone like Ananda, someone who touches the hearts of everyone she meets, someone who will be missed by the music world greatly. What a wonderful tribute to a giant in the industry."

"Holy crap." Ananda turned to me. "I never knew they felt that way about me. I thought I was the butt of all their jokes!"

I draped an arm around her shoulder. "Never underestimate how much people love you."

The host moved on to close the show. I turned the tv off. Ananda stuffed the last of her clothes into the bag and zipped it shut. She reached for a rose from a nearby bouquet, snapped the stem in half, and tucked the flower behind her ear. "I'm ready."

"Do you want your sunglasses?" Hayden asked. "The paparazzi will be waiting."

"No. You can have them. I don't think I'll need them anymore."

I opened the door and saw a crowd of people. Both uber-famous celebrities and stagehands crowded around. They parted for us to pass, babbling encouraging words and touching Ananda's shoulders as she walked by. She smiled at them, shining like a star.

At the end of the hallway, a beefy security guard held open

the back door.

"Take care of yourself," he said to Ananda.

"Thanks. You too."

We stepped out into the warm night. The paparazzi were there. Ananda let herself be photographed. This time, I stayed right beside her. I didn't mind being photographed. Being there with Ananda and Hayden felt as natural as breathing.

After a minute, we waved goodbye to the paps and walked to our rental SUV in silence. When we were all in, we closed the doors and everything muted. I sat there for a moment, flashes of light echoing behind my eyes when I blinked. I'd never be a part of that chaotic, all-consuming, hungry world again. It felt like the stress I'd been carrying for the past couple of months dissolved into a thousand birds in flight.

We drove to the treatment center in silence. The only sounds were the voice navigation system and the clicking of the turn signal. When we sped onto the highway, the road whipped by in a blur of lights and buildings. Ananda sat in the back seat, eyes closed, looking still and serene. From time to time, one of us sighed and glanced at each other, but we didn't talk. We didn't have to, because we knew each other so well.

The voice-over directions led us onto a boulevard. Soon enough, it told us to turn onto the road that led us to the Purple Lotus Rehab and Rest Resort.

It was hard for me to believe Ananda was going away. I wanted to keep her close, just as I always had. Jared was right. She was like a drug I was addicted to.

I put the SUV in park near the white modern building with a neon purple lotus in the window. Mountain ranges crested one side of the horizon, and a pearlescent moon rose amidst the stars.

"So what now, Ananda? You can do pretty much whatever you want. Is there anything you always wanted to do?"

Her eyes fluttered to meet mine, shy. She scooted closer. "I always wanted to be a model. I told you I was one, but I lied."

"It's okay." I touched her hand.

"But remember all the modeling clothes I had? The ones

that I said were from my gigs? Didn't you ever wonder how I got those?"

I nodded, recalling the well-cut garments with no tags. The detail was exquisite. They had the most intricate beading, the deftest silhouettes, and the perfect choice of fabric. After Kitty told me she'd never modeled, I'd assumed she stole them from someone and cut the tags out.

"Where did you get those?" I asked.

"I made them. That's what I really want to do."

"What? You made them yourself?"

"Yeah. When you're almost six feet tall, you pretty much need to have a tailor or make your own clothes. But I could never tell you I made them because I lied about being a model."

"You'll be a fabulous designer," Hayden said.

"Thanks."

Hayden's phone pinged. She wrestled it out of her pocket. Her eyes grew wide.

"Oh my God," she said. "You guys aren't going to believe this. Rosie was real!"

"What?" I asked.

"I've been doing research on Rosie, the ghost at the House of Transformation." She glanced from me to Ananda. "Ananda asked me to find out if she ever lived there. I looked through census records for weeks, but she didn't show up. So I went to the ancestry site, searched for the people who lived at your house, and contacted the current-day, living relatives. One of them just got back to me with a birth record for a Rose-Marie Kanouse. She lived at the House of Transformation. She was born in 1902 and she died in 1909 of tuberculosis. She was between the census reports — that's why I didn't find her before."

Ananda gasped, looking at me. "You were right! All this time, you were right about Rosie! How did you know?"

I felt as if the ground gave way beneath me. I shook my head. "I don't know, it's probably just a coincidence."

"No, it's not," Ananda said. "You really are a spiritual person. If you ever wanted proof, here it is."

"It- it must've been the drugs," I stammered.

"You saw Rosie before Kitty ever came to the house and gave you clemeral, remember?"

I nodded. Maybe I really had communicated with a ghost at the House of Transformation.

Hayden poked her head up. "But this isn't just about you, Mag. This means those other spirits must've been real too. You didn't imagine those things."

Ananda tilted her head back. "That means I'm not crazy. All this time I thought I was crazy for feeling everything that happened there — the spirits, the portals, and I'm not crazy."

I wanted to say it wasn't definitive proof, but I wasn't so sure anymore. In a way, it *was* proof, but I had no idea what it meant. A quote from Shakespeare rose in my mind.

There are more things in heaven and earth than are dreamt of in your philosophy.

I shivered at the thought of Yes, Ricky, and Rosie floating above the rubble of the house. Maybe it *was* real. Maybe their souls were at peace. Maybe Blossom was right, and everything really did happen for a reason.

"I have to tell you something." My heart trembled. "If Rosie is real, that means Yes and Ricky are okay. I saw them with her. They were together, and they were happy."

Tears rimmed my eyes. It'd been years since I'd spoken about them. The last time was with Kitty when I saw them above the burned house. I hadn't even told John because he thought ghosts weren't real. It was a relief to finally talk about it. I felt something in my heart give out, like I'd been keeping a shard of ice there that had finally melted.

Ananda reached out to me, tears sliding down her face. "I needed to hear that. I hoped they were at peace. I always felt so guilty."

I searched her eyes, my breath ragged.

She swallowed hard. "Jared and I put the xyritav in the food. The spirits told us to do it. We thought we'd be protected. I felt so guilty when I woke up in the ambulance and saw what was happening. I ran away as fast as I could and left town. When you reached out to me, all those years ago, I thought you knew I did it. I felt terrible – that's why I couldn't respond."

I shook my head, emotion building inside of me. The first day she'd showed up at my apartment, she tried to ask me about the ghosts. I'd shut her down, just like my other therapist had when I'd brought them up. I'd stopped her healing process.

"I'm so sorry."

She wiped her face. "I'm so sorry too."

I tried to breathe but I needed air. I opened the car door and ambled outside. Ananda and Hayden got out too.

We looked up in silence at the stars and moon.

Hayden's phone pinged again.

"For what it's worth," she said, "your social media is blowing up."

We gathered around her phone as she scrolled through page after page of messages.

Take care @AnandaDawn love you!!!!!

Better rehab than the grave @AnandaDawn! I'll miss you.

Love love love @AnandaDawn.

Curtain falls on the singing career of @AnandaDawn, but what's next? Can't wait.

"Whoa, this one's from Cypress!" Hayden said.

Get better @AnandaDawn! You're an inspiration to us all and we love you!

"Oh my Goddess, Cypress said I'm an inspiration?" She sniffled back tears and reached for Hayden.

"Thank you so much for all you did. I'm going to miss you two."

"Not as much as we'll miss you," Hayden said, her eyes flushed with tears.

"I doubt it."

We hugged, Ananda's cinquefoil perfume once again mesmerizing me. I flashed back to the House of Transformation collaging days, then back to the first time I ever met her, with her velvet coat and startling green eyes.

"I'll visit you soon," I said. "I promise."

"I hope so. But Mag?" A tear ran down her cheek.

"Yeah?"

"Sometimes you hide from life. Don't give up on your dreams again. Don't go back to being complacent. You deserve a bigger life."

I nodded. I knew in my heart it was true. "Okay," I squeaked. "I'll try."

I wanted Ananda to call off the rehab, so we could be besties again, with massage and yoga and art, but I knew she needed the treatment center. All her life, she'd wanted someone to take care of her, and now she was finally at the right place for that to happen.

She picked up her bags and sniffed, a half-smile on her face. The doors opened automatically. She walked into the glass-front entry of the building, onto the lavender carpet, and stood in front of a white desk. A woman with kind eyes passed her a clipboard with papers.

I watched, riveted, as if some force prevented me from leaving. I thought about going in with her, even though I didn't have a problem. I just wanted to be near her again.

Ananda waved to us.

I willed myself to wave back too, but it took so much effort. I wondered if she might change her mind and come running out, wearing her million-dollar smile, but she didn't.

Ananda turned and disappeared down a hallway.

"Is this for real?" Hayden murmured. "I feel like I'm dreaming."

"Me too. But I guess this is what she needed all along."

"I think we helped. At least she's not morbid anymore, right?"

I nodded. We stood in silence for another minute before we went back to the car.

The hotel suite was eerily quiet without Ananda. The crazed fury before the show was evident — towels lay crumpled on the floor, and makeup and clothing were strewn everywhere.

"What a mess." Hayden started to pick through everything.

"Wait." I stopped her, an intense pang flinching in my heart.

"Don't pack it up just yet."

"Why not?" she asked, peering at me.

I never let her see me like this — cracked, flawed. I was supposed to be the strong one in our friendship, but I couldn't hide it anymore. The reality of the situation sank in. I wouldn't be seeing Ananda anymore.

"Let's pretend she's still here, just in the other room. We can clean up tomorrow."

Hayden dropped the clothing and nodded. "I have an idea. Let's order room service and watch a silly movie."

A grin spread over my face. I couldn't imagine a better time.

The next day, Hayden and I went out to breakfast just like normal people. After all those months of living like shut-ins and running like crazy, it was nice to feel the sun on my face and not care who saw us. No paparazzi followed us from the hotel. We were nobodies again. We ate at a fancy patio restaurant without any interruptions.

After we ate, we sat there, soaking in the sunshine and drinking coffee. Hayden bought our plane tickets back to St. Paul while I checked my email. Grass Riot, a publishing house in Baltimore, wanted to publish a book about my time at the House of Transformation, as long as I signed a contract I wouldn't pull it from the shelves like I had with *Analyzing Ananda*. They gave me complete editing rights. Their deal was a hell of a lot better, too. I wrote back and told them I'd think about it.

Jared emailed to say he'd successfully documented that five hundred of the one-star reviews of Ananda's song were from Yellow Records. He filed a case against them and said they'd go to court in a few months. The news would hit the headlines tomorrow. In the meantime, itunes removed the ratings. The song shot up to 3.8 stars.

I wrote back to thank him, and ask if he wanted to get together sometime. For all Jared's faults, I still liked him. His remorse was proof he'd never anticipated the xyritav would make people sick on that fateful night.

Ananda wrote too, saying she was having a great time in rehab. She'd met another celebrity there, and they were hanging out. Their sponsors were really nice and the food was magnificent. Kitty arrived right after she saw the Grammy performance. She was going through detox and puking a lot, but Ananda was helping her.

There was also an email from Brad — just his phone number. I smiled. It was just like him: simple, suggestive, open-ended.

"What are you smiling about?" Hayden asked.

"Brad actually wrote me. I can't believe it."

She laughed. "Of course he did. You still like him, right?"

"I guess." I shrugged.

"I thought so. That's why I asked him to remix Ananda's song."

I looked at her. Clever minx. "Do you think there's a chance for us?"

"Yes, I do, and you're welcome."

I stood up and hugged her. "Thanks. I'll be right back."

I walked out of the café to a sunny street corner with a lamppost and a newsstand. I took a deep breath and touched Brad's number in the email.

As it rang, my heart fluttered faster, and I felt the sweet confusion that always happened whenever I talked with him.

"Hello?"

"Hi."

Epilogue: Six months later

In her first interview since leaving the Purple Lotus Rehab and Rest Resort, Ananda sat with Richard Trucco in front of a studio audience. She looked more radiant than ever, especially with her new auburn hair shade. She sipped from a glass of water, confidence oozing from her.

He brushed a greasy lock of hair behind his ears. "Can we talk about your addiction?"

"Sure."

"You were addicted to xyritav, am I correct?"

"Yes, but I've been sober for almost seven months."

"And you think that's going to last?"

She nodded and paused until she felt the entire audience lean forward, waiting for her response. "I'm a different person now than I was before."

"Different how?"

"I know who I am now. My former manager Mag always said I did things the hard way, and this is a perfect example. I never knew how to be myself. I used to hide that with xyritav. Now, I'm at peace with who I am. I've been doing a lot of yoga, meditation, and therapy. I'm happier now than I ever have been."

"How did the decision to go to rehab come about? Did they 'try to make you go to rehab, and you said no,' to quote an Amy Winehouse song?"

She smiled but shook her head. "I decided to go when the moment was right. While I was there, I received so many letters of support from my fans. They really helped me turn that corner for good."

The audience applauded and stood up, giving Ananda her first standing ovation since the Grammys.

"Ahem," the Greaseball said, trying to take back the interview. "In your newly released autobiography, you reveal a lot about your history, your parents, and you set the record straight about some lies you told in the past. Could you read from your book?"

"Sure." She cleared her throat.

"I was born in the middle of the night. Maybe that's why I love nighttime so much. My first memory is looking at the moon.

My mother was a cafeteria worker at an elementary school, and my father was a drifter. He left before he knew my mom was pregnant, and she never heard from him again. People said she was a wonderful person. She loved parties and meeting new people. After post-partum depression set in, her life started to collapse. My memories of her are tinged with sadness, because in the end, she didn't have a support system, and her mental illness started taking over. It's hard to say how bad things were, because I didn't have a frame of reference, and you can work as a lunch-lady and hide disorders pretty easily. She slipped through the cracks for years.

When I got older, I saw how strange she was. I saw how much pain she was in, and how hard it was for her to even leave the apartment. We'd stay in, imagine elaborate characters, and dress up. Our plays lasted for days. We made all our own costumes, and if we didn't have any fabric, we'd use the sheets or the curtains. She taught me how to sew. We didn't have very much, but we had our imaginations.

We had some hungry times, where we had to be careful with every cup of flour and egg. It was partially because the food stamps went so quickly, but also because my mother was agoraphobic. I remember her clinging to the grocery cart and not reprimanding me for my behavior, even when I turned cartwheels in the aisles and ate all the free samples.

About the time I was ten, my mother made me walk to the grocery alone because her agoraphobia was so bad. I loved it. I hung out and read fashion magazines for hours with a can of orange soda. I never got in trouble.

By the time I was a teenager, I stayed out as late as I wanted. I stayed at friends' houses and started smoking cigarettes. The school couldn't do anything except tell my mom when I missed school. Since I didn't get in trouble with her, I kept doing whatever I wanted.

Eventually, my mom missed a lot of work. We were kicked out of the apartment. My grandparents took us in, but they didn't enforce rules either. No one really talked in our household. We just sort of lived together. My grandparents bought groceries, which cut off my excuse to hang out at the grocery.

It was around that time, at sixteen, that I started using. Clemeral was the easiest drug to get into because everyone at high school had it. It was mellow and the effects were easy to conceal. Mostly, I liked it because it took away my sense of dread. I knew I was growing up, and I had no idea where I fit into the world. Clemeral was like a dream where everything was okay. I didn't worry about fitting in with the rich girls, didn't worry about passing my classes, and I didn't worry about the future. I knew I wanted a lot out of life, and I needed to work to get it, but clemeral made me feel like I already had it.

Of course, it was an elaborate illusion that faded after a couple of hours. That's when my addiction began. I started selling it in high school to sustain my habit.

I changed my name the same day I was kicked out of high school. I was hiding out in a grove of trees by my house, reading a book I'd nicked from the used bookstore about the world's religions when I came across the word Ananda. In Hinduism and Buddhism, it means extreme happiness, or bliss, and that's what I identified with more than anything else. I was bliss. I was happiness, as long as I had clemeral.

Xyritav is another story. It was beyond bliss. It made my illusory childhood worlds of play come alive again — all the mythology, symbolism, and elation. I stayed at her place and built up my clientele, all the while escaping to another realm where I was exactly who I wanted to be.

I started feeling depressed around this time. Maybe intuitively, I knew I needed some kind of medicine. Some days, I felt like I was stuck in the bottom of the darkest cave until I took it again. It was a vicious cycle. I'm not proud of self-medicating, but without health insurance, the cost of seeing a doctor and getting treatment was unthinkable. I lived one day at a time because I couldn't foresee a future at all."

Ananda closed the book and let it fall on her lap. The audience sighed.

Richard Trucco shook his head. "It sounds like you made the best of a bad childhood and tried to cover up what you didn't like. What about some of the things you made up, or lied about?"

She shrugged. "I did make up a lot, but some of the lies weren't my fault. I *was* interviewed for my first biography, but the writer didn't use my story. My manager controlled my image, and he made up stuff for that book."

"What about your other lies? You told people you were a fashion model when you weren't."

"Maybe I was living in the future," she said, flashing her million-dollar smile.

The audience went crazy again, cheering and clapping.

She waited until they died down. "But you're right. I was only an art model for my friends. I think I lied about it because my imagination was always so vivid. It was my only escape from how boring my life was, and most of the time, I preferred it to the real world. It's taken me a while to adjust to real life, but I'm all the better for it."

"You also said you were Anaïs Nin in a past life."

"Can you prove I wasn't?" she asked with a raised eyebrow.

"Err, no?" he stammered.

"Well, then." She smiled.

"Maybe you can tell me about your fascination with art. Why do you love art so much?"

"Art is everything. It's creativity and self-expression, and it lasts beyond a lifetime. It's like another world to get lost in."

"Interesting. Did you go to art school?"

"No, but I don't think you need an art degree to appreciate art, am I right?" she asked the audience, raising her palms.

The audience resounded in applause and stood up again.

"I am art!" Ananda said, "and you are art. And you! And you!"

She laughed and Trucco laughed along with her.

"Alright. What else do you have going on in your life?"

"I finally have my own fashion line called Yes. It'll be debuting at Fashion Week in New York City in a couple of weeks. I'll be modeling in the show. Right now we're really exclusive, but we have a whole line of dresses, skirts, and blouses. I hope to expand the line next year for a younger look I'm calling Hayden, and a minimalist artistic look I'm calling

Mag."

"There's a rumor," Trucco said, tapping a pencil against his lip. "There's a rumor that a few years ago, you were told to wear a certain designer's gown at the Grammys, and you said you'd rather go naked than wear that, and that's why you appeared naked on stage when you presented an award."

"That's correct, but my manager also put xyritav in my water that night."

"I was shocked to learn you sewed some of those gorgeous gowns we've seen on you over the years, including those from your time at the House of Transformation. Can we see some of those?"

Jared's photos played on the screen behind them. The audience cooed.

Ananda pointed to one on screen. "A replica of that one is going in the current line, and so is this." She stood to showcase her sparkling dress.

"Isn't she beautiful?" Trucco asked.

The audience responded in applause.

"What happened with Yellow Records?" he asked.

"That was pretty insane. When I released my single earlier this year, they wrote five hundred negative reviews of it. Can you believe it? But they got caught, and now they're paying for it."

"Any plans for the money?"

"I'm donating it all to charities. Speaking of which, I created my own charity called *It's Real*. It's like the *It Gets Better* project, only we're raising awareness of mental health."

"We need more awareness about that issue, and there's no better person to do it than you. By the way, congratulations on your recent Grammy nomination!"

"Thanks." Ananda blushed. "I wasn't expecting that at all. I don't think I'll win, but it's an honor to be nominated."

"Why don't you think you'll win? It's a catchy tune."

Brad's remix bumped through the speakers. The Greaseball got up to dance and extended a hand to Ananda. She shook her head, but after a beat, she rose and danced with him, hands in the air, smiling. A few members in the audience danced too.

The music tapered off and Ananda and the Greaseball took their seats, laughing. She took a drink of water while he adjusted his tie.

"So what's new with your music? Any new songs?"

"I've been singing to myself when I sew. The sewing machine makes a rhythm, and it's really inspired me lately."

"Really? When will your next album be released?"

"I don't know. All I know is I've wanted to design clothes for years, and I'm not locked into a record contract anymore. I actually have some autonomy with my life now, so that's what I'm focused on."

"Sweet freedom, huh?"

"That's the best thing there is." She beamed.

"Well, I'm afraid that's all the time we have, but thank you, Miss Dawn. You've been a great guest. You're so talented!"

"Thanks Richard," she said. "It's actually been a pleasure."

At the New Beginnings Center, I smiled for the cameras and cut the enormous red ribbon wrapped around the newly built coffeehouse addition. Cameras flashed spastically, and I started to feel a little dizzy.

Brad reached out a hand to steady me and I held him, feeling the weight of his strong arms. It was so nice to have him nearby, especially since he'd contributed nearly a quarter of the funds. The expansion included six bedrooms, two bathrooms, a commercial coffeehouse, and a state-of-the-art kitchen. The coffeehouse was a particularly brilliant idea to provide the girls with an income, job experience, and a safe place to hang out.

Tanya smiled at me and gave me an enormous hug. She'd gotten quite good at turning out scones and muffins.

Hayden had managed the kitchen operations before she left last week to be Ananda's personal assistant again. She wrote, saying the fashion business was a huge change, and Ananda was running all her own social media, much to her surprise.

I was worried about Ananda's image after she 'dropped the A-bomb' on stage several months ago, but she gained thousands of fans since then, and is more popular than ever. Several other celebrities have copied her, but Ananda was credited for starting the trend to go transparent with her faults and addictions. Even though she wasn't the first musician to go rogue off her label, she's credited for a widespread movement among the industry, especially the former Yellow Records artists.

In a strange turn of events, the media actually praised her for getting help instead of tearing her down, perhaps because the music industry had too many losses with the old system of hiding flaws. She even got a magazine cover on Us Weekly that called her 'Ananda the Brave.' Her transparency changed the way a lot of celebrities view therapy and mental health. Her book, which revealed her childhood and her perpetual misadventures with her manager and publicist, is continuously sold out, with the exception of e-books.

It turned out she only needed a couple of months of rehab, much to the chagrin of the press junkets who speculated she'd be there for several months or a year. Of course, anyone who knew her knew she'd land on her feet, cat that she is. As soon as she was out of rehab, she moved all her belongings out of her LA rental to start anew. She settled on San Francisco.

Much to my disbelief, she's seeing my parents as therapists. She asked both of them to work with her at the same time so she could get 'double the impact.' Even though they're retired, they made a special case just for her. Subconsciously, I think she wanted to mimic a healthy relationship with people the same age as her parents. I hear she's getting a lot from it. Dad said he doesn't remember calling her a dirty hippie fairy, but said he always found her intriguing. Now, they've grown to love her like a second daughter. No surprise there, of course. Everyone loves her.

Ananda's fashion line is hotly anticipated by the fashion community. She only made a few thousand garments of each style — something virtually unheard of for her caliber. She has no shortage of orders, but she handpicks each boutique to make sure it reflects her artistic ideas. There was even a story in the New York Times about the harried remodeling of boutiques all over the world to compete for having her exclusive line.

Ananda left Kitty back in rehab. From what I can gather, they had another catastrophic argument. When I visited Kitty, poolside, with a carrot-ginger-beet juice, she didn't want to talk about it, but said she was having a great time in rehab and didn't want to leave. The yoga, meditation, architecture, and food all looked so good, I was tempted to check myself in for a few days, even though I didn't have an addiction. Kitty is currently recording the audio version of Ananda's book while in rehab. She snidely mentioned Ananda and I 'weren't the only ones offered book deals.' When I asked her about the rumor that a producer might be interested in her for a reality tv show, she just smiled and said she was sworn to secrecy, and couldn't tell me about *any* of her offers at the moment.

Jared convicted the Yellow Records executives for slander in a fiercely fought court case. Investigation revealed that Yellow Records left hundreds of bad reviews for several other recording artists who went rogue or were fired. Jared even started a case for laws concerning paparazzi, since that was part of Ananda's problem. He said he's optimistic he can change the laws so the people and companies supporting the behavior can be charged with harassment.

The case against Ananda's former manager for spiking her water with xyritav was dismissed without grounds of evidence, but the public largely took Ananda's side. Hayden was in touch with Jared almost every day when they set up *It's Real.* Jared never sent a bill for his work, and when Hayden asked him about it, he said he owed us.

He never responded to my emails, except to decline meeting up, saying he was too busy. I wonder if he's still ashamed. My last memory of him was the guilt-stricken face slowly backing away from the window that night the paramedics came. That image will never be erased from my mind. I know accidents and mistakes happen, and I've forgiven him. I just wish he could forgive himself.

Yes used to say 'everything happens for a reason.' I have to imagine that if anyone got to choose the time of her passing, it'd be her. I haven't done anything with the knowledge that I may have communicated with ghosts, or that Ananda and Jared were responsible for eight deaths that happened that night. Sometimes, though, when I think about Rosie, or Yes, or Ricky, I breathe easier, knowing if my visions are true, the other side may be a place of great elation and love.

The media moved on to a new scandalous starlet. Her name is Shiloh Bridges. She was a child actress who was most recently in the news for appearing naked at a dance club in LA and making out with several strangers. Of course, the Greaseball published racy photos of Shiloh at the club, kissing men and women, with full tongue action. It sparked a lot of news and internet chatter. It's an echo of Ananda's sensualism and her naked appearance at the Grammys, but Shiloh's exhibitionism seems to be shallower, without meaning or flair. However, because of those photographs, millions more people know her name, and people are already speculating about what crazy thing she's going to do next, just as they had with Ananda.

The falling of an ingénue is like a ten-car pileup. It's hard to look away. It's the shocking desecration of society's morals. Even though I know that, I can't help but be shocked at what Shiloh does, nor can I tear my eyes away. As much as I admire her for breaking the societal restraint, I have to resist demonizing her in my mind. Her actions, just like Ananda's, spark a subconscious love-hate thought cycle in people. We're fascinated by contradictions like her because we love to solve problems. We mull it over in our minds and read the click-bait as soon as it pops up in the sidebar. As much as the cycle is disturbing on a psychological level, I'm relieved to know there's a method behind the madness. I can only hope Shiloh has the perseverance to survive the ordeal and pull through like Ananda did.

Now that the pressure is off Ananda, she's actually living her life. The paparazzi backed off almost completely since her confession. She rarely appears in magazines nowadays, and if so, it's to plug her clothing line. She told me she can walk around her neighborhood in San Francisco without being harassed, which is a giant step for her. She's still recognized every time she goes out, and still gets asked for the occasional picture or autograph, but people play it cool most of the time. Something about her has settled into place, and people respect her now. Perhaps it's her own self-respect shining through. She compares her new life to the removal of a thousand veils, and said she can finally breathe again.

I only see John once a month now. It's a big change from when I saw him every week. I just don't have as many issues now. He said he feels we're done, but I keep making the next appointment, just in case. But who knows. Maybe next month, I won't make another appointment.

The State Board hasn't reinstated my therapist license yet. I try not to linger on it, even though I miss being a therapist and making a difference. I asked Mary to investigate. She told me a handful of stuffy people are keeping me from being voted back in.

"They're the ones who really need therapy," she said, which made me laugh despite my bitterness.

On a positive note, the money I made from being Ananda's manager is enough to carry me through many years. She gave me a full year's salary. I'd tried to refuse it, especially since I was only her manager for a few months, but she didn't listen to logic, which is no surprise.

I've thought a lot about what Ananda said, about how my life should be bigger. I decided to do something I've always wanted to do. I enrolled at the Art Institute of New York City. I'll have my own apartment a couple of blocks from Brad's loft, where I visit from time to time.

I love New York. I haven't gotten used to the smell yet, and the fashion is way more stylish and minimalist than Minnesota's, but I'm adapting. Already, I have a favorite coffeehouse and bakery, and I feel my heart blooming every time I visit.

Brad made quite a bit of money for his remix of Ananda's song. He was able to quit his job to make remixes for other musicians. If it's anywhere near as profitable as Ananda's song was, he'll never have to work a 9-5 job again.

I'm not sure where things will go with me and Brad, but right now, we're happy. It's like we never broke up. We're taking it slow, even though I want to stay with him every night. We still joke about surviving Hurricane Ananda, but we both feel like she made it up to us.

Sometimes I think we all owe her ex-manager a debt of gratitude, even if he did deceive her. More than that, though, we owe it to Ananda's genius, her recovery, and most important, our friendship. I hate to think what might've happened if Ananda hadn't come to me. What if she'd gone to Kitty instead? What if I hadn't found her in LA? There were so many close calls. In my meditations, which I picked up again recently, I practice 'a moment of gratitude.' Inevitably, I think of Ananda and smile.

I started transforming too, something I never thought possible before Ananda came back into my life. Just the other day, as I walked around Soho, I felt my usual panic grip me. I started to name my fears, except I couldn't. I searched my soul and couldn't name a single fear. I realized my fear of the unknown had become excitement for the unknown. My fears of losing my job and being socially ostracized turned out to be something I'd lived through. What was the worst-case scenario I'd been so worried about? Finding myself all over again? I'm living in a completely new world, but most importantly, I'm actually living.

I saw Stevey at his gallery near Union Square. He gained some weight and a few wrinkles, and was elated to see me again. He offered to show my first set of work, which I readily agreed to. It'll be my first show since the one at his warehouse all those years ago. He informed me his rate went up, but he can sell whatever I give him. He'd kept one of my old collage prints, which apparently went up in value tremendously. The yuppie couple who bought the collage prints recently made a fortune from the pieces they sold. Our old collages even had a small article in Current Art magazine. Since then, google searches for my art have been in the thousands every month. Several companies offered to distribute it, which is tempting, but I've been too busy lately to pursue it.

Stevey said he sees Barry every year or so when they vacation on Fire Island, and he's doing well, considering. Barry found cancer on one of his feet, but he's in treatment. Much to his regret, he sold our print several years ago when Ananda's popularity first began to spike. However, he has a standing order for a print of everything I make for the new show.

Stevey always asks about Ananda — specifically if she can make an appearance for my show. I promised I'd invite her, but we both know how busy she is.

Art school starts in four weeks. In the meantime, Ananda surprised me with a weeklong vacation to Europe for the two of us. She said she was working on fulfilling all the promises she'd ever made, and this was an important one. We'll meet in Paris at *L'Hôtel Vernet* next week.

She seems healthier than ever, and surer of herself. She has a kind of peace I never saw in her before, as if the green fire in her eyes has finally quelled, and a moss-covered forest sprung up in its place.

Until my vacation, I've been assisting with the direction and scope of *It's Real*. The web page is up, and Hayden is working on getting more celebrity videos. We have a few big names so far. Even though I'm not a therapist anymore, I'm thrilled I can still make a difference, this time for people all over the world. Once art school starts up, I'll go to quarterly meetings and be on the board. It's such an honor to be part of it. If it's one tenth as successful as the *It Gets Better* project, it'll be a success. Even if we only save one person, our work will not have been wasted.

Sometimes I drop by the New Beginnings Center and volunteer. The new counselor Caroline hired has a trustworthy manner and sleepy brown eyes. I instantly liked him. He works out of my old office. When I drop by with a letter for him, or to ask where the cleaning supplies are kept nowadays, I'm always surprised at how different the raspberry-colored walls look. I thought I'd miss the rich color, but find it no longer suits me. It's too intense, too solid.

After a long day of cleaning floors or doing dishes at the center, I eat dinner with everyone. It was always my favorite moment of the day when I was a therapist, and it's still great. The girls who've known me for a while fawn over me. The new ones are shyer, but there's one thing they have in common. They all want to know about Ananda.

"Tell us a story about Ananda."

"What was it like working with her?"

"What was she like when she was young?"

That last question makes me feel as if age is creeping up on me. I never know what to say. It's hard to talk about her. She was such a dichotomy — exciting and disappointing, hot and cold, loving and distant, all mine and never mine. And then there's the new Ananda, who overcame everything and got where she is today. She removed herself from all expectations, and yet is still in everyone's good graces. It makes me think my book about what really happened at the House of Transformation might be something people would read after all.

Looking back at our time together, I'm struck by how young we were. We thought we knew what the world was. We had universe-sized dreams, rich with possibility. Some of them actually came true. I actually am a world-renowned artist. Ananda actually is a supermodel with her own line of clothing. Brad really is a top-ten musician, and Kitty is fabulous, and always will be, whatever she decides to do.

Even though not all of us made it out of the House of Transformation alive, and we all left with some regrets, those who made it out are alright. Even Kitty is exactly where she wants to be. It makes me wonder if Yes and Rosie might be pulling strings for us in the otherworld.

Sometimes I find myself wondering how Ananda did it — she was almost completely self-made. What if my loving parents had abandoned me? What if my role models were rock stars instead of hard-working adults? It's something I can't even conceive of. I almost certainly would be an emotionally stunted adult. I never would've become an Ananda Dawn.

Lately, I've come to believe that, more than anything, we are what we make of ourselves. Ananda was a liar and a dreamer before she was discovered. Her life would've been easier if she was a wealthy socialite or an educated or working-class girl, but instead, her story is one of reinvention, creativity, determination, and triumph against so many odds.

And so what if her bright light exposed so many shadows? I love her all the more for it, for the same reason as everyone else loves her — for her shadows, her light, and everything in between.

Afterword

There should be a word in the English language for how our culture reveres celebrities, for how we yearn to see both their accomplishments and trials, for our contradictory mixture of awe, empathy, and avarice. It is this complex emotion I wanted to capture in the writing of this book.

Although society has lost countless artistic geniuses and musicians to untimely deaths, the one that affected me the most was Amy Winehouse. She had so much talent and potential. When I learned of her passing, I mourned for days. I wished someone could've saved her from her own self-destruction. At times, when writing, I imagined Ananda dealing with the same out-of-control spiral, but with a breakthrough instead of a continued break down.

Other times, I imagined Ananda as if Marilyn Monroe was born into this era, with its unique challenges. There is no denying Monroe's nearly universal appeal, and yet her inner life revealed insomnia, perfectionism, feelings of unlovability, and post-traumatic stress, likely from an unstable upbringing in the foster system and consequent marriage failures. Her search for unconditional love is one everyone can relate to.

This project started from 2005 to 2009, and sat untouched on an old computer drive until it was finished in 2013 with the help of NaNoWriMo, and edited a thousand times from 2013-2015.

Five percent of the profits from this book will go to Daybreak, a shelter for runaway and homeless youth. Learn more about Daybreak at: http://daybreakdayton.org.

Acknowledgments

There are so many people who inspired me in so many ways for this novel. First, I thank my husband Tim. He not only saved this early file from an archaic word formatting program, but also has been a constant comfort. His creative work ethic inspires me every day. I also thank him for bringing my cover idea to beautiful fruition, for editing assistance, and for being a technical whiz in general.

For writing advice on selected early chapters, I thank Robert Smythe, Luke See, Alexandra Lander, Duante Beddingfield, and the Dayton Writers group from 2005-2007.

Of my support group, I thank my shining star Kristl, without whom this book would've been shelved many times. Thanks also to Matthew Temple for support, Andrea Hutson for all the yummy food, Soul Fire Tribe, Judy and Dave VerValin, Nicki Ojeda, Kari Himes, Mike Wishnewski, Vida Valentine, Susan Roper, M.R., E.G., and all my other amazing friends. Your work inspires my work. I appreciate it more than you know.

About the author

Astrea Taylor is the author of House of Transformation. She has lived in several cities in the United States, but resides in Dayton, Ohio. She is a co-leader of Soul Fire Tribe, a fire dance performance group.

Currently, she's working on a collection of short stories, a story about a doomed circus, and a Young Adult trilogy about a demon who just wants to go to heaven.

Keep in touch at https://www.facebook.com/AstreaTaylor.

www.ingramcontent.com/pod-product-compliance
Lightning Source LLC
Chambersburg PA
CBHW051211120726
47905CB00004B/1069